MONKEY KING

Vol. 07

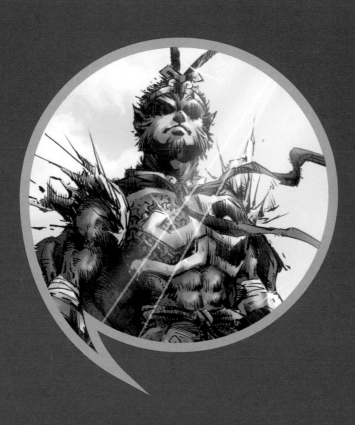

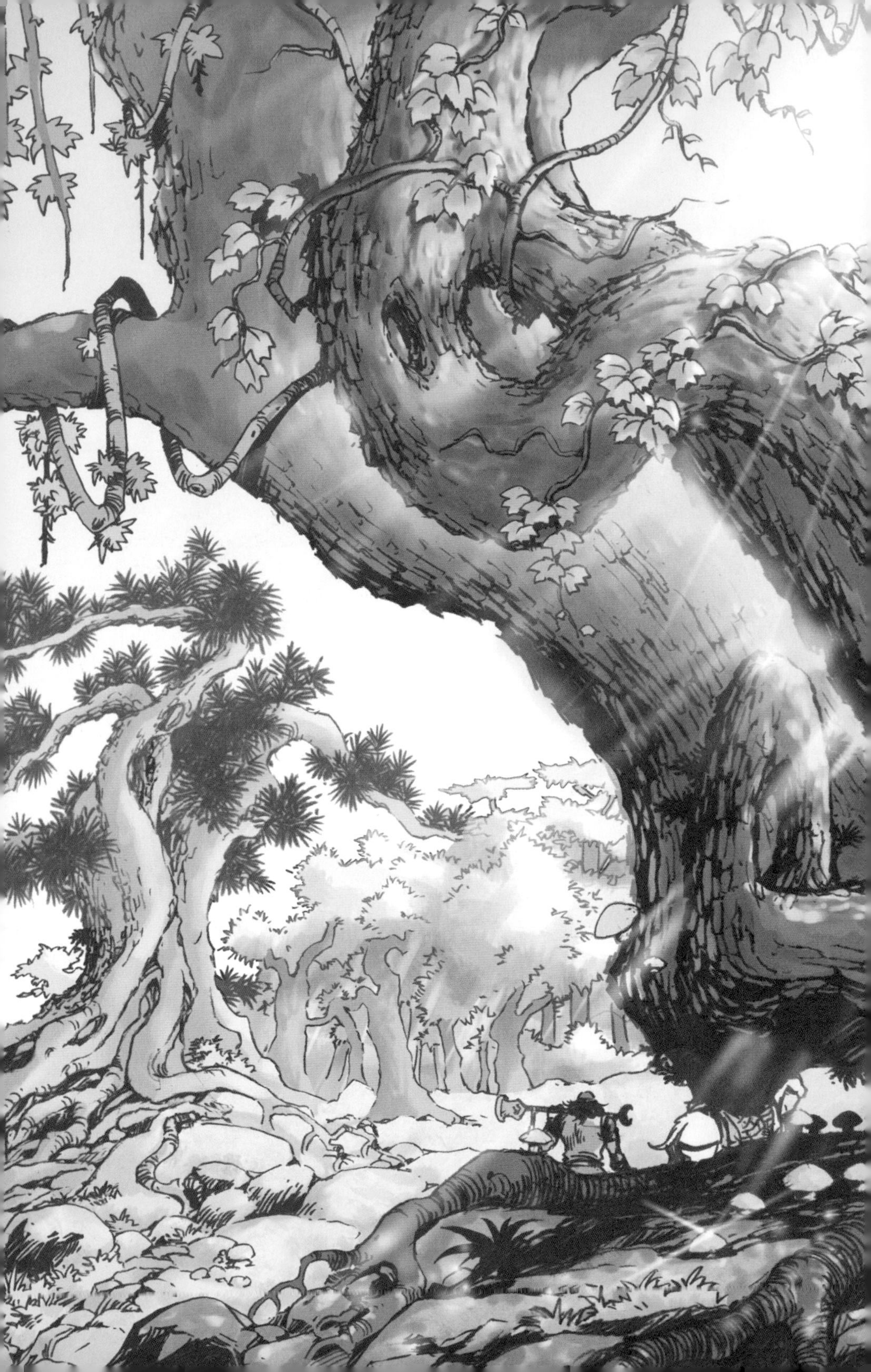

MONKEY KING Vol. 07

The Expulsion of Sun Wu Kong

Created by WEI DONG CHEN

Wei Dong Chen, a highly acclaimed and beloved artist, and an influential leader in the "New Chinese Cartoon" trend, is the founder of Creator World in Tianjin, the largest comics studio in China. Recently the Chinese government entrusted him with the role of general manager of the Beijing Book Fair, and his reputation as a pillar of Chinese comics has brought him many students. He has published more than three hundred cartoons, which have been recognized for their strong literary value not only in Korea, but in Europe and Japan, as well. Free spirited and energetic, Wei Dong Chen's positivist philosophy is reflected in the wisdom of his work. He is published serially in numerous publications while continuing to conceive projects that explore new dimensions of the form.

Illustrated by CHAO PENG

Chao Peng is considered one of Wei Dong Chen's greatest students, and is the director of cartoon at Creator World in Tianjin. One of the most highly regarded cartoonists in China today, Chao Peng's fantastic technique and expression of Chinese culture have won him the acclaim of cartoon lovers throughout China. His other works include "My Pet" and "Searching for the World of Self".

Original story
"The Journey to The West" by Wu, Cheng En

Editing & Designing
Sun Media, Design Hongs, David Teez, Jonathan Evans,
YK Kim, HJ Lee, SH Lee, Qing Shao, Xiao Nan Li, Ke Hu

✳ Characters

THE WHITE BONE GOBLIN

The White Bone Goblin sleeps deep within the mountains, and can transfigure into multiple human likenesses. When she senses San Zang and his disciples passing through her realm, the White Bone Goblin pursues him, as she has heard rumors that the priest's flesh can grant immortality if eaten. Her disguises fool everyone but Sun Wu Kong, whose repeated attempts to destroy the monster severely test the loyalty of the group and the compassion of San Zang.

THE DEVIL OF MOUNT DAOWAN

When Sun Wu Kong was defeated by the army of the Jade Emperor, the armies of Heaven set fire to Spring Mountain, killing most of the monkeys who lived there. Those who were left were either hunted down by bands of marauders or enslaved by the Devil of Mount DaoWan, who, like the Evil King before him, makes the mistake of claiming Sun Wu Kong's title as supreme ruler of Spring Mountain.

THE YELLOW ROBE DEMON

The Yellow Robe Demon lived among the heavenly gods until the day he fell in love with the Jade Lady, who was born to earth as a princess in the BaoXiang Kingdom. The demon fell to the earth to live as a monster, then kidnapped and married the princess. Though he loves his wife and tries to win the approval of her father, the Yellow Robe Demon is a treacherous being who first tries to eat San Zang and then turns the priest into a tiger.

THE JADE LADY

The Jade Lady was once a Taoist fairy who was born to earth as the third daughter of the king of BaoXiang. Thirty years ago, her former lover, the Yellow Robe Demon, kidnapped her and made her his wife. While she has great affection for her husband and children, the Jade Lady misses her father and resents her husband for separating them. She makes contact with her father through San Zang, who is not very talented at defeating monsters, but who has a few disciples that might get the job done.

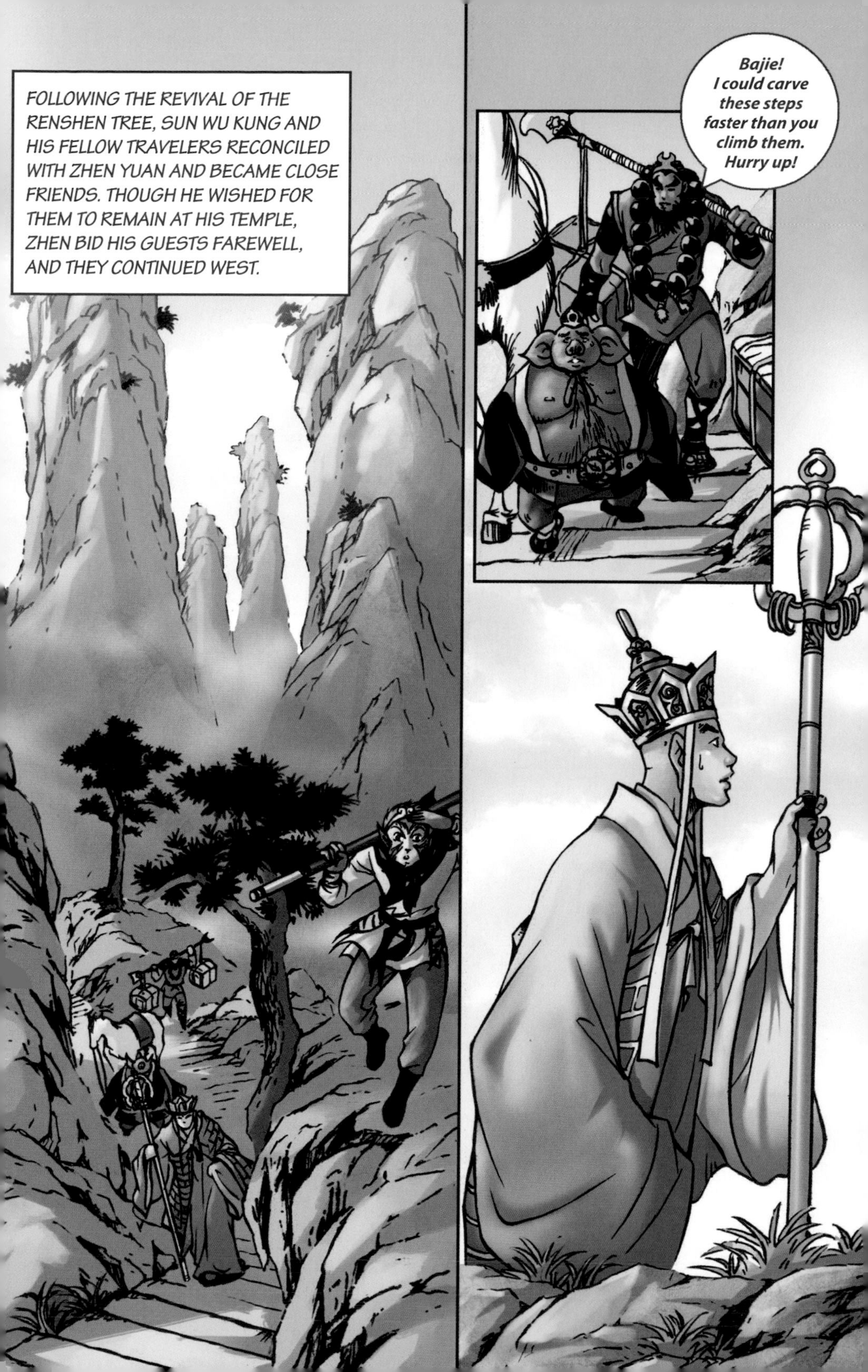
FOLLOWING THE REVIVAL OF THE RENSHEN TREE, SUN WU KUNG AND HIS FELLOW TRAVELERS RECONCILED WITH ZHEN YUAN AND BECAME CLOSE FRIENDS. THOUGH HE WISHED FOR THEM TO REMAIN AT HIS TEMPLE, ZHEN BID HIS GUESTS FAREWELL, AND THEY CONTINUED WEST.
Bajie! I could carve these steps faster than you climb them. Hurry up!

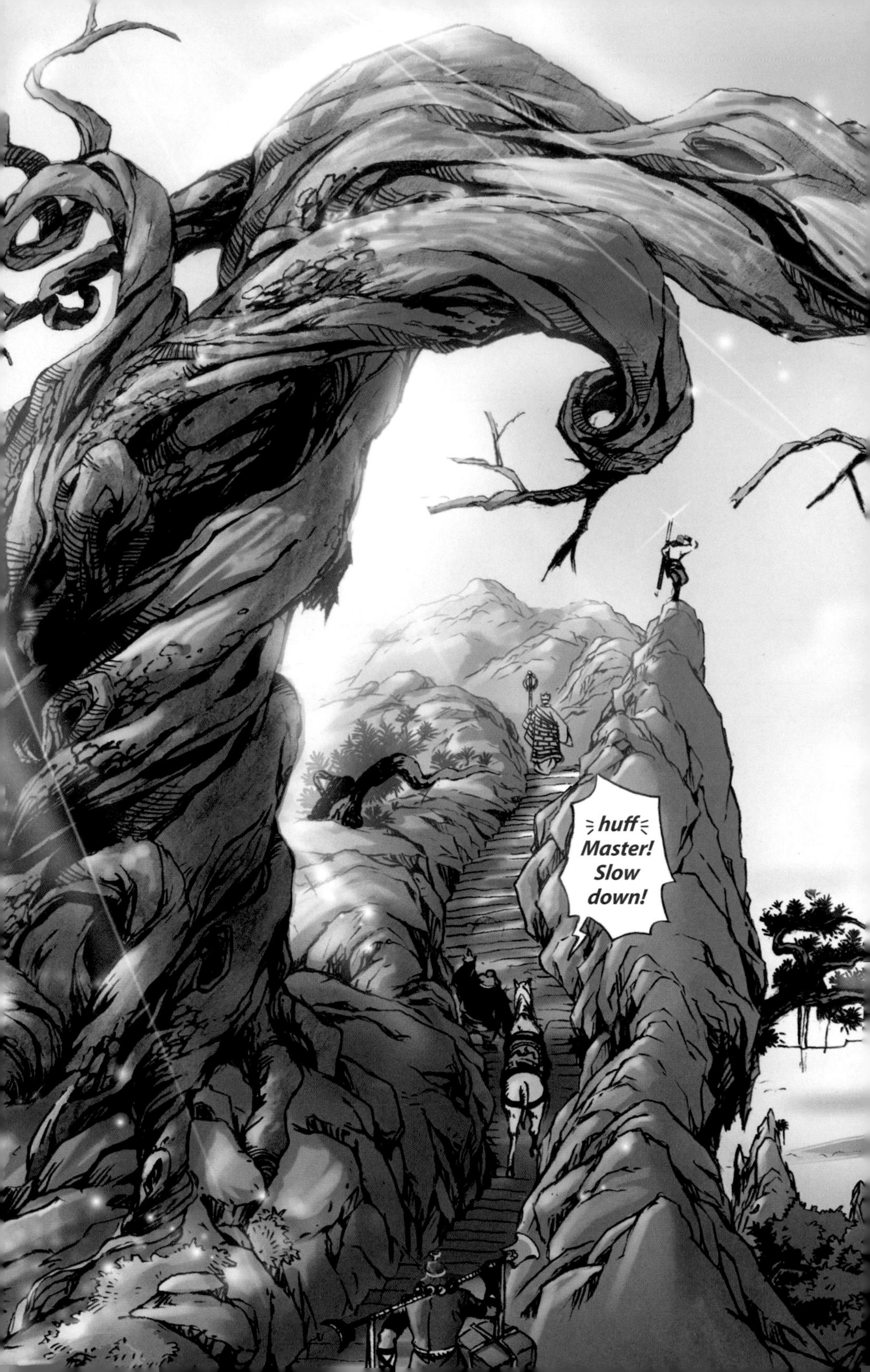
huff
Master! Slow down!

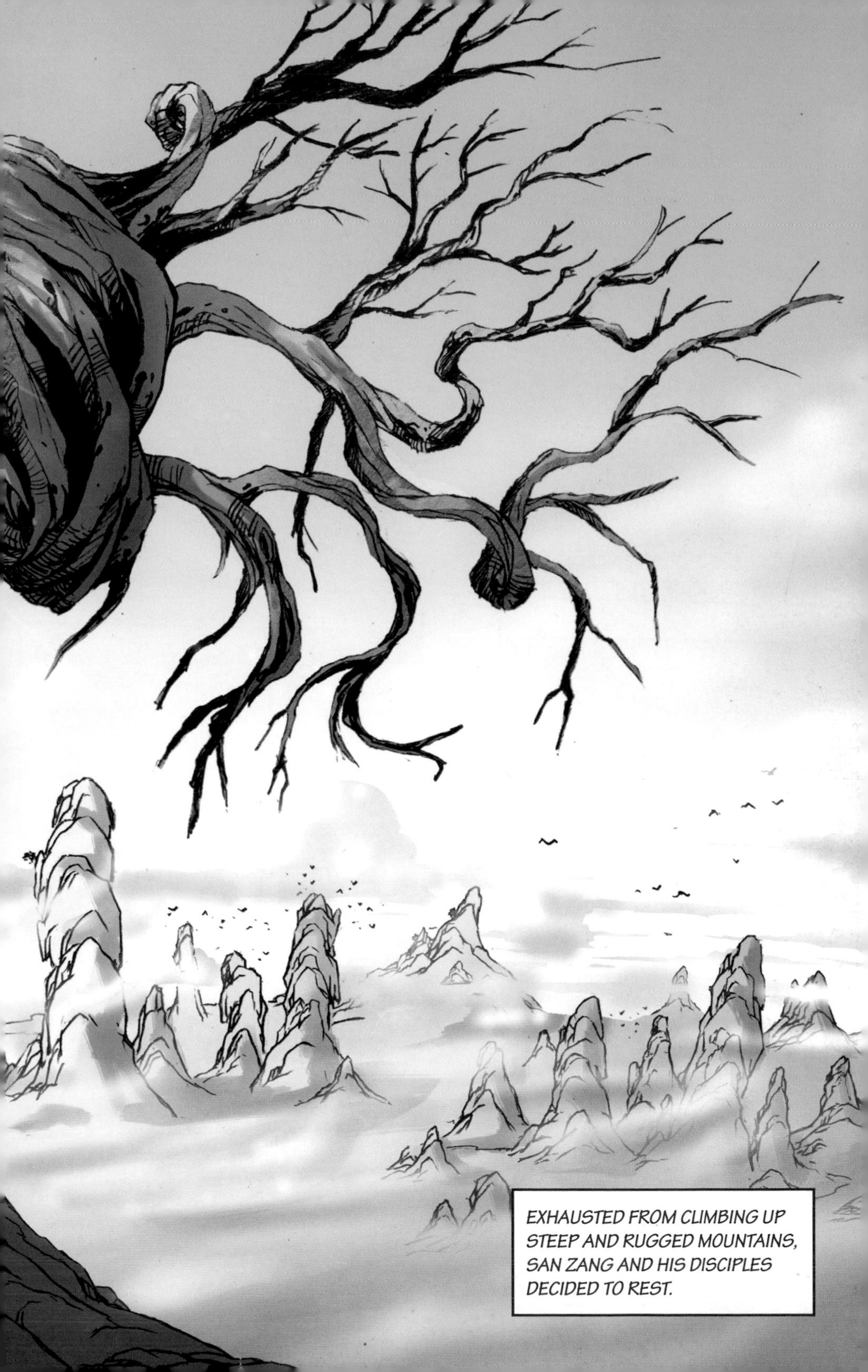
EXHAUSTED FROM CLIMBING UP STEEP AND RUGGED MOUNTAINS, SAN ZANG AND HIS DISCIPLES DECIDED TO REST.

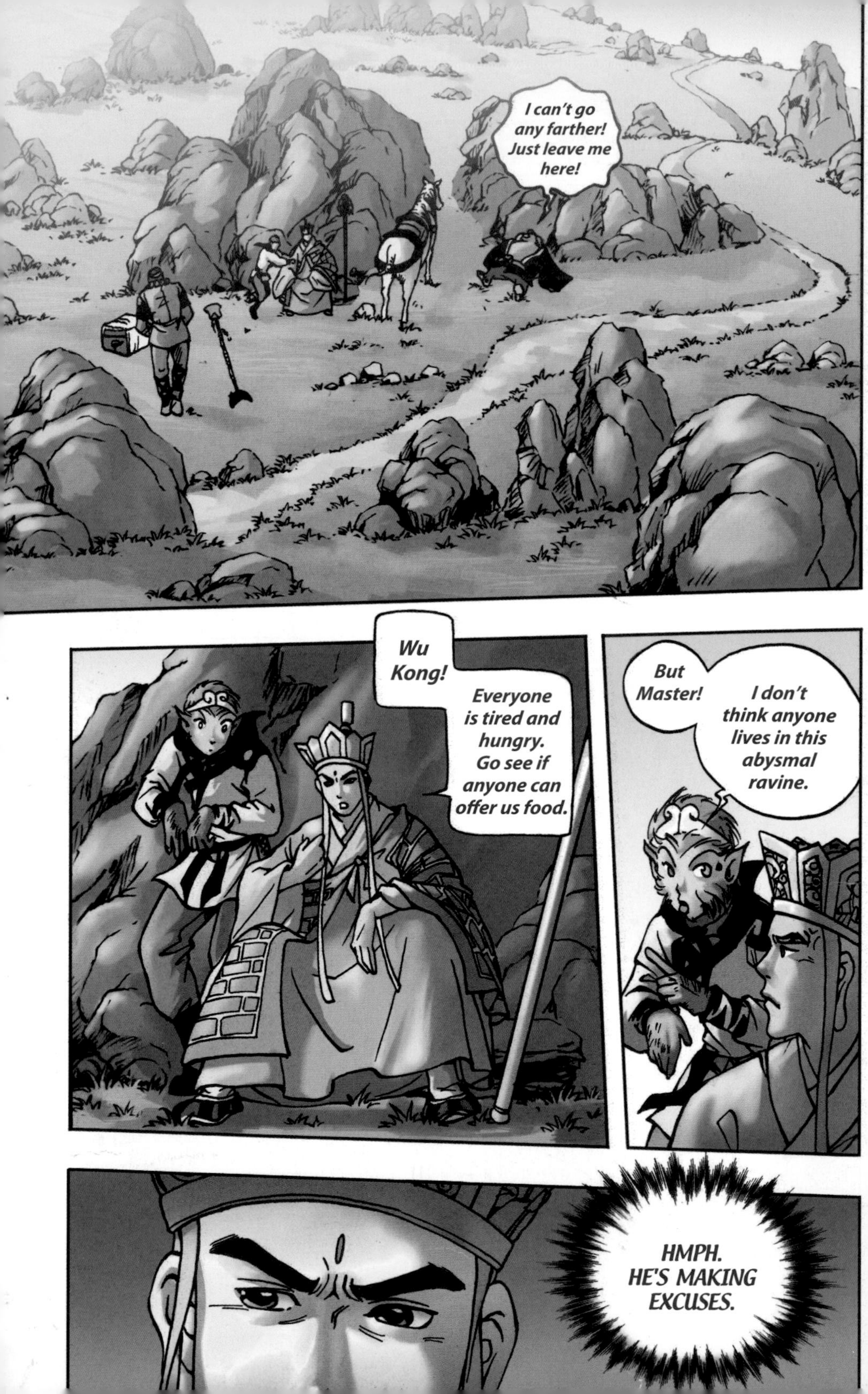
I can't go any farther! Just leave me here!
Wu Kong!
Everyone is tired and hungry. Go see if anyone can offer us food.
But Master!
I don't think anyone lives in this abysmal ravine.
HMPH. HE'S MAKING EXCUSES.

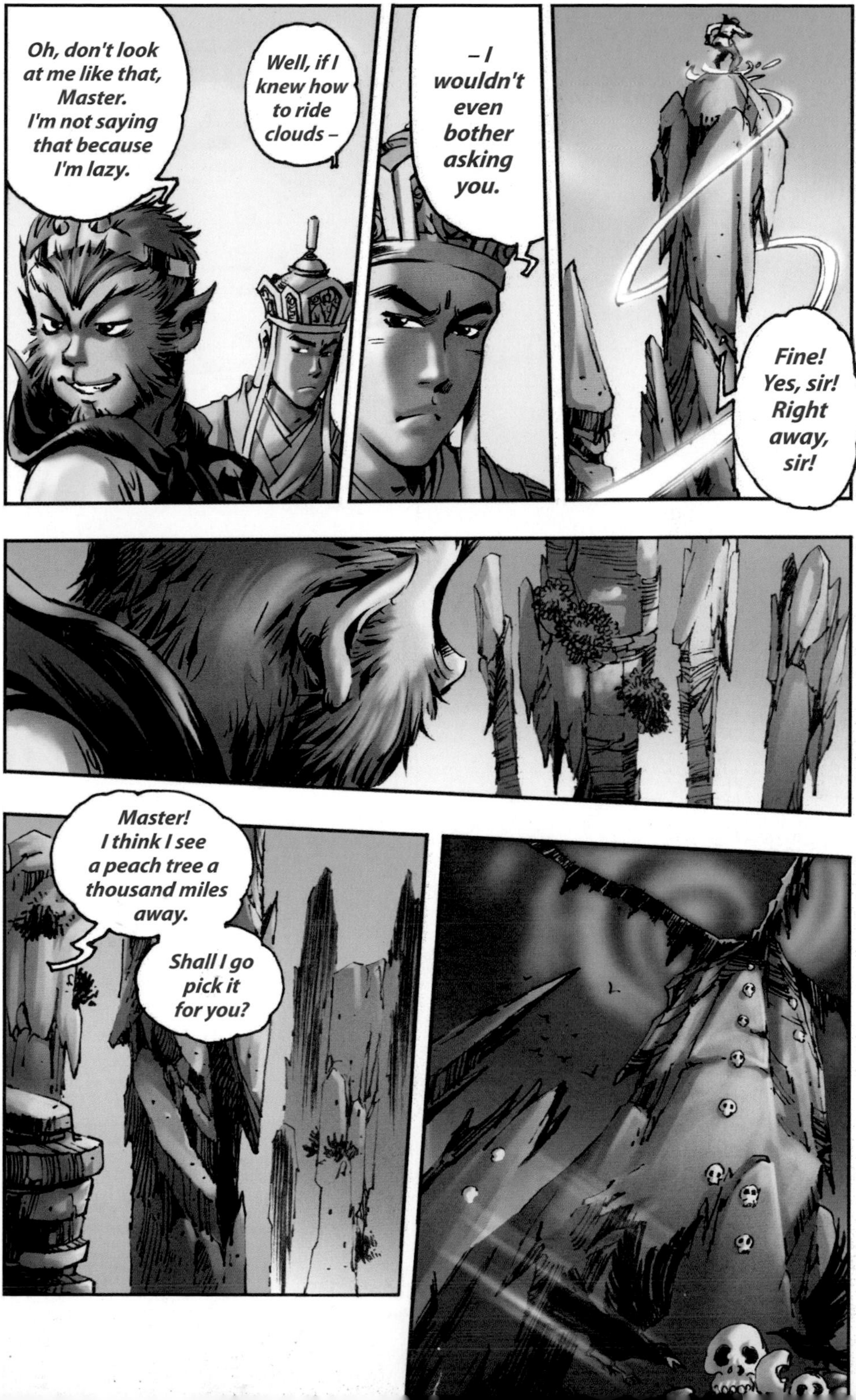
Oh, don't look at me like that, Master. I'm not saying that because I'm lazy.
Well, if I knew how to ride clouds –
– I wouldn't even bother asking you.
Fine! Yes, sir! Right away, sir!
Master! I think I see a peach tree a thousand miles away.
Shall I go pick it for you?

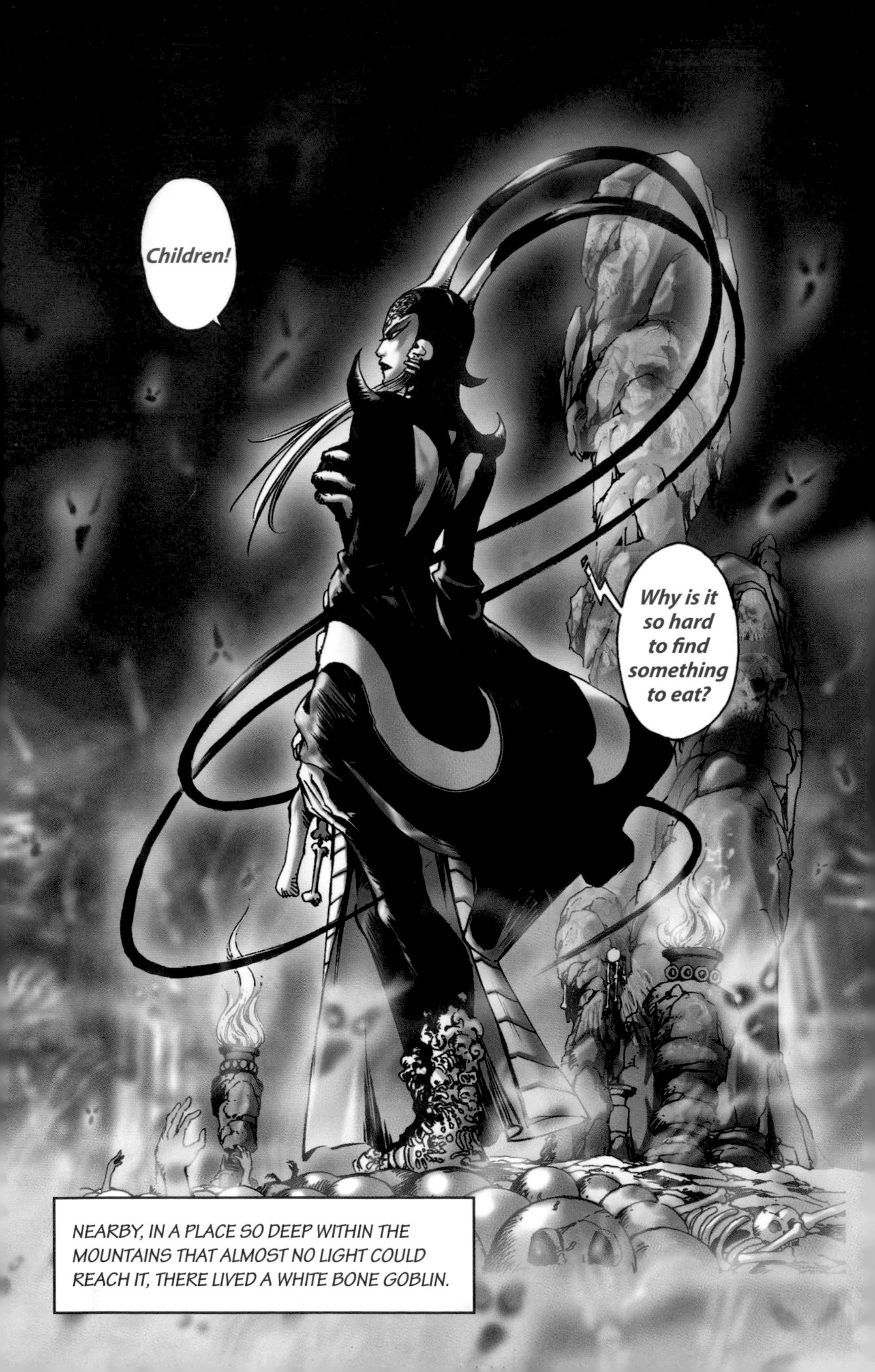
Children!
Why is it so hard to find something to eat?
NEARBY, IN A PLACE SO DEEP WITHIN THE MOUNTAINS THAT ALMOST NO LIGHT COULD REACH IT, THERE LIVED A WHITE BONE GOBLIN.

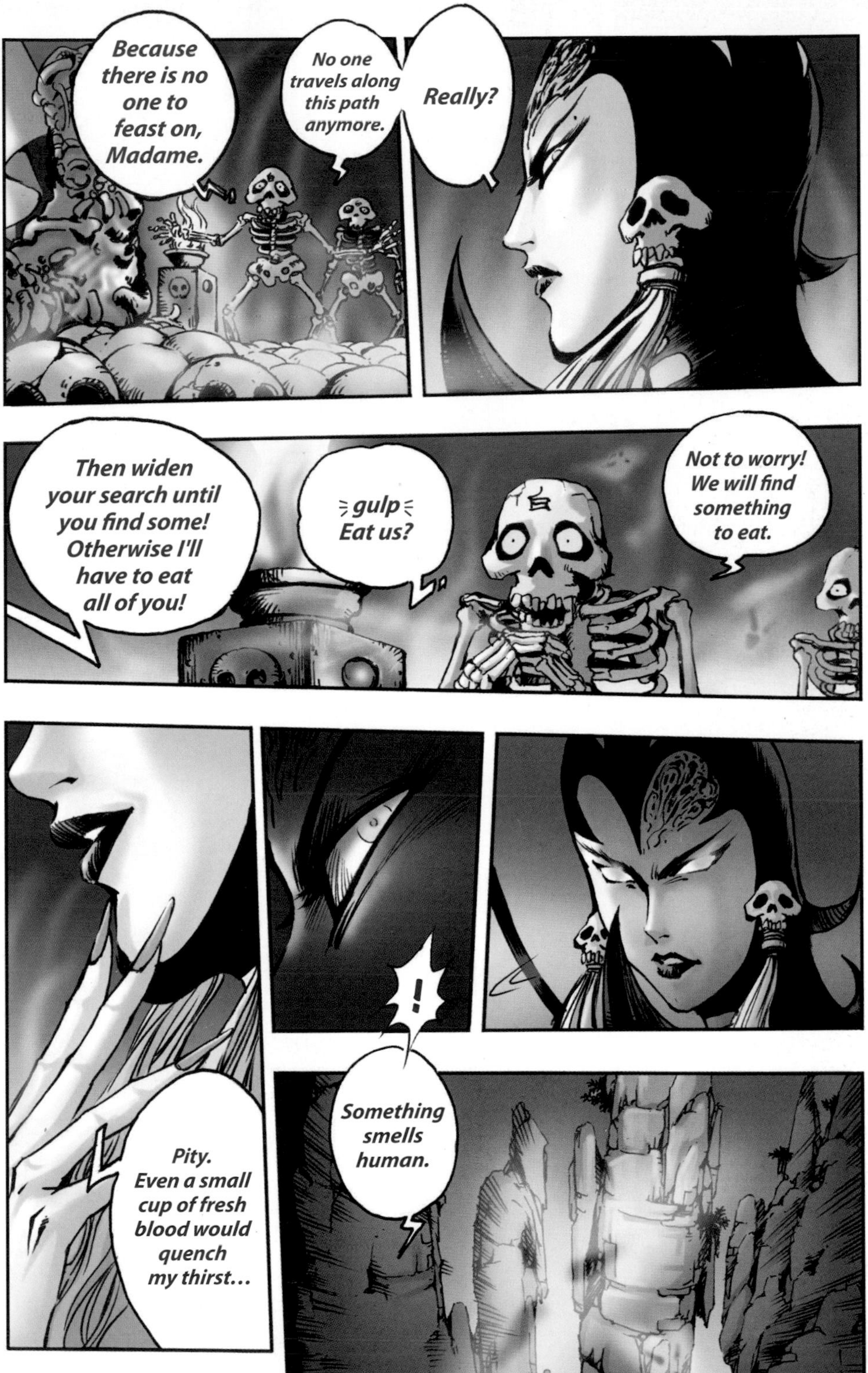

Because there is no one to feast on, Madame.
No one travels along this path anymore.
Really?
Then widen your search until you find some! Otherwise I'll have to eat all of you!
gulp Eat us?
Not to worry! We will find something to eat.
Pity. Even a small cup of fresh blood would quench my thirst…
!
Something smells human.

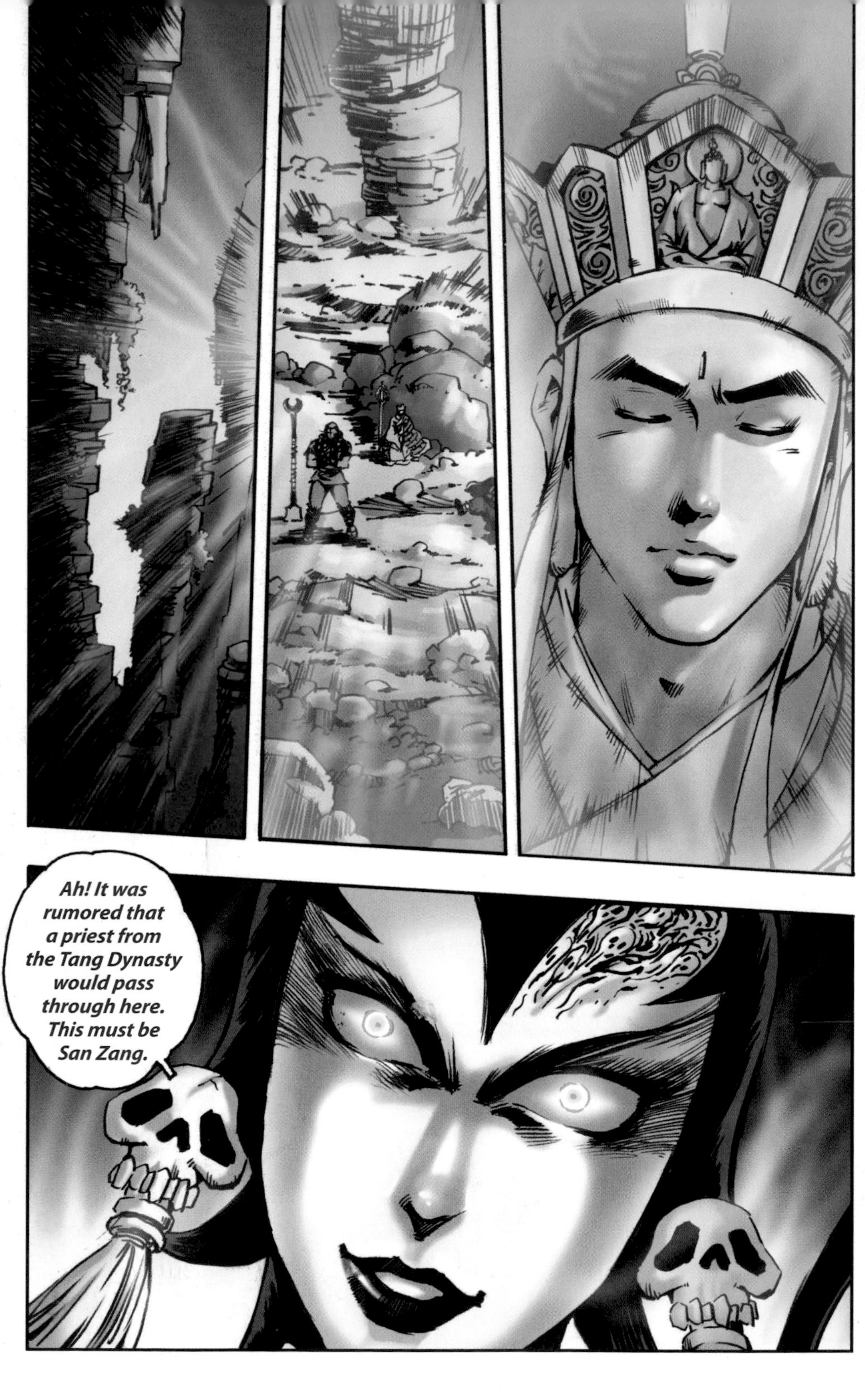
Ah! It was rumored that a priest from the Tang Dynasty would pass through here. This must be San Zang.

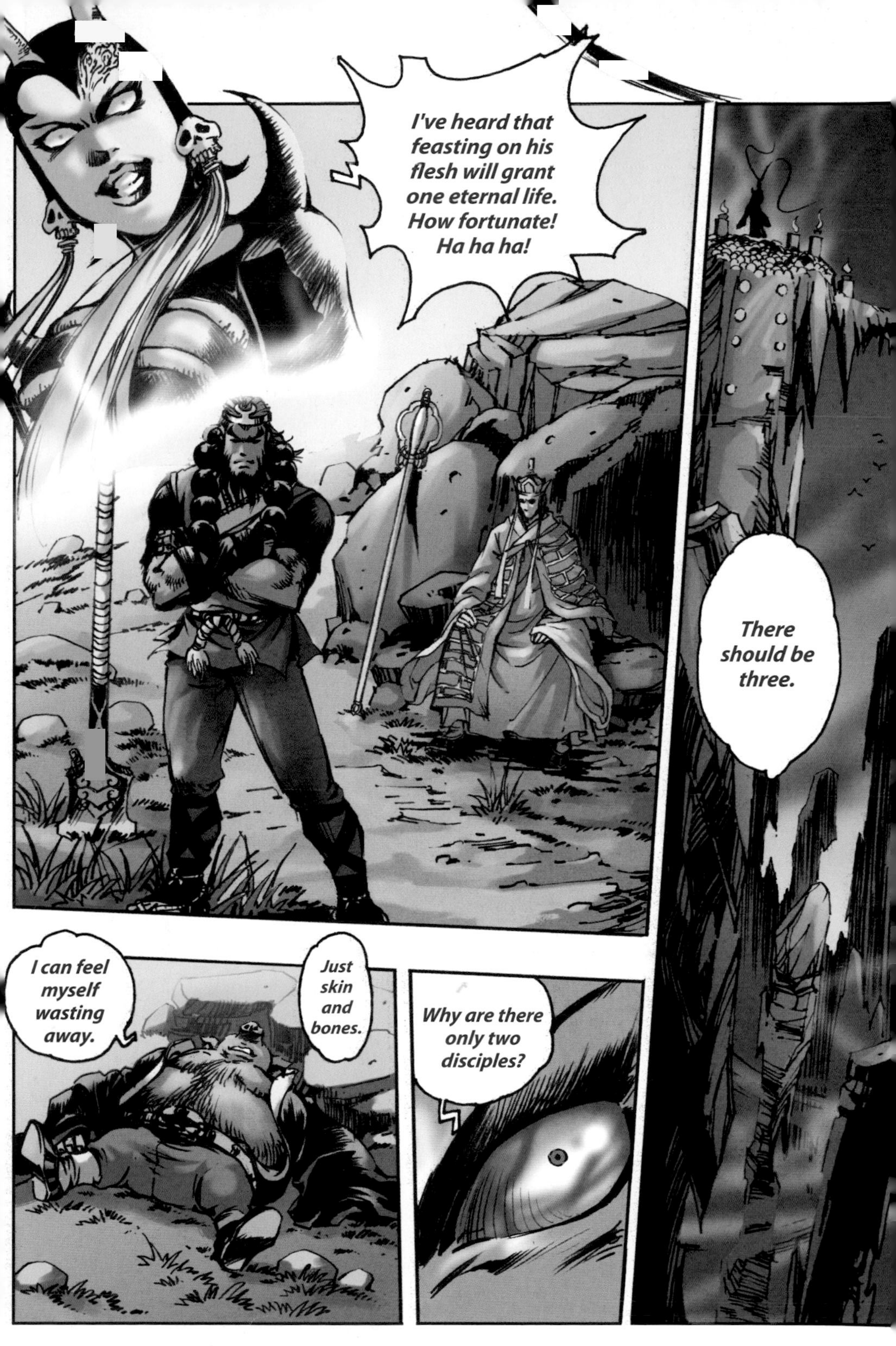
I've heard that feasting on his flesh will grant one eternal life. How fortunate! Ha ha ha!
There should be three.
I can feel myself wasting away.
Just skin and bones.
Why are there only two disciples?

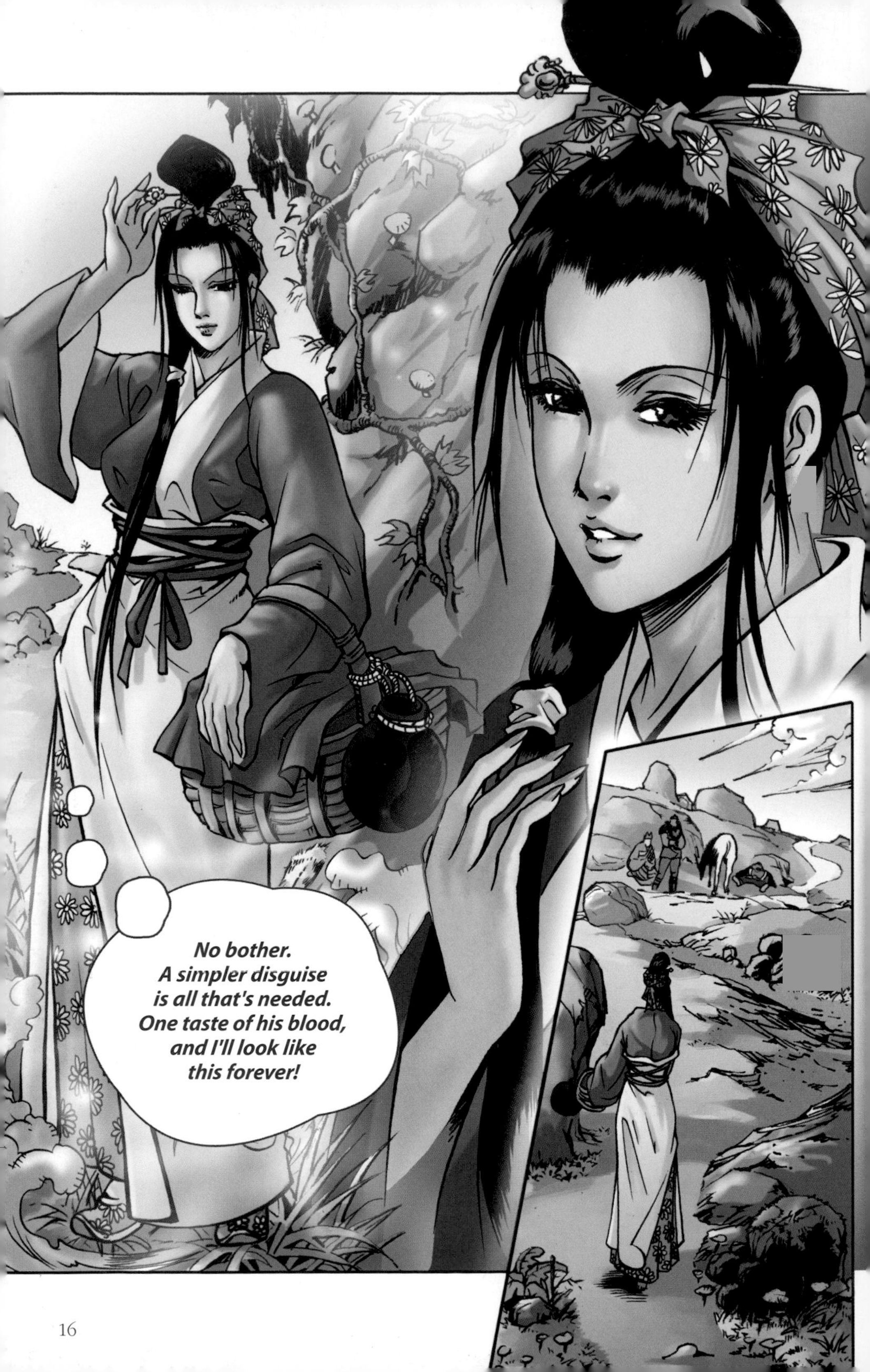
No bother. A simpler disguise is all that's needed. One taste of his blood, and I'll look like this forever!

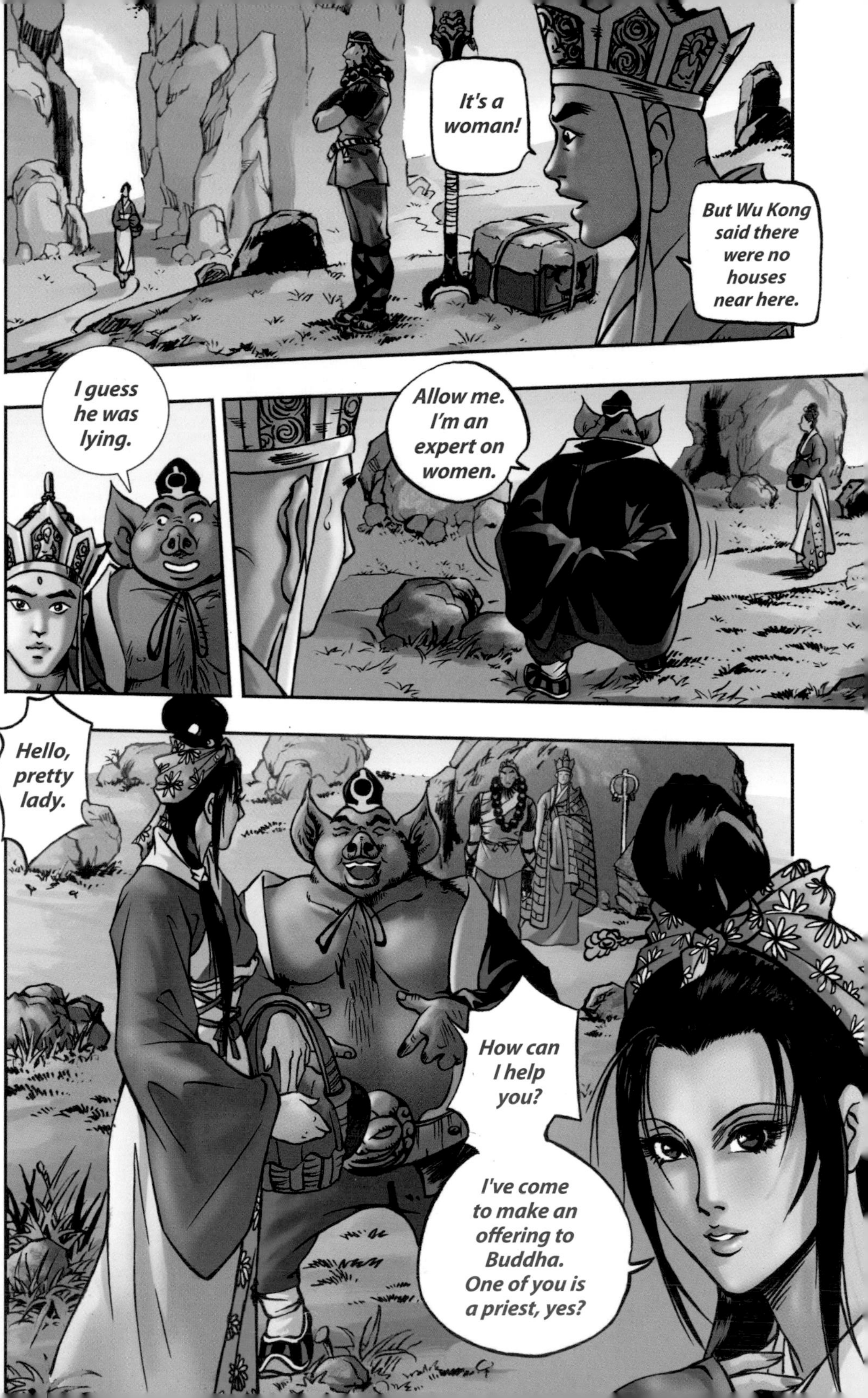
It's a woman!
But Wu Kong said there were no houses near here.
I guess he was lying.
Allow me. I'm an expert on women.
Hello, pretty lady.
How can I help you?
I've come to make an offering to Buddha. One of you is a priest, yes?

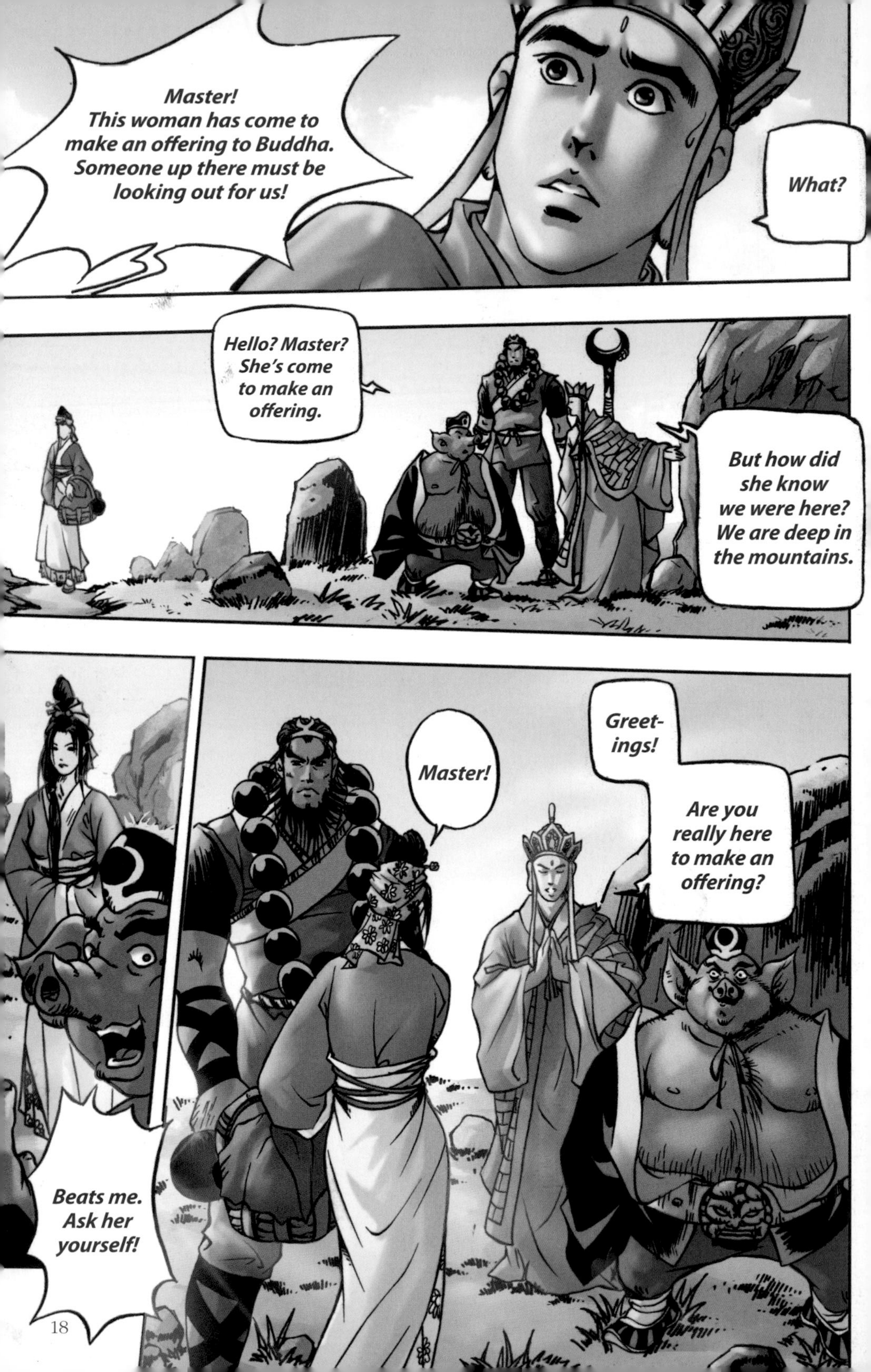

Master! This woman has come to make an offering to Buddha. Someone up there must be looking out for us!
What?
Hello? Master? She's come to make an offering.
But how did she know we were here? We are deep in the mountains.
Greet-ings!
Are you really here to make an offering?
Master!
Beats me. Ask her yourself!

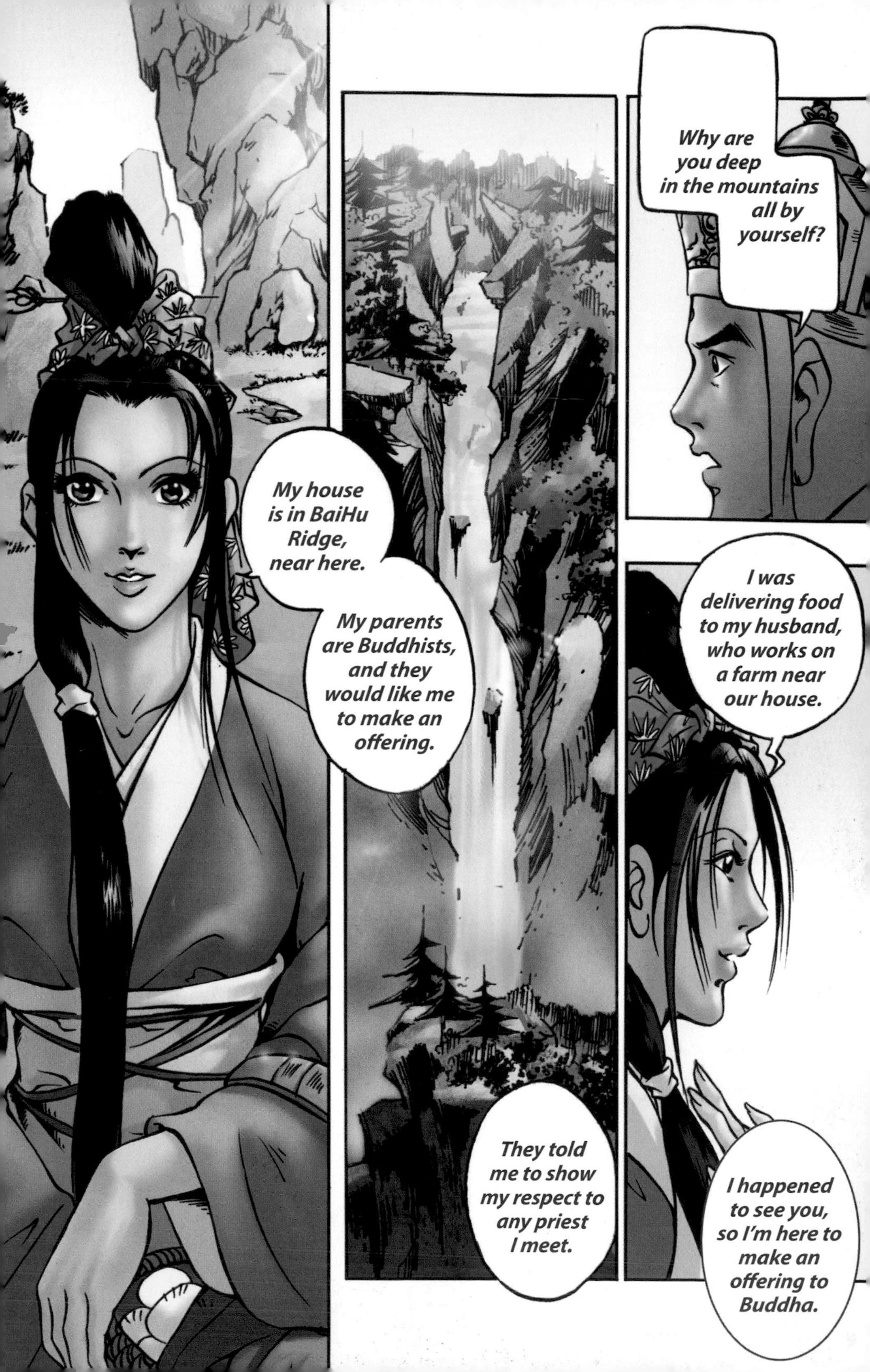
My house is in BaiHu Ridge, near here.
My parents are Buddhists, and they would like me to make an offering.
They told me to show my respect to any priest I meet.
Why are you deep in the mountains all by yourself?
I was delivering food to my husband, who works on a farm near our house.
I happened to see you, so I'm here to make an offering to Buddha.

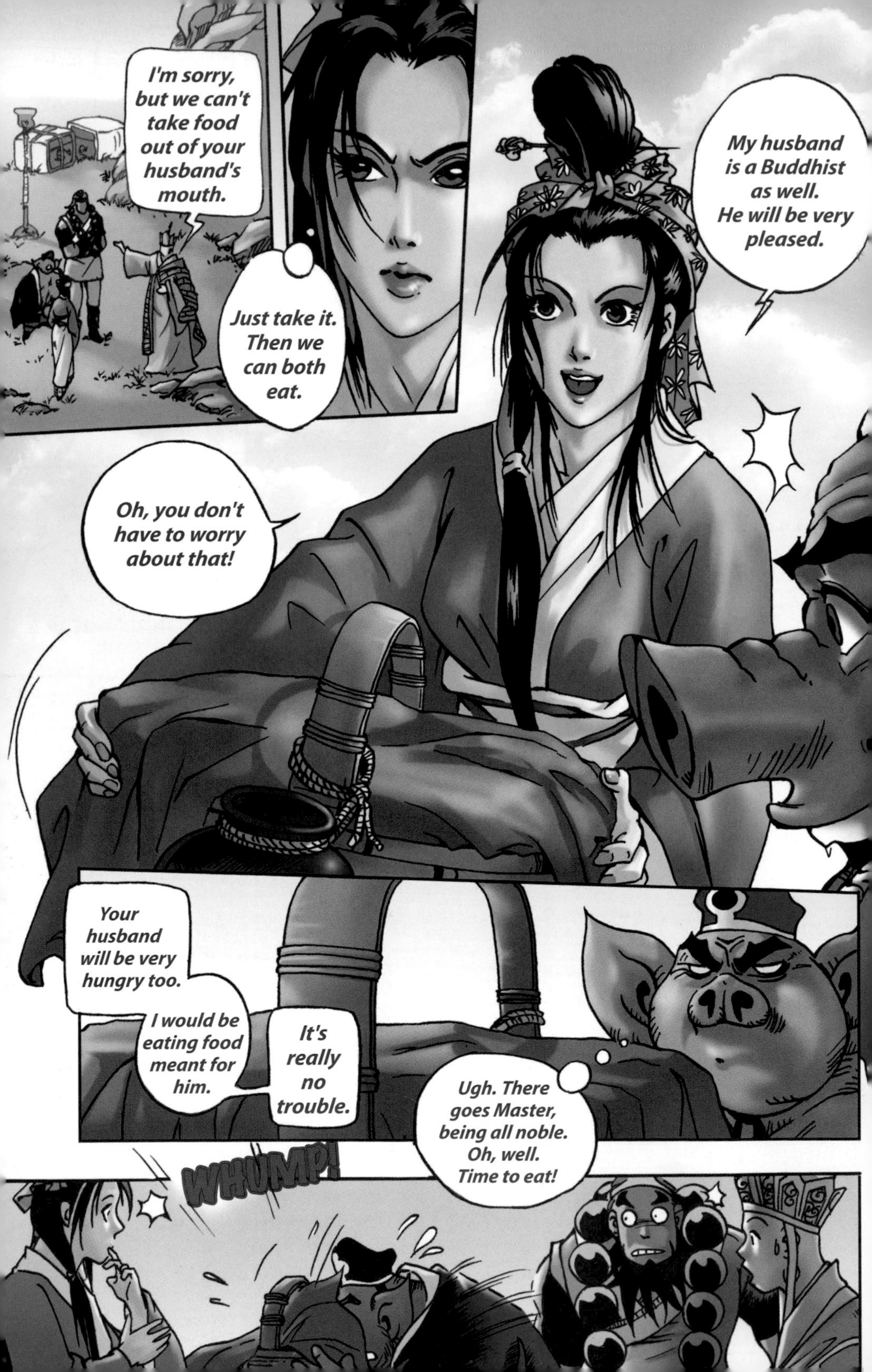

I'm sorry, but we can't take food out of your husband's mouth.
Just take it. Then we can both eat.
My husband is a Buddhist as well. He will be very pleased.
Oh, you don't have to worry about that!
Your husband will be very hungry too.
I would be eating food meant for him.
It's really no trouble.
Ugh. There goes Master, being all noble. Oh, well. Time to eat!
WHUMP!

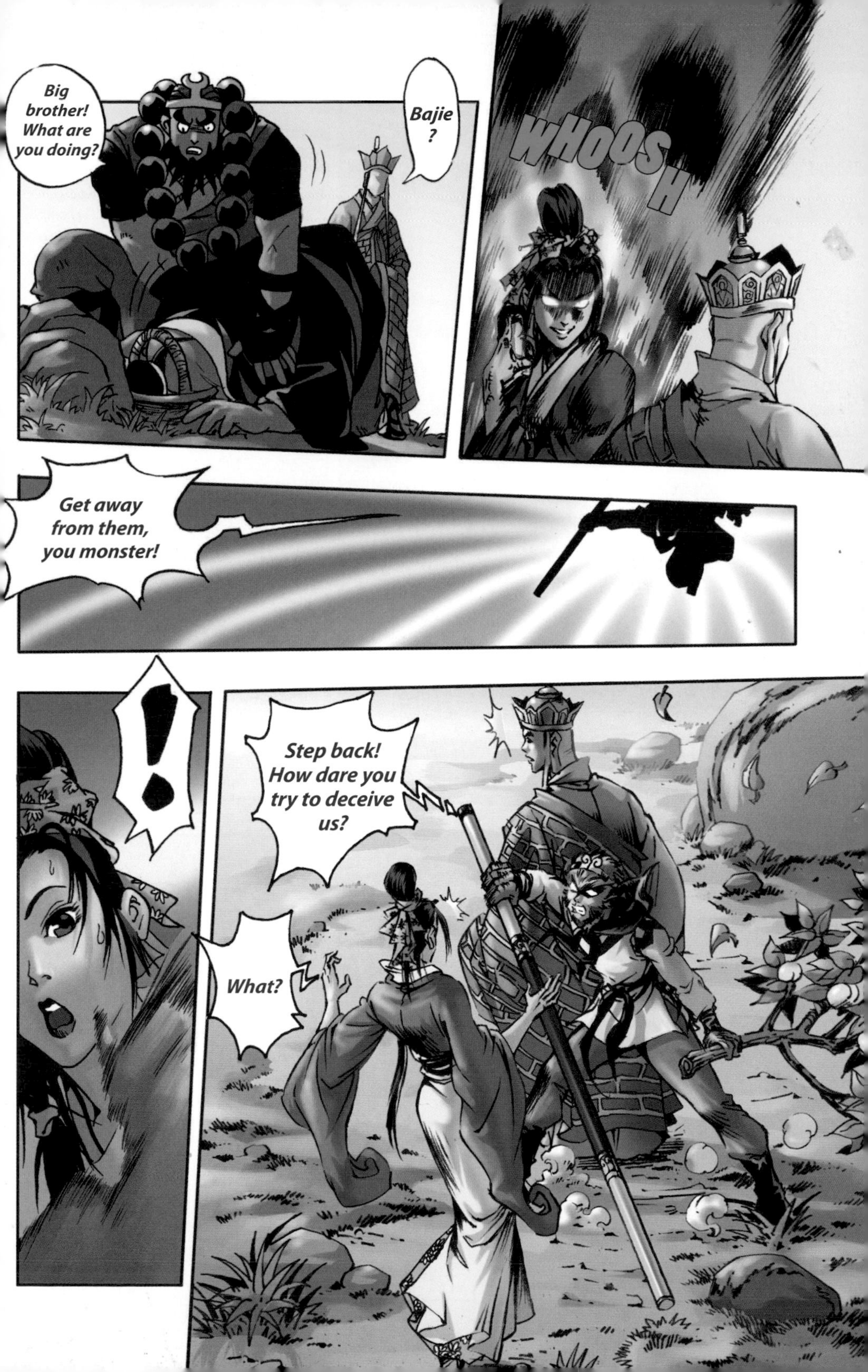

Big brother! What are you doing?
Bajie ?
WHOOSH
Get away from them, you monster!
!
Step back! How dare you try to deceive us?
What?

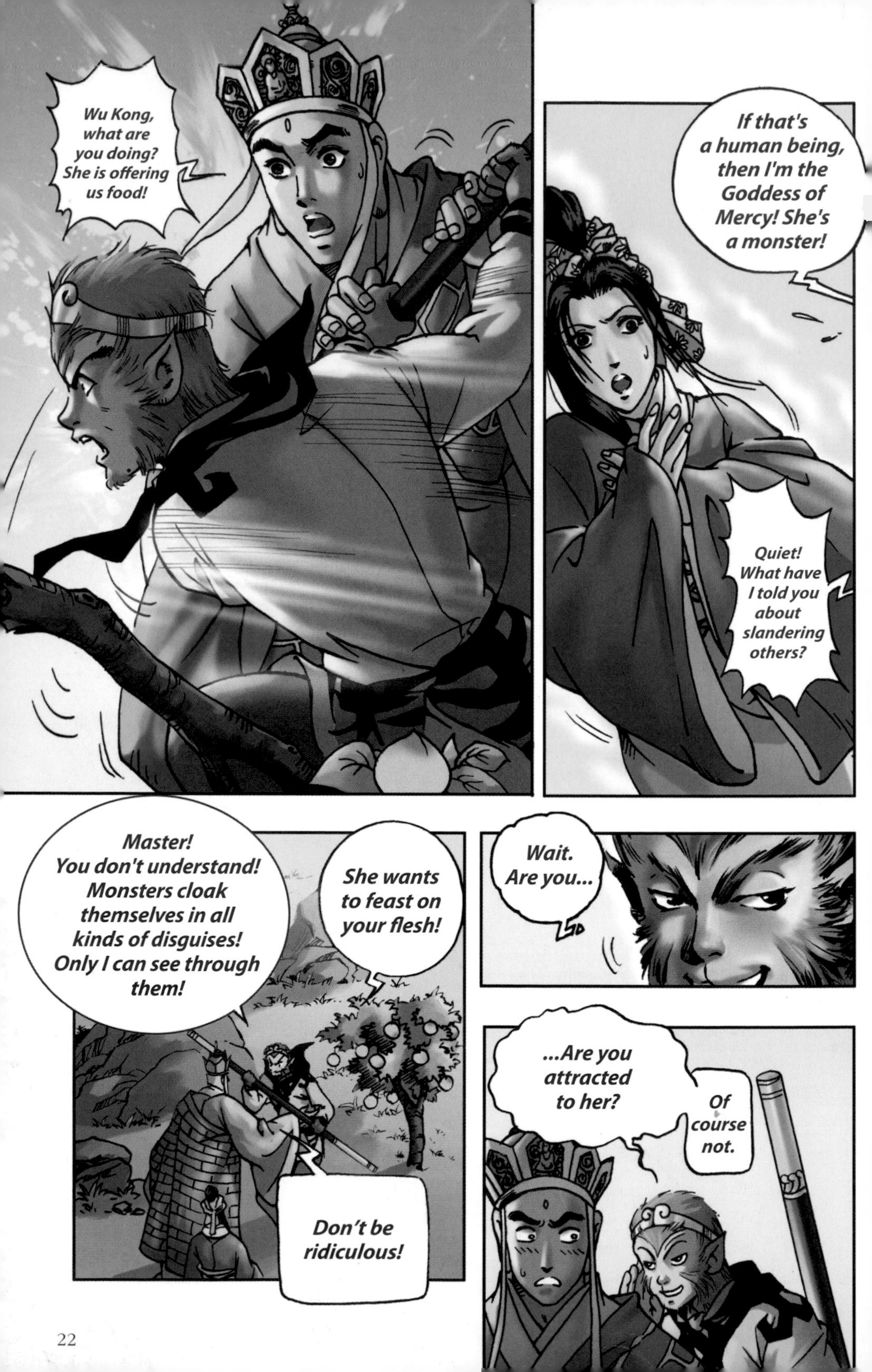
Wu Kong, what are you doing? She is offering us food!
If that's a human being, then I'm the Goddess of Mercy! She's a monster!
Quiet! What have I told you about slandering others?
Master! You don't understand! Monsters cloak themselves in all kinds of disguises! Only I can see through them!
She wants to feast on your flesh!
Don't be ridiculous!
Wait. Are you...
...Are you attracted to her?
Of course not.

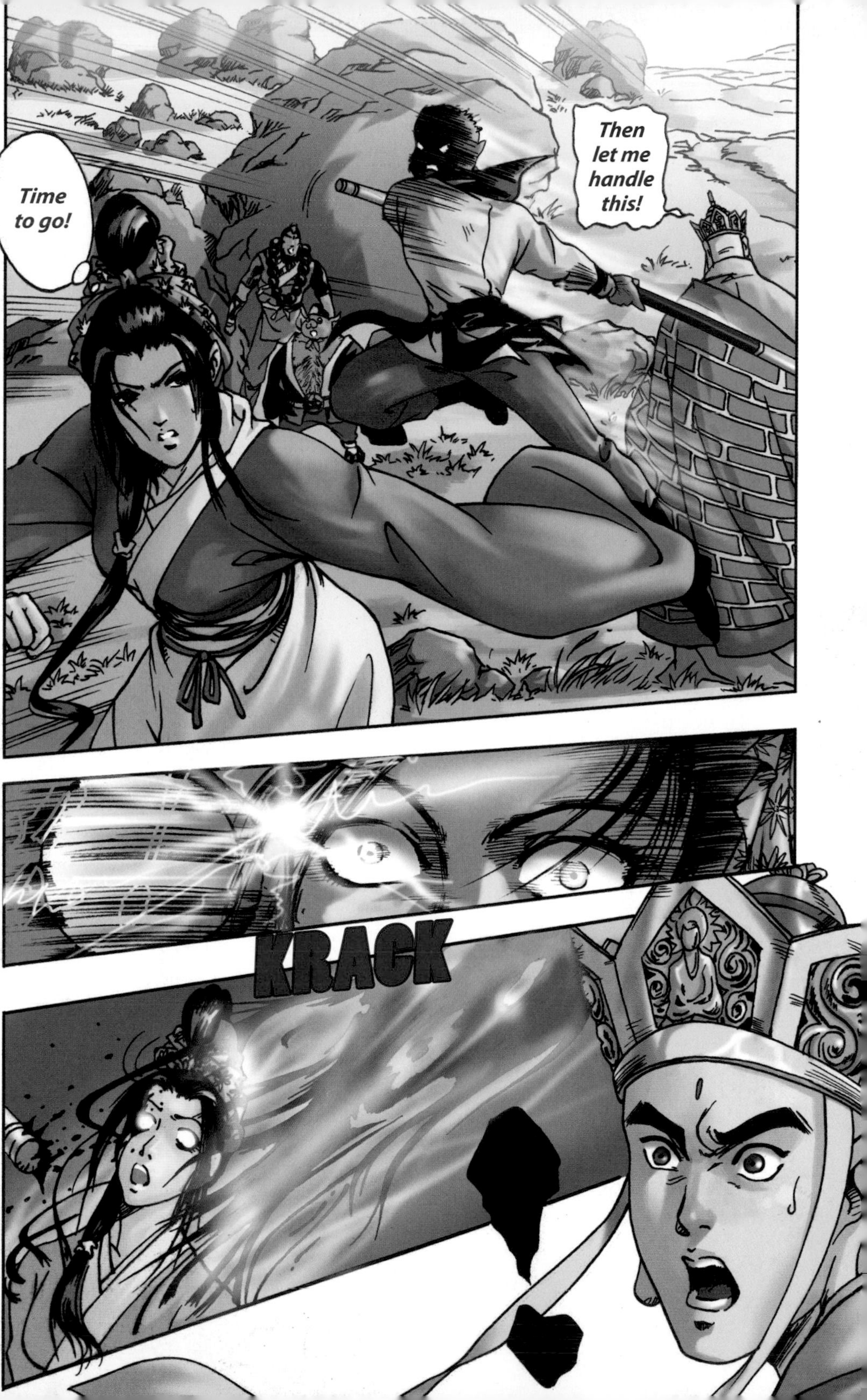
Time to go!
Then let me handle this!
KRACK

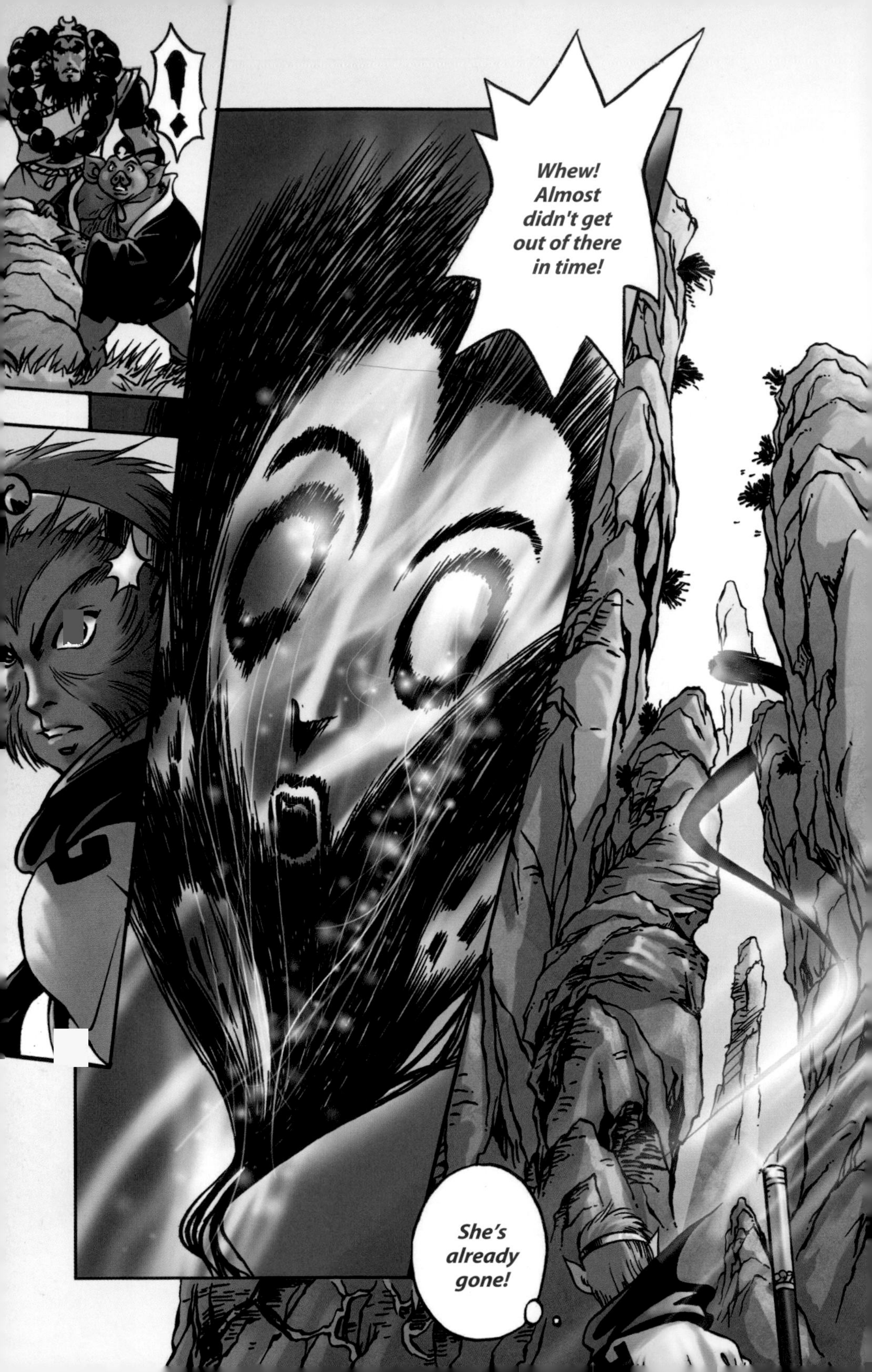
!
Whew! Almost didn't get out of there in time!
She's already gone!

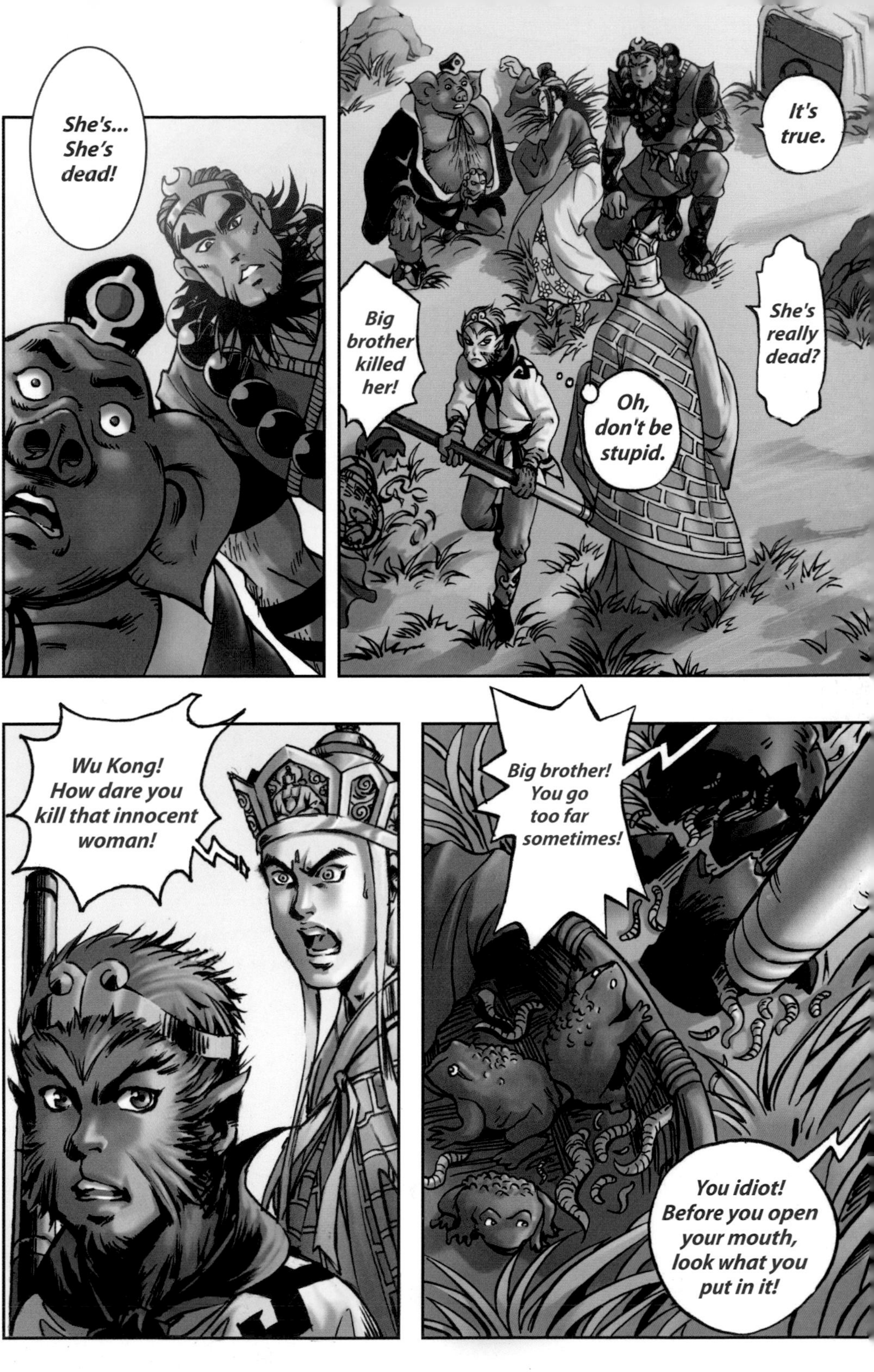
She's... She's dead!
It's true.
Big brother killed her!
She's really dead?
Oh, don't be stupid.
Wu Kong! How dare you kill that innocent woman!
Big brother! You go too far sometimes!
You idiot! Before you open your mouth, look what you put in it!

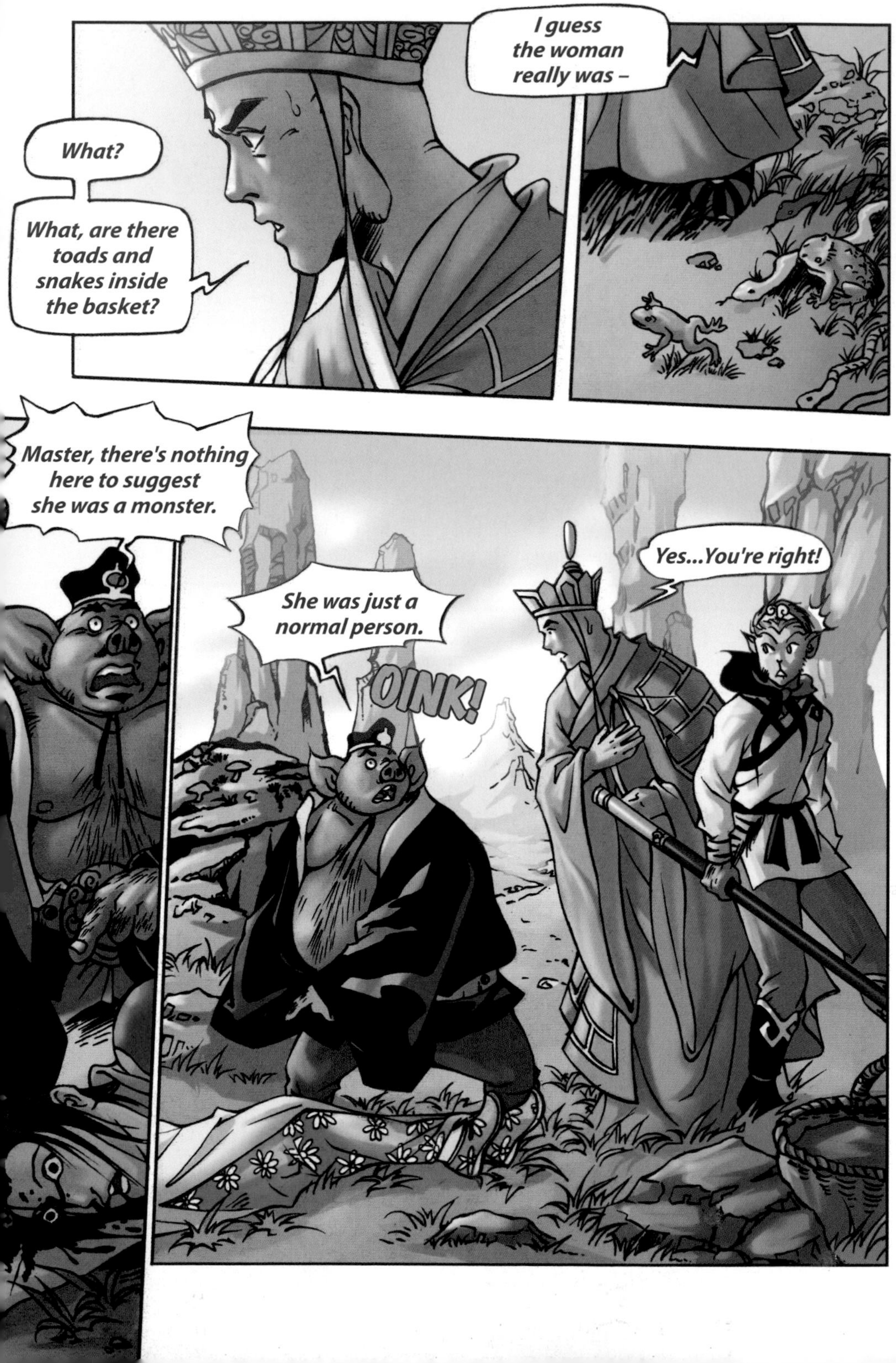
I guess the woman really was –
What?
What, are there toads and snakes inside the basket?
Master, there's nothing here to suggest she was a monster.
She was just a normal person.
OINK!
Yes...You're right!

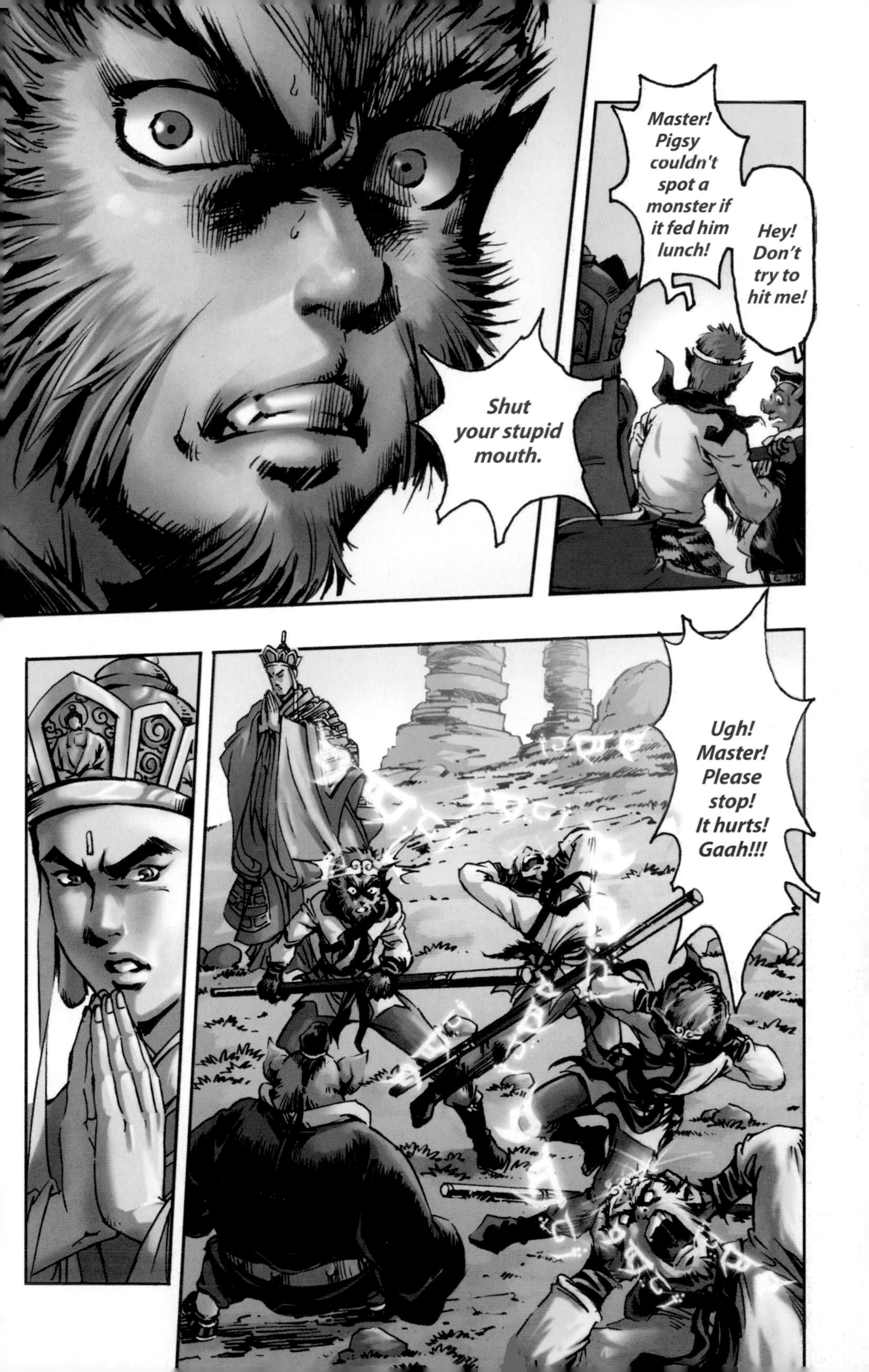
Shut your stupid mouth.
Master! Pigsy couldn't spot a monster if it fed him lunch!
Hey! Don't try to hit me!
Ugh! Master! Please stop! It hurts! Gaah!!!

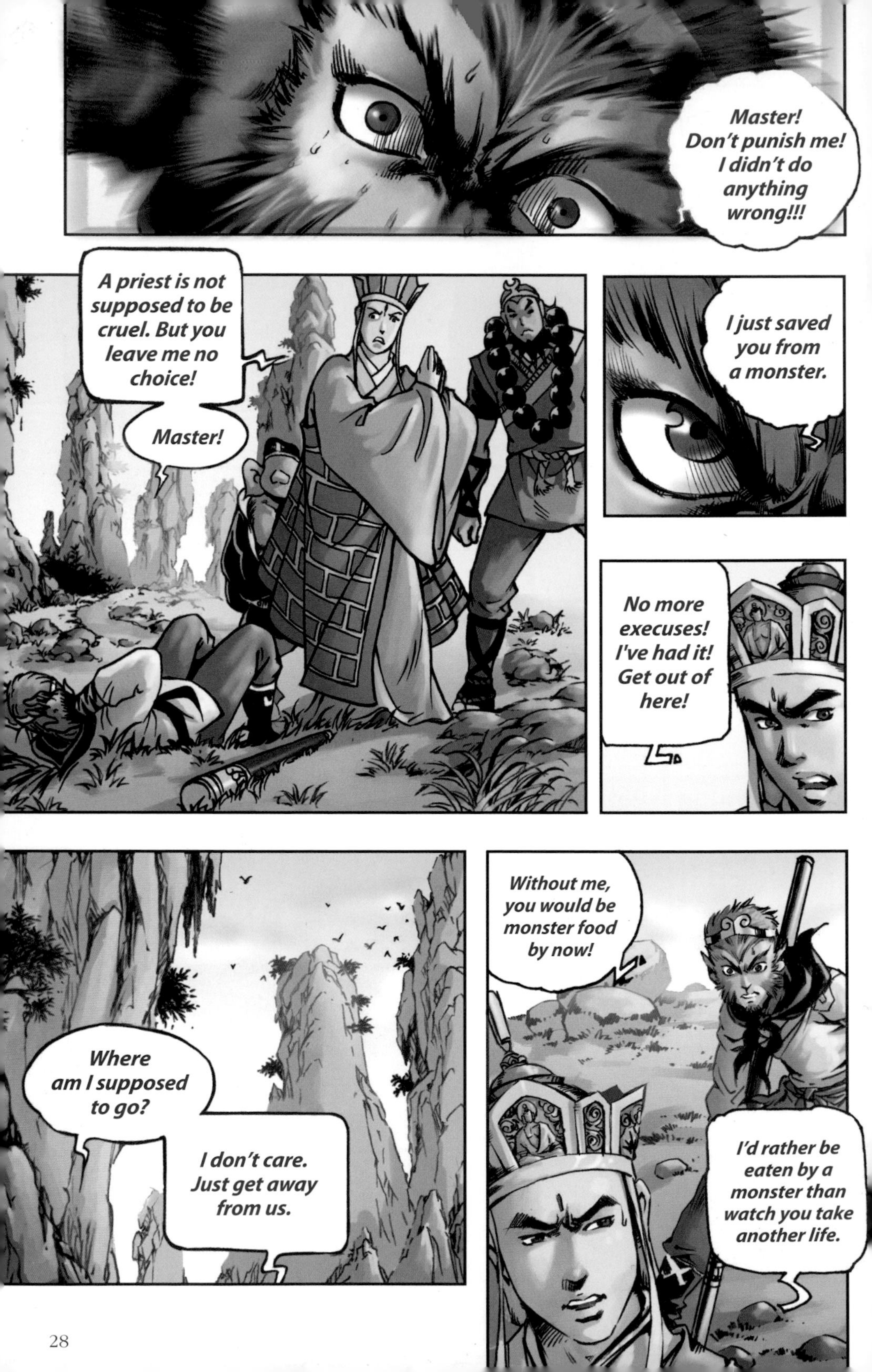
Master! Don't punish me! I didn't do anything wrong!!!
A priest is not supposed to be cruel. But you leave me no choice!
Master!
I just saved you from a monster.
No more execuses! I've had it! Get out of here!
Where am I supposed to go?
I don't care. Just get away from us.
Without me, you would be monster food by now!
I'd rather be eaten by a monster than watch you take another life.

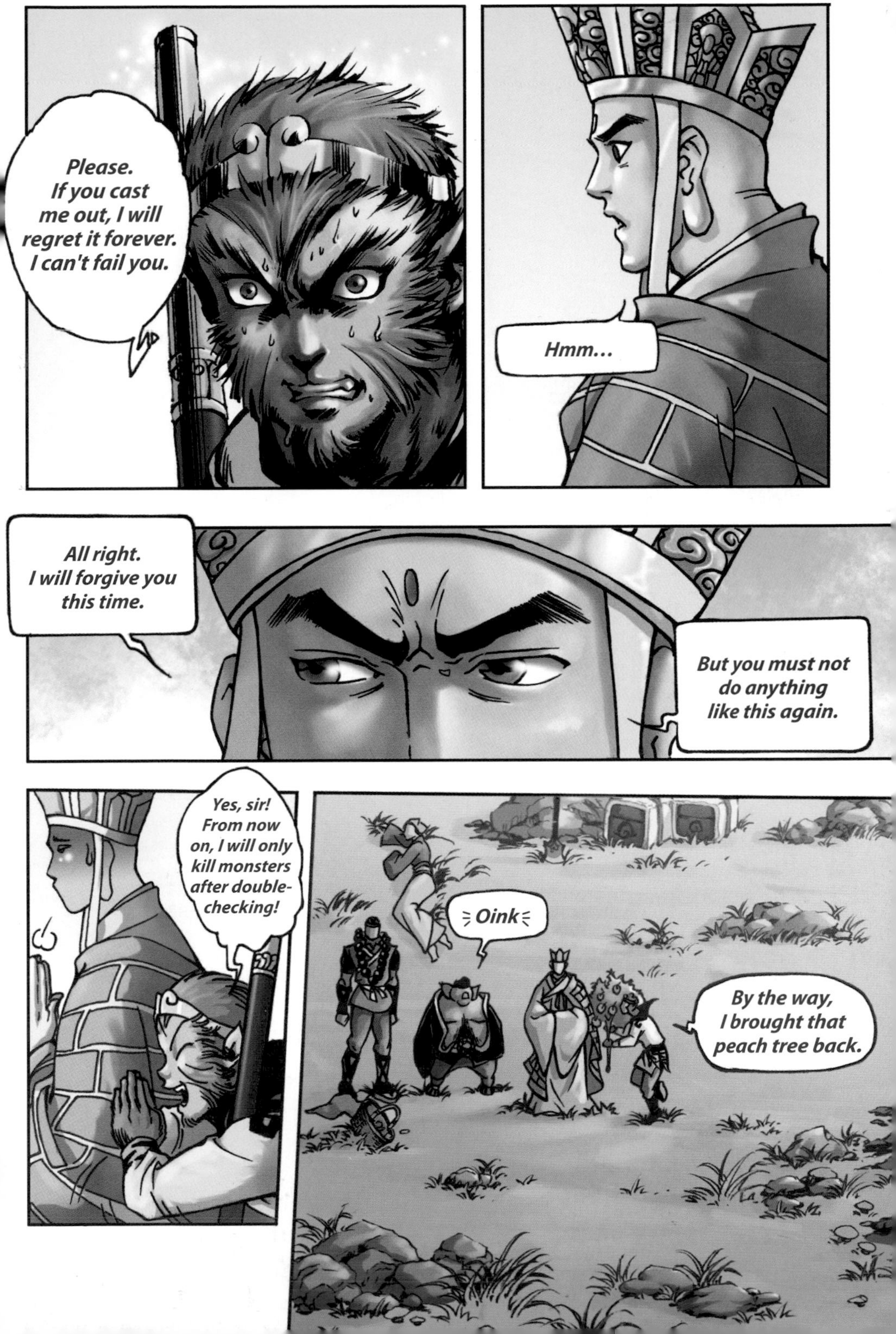
Please.
If you cast me out, I will regret it forever. I can't fail you.
Hmm…
All right. I will forgive you this time.
But you must not do anything like this again.
Yes, sir! From now on, I will only kill monsters after double-checking!
Oink
By the way, I brought that peach tree back.

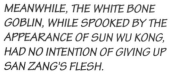

MEANWHILE, THE WHITE BONE GOBLIN, WHILE SPOOKED BY THE APPEARANCE OF SUN WU KONG, HAD NO INTENTION OF GIVING UP SAN ZANG'S FLESH.

Sun Wu Kong! It's just as I've heard. I'm lucky to be alive!

I must get rid of him, or I'll never be able to eat San Zang's heart.

Do you want us to go?

Don't be foolish! You're no match for him!

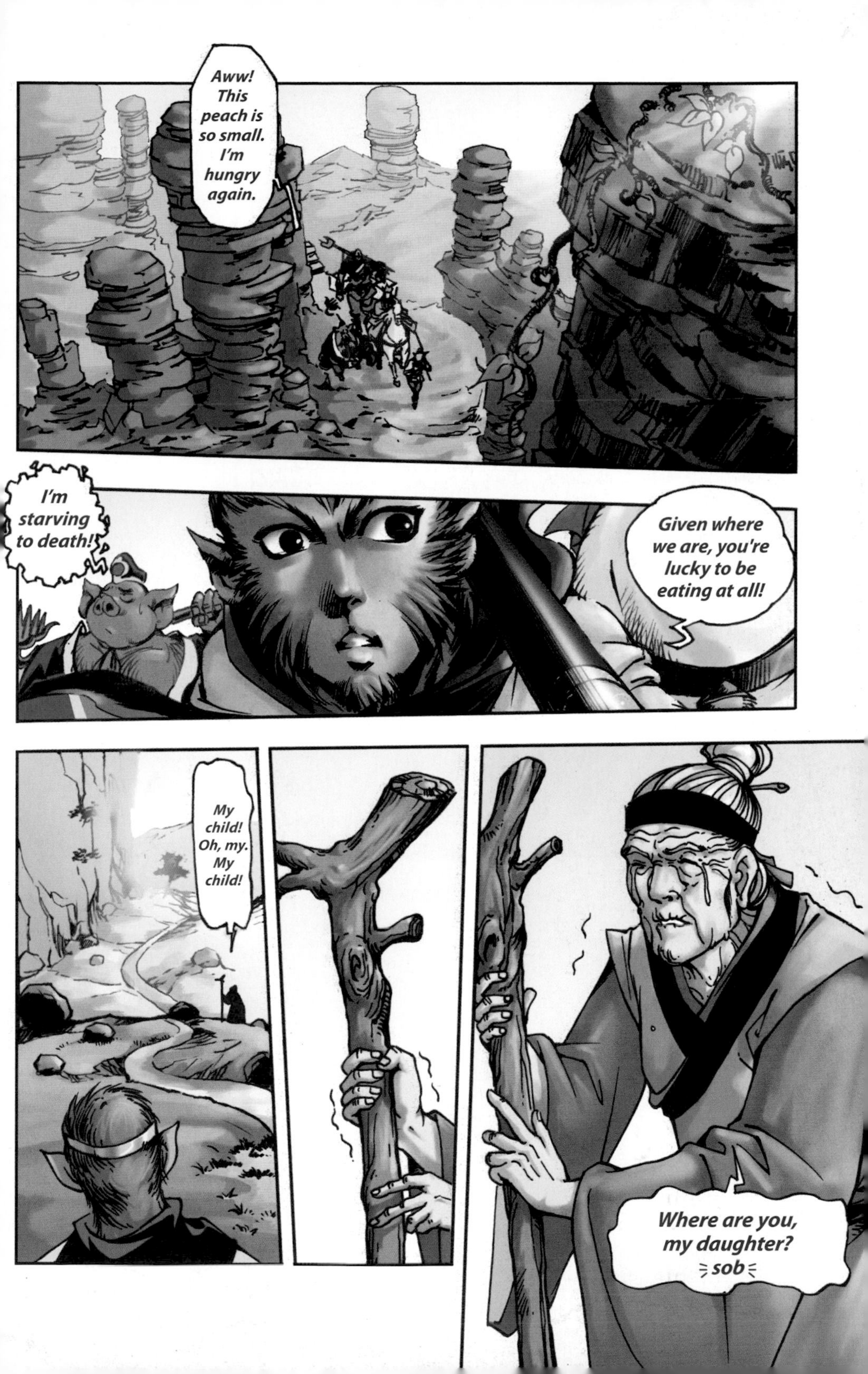
Aww! This peach is so small. I'm hungry again.
I'm starving to death!
Given where we are, you're lucky to be eating at all!
My child! Oh, my. My child!
Where are you, my daughter?
sob

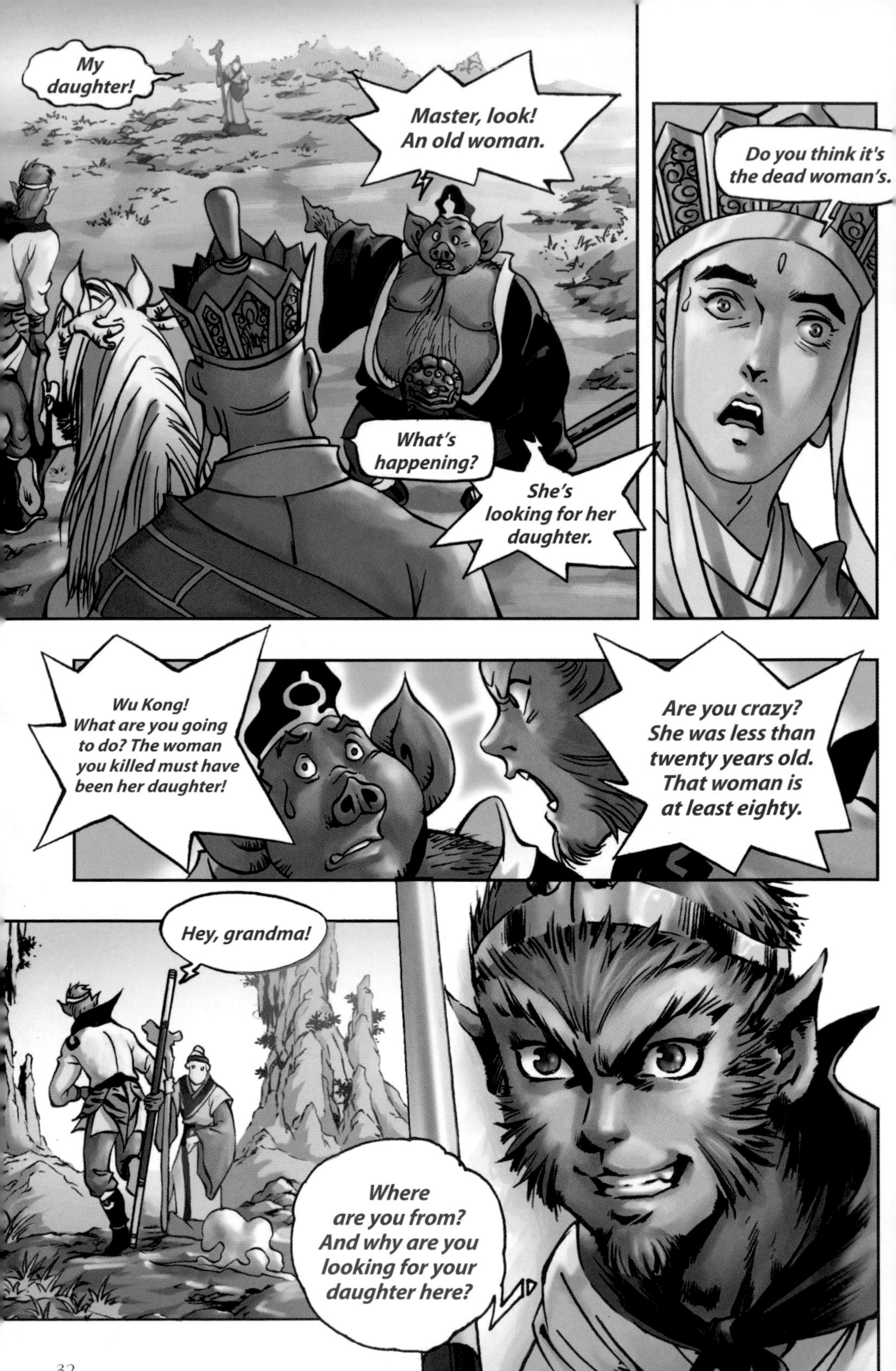
My daughter!
Master, look! An old woman.
Do you think it's the dead woman's.
What's happening?
She's looking for her daughter.
Wu Kong! What are you going to do? The woman you killed must have been her daughter!
Are you crazy? She was less than twenty years old. That woman is at least eighty.
Hey, grandma!
Where are you from? And why are you looking for your daughter here?

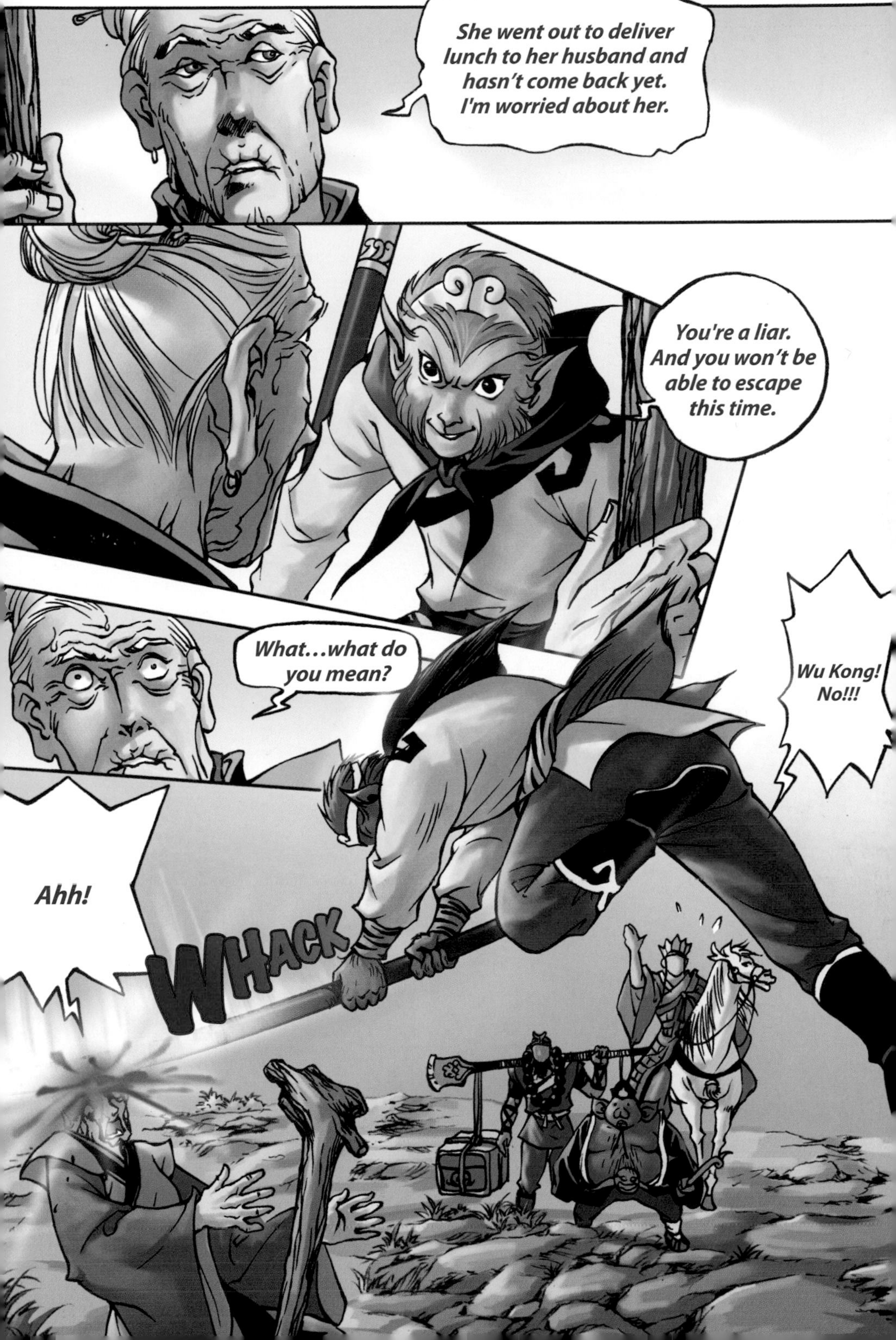
She went out to deliver lunch to her husband and hasn't come back yet. I'm worried about her.
You're a liar. And you won't be able to escape this time.
What…what do you mean?
Wu Kong! No!!!
Ahh!
WHACK

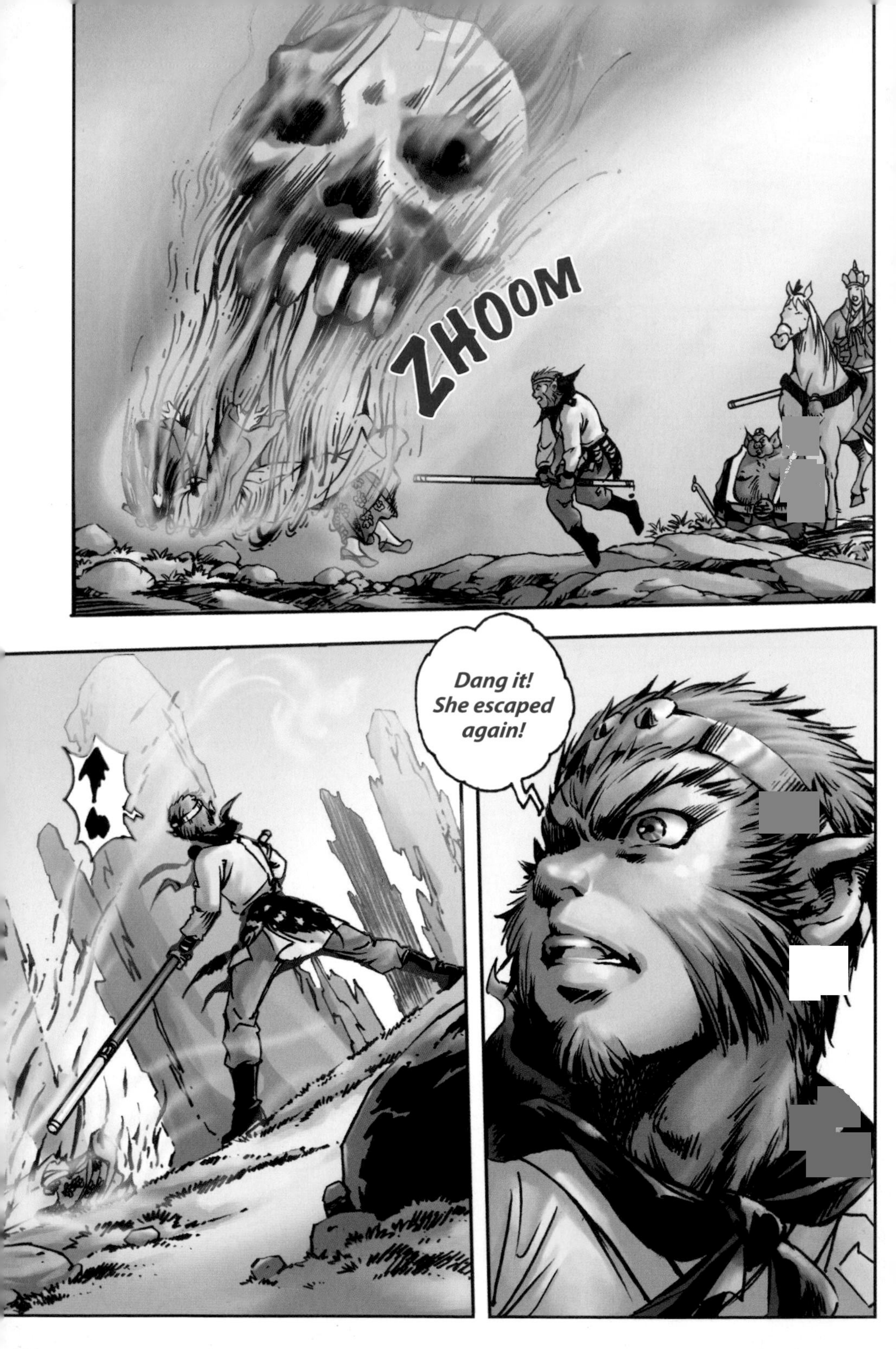
ZHOOM
Dang it! She escaped again!

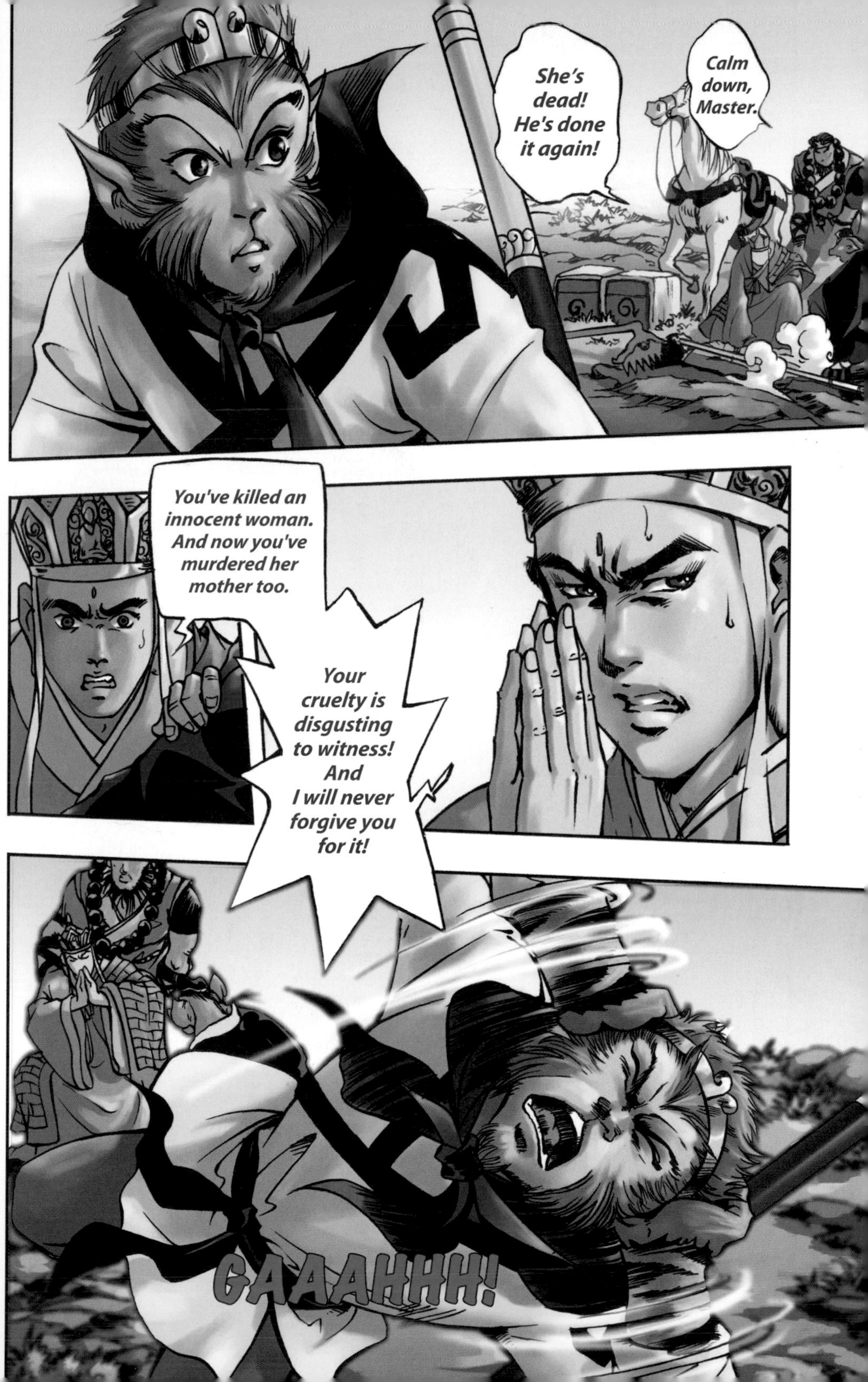
She's dead! He's done it again!
Calm down, Master.
You've killed an innocent woman. And now you've murdered her mother too.
Your cruelty is disgusting to witness! And I will never forgive you for it!
GAAAHHH!

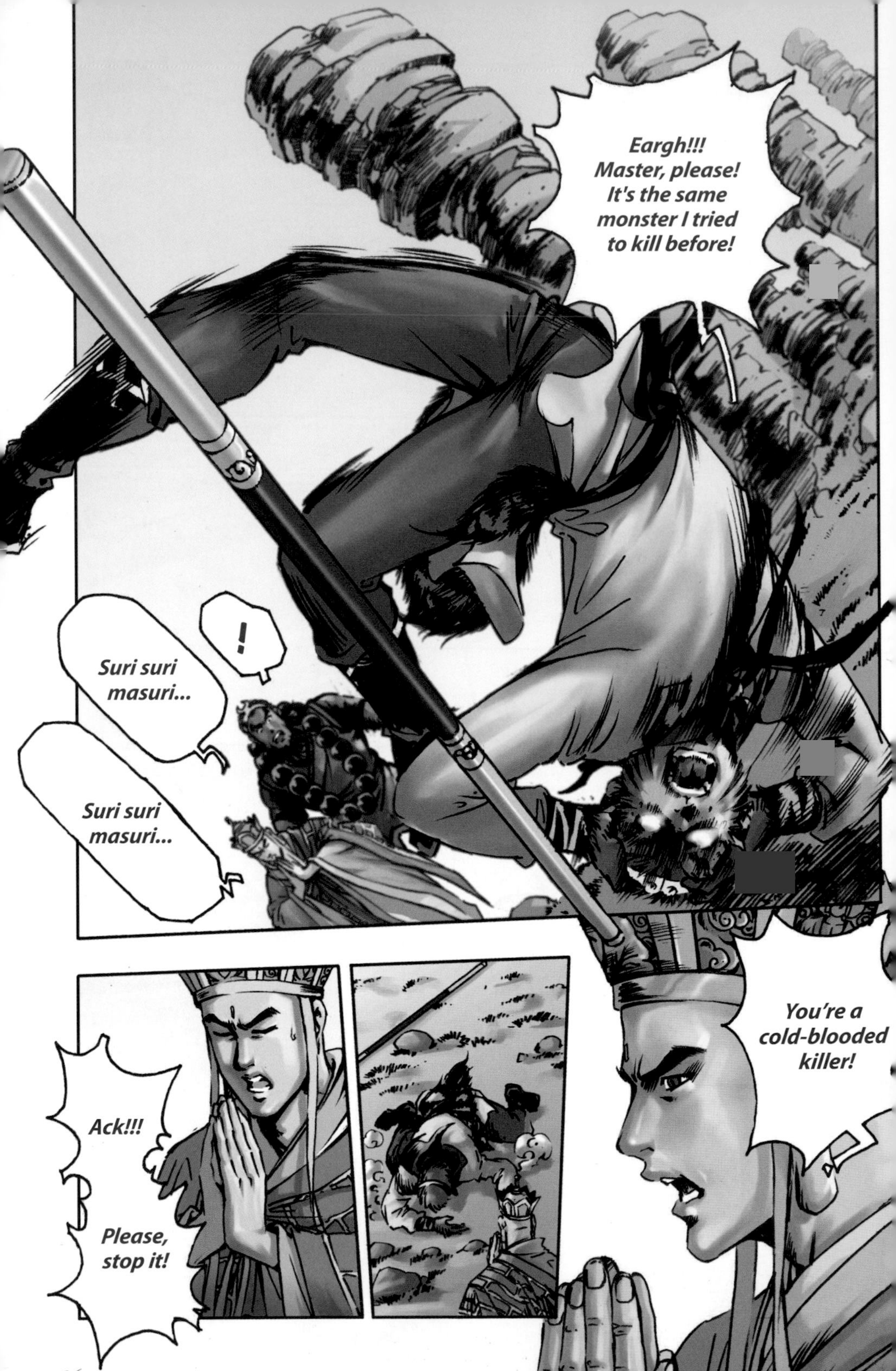
Eargh!!! Master, please! It's the same monster I tried to kill before!
!
Suri suri masuri...
Suri suri masuri...
Ack!!!
Please, stop it!
You're a cold-blooded killer!

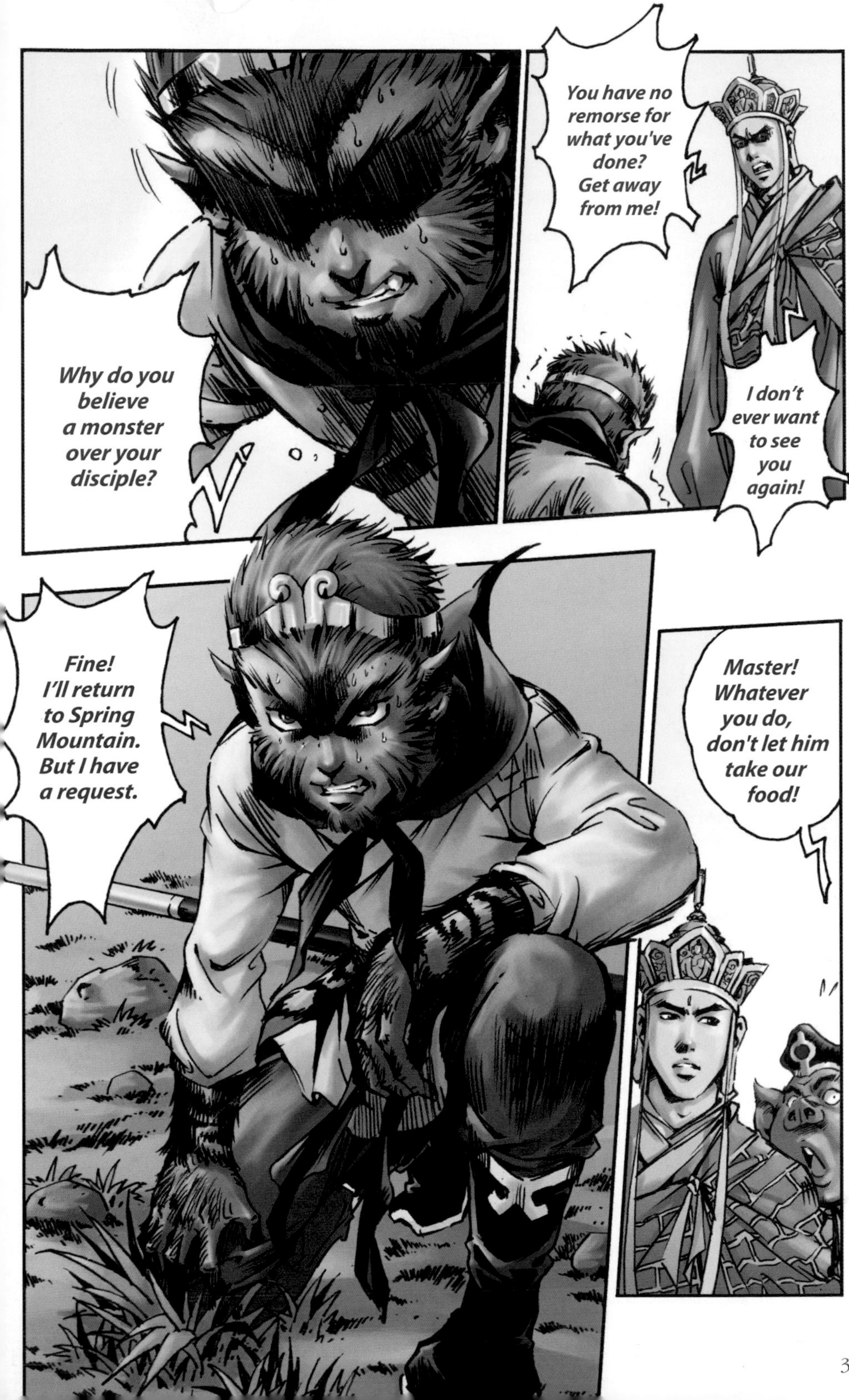
You have no remorse for what you've done? Get away from me!
Why do you believe a monster over your disciple?
I don't ever want to see you again!
Fine! I'll return to Spring Mountain. But I have a request.
Master! Whatever you do, don't let him take our food!

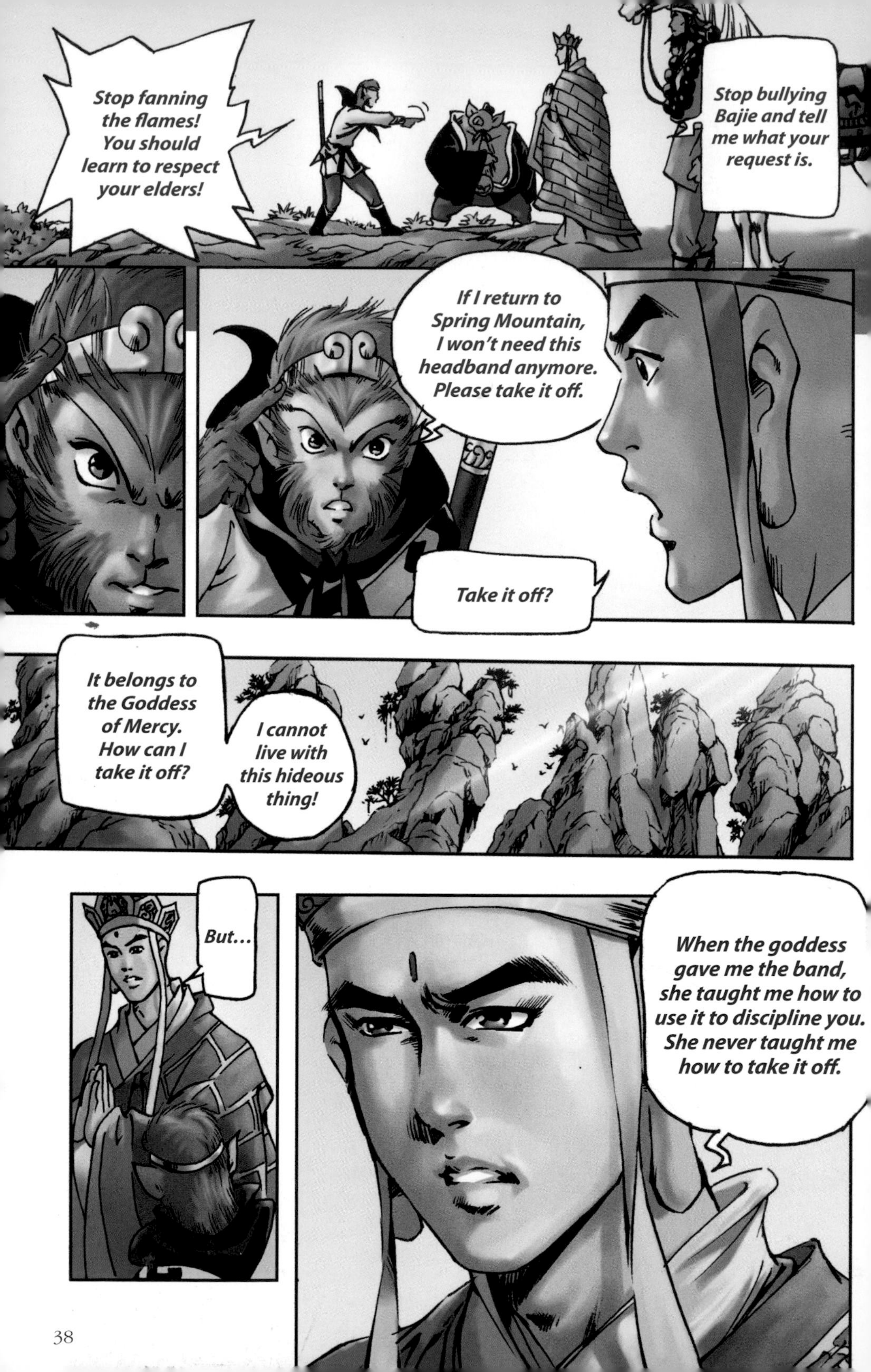
Stop fanning the flames! You should learn to respect your elders!
Stop bullying Bajie and tell me what your request is.
If I return to Spring Mountain, I won't need this headband anymore. Please take it off.
Take it off?
It belongs to the Goddess of Mercy. How can I take it off?
I cannot live with this hideous thing!
But…
When the goddess gave me the band, she taught me how to use it to discipline you. She never taught me how to take it off.

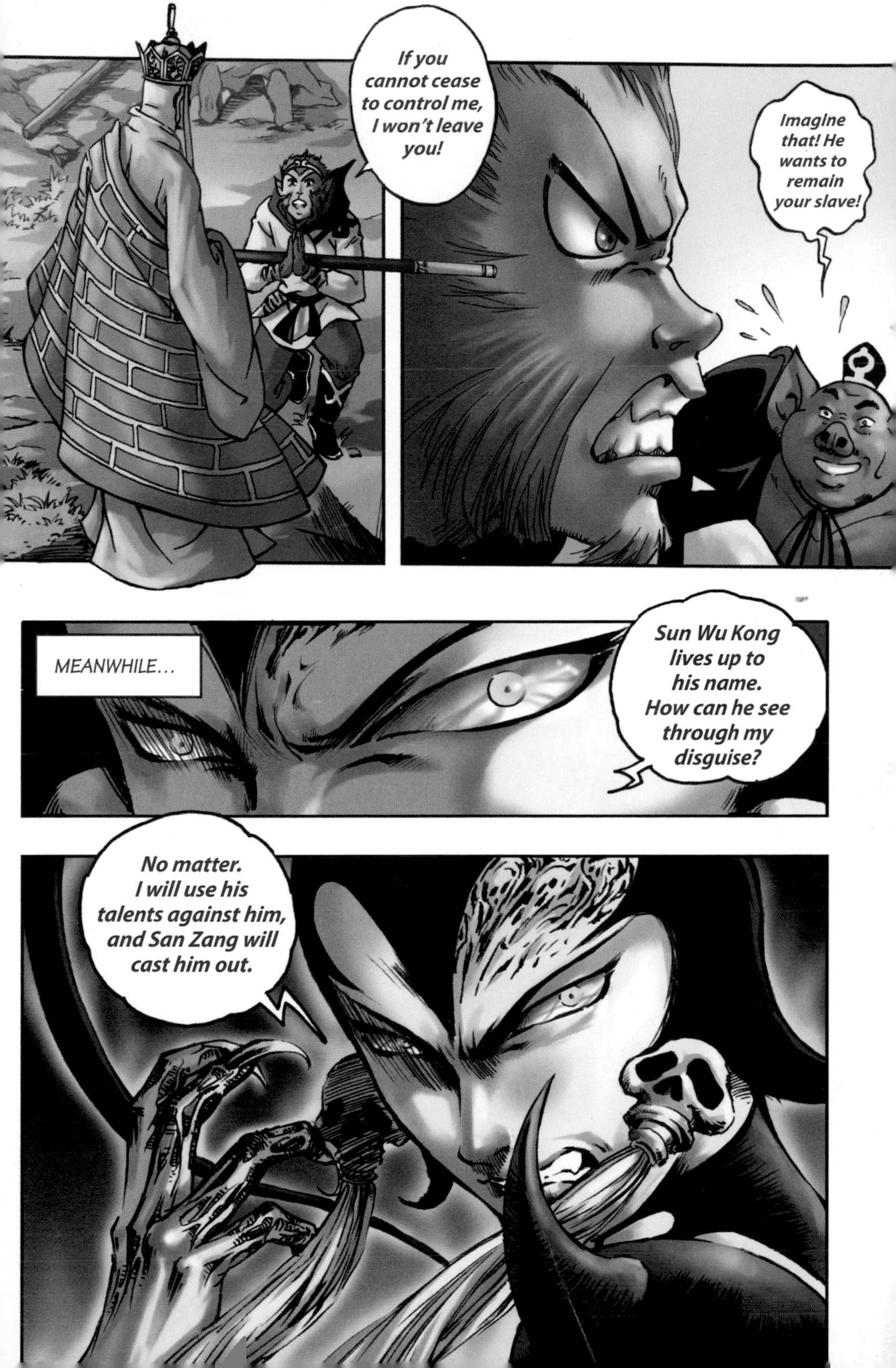
If you cannot cease to control me, I won't leave you!
Imagine that! He wants to remain your slave!
MEANWHILE...
Sun Wu Kong lives up to his name. How can he see through my disguise?
No matter. I will use his talents against him, and San Zang will cast him out.

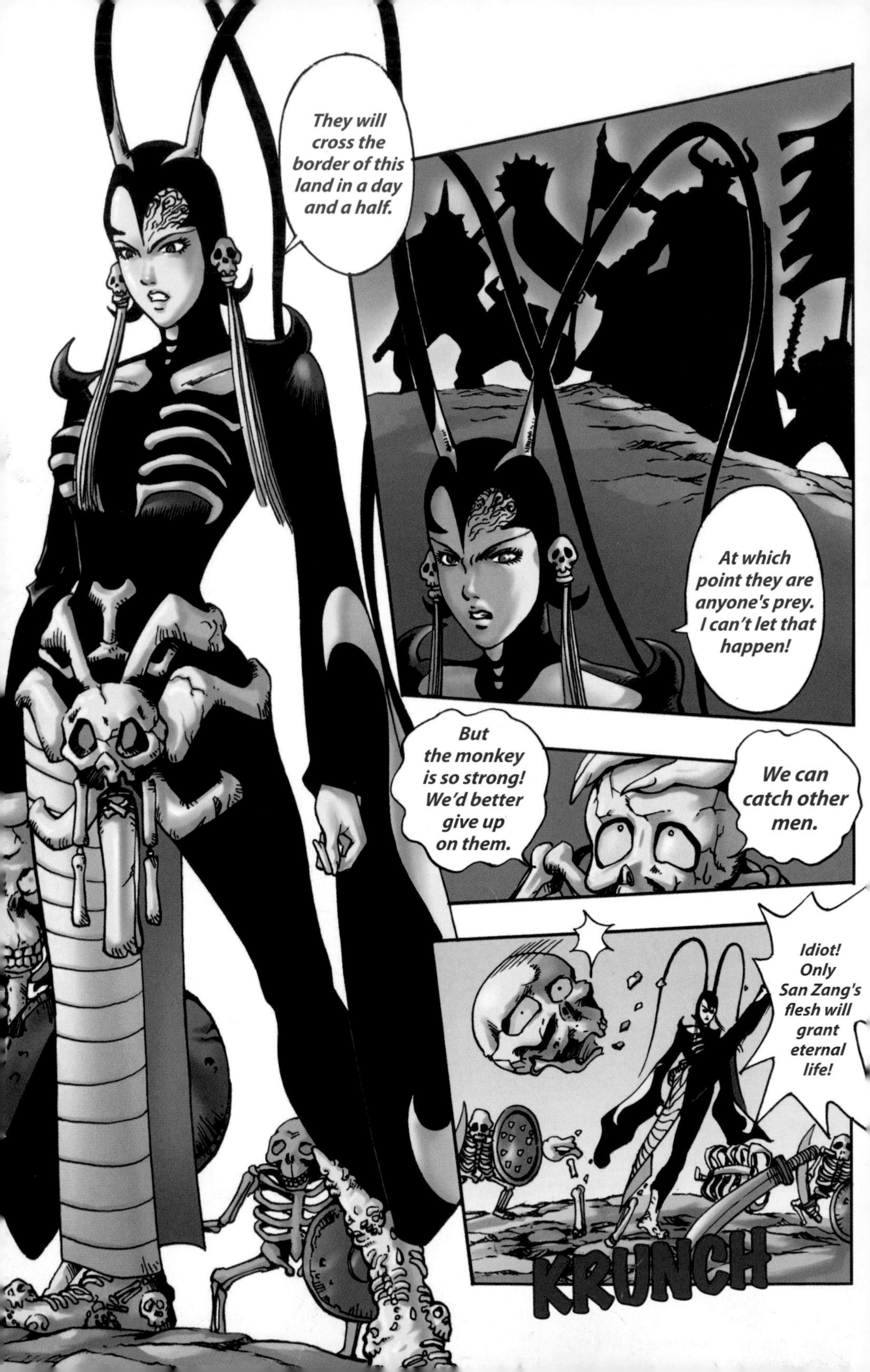
They will cross the border of this land in a day and a half.
At which point they are anyone's prey. I can't let that happen!
But the monkey is so strong! We'd better give up on them.
We can catch other men.
Idiot! Only San Zang's flesh will grant eternal life!
KRUNCH

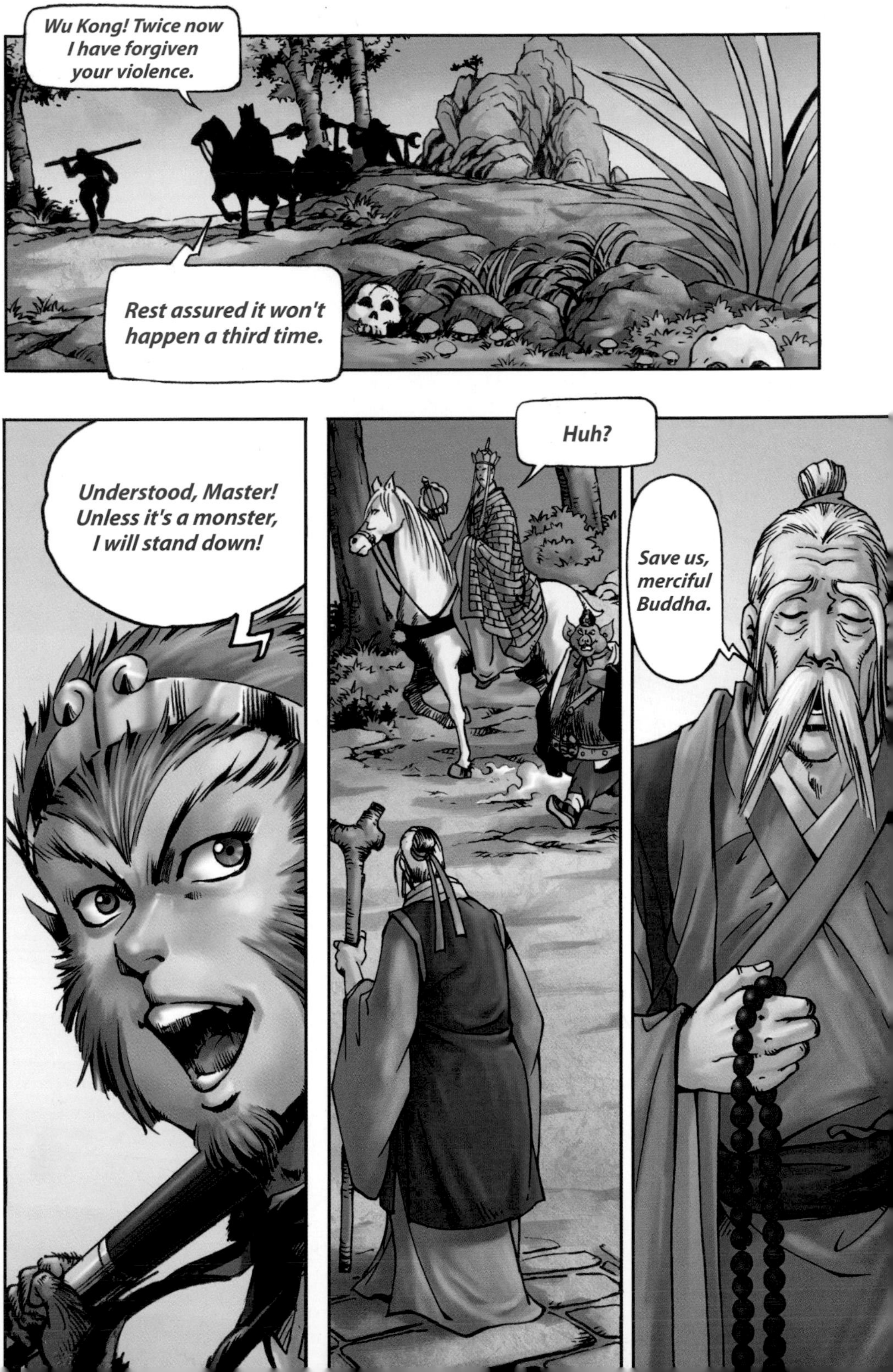

Wu Kong! Twice now I have forgiven your violence.
Rest assured it won't happen a third time.
Understood, Master! Unless it's a monster, I will stand down!
Huh?
Save us, merciful Buddha.

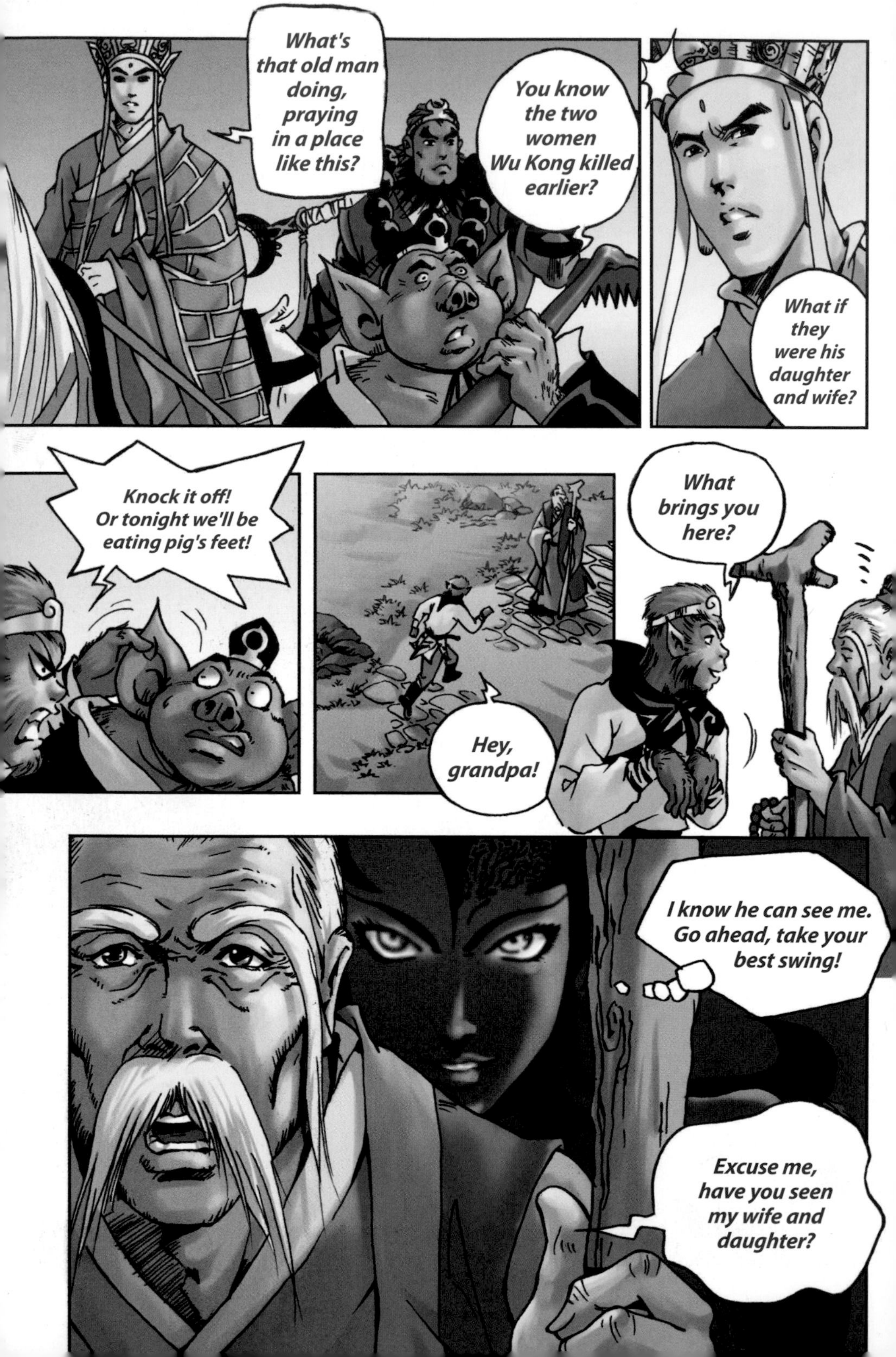
What's that old man doing, praying in a place like this?
You know the two women Wu Kong killed earlier?
What if they were his daughter and wife?
Knock it off! Or tonight we'll be eating pig's feet!
Hey, grandpa!
What brings you here?
I know he can see me. Go ahead, take your best swing!
Excuse me, have you seen my wife and daughter?

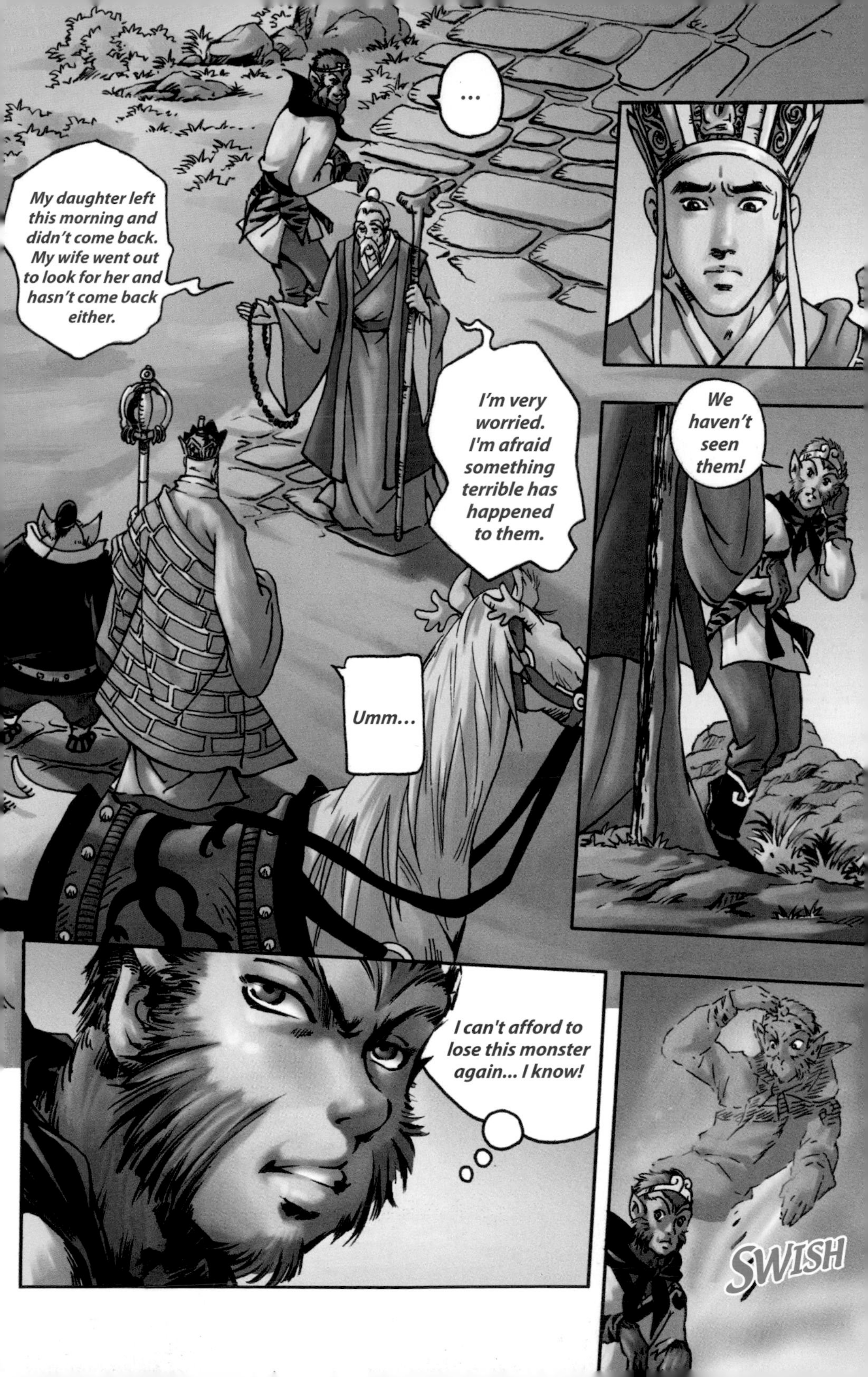
...
My daughter left this morning and didn't come back. My wife went out to look for her and hasn't come back either.
I'm very worried. I'm afraid something terrible has happened to them.
We haven't seen them!
Umm...
I can't afford to lose this monster again... I know!
SWISH

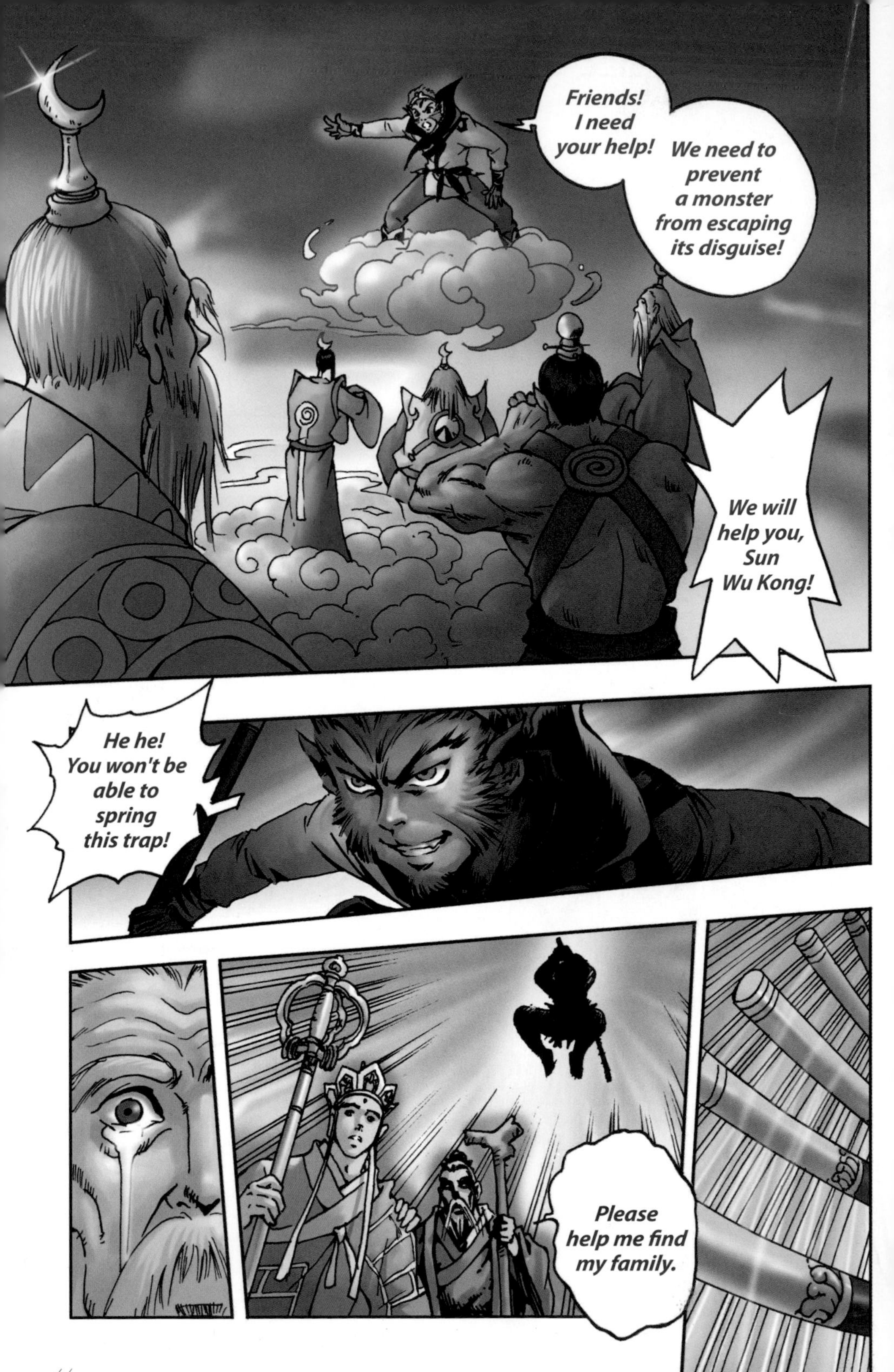

Friends! I need your help!
We need to prevent a monster from escaping its disguise!
We will help you, Sun Wu Kong!
He he! You won't be able to spring this trap!
Please help me find my family.

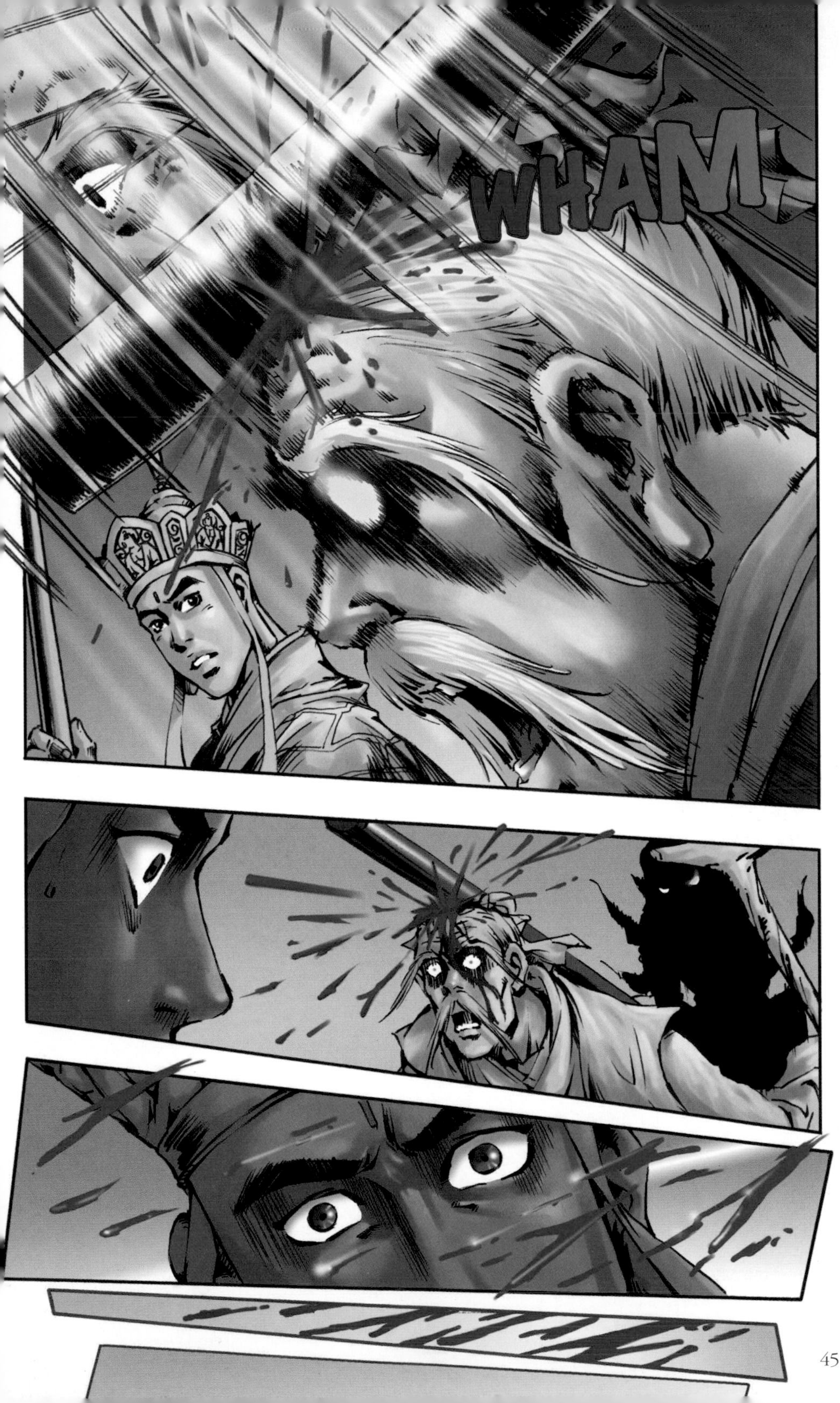
WHAM

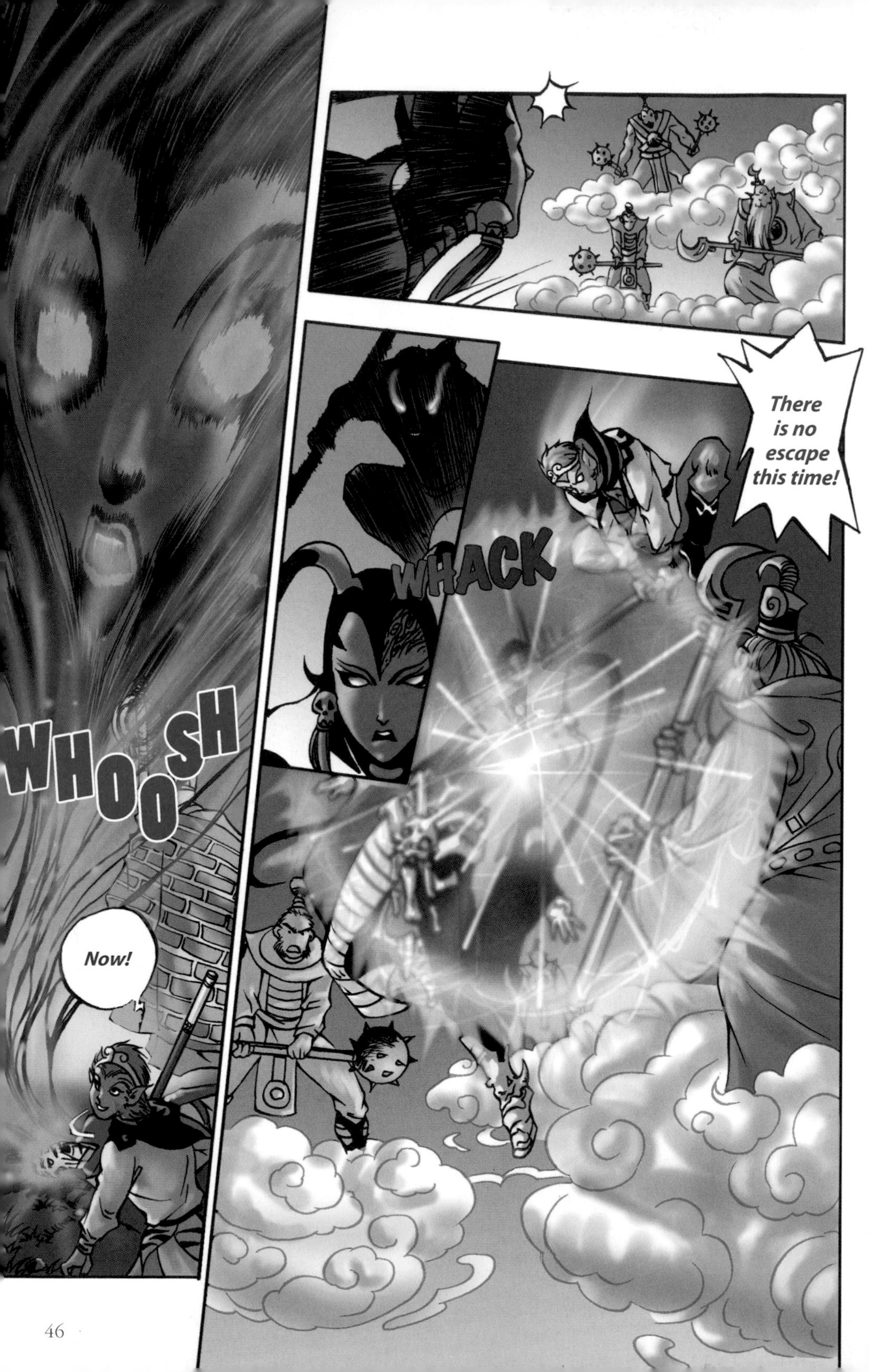
WHOOSH
Now!
There is no escape this time!
WHACK

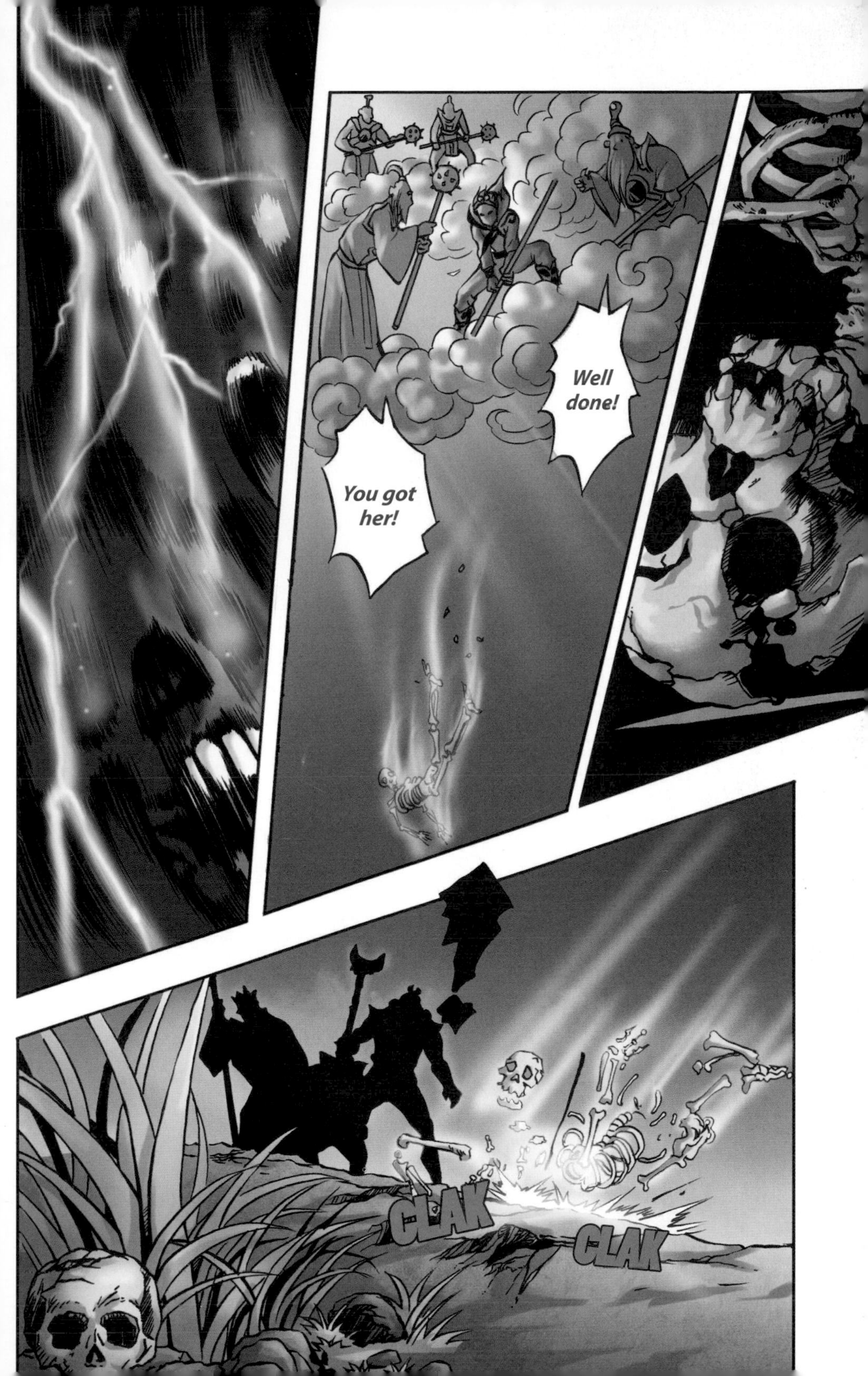
Well done!
You got her!
CLAK
CLAK

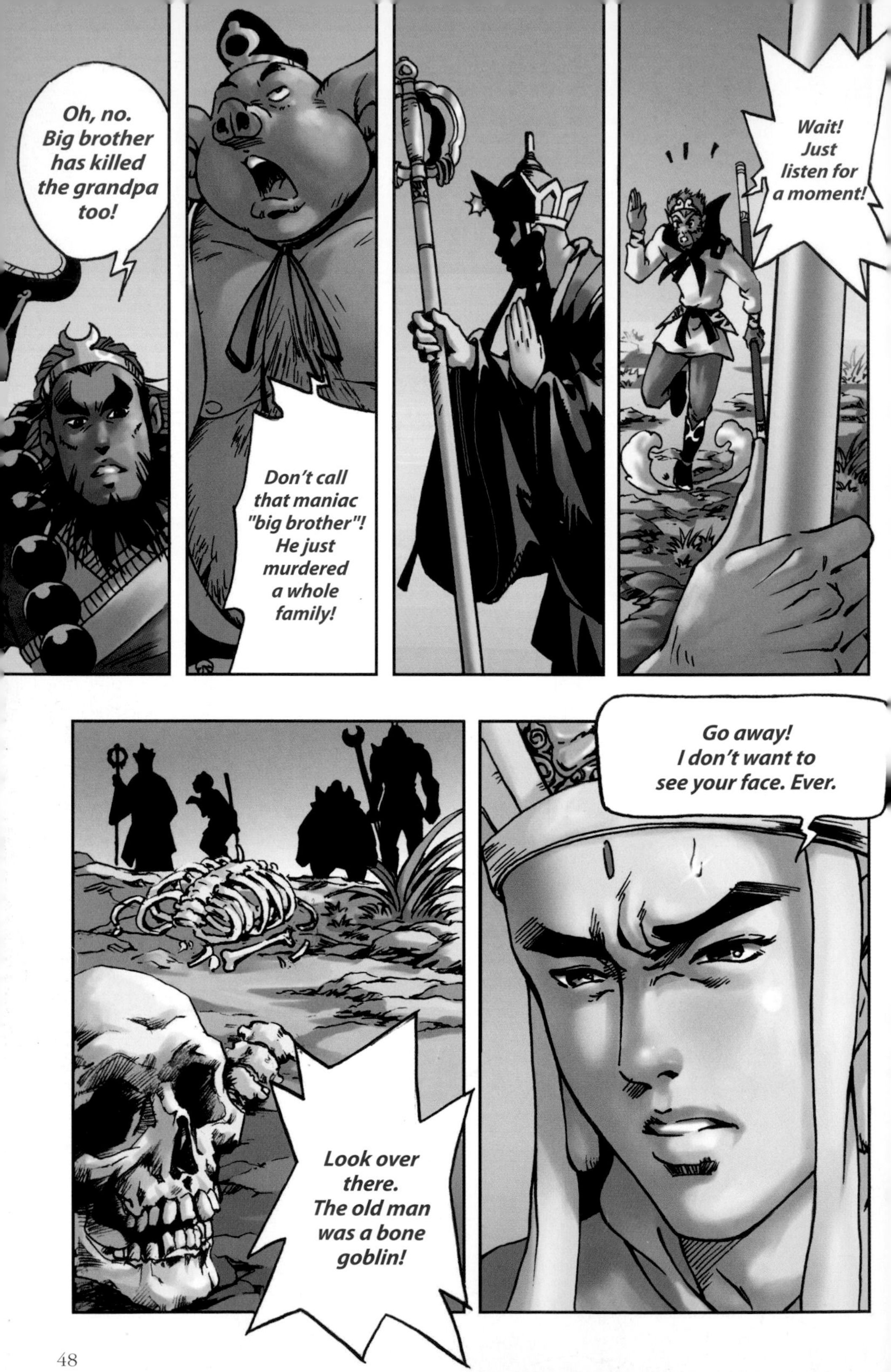
Oh, no. Big brother has killed the grandpa too!
Don't call that maniac "big brother"! He just murdered a whole family!
Wait! Just listen for a moment!
Look over there. The old man was a bone goblin!
Go away! I don't want to see your face. Ever.

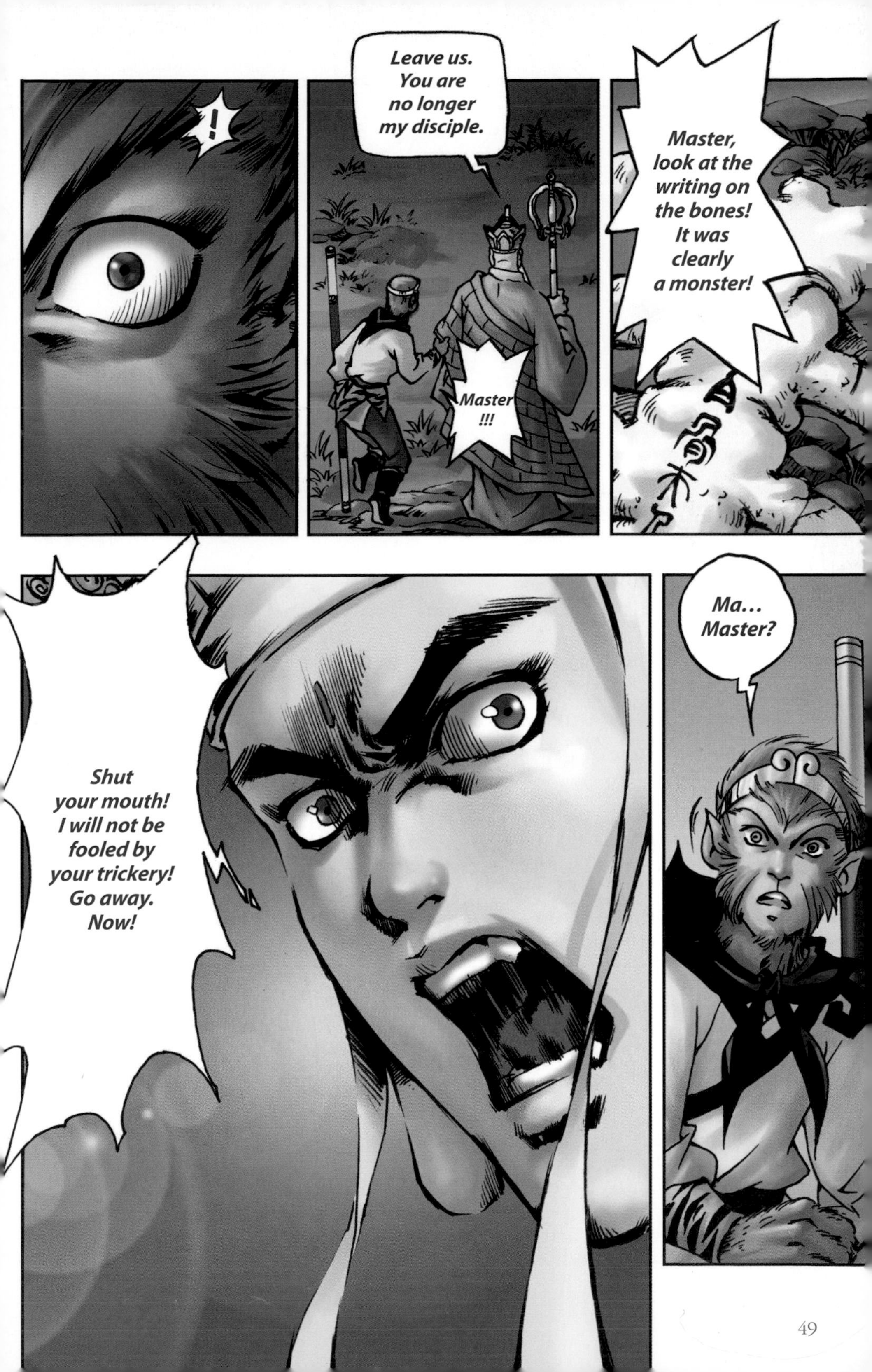
!
Leave us. You are no longer my disciple.
Master !!!
Master, look at the writing on the bones! It was clearly a monster!
Shut your mouth! I will not be fooled by your trickery! Go away. Now!
Ma… Master?

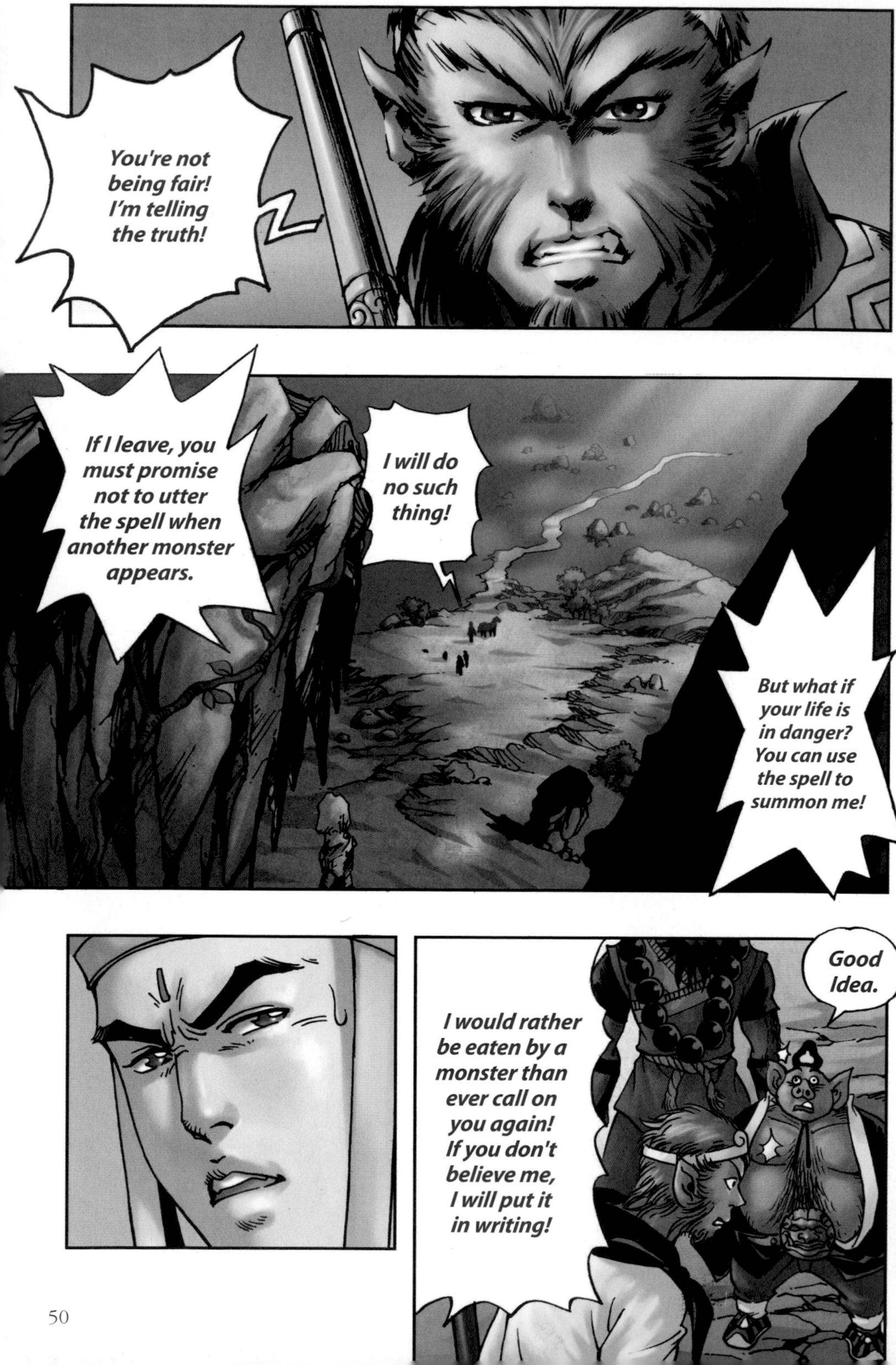
You're not being fair! I'm telling the truth!
If I leave, you must promise not to utter the spell when another monster appears.
I will do no such thing!
But what if your life is in danger? You can use the spell to summon me!
I would rather be eaten by a monster than ever call on you again! If you don't believe me, I will put it in writing!
Good Idea.

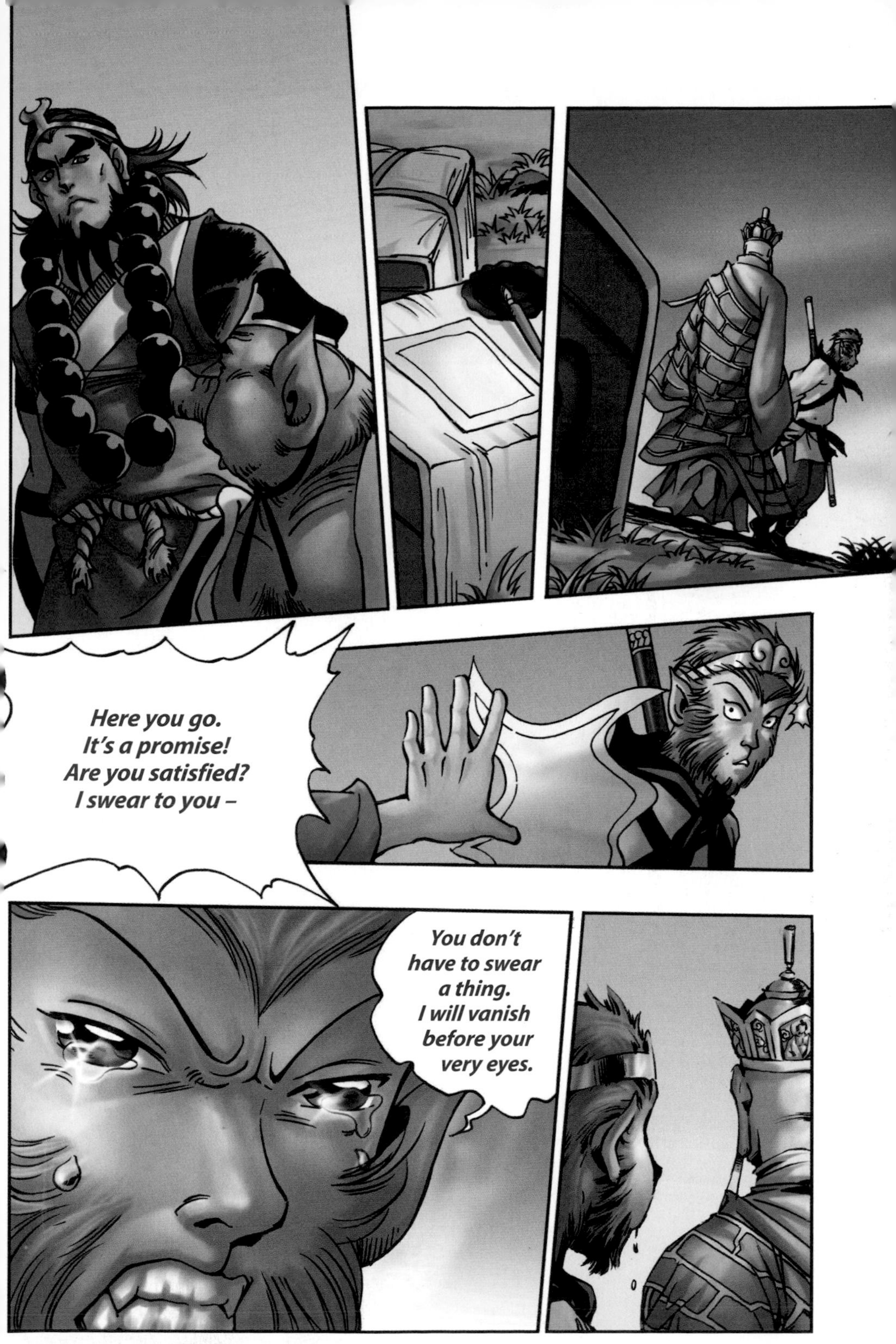
Here you go.
It's a promise!
Are you satisfied?
I swear to you –
You don't have to swear a thing. I will vanish before your very eyes.

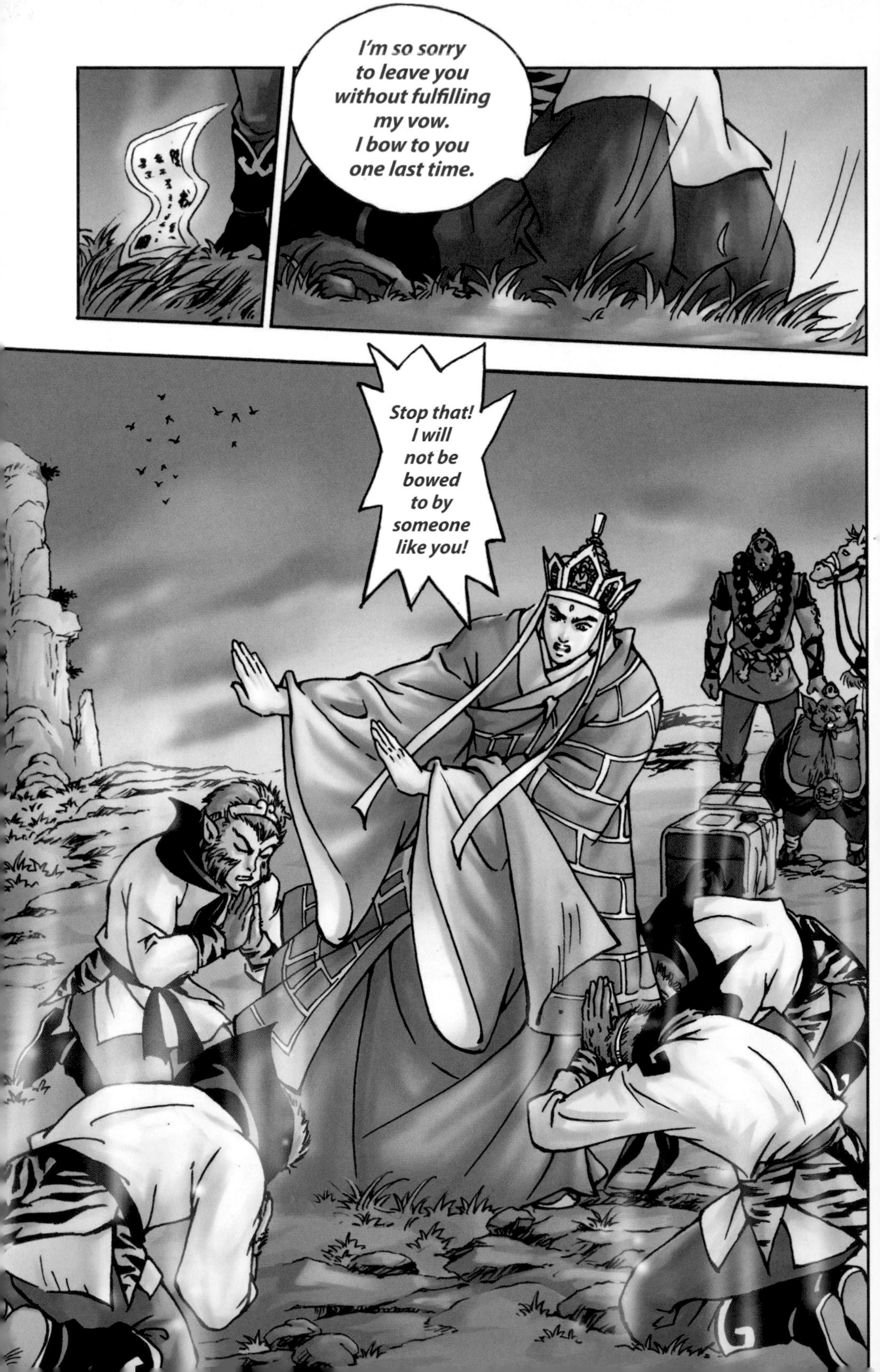
I'm so sorry to leave you without fulfilling my vow. I bow to you one last time.
Stop that! I will not be bowed to by someone like you!

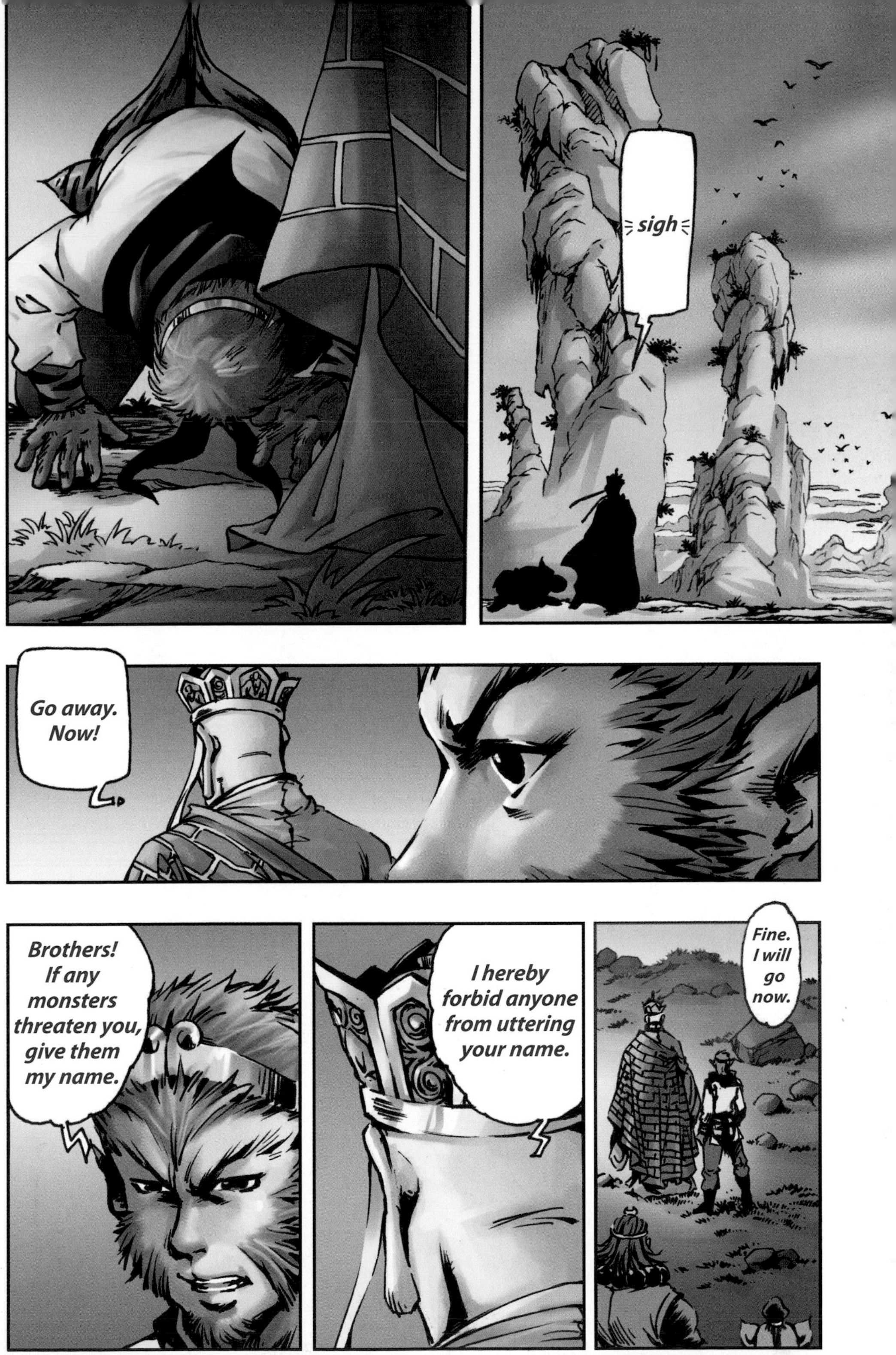
sigh
Go away. Now!
Brothers! If any monsters threaten you, give them my name.
I hereby forbid anyone from uttering your name.
Fine. I will go now.

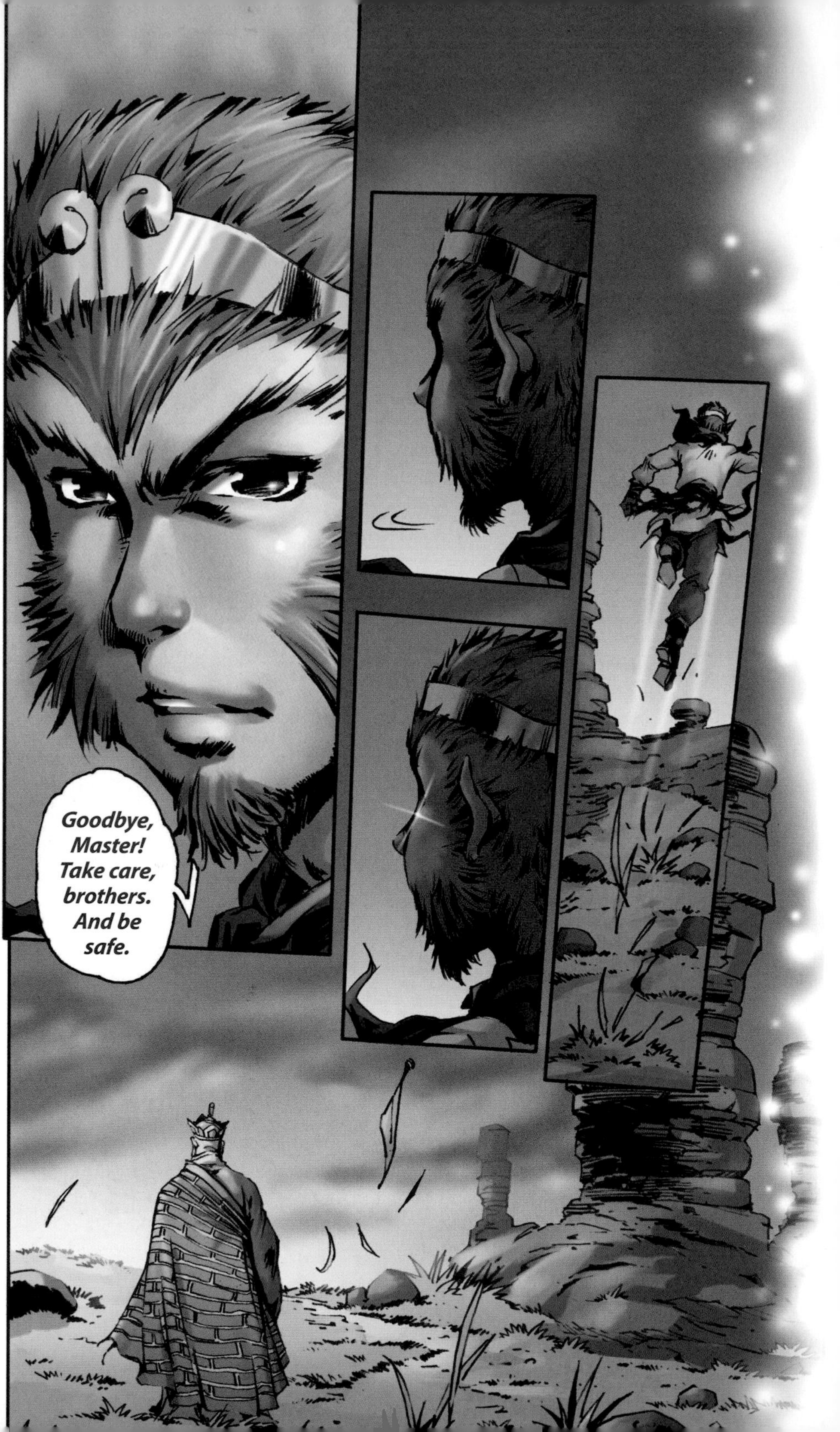
Goodbye, Master! Take care, brothers. And be safe.

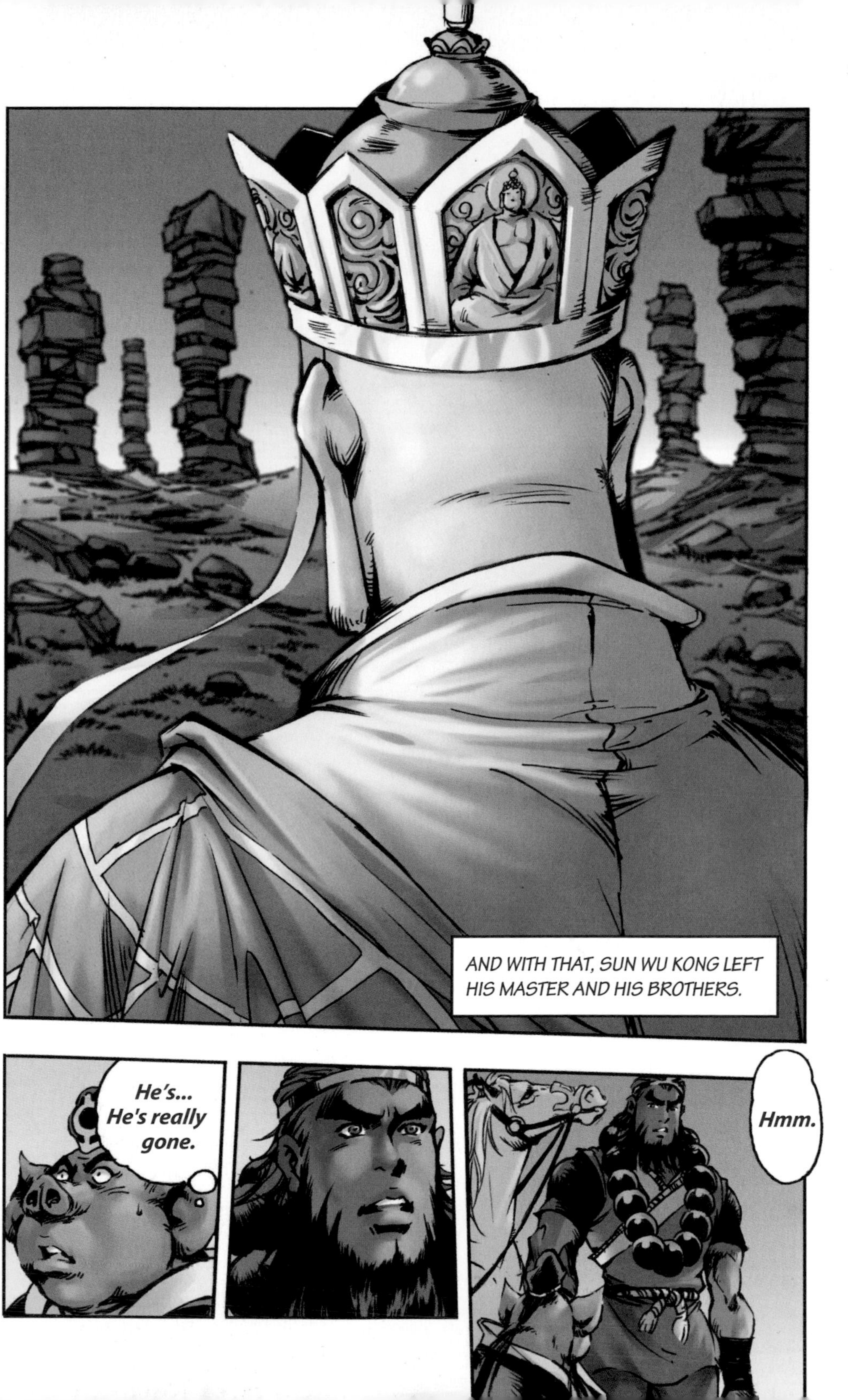
AND WITH THAT, SUN WU KONG LEFT HIS MASTER AND HIS BROTHERS.
He's... He's really gone.
Hmm.

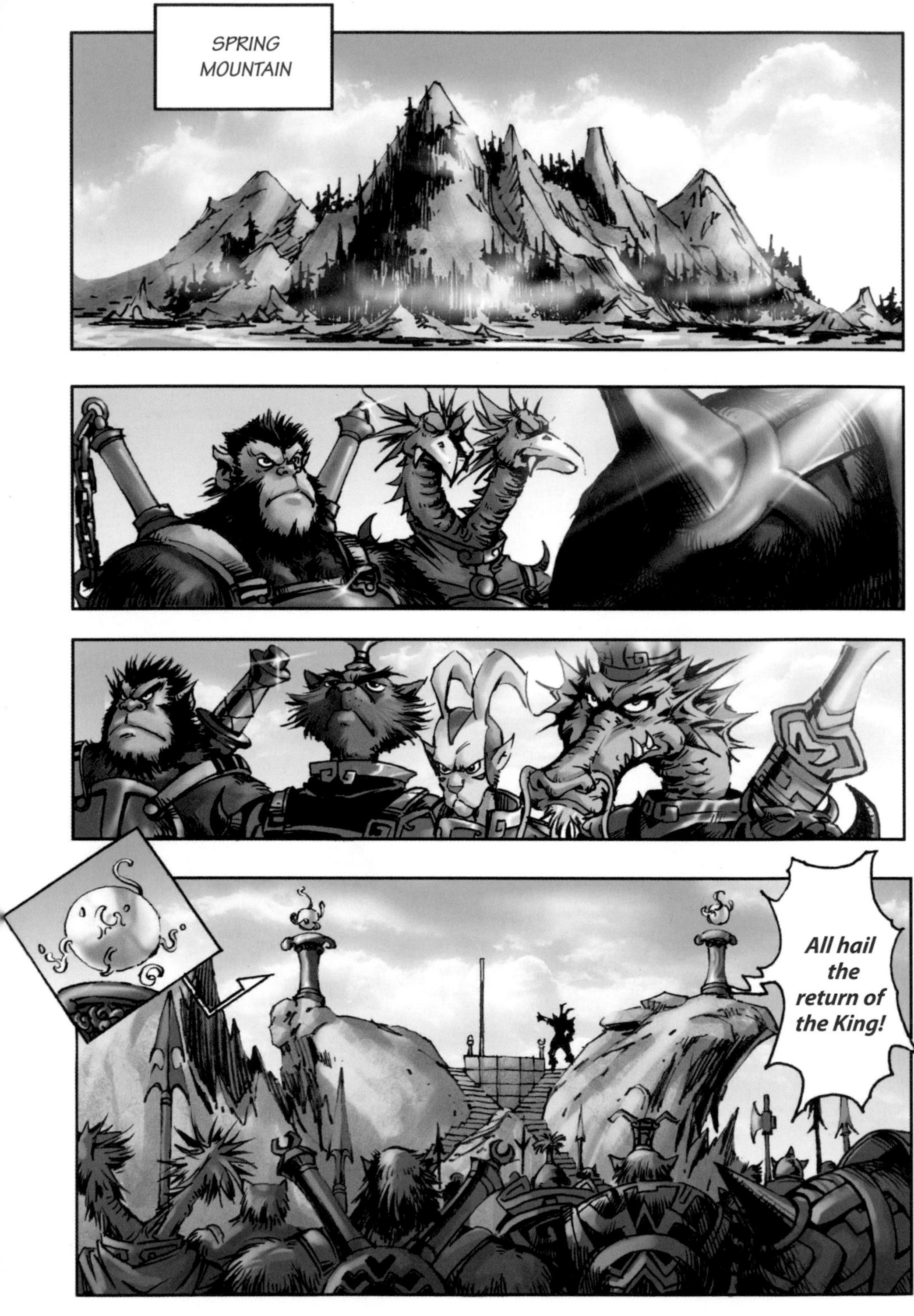
SPRING MOUNTAIN
All hail the return of the King!

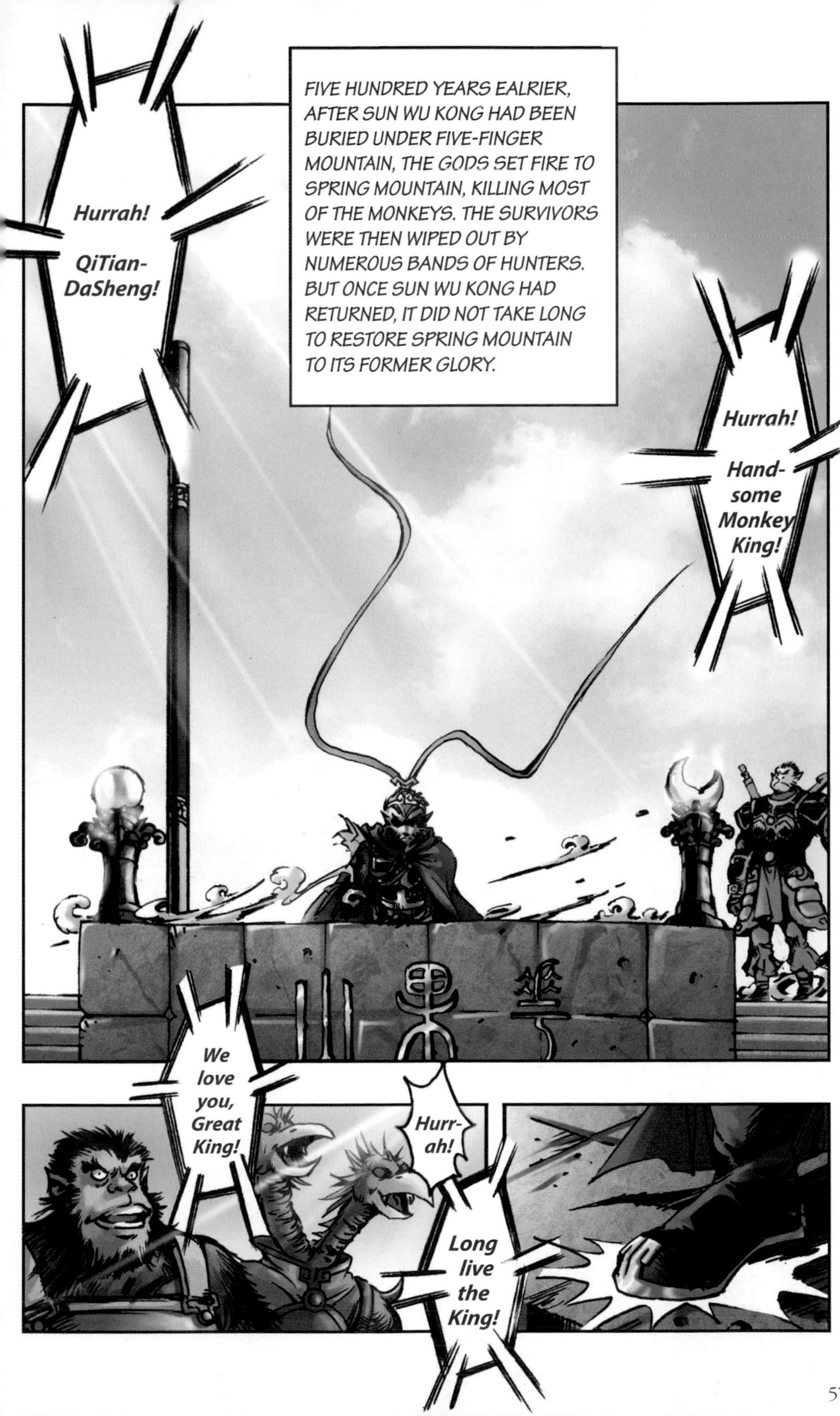
FIVE HUNDRED YEARS EALRIER, AFTER SUN WU KONG HAD BEEN BURIED UNDER FIVE-FINGER MOUNTAIN, THE GODS SET FIRE TO SPRING MOUNTAIN, KILLING MOST OF THE MONKEYS. THE SURVIVORS WERE THEN WIPED OUT BY NUMEROUS BANDS OF HUNTERS. BUT ONCE SUN WU KONG HAD RETURNED, IT DID NOT TAKE LONG TO RESTORE SPRING MOUNTAIN TO ITS FORMER GLORY.
Hurrah! QiTian-DaSheng!
Hurrah! Hand-some Monkey King!
We love you, Great King!
Hurr-ah!
Long live the King!

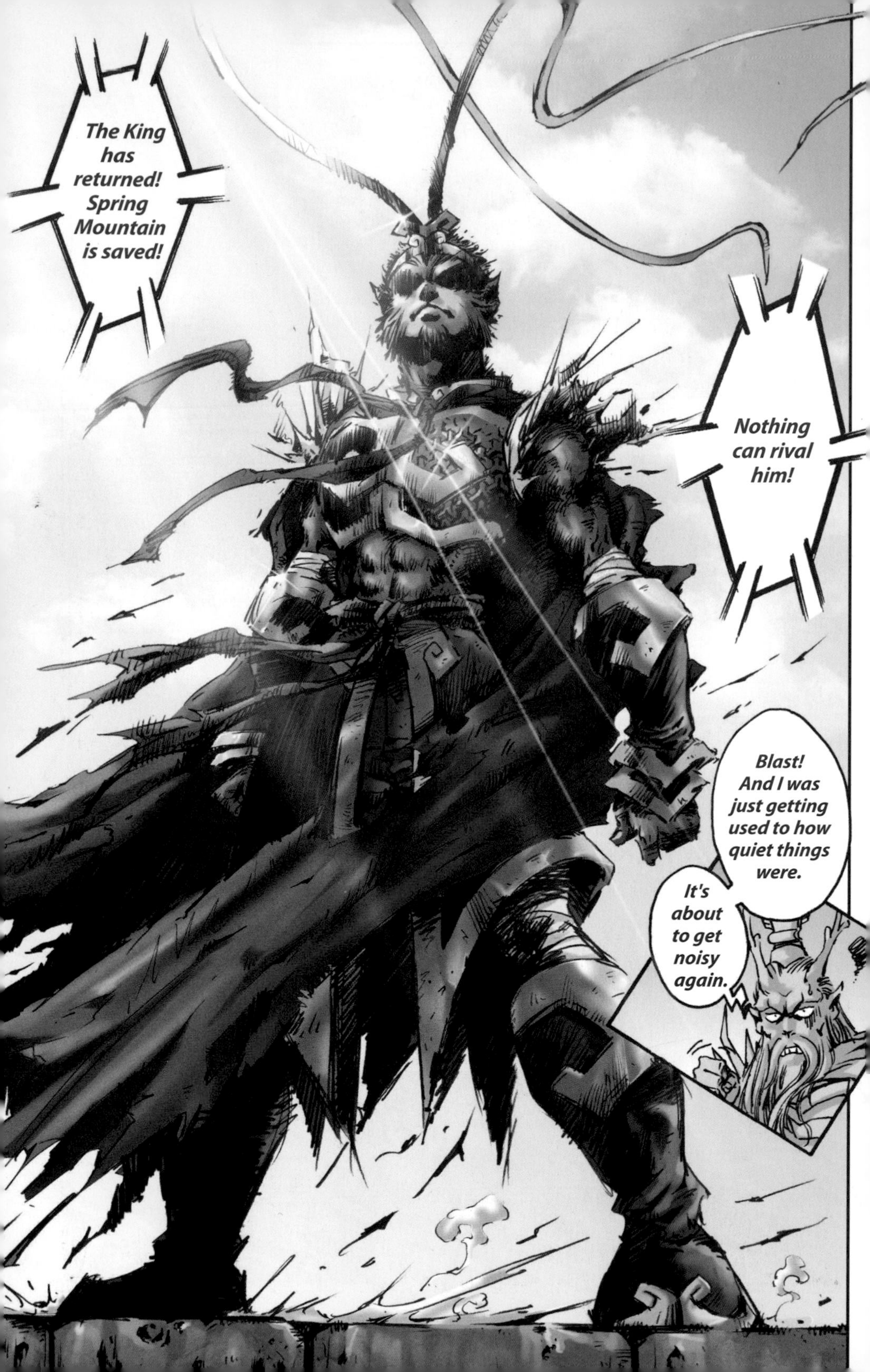
The King has returned! Spring Mountain is saved!
Nothing can rival him!
Blast! And I was just getting used to how quiet things were.
It's about to get noisy again.

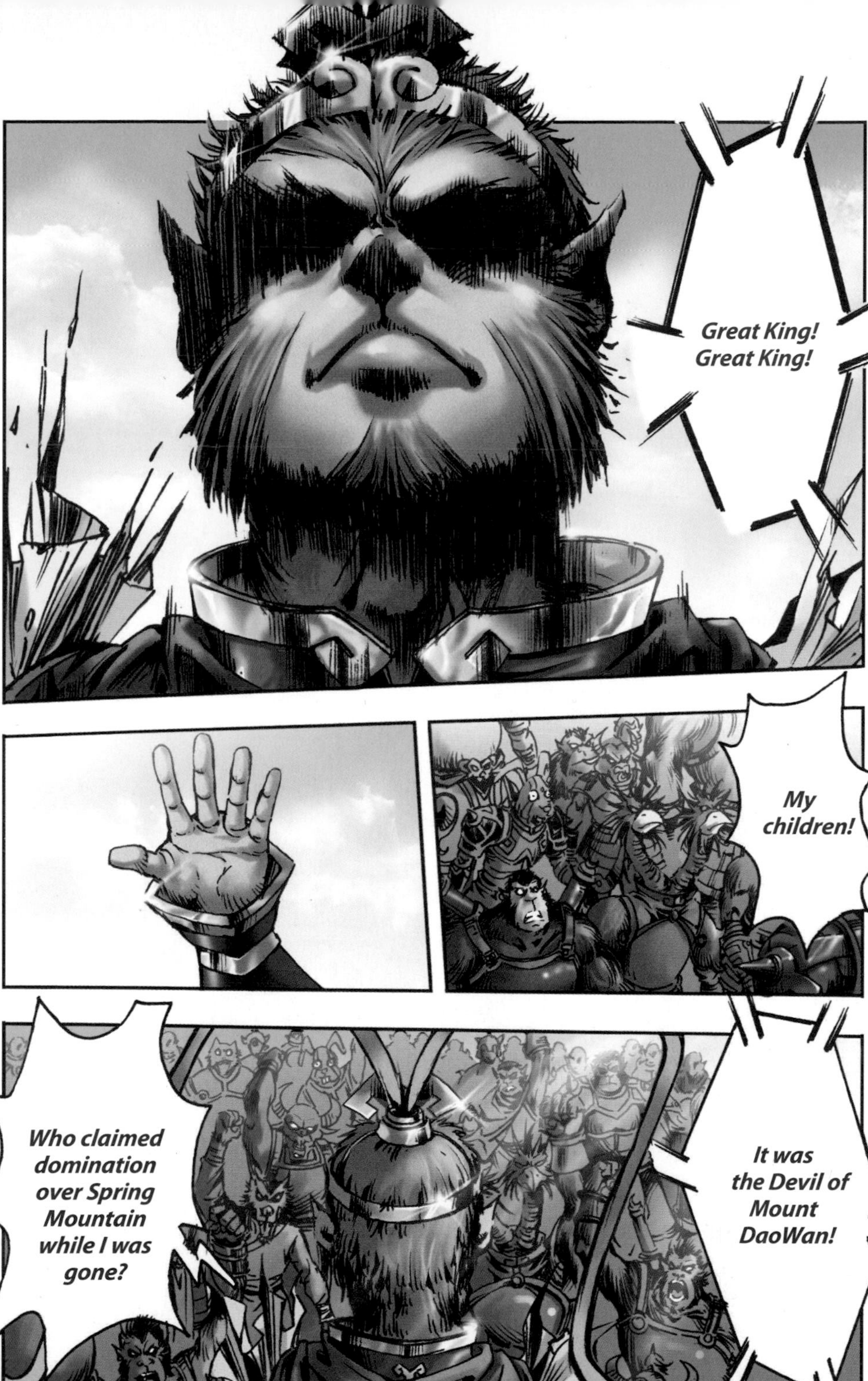
Great King!
Great King!
My children!
Who claimed domination over Spring Mountain while I was gone?
It was the Devil of Mount DaoWan!

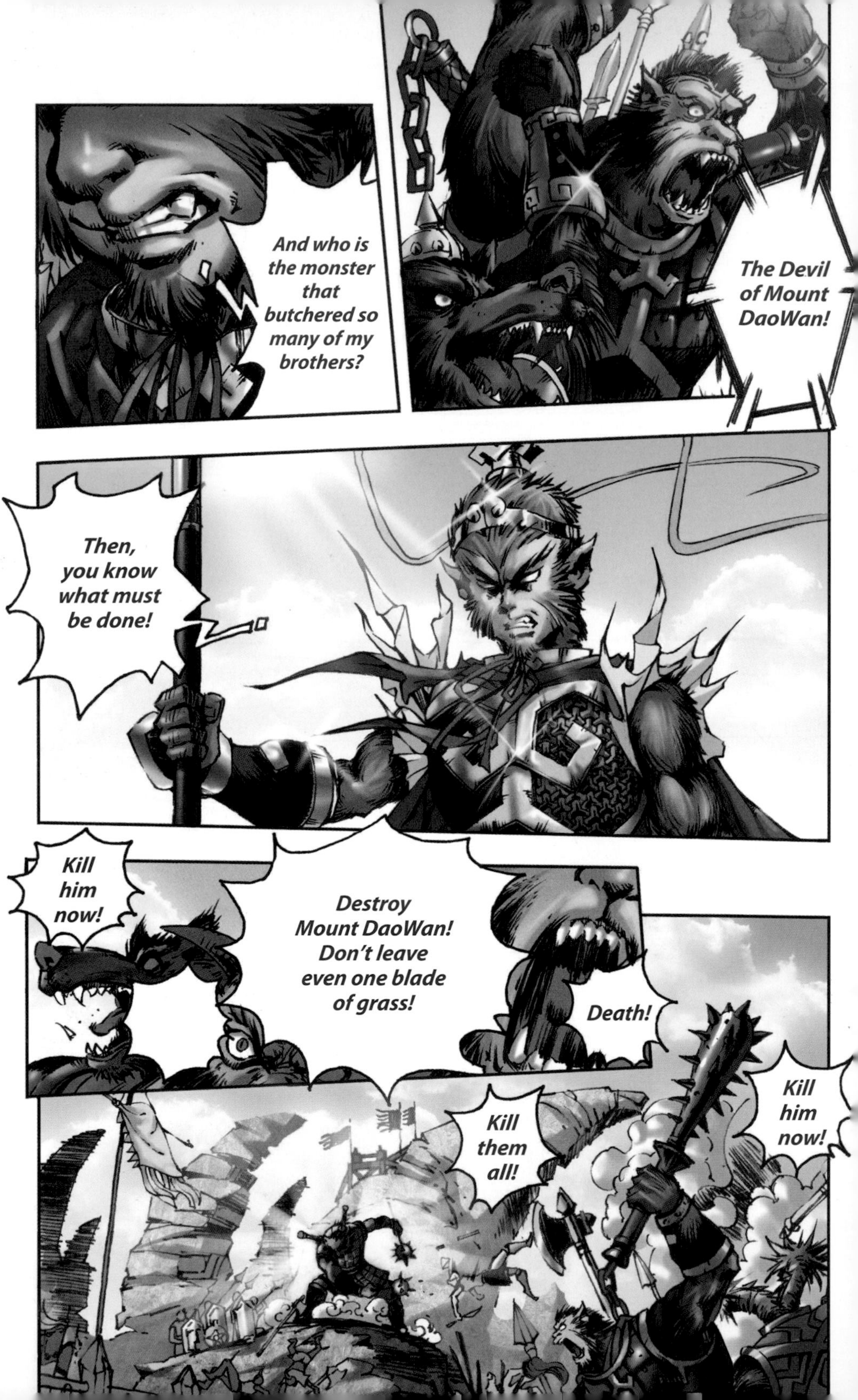
And who is the monster that butchered so many of my brothers?
The Devil of Mount DaoWan!
Then, you know what must be done!
Kill him now!
Destroy Mount DaoWan! Don't leave even one blade of grass!
Death!
Kill them all!
Kill him now!

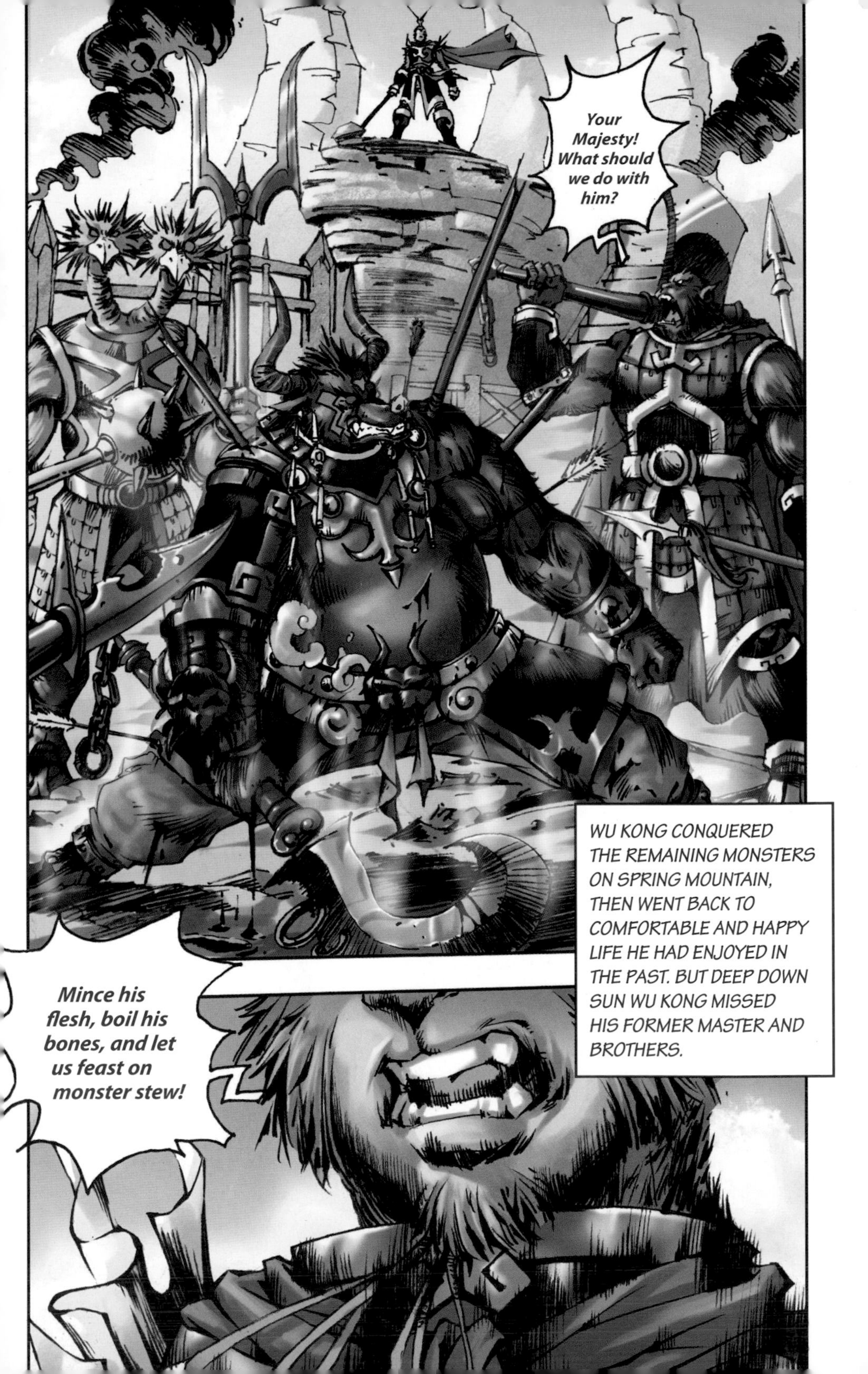
Your Majesty! What should we do with him?
WU KONG CONQUERED THE REMAINING MONSTERS ON SPRING MOUNTAIN, THEN WENT BACK TO COMFORTABLE AND HAPPY LIFE HE HAD ENJOYED IN THE PAST. BUT DEEP DOWN SUN WU KONG MISSED HIS FORMER MASTER AND BROTHERS.
Mince his flesh, boil his bones, and let us feast on monster stew!

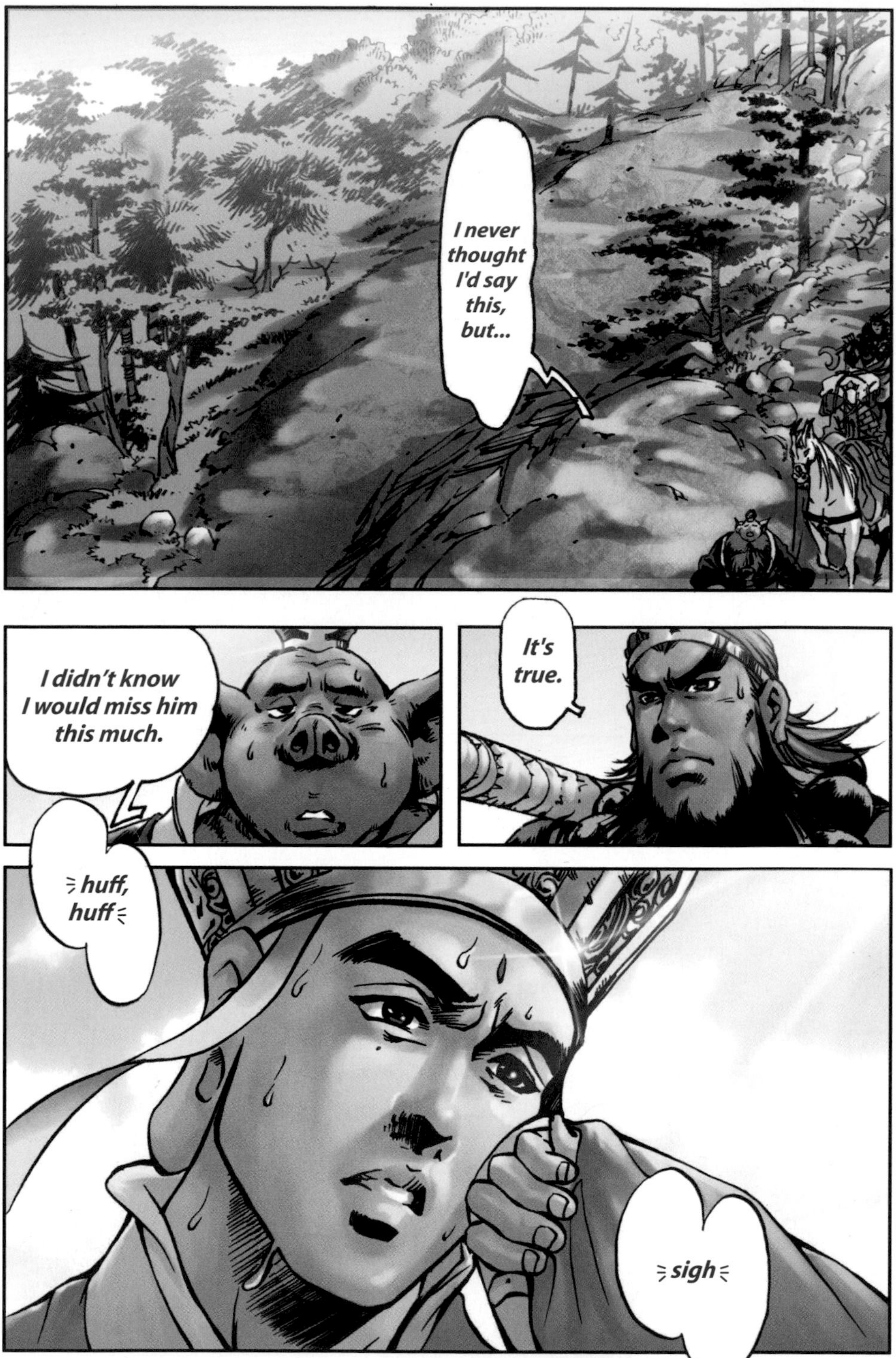
I never thought I'd say this, but...
I didn't know I would miss him this much.
It's true.
huff, huff
sigh

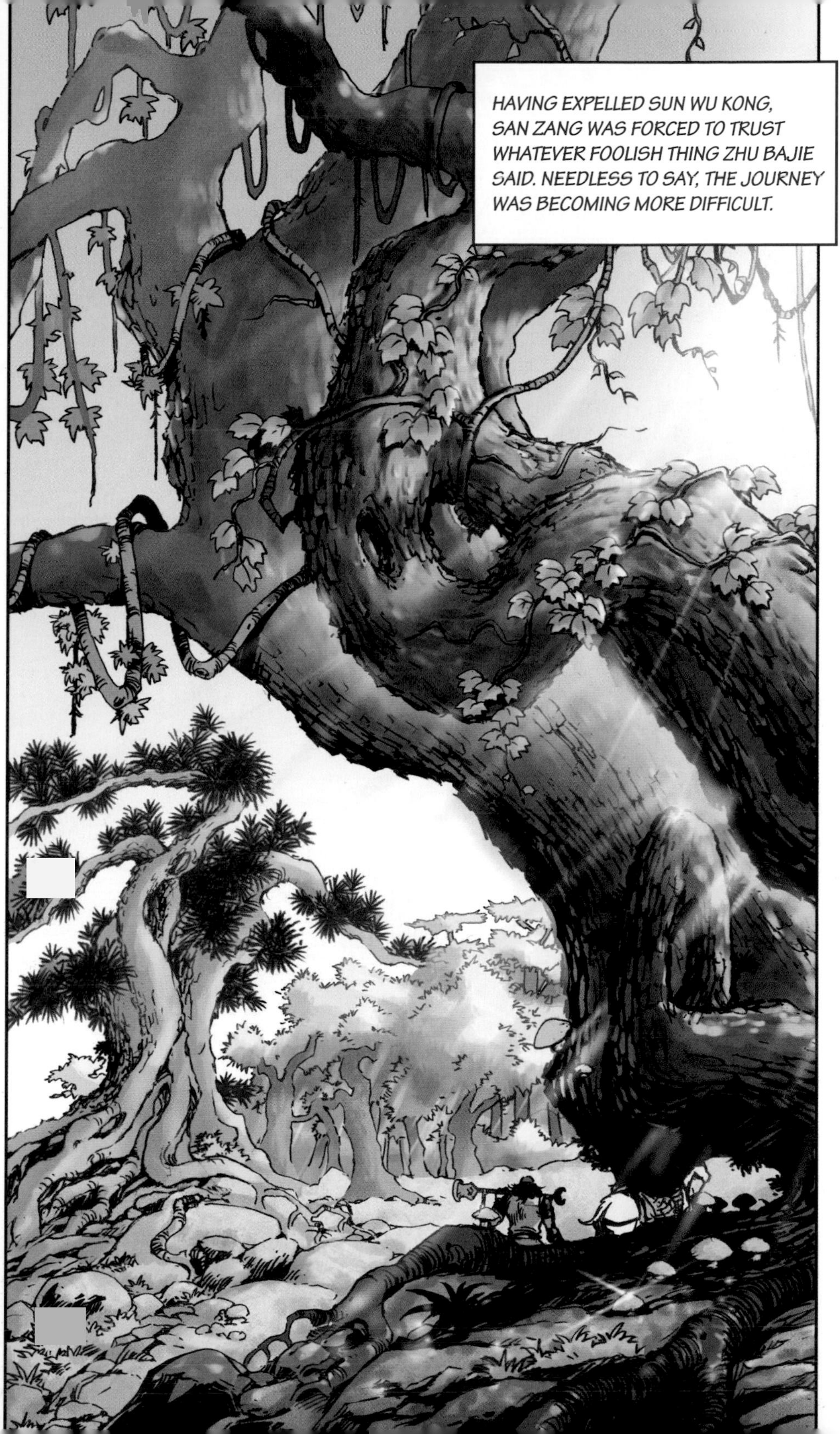
HAVING EXPELLED SUN WU KONG, SAN ZANG WAS FORCED TO TRUST WHATEVER FOOLISH THING ZHU BAJIE SAID. NEEDLESS TO SAY, THE JOURNEY WAS BECOMING MORE DIFFICULT.

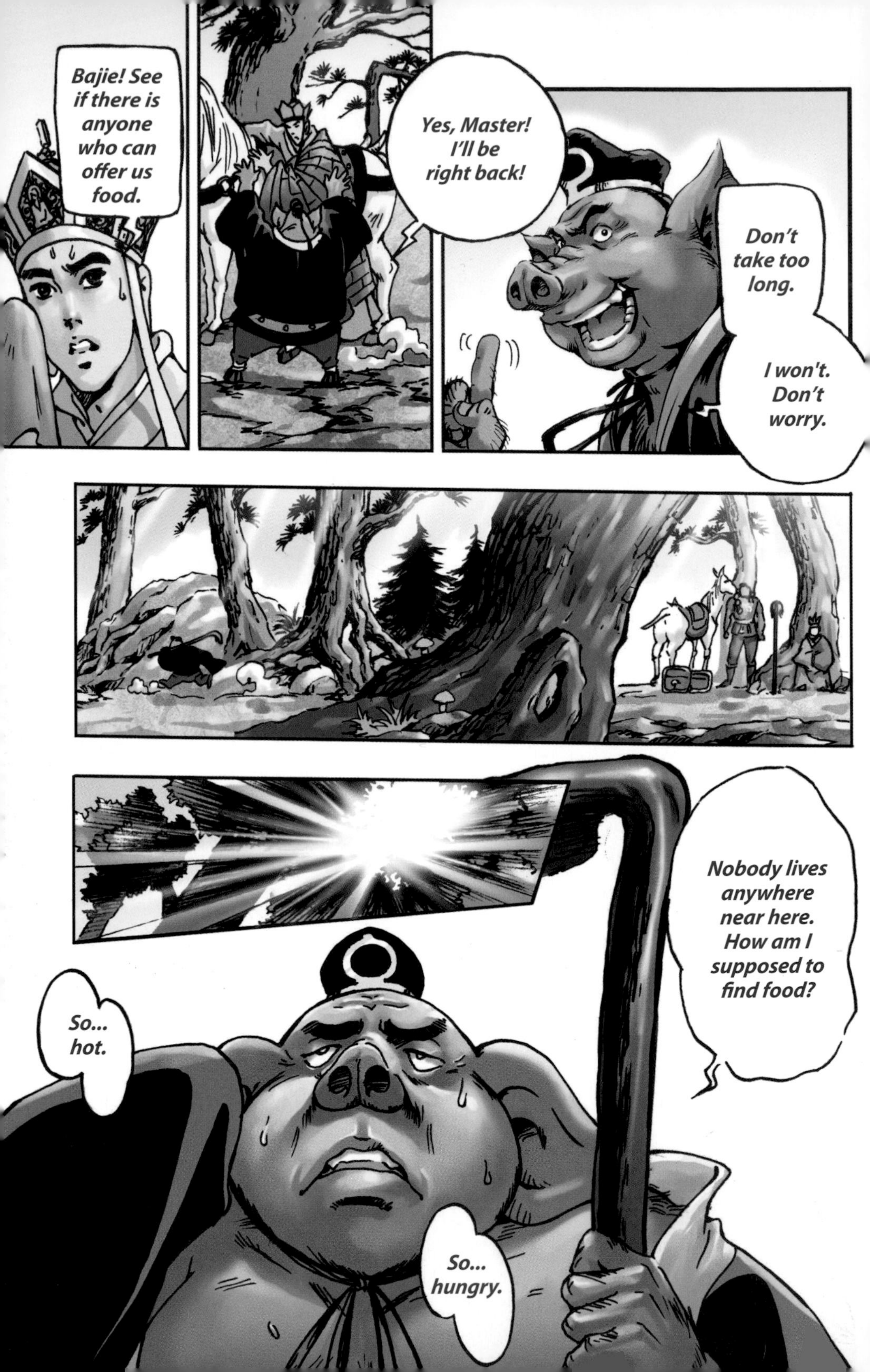
Bajie! See if there is anyone who can offer us food.
Yes, Master! I'll be right back!
Don't take too long.
I won't. Don't worry.
Nobody lives anywhere near here. How am I supposed to find food?
So... hot.
So... hungry.

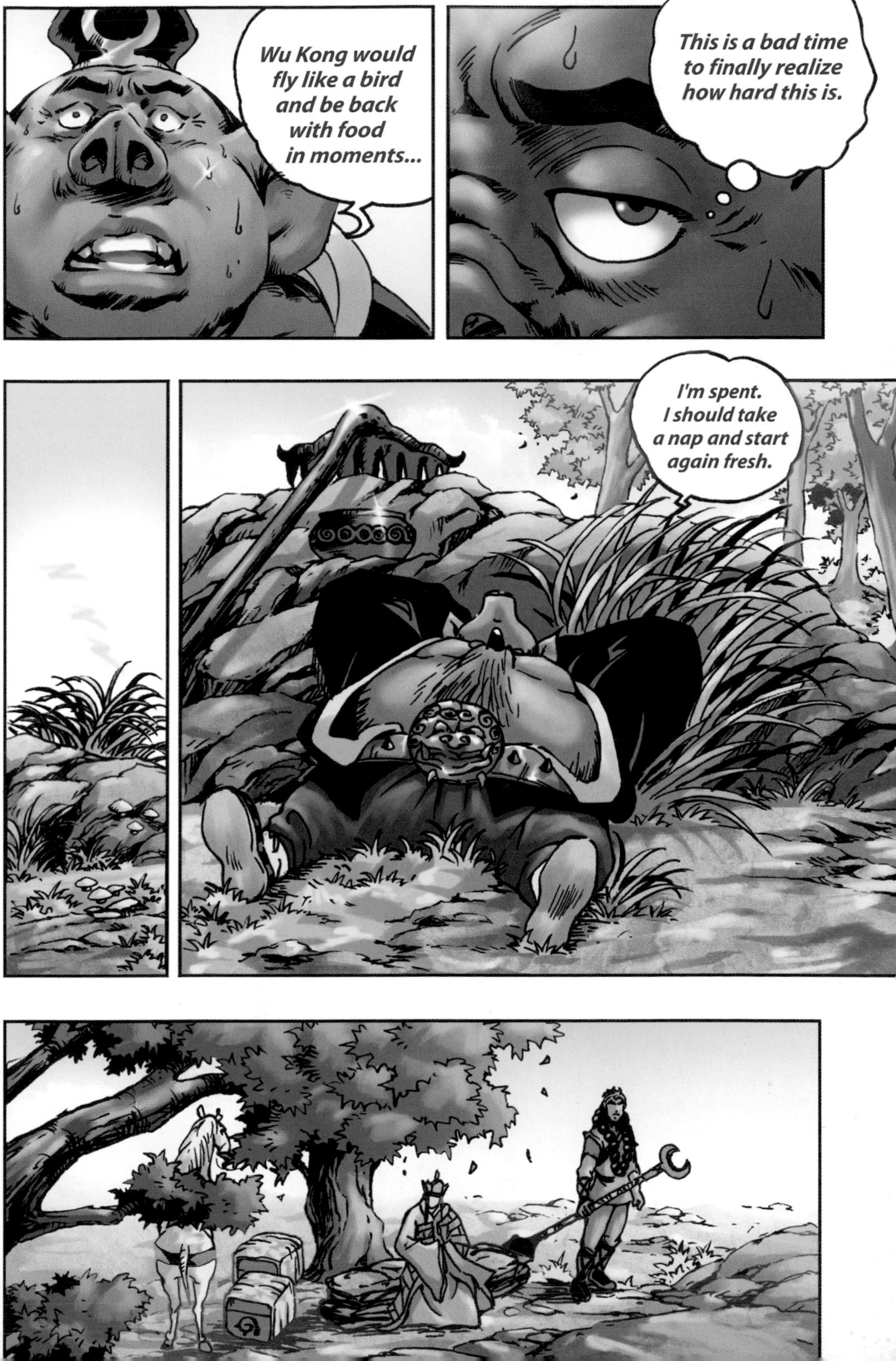
Wu Kong would fly like a bird and be back with food in moments...
This is a bad time to finally realize how hard this is.
I'm spent. I should take a nap and start again fresh.

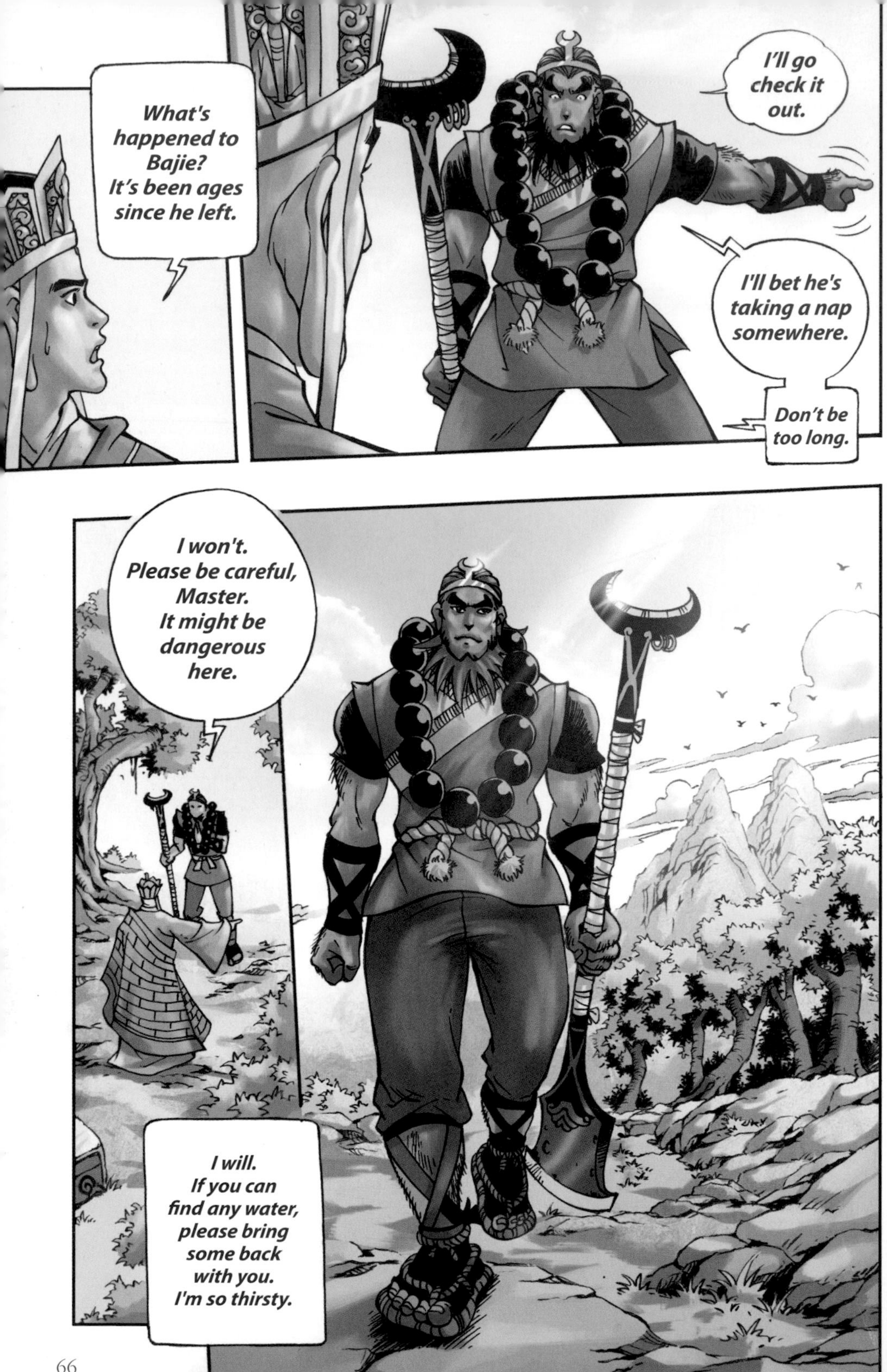
What's happened to Bajie? It's been ages since he left.
I'll go check it out.
I'll bet he's taking a nap somewhere.
Don't be too long.
I won't. Please be careful, Master. It might be dangerous here.
I will. If you can find any water, please bring some back with you. I'm so thirsty.

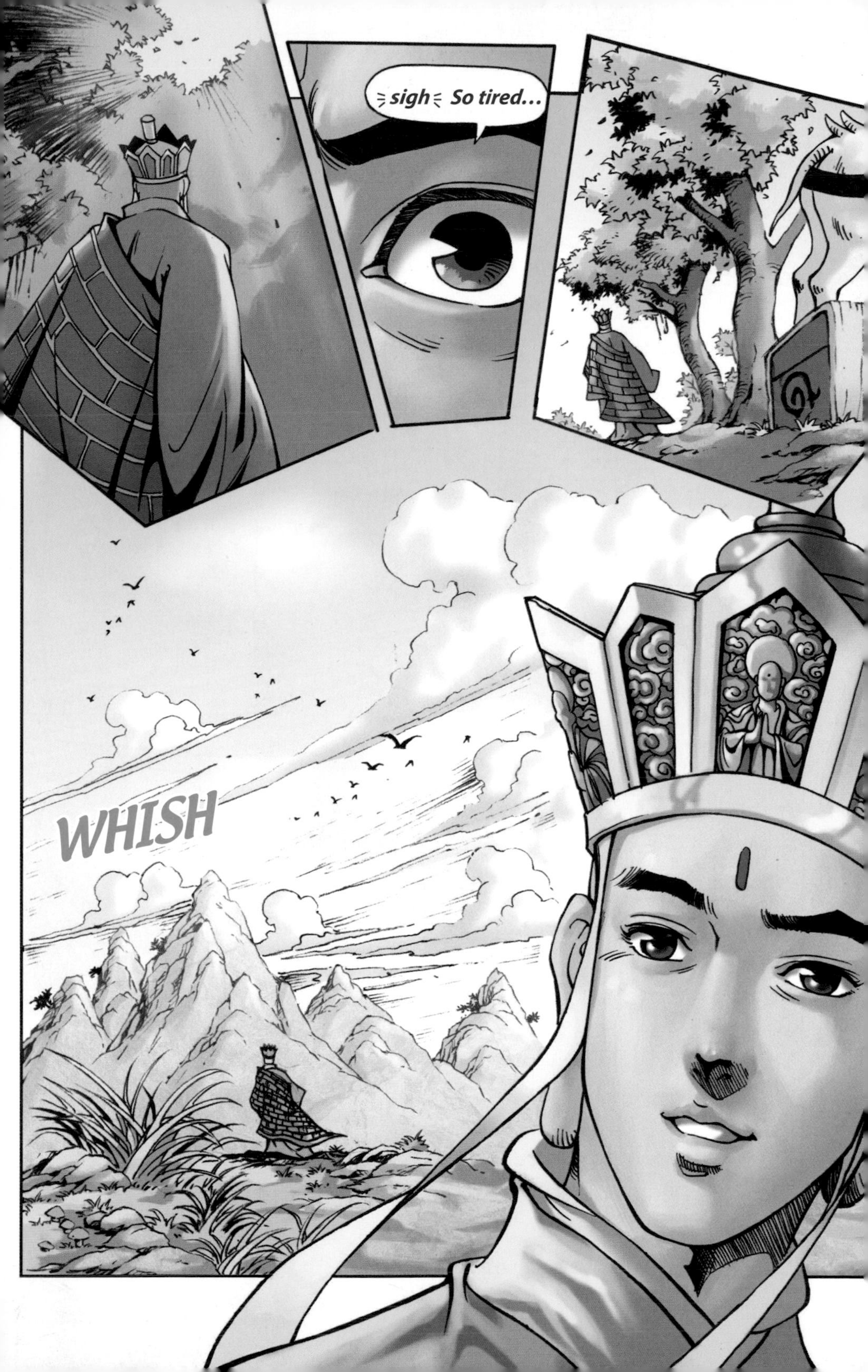
sigh So tired...
WHISH

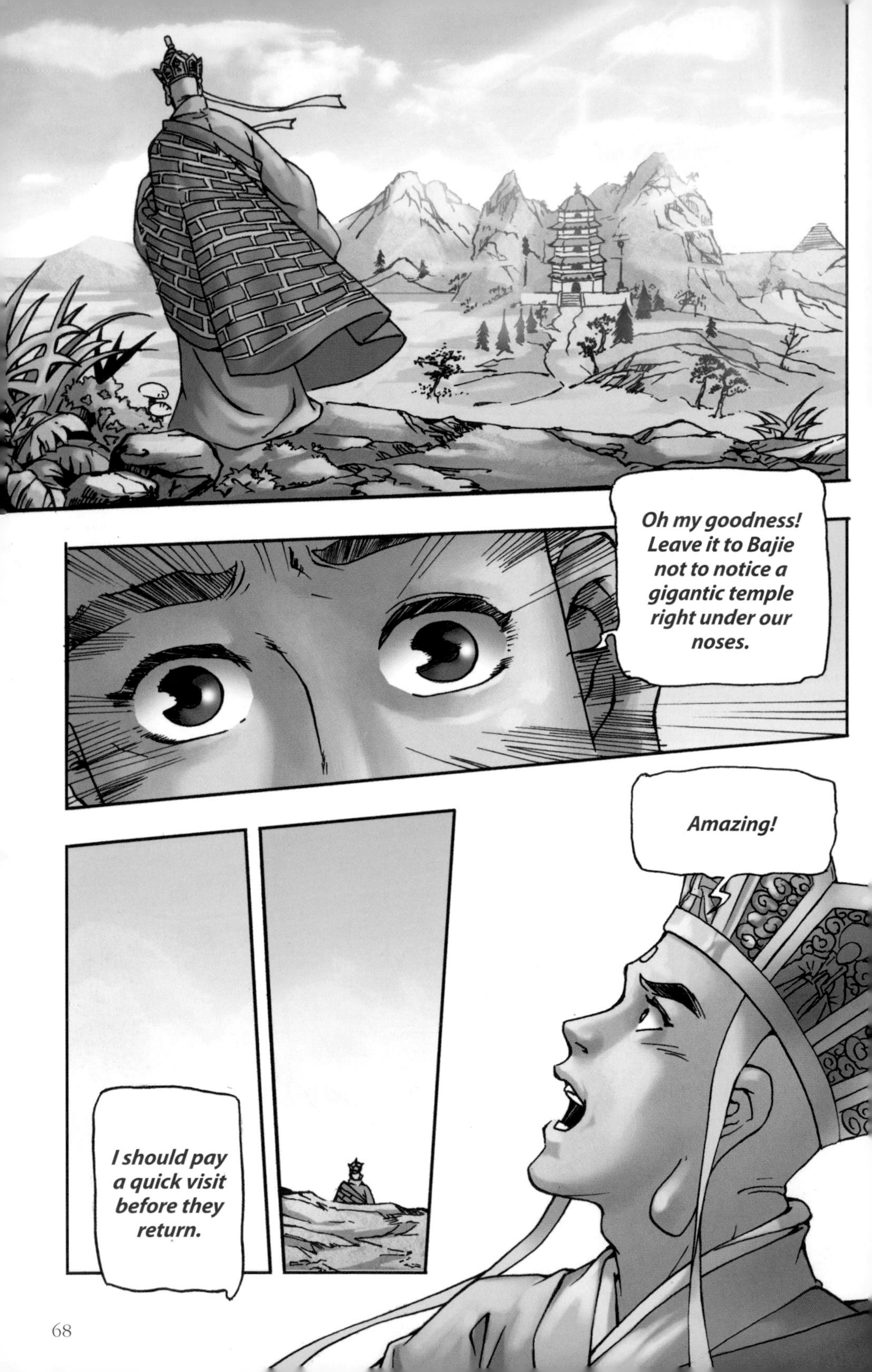
Oh my goodness! Leave it to Bajie not to notice a gigantic temple right under our noses.
Amazing!
I should pay a quick visit before they return.

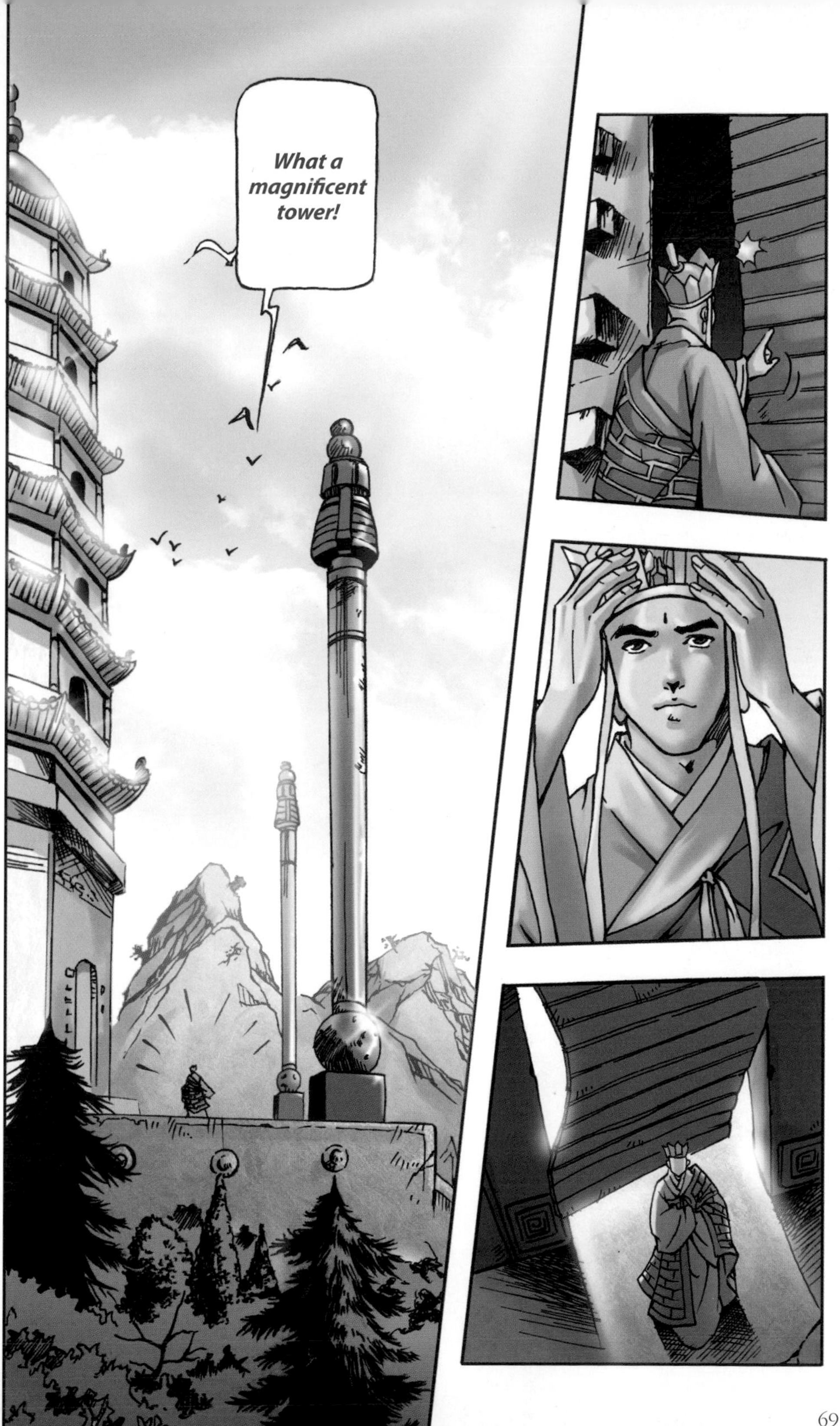
What a magnificent tower!

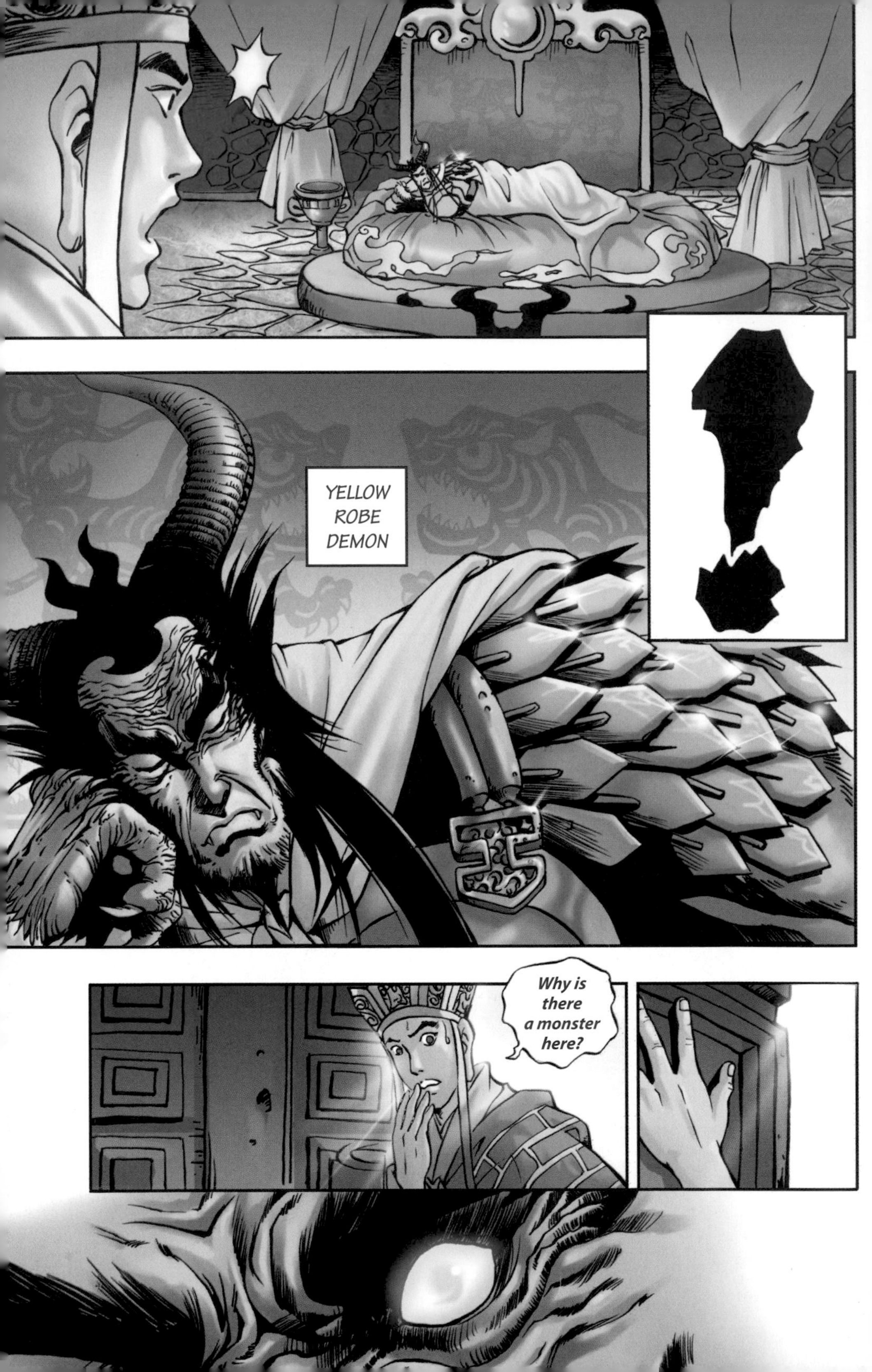
YELLOW
ROBE
DEMON
Why is there a monster here?

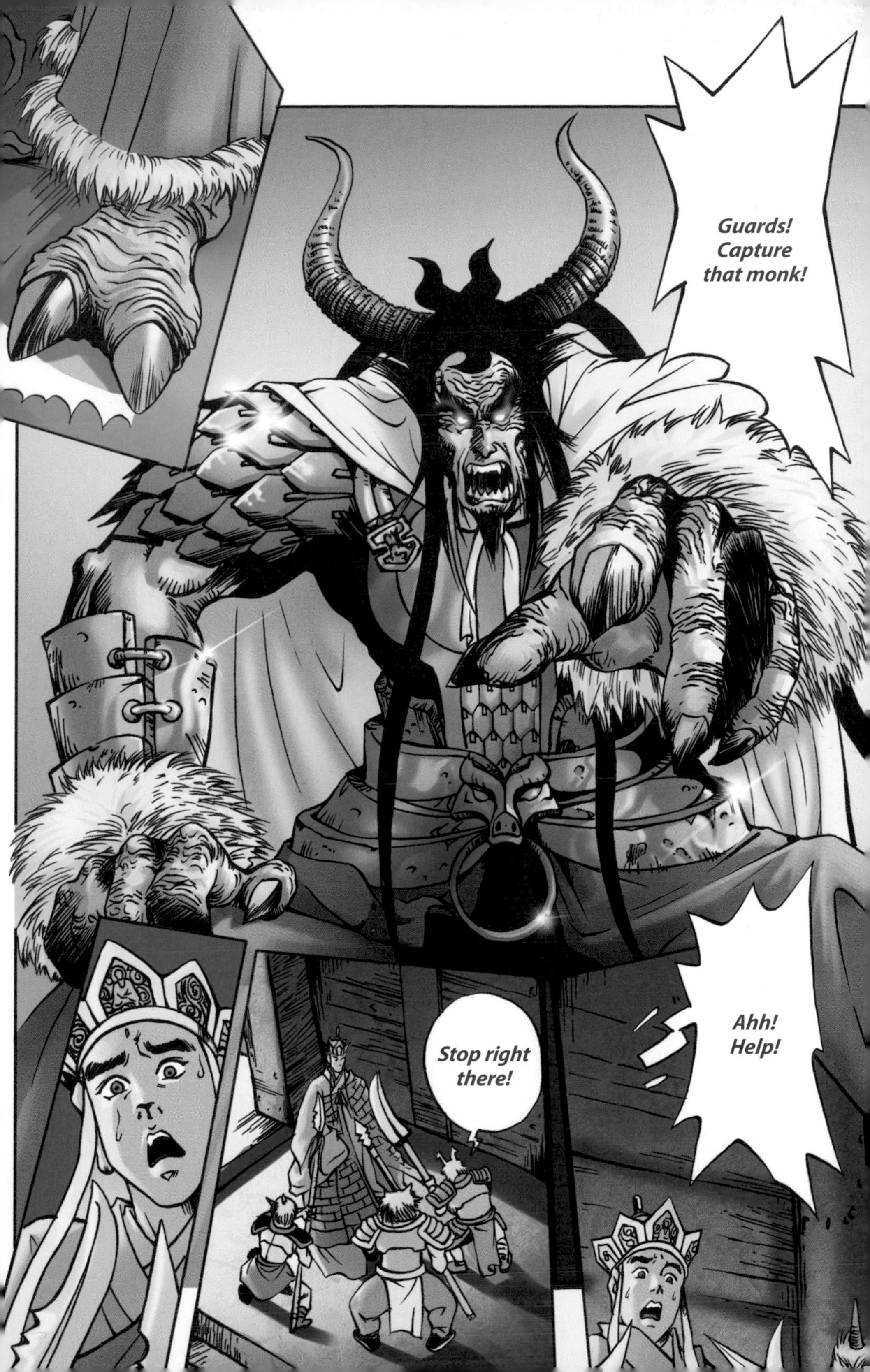
Guards! Capture that monk!
Stop right there!
Ahh! Help!

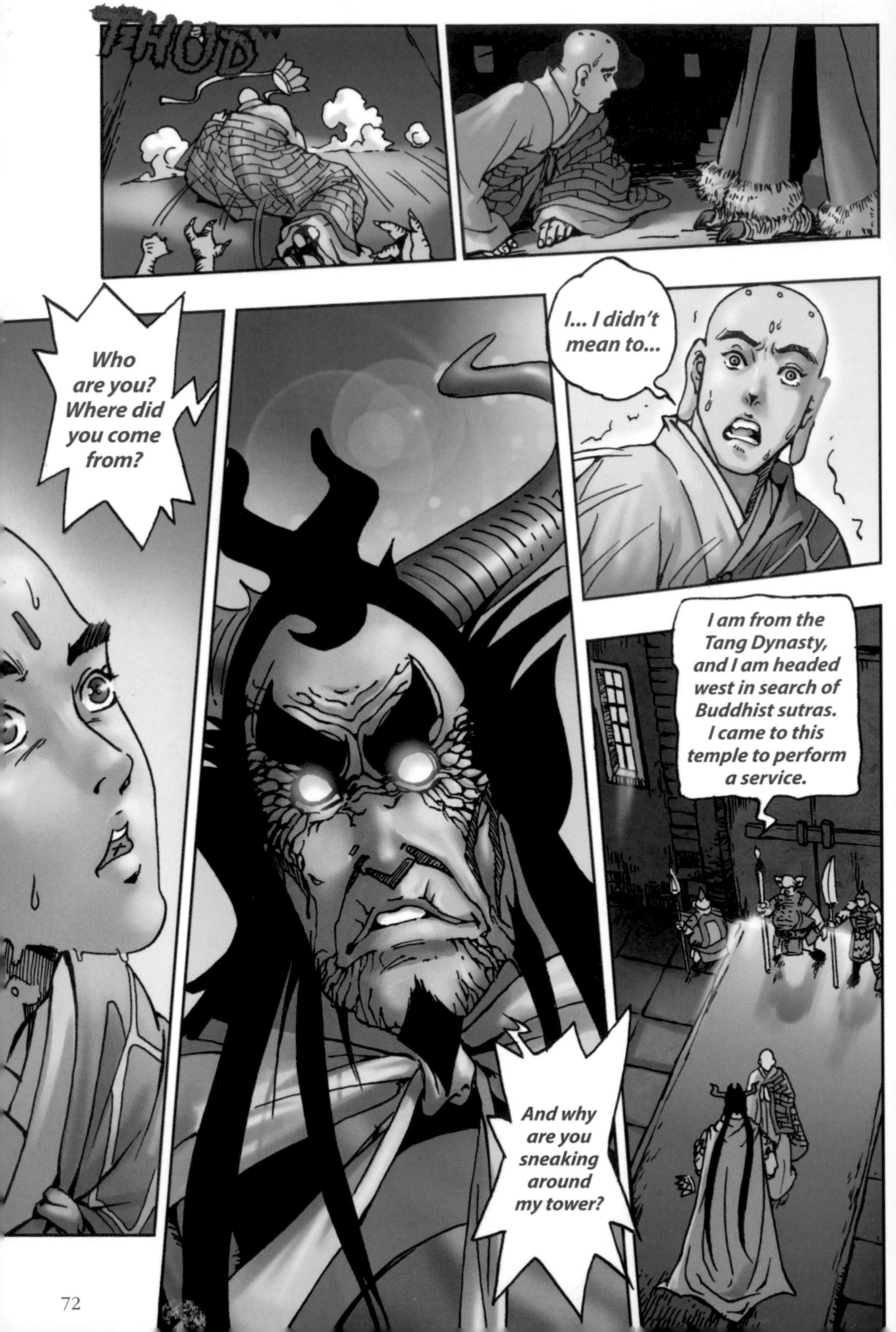
THUD
I... I didn't mean to...
Who are you? Where did you come from?
And why are you sneaking around my tower?
I am from the Tang Dynasty, and I am headed west in search of Buddhist sutras. I came to this temple to perform a service.

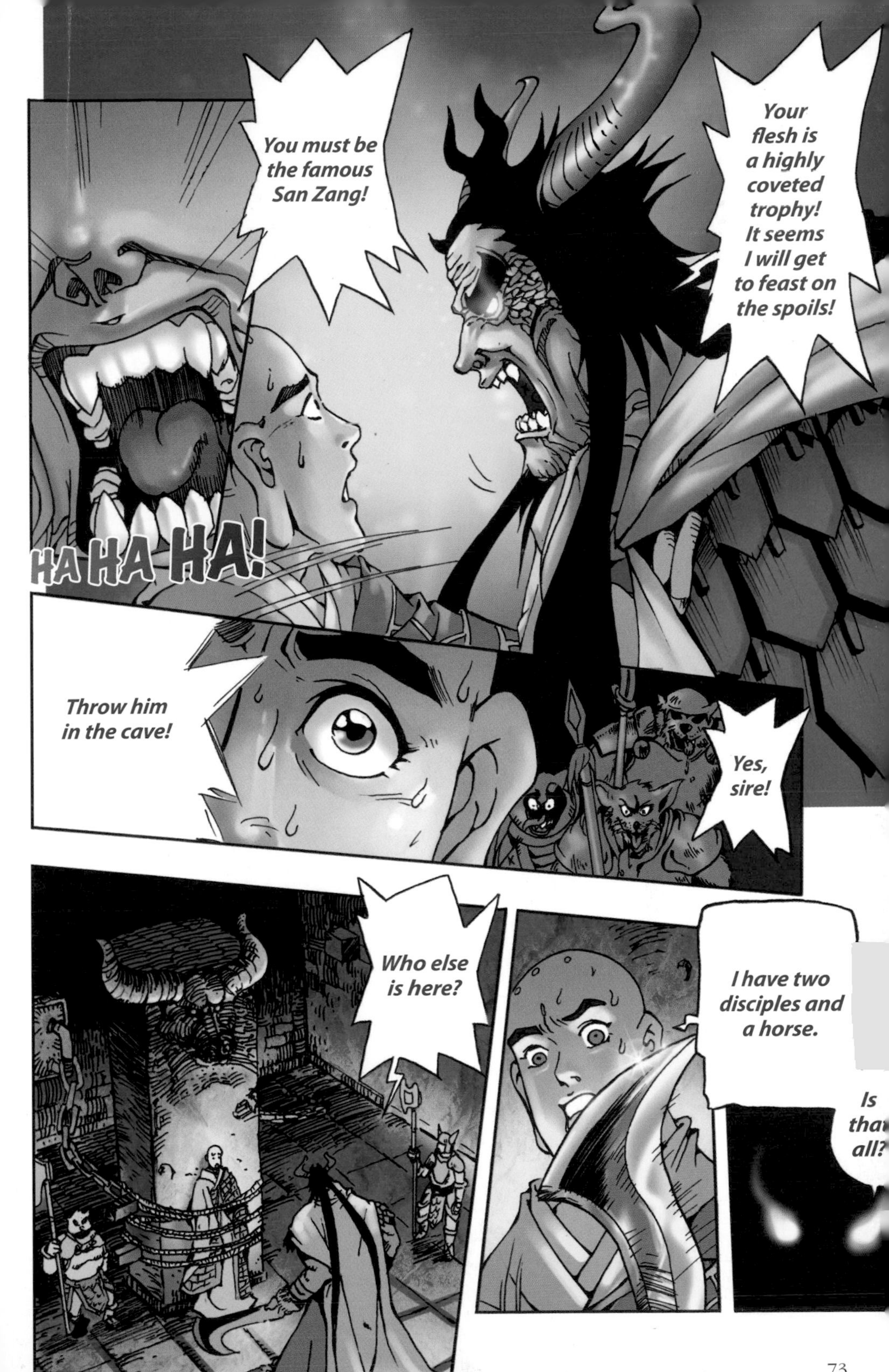
You must be the famous San Zang!
Your flesh is a highly coveted trophy! It seems I will get to feast on the spoils!
HA HA HA!
Throw him in the cave!
Yes, sire!
Who else is here?
I have two disciples and a horse.
Is tha all?

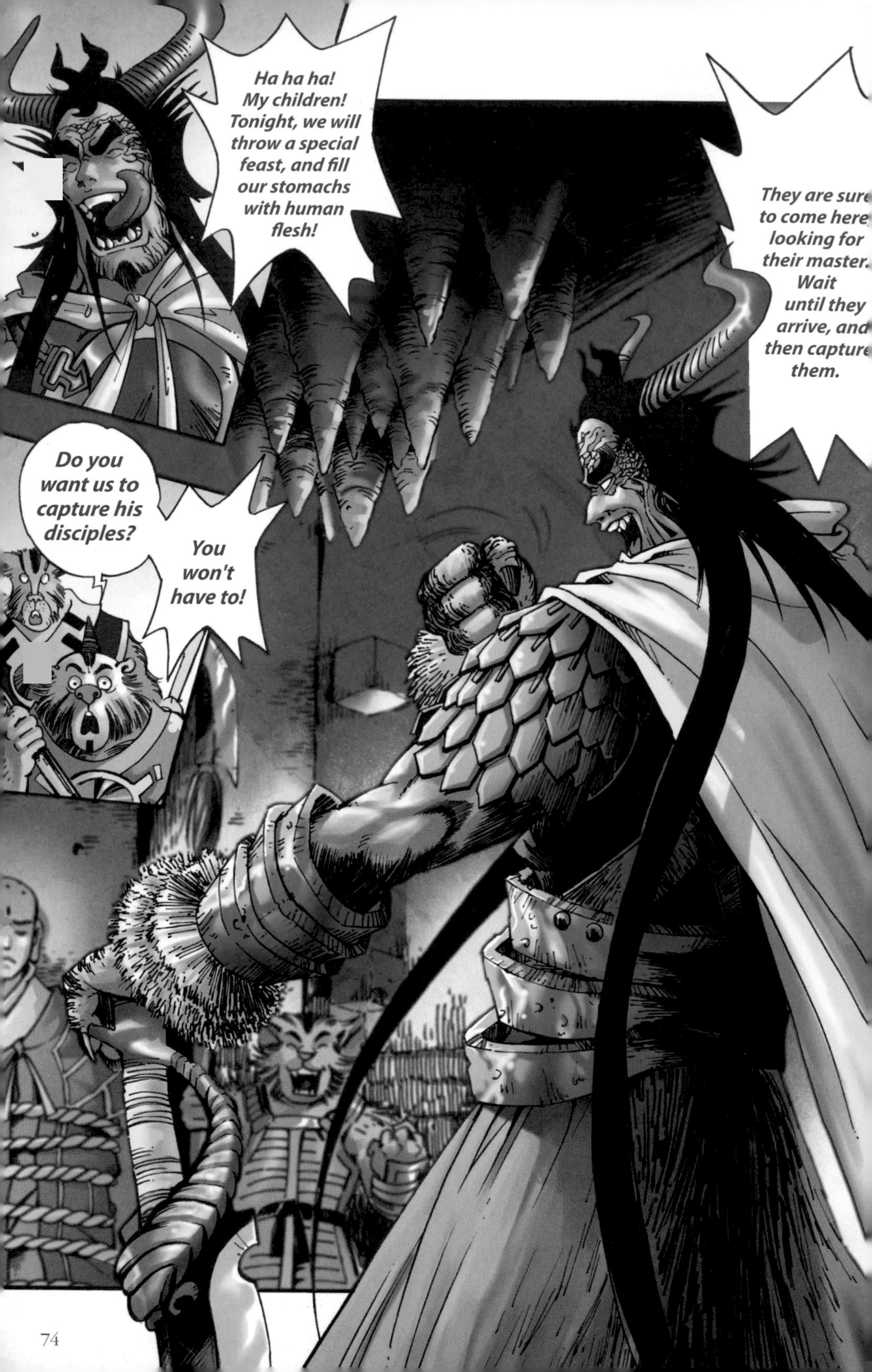
Ha ha ha! My children! Tonight, we will throw a special feast, and fill our stomachs with human flesh!
Do you want us to capture his disciples?
You won't have to!
They are sure to come here looking for their master. Wait until they arrive, and then capture them.

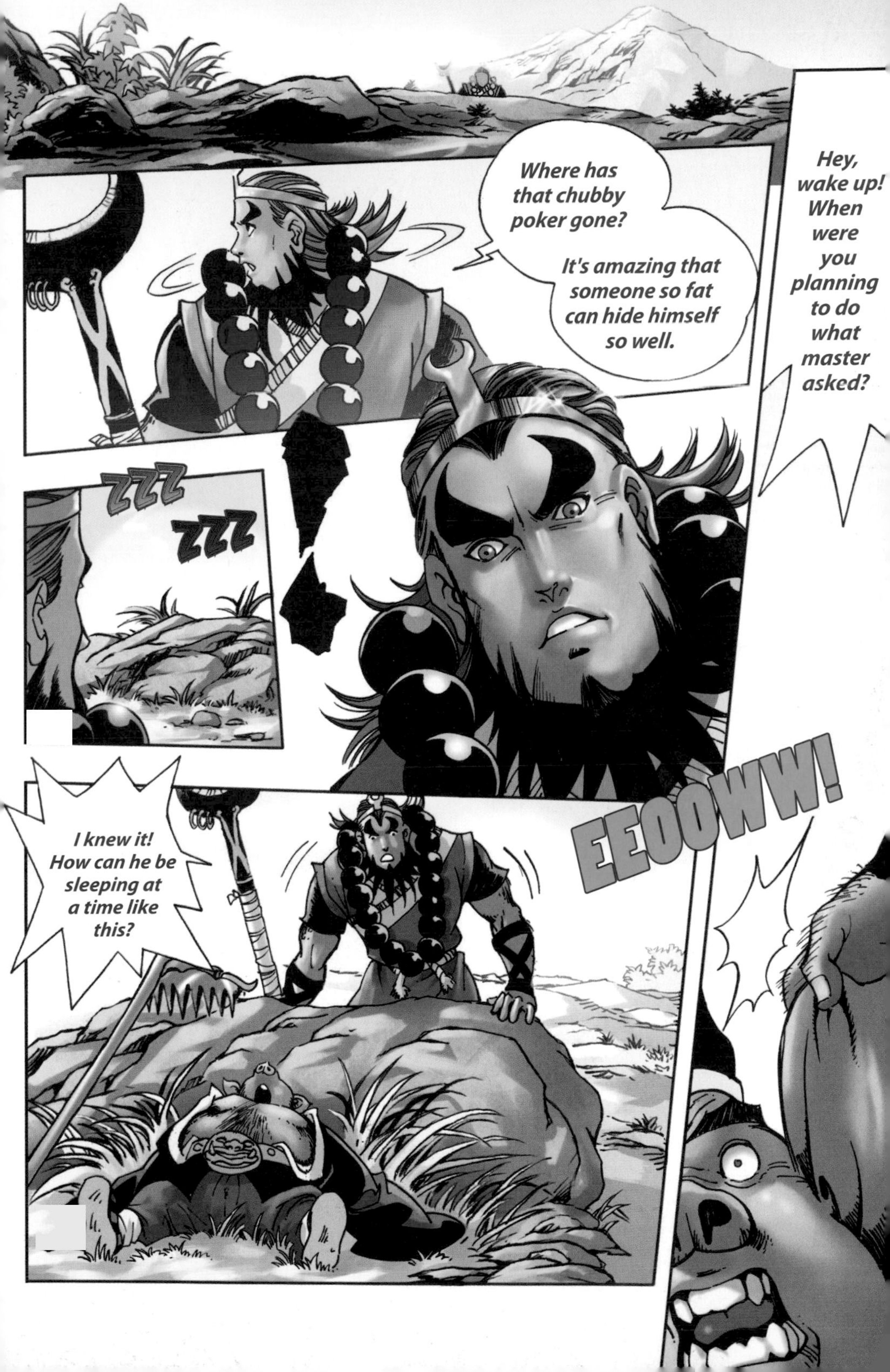
Where has that chubby poker gone?
It's amazing that someone so fat can hide himself so well.
Hey, wake up! When were you planning to do what master asked?
ZZZ
ZZZ
I knew it! How can he be sleeping at a time like this?
EEOOWW!

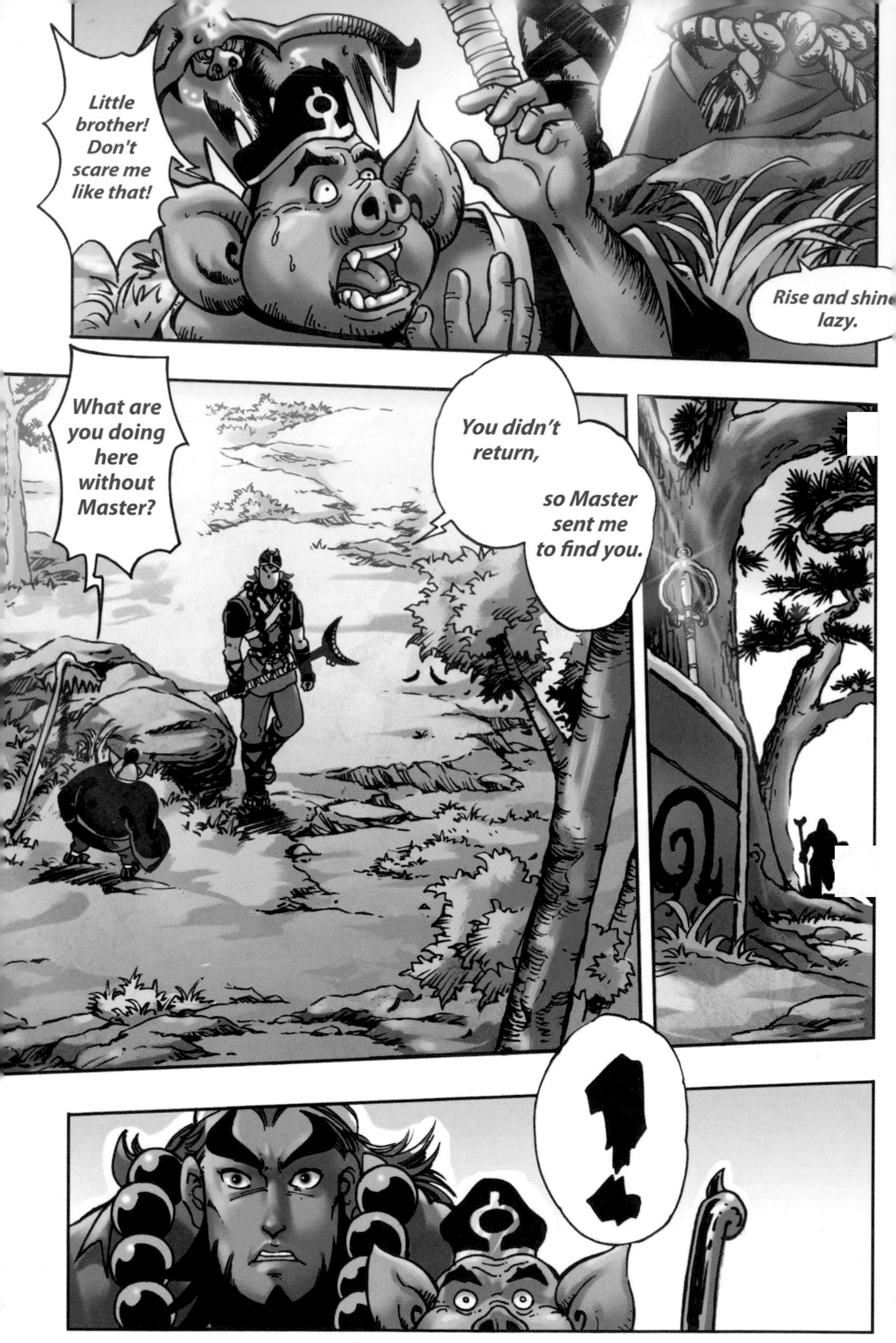
Little brother! Don't scare me like that!
Rise and shine lazy.
What are you doing here without Master?
You didn't return,
so Master sent me to find you.
!

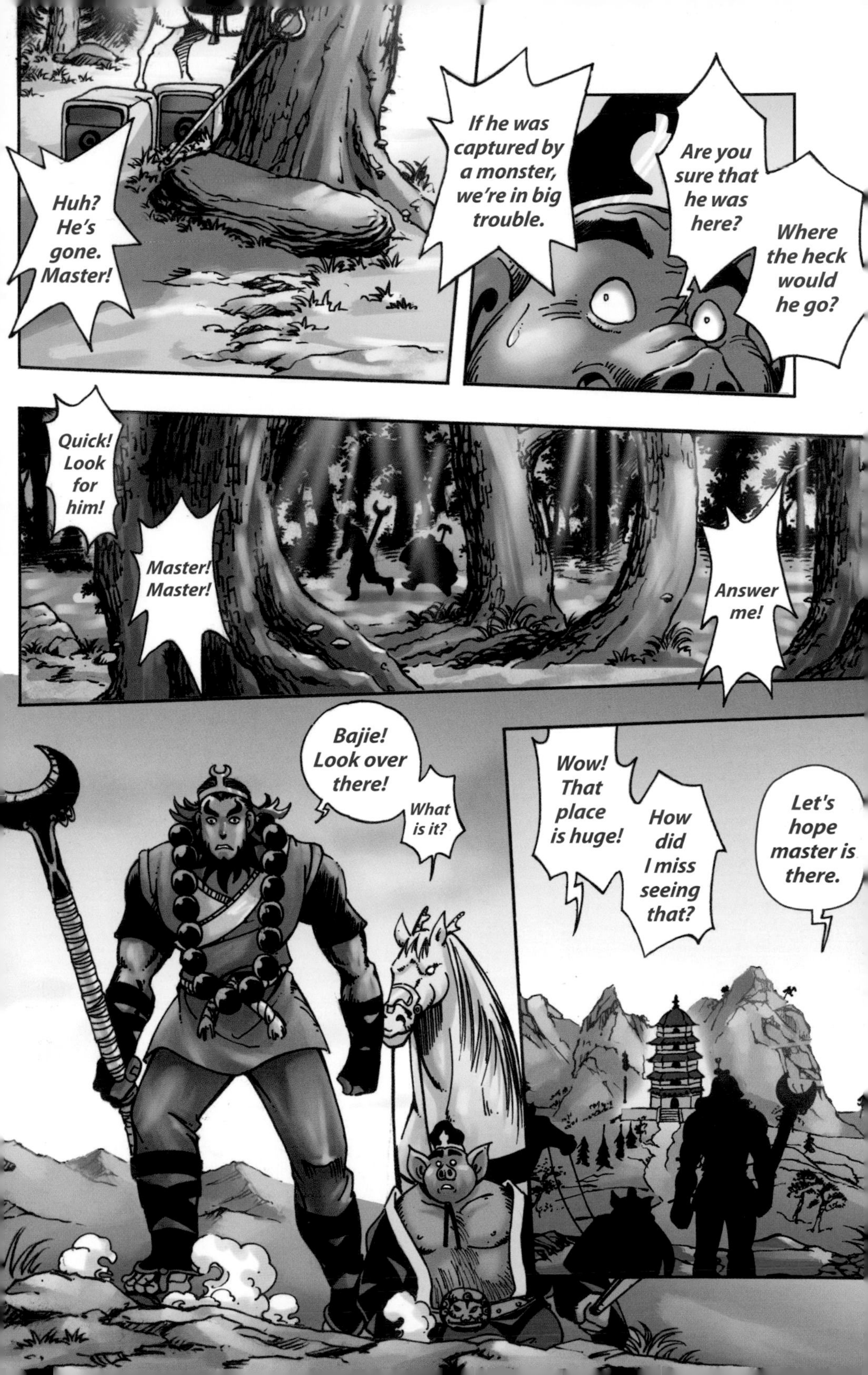
Huh? He's gone. Master!
If he was captured by a monster, we're in big trouble.
Are you sure that he was here?
Where the heck would he go?
Quick! Look for him!
Master! Master!
Answer me!
Bajie! Look over there!
What is it?
Wow! That place is huge!
How did I miss seeing that?
Let's hope master is there.

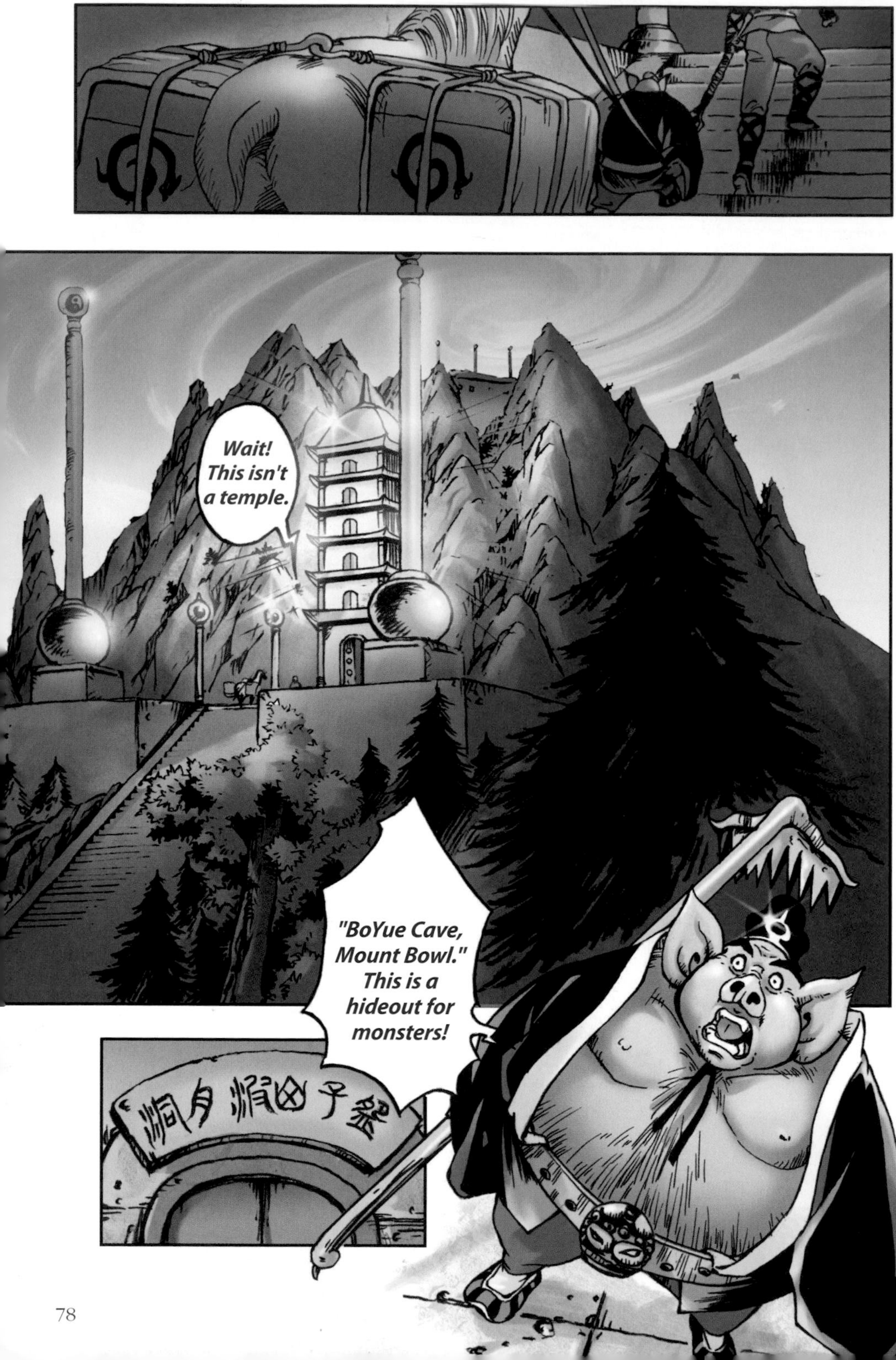
Wait! This isn't a temple.
"BoYue Cave, Mount Bowl."
This is a hideout for monsters!

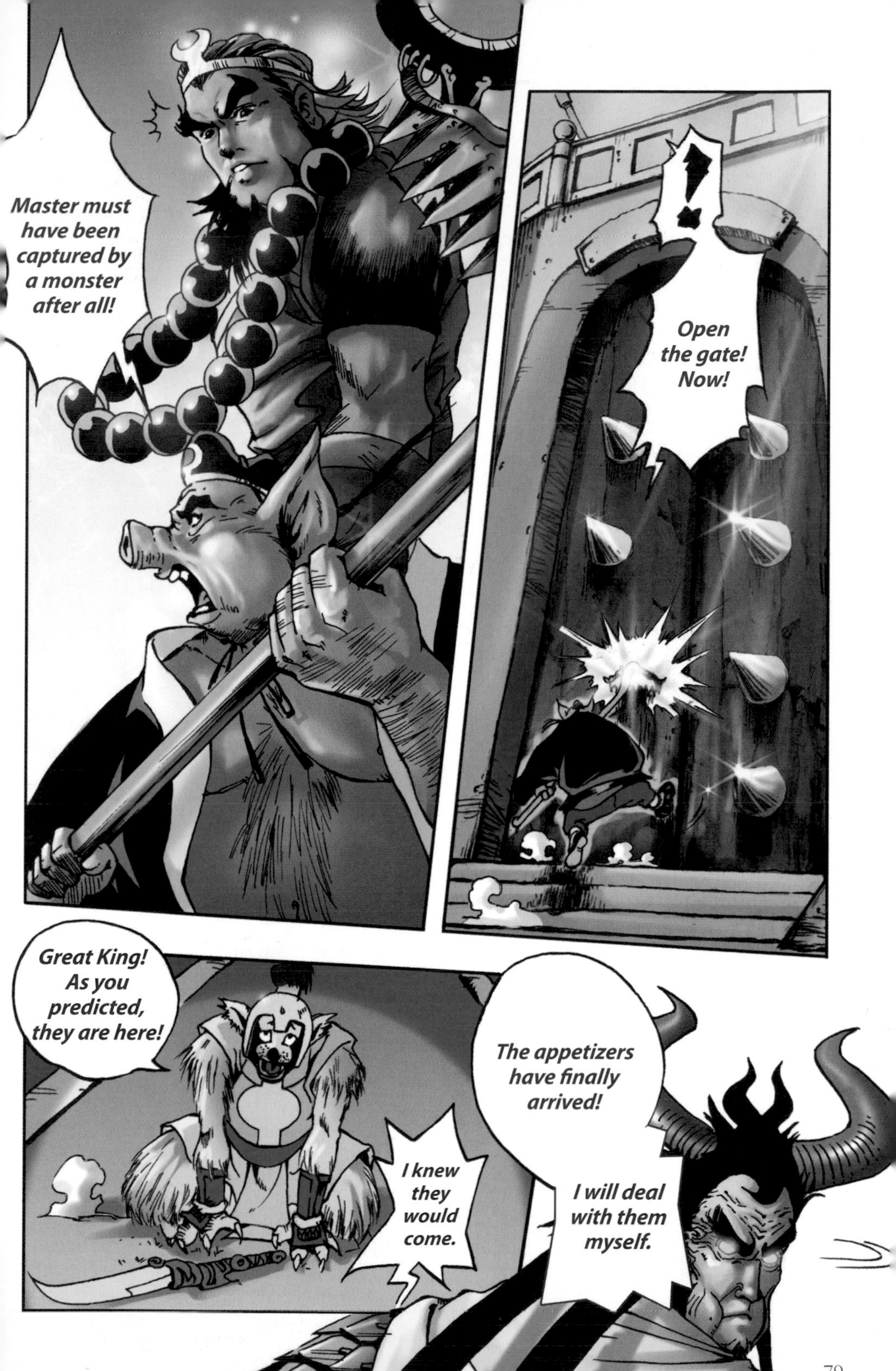

Master must have been captured by a monster after all!
Open the gate! Now!
Great King! As you predicted, they are here!
I knew they would come.
The appetizers have finally arrived!
I will deal with them myself.

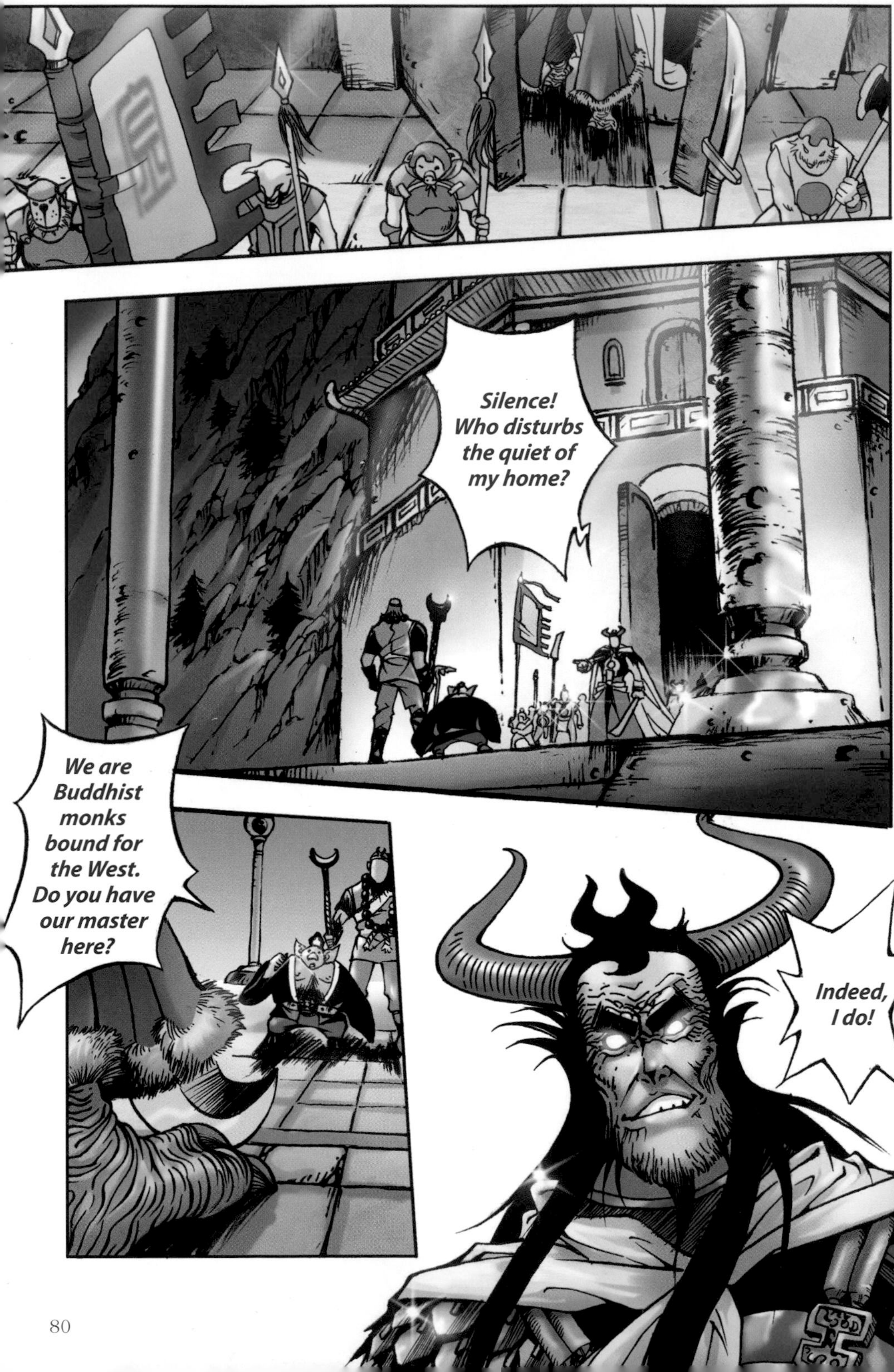
Silence! Who disturbs the quiet of my home?
We are Buddhist monks bound for the West. Do you have our master here?
Indeed, I do!

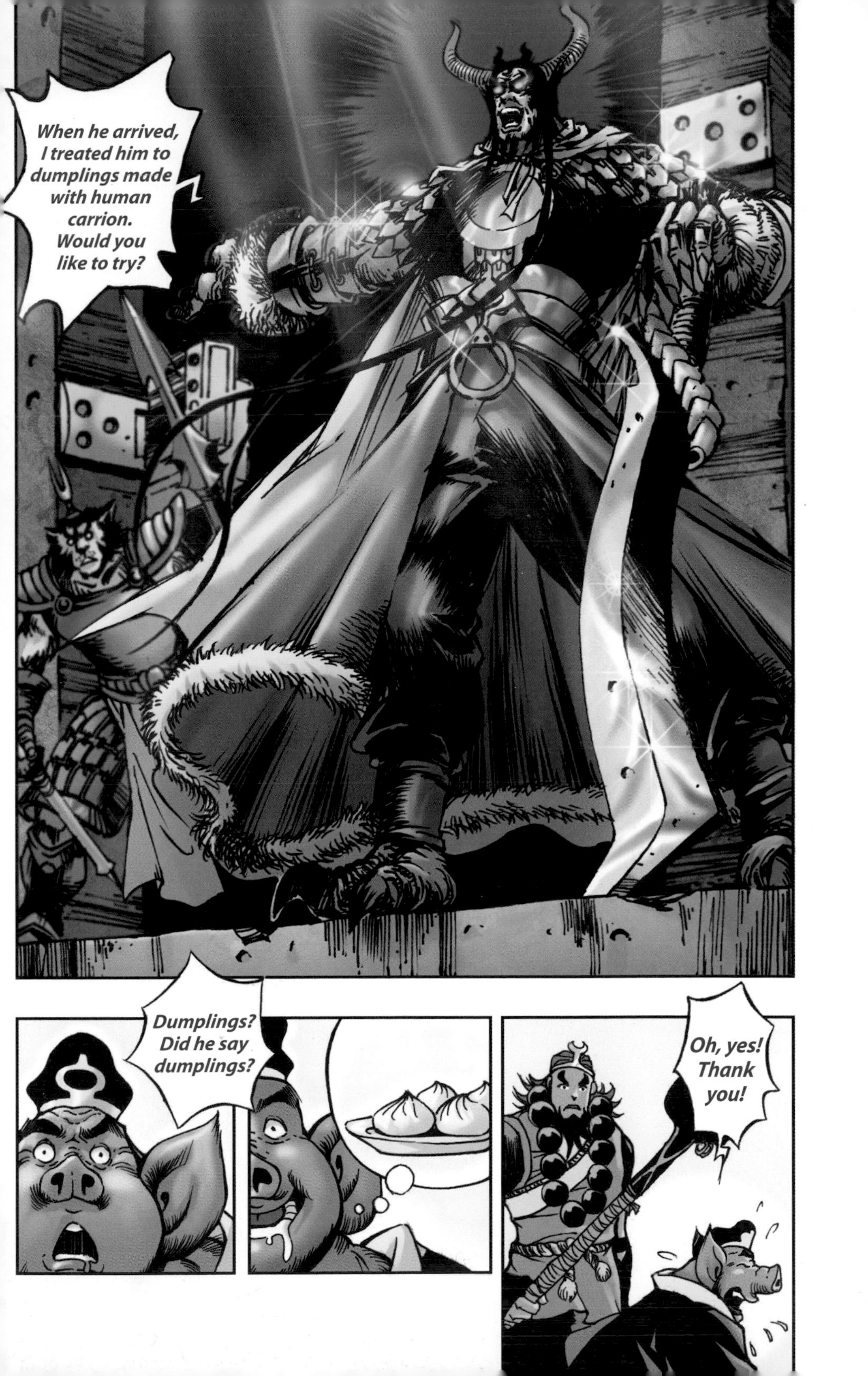
When he arrived, I treated him to dumplings made with human carrion. Would you like to try?
Dumplings? Did he say dumplings?
Oh, yes! Thank you!

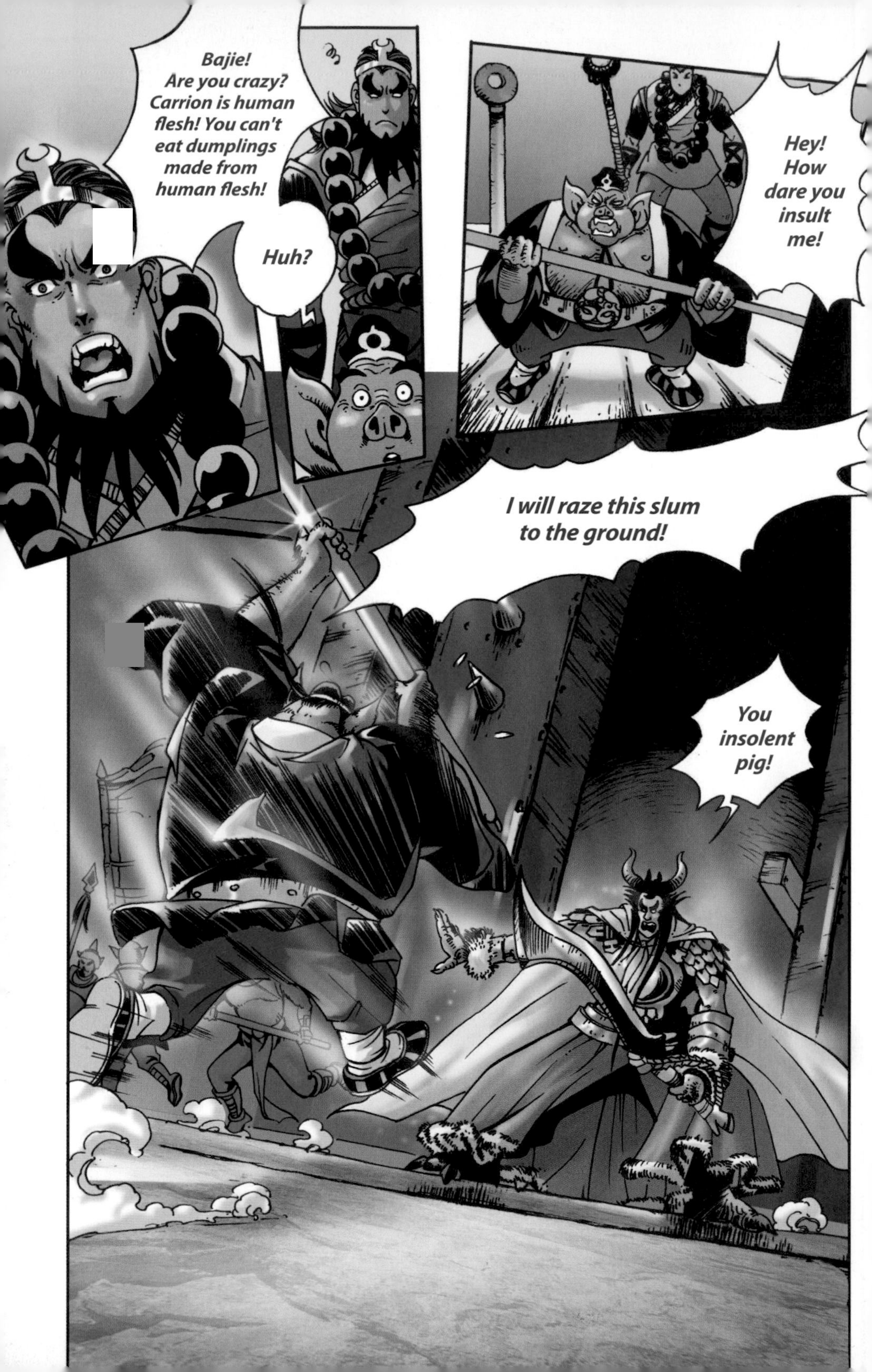
Bajie! Are you crazy? Carrion is human flesh! You can't eat dumplings made from human flesh!
Huh?
Hey! How dare you insult me!
I will raze this slum to the ground!
You insolent pig!

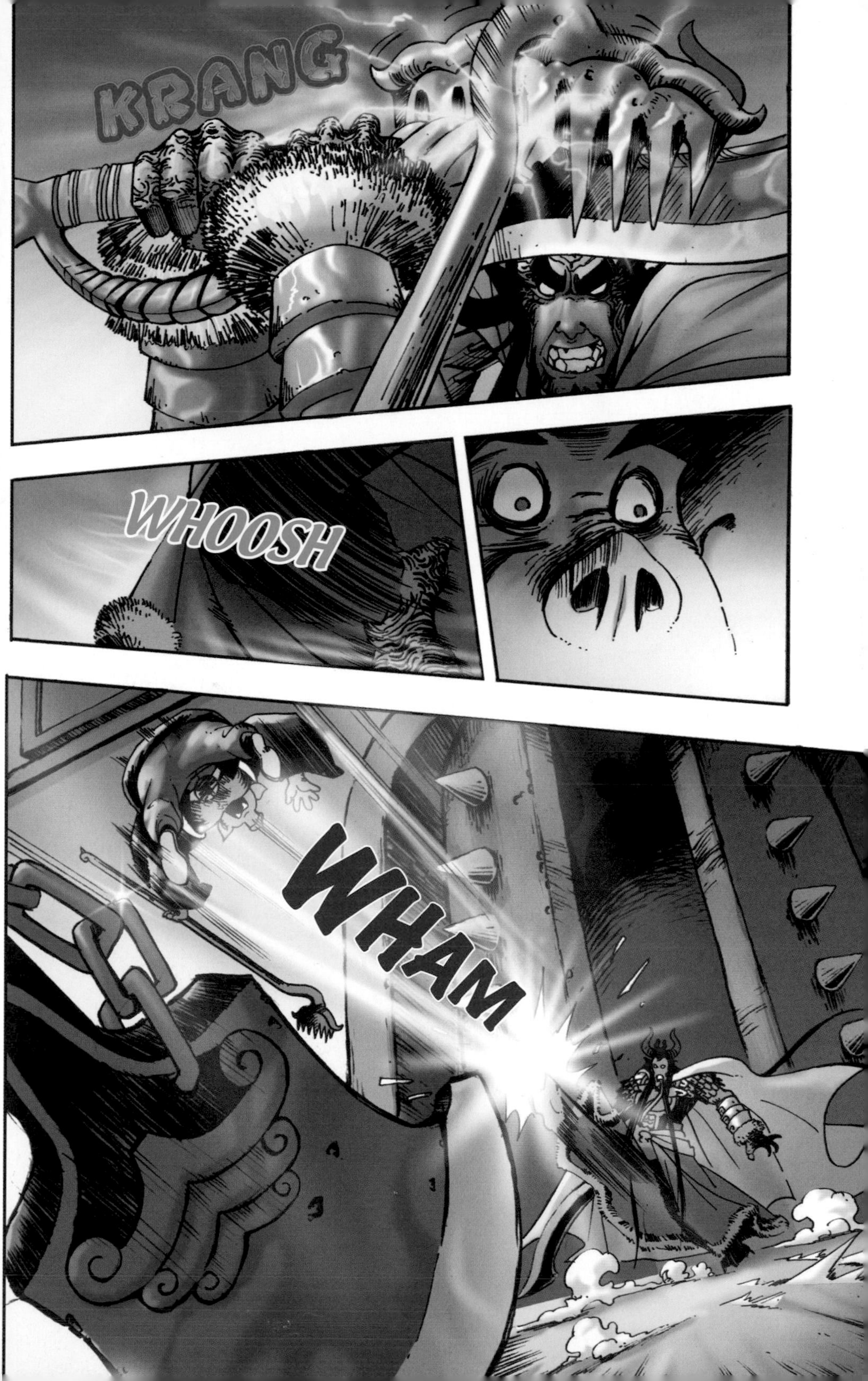
KRANG
WHOOSH
WHAM

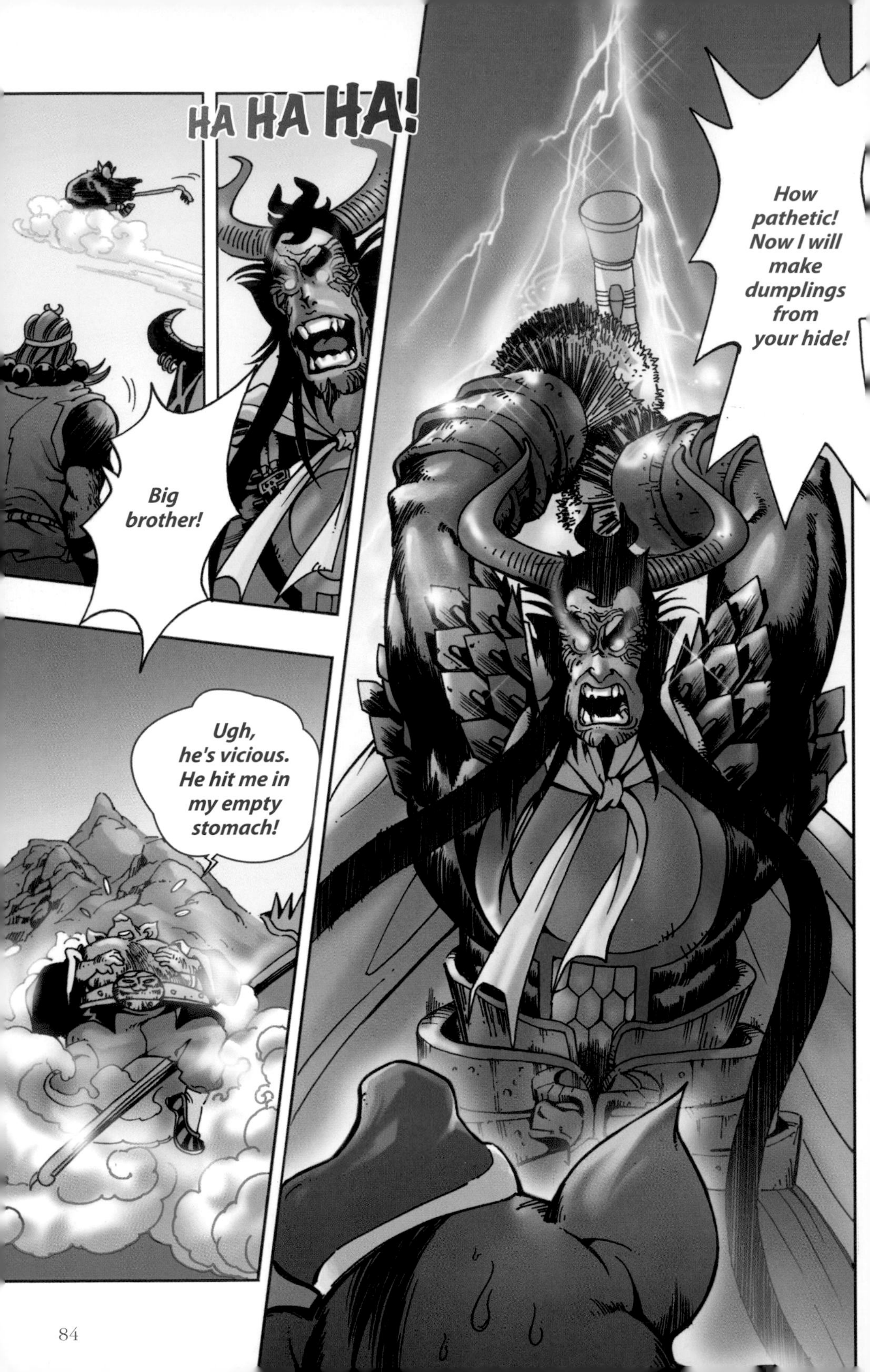
HA HA HA!
How pathetic! Now I will make dumplings from your hide!
Big brother!
Ugh, he's vicious. He hit me in my empty stomach!

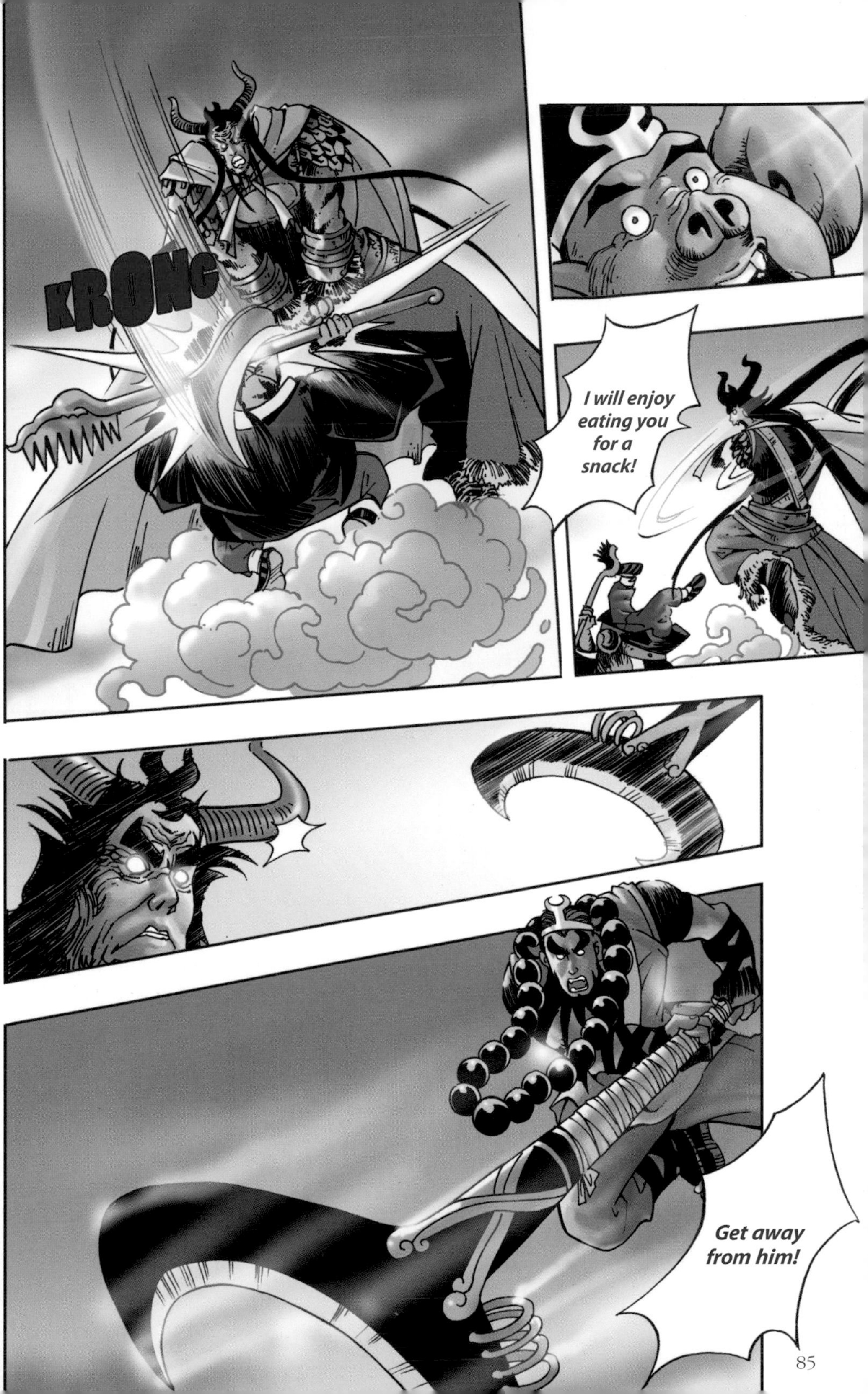
KRONG
I will enjoy eating you for a snack!
Get away from him!

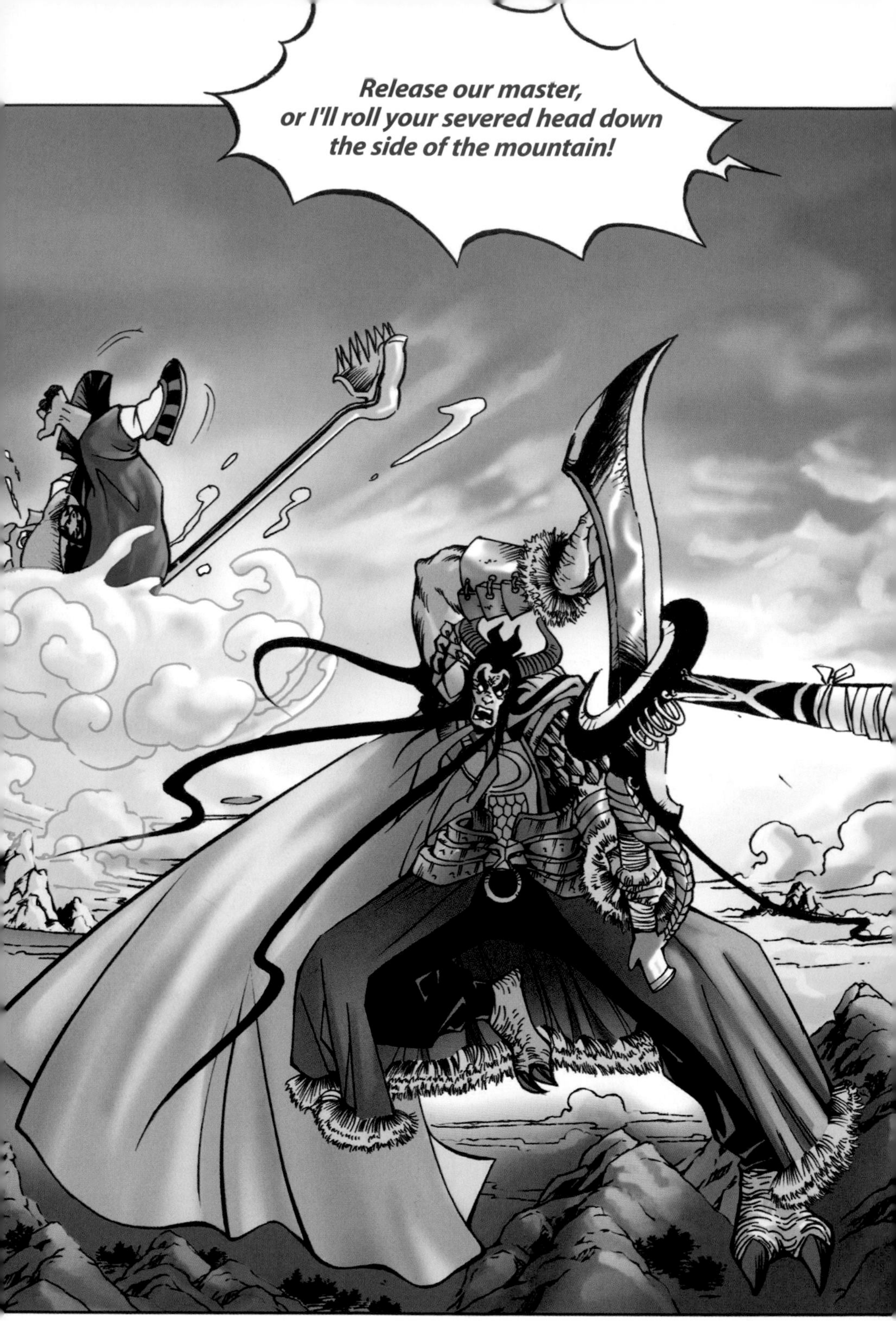
Release our master, or I'll roll your severed head down the side of the mountain!

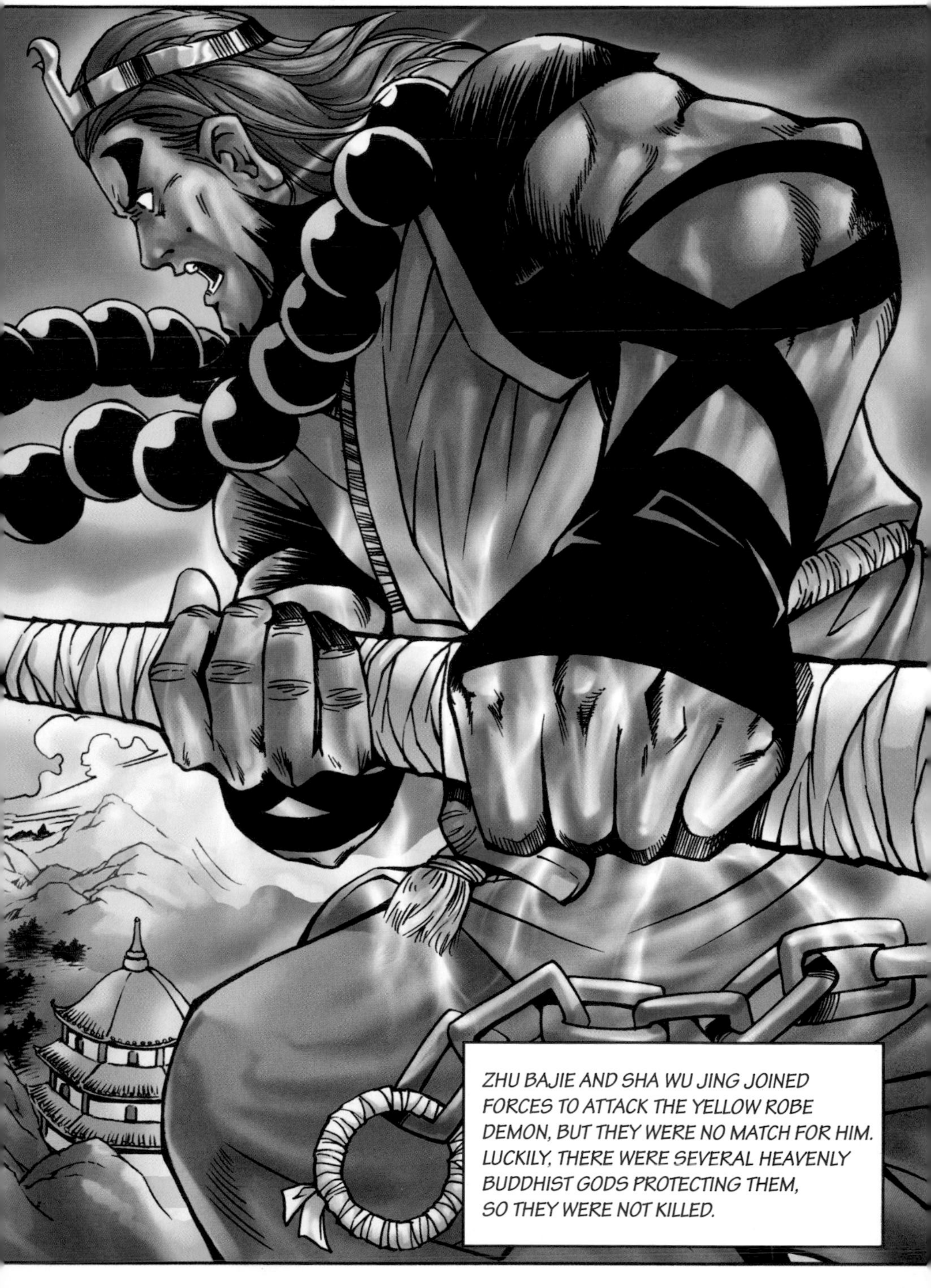
ZHU BAJIE AND SHA WU JING JOINED
FORCES TO ATTACK THE YELLOW ROBE
DEMON, BUT THEY WERE NO MATCH FOR HIM.
LUCKILY, THERE WERE SEVERAL HEAVENLY
BUDDHIST GODS PROTECTING THEM,
SO THEY WERE NOT KILLED.

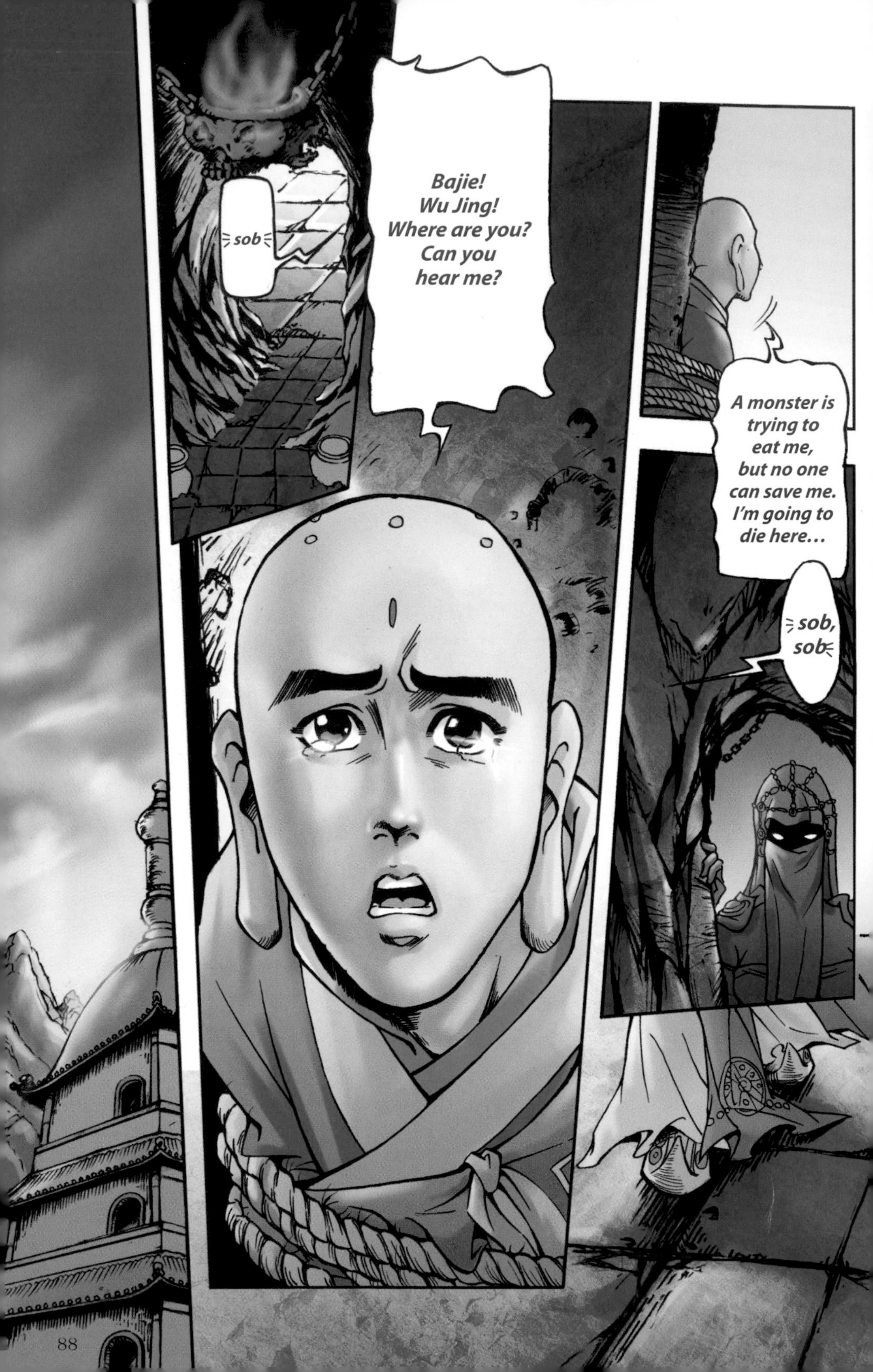
sob
Bajie! Wu Jing! Where are you? Can you hear me?
A monster is trying to eat me, but no one can save me. I'm going to die here…
sob, sob

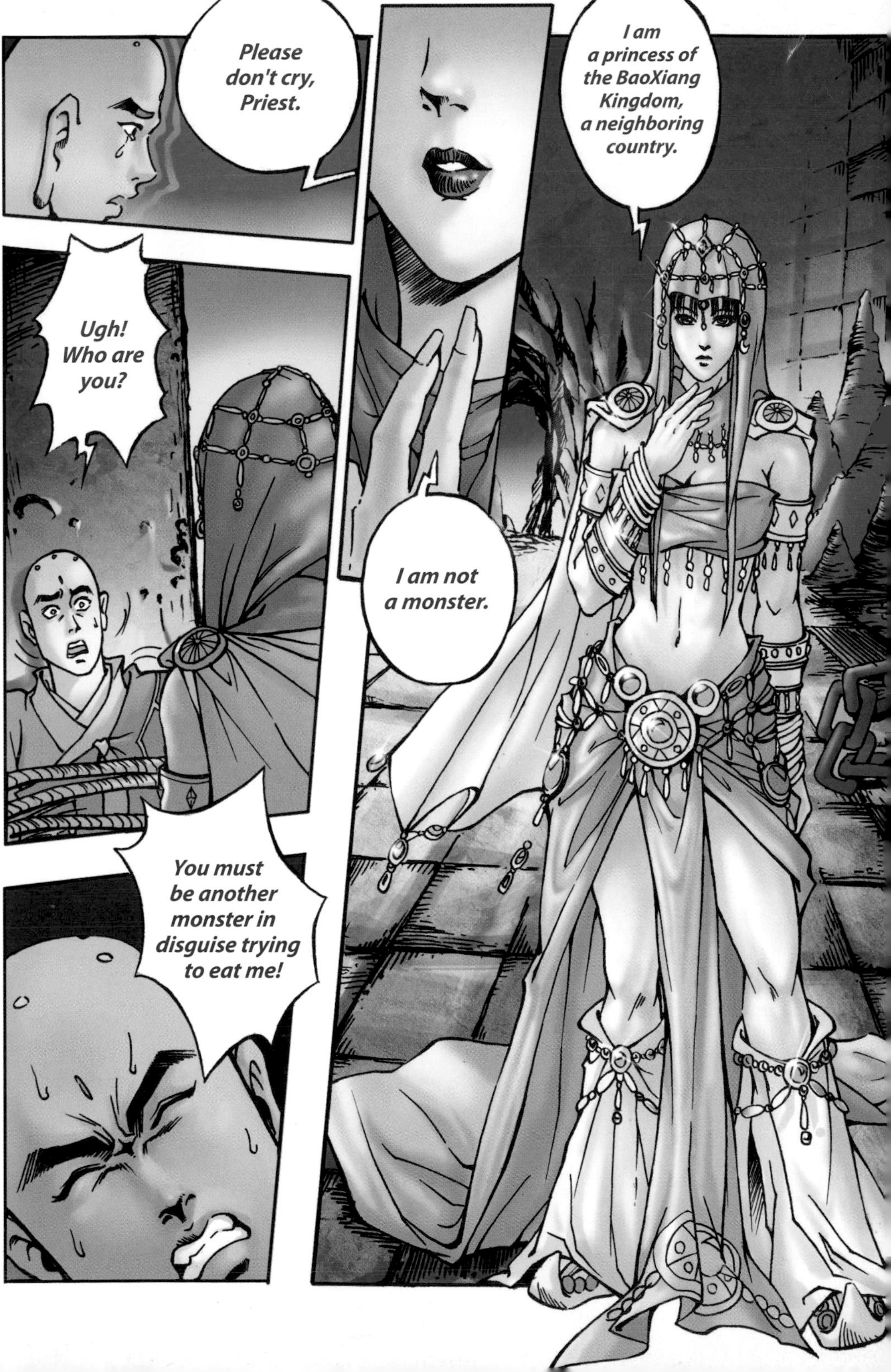
Please don't cry, Priest.
I am a princess of the BaoXiang Kingdom, a neighboring country.
Ugh! Who are you?
I am not a monster.
You must be another monster in disguise trying to eat me!

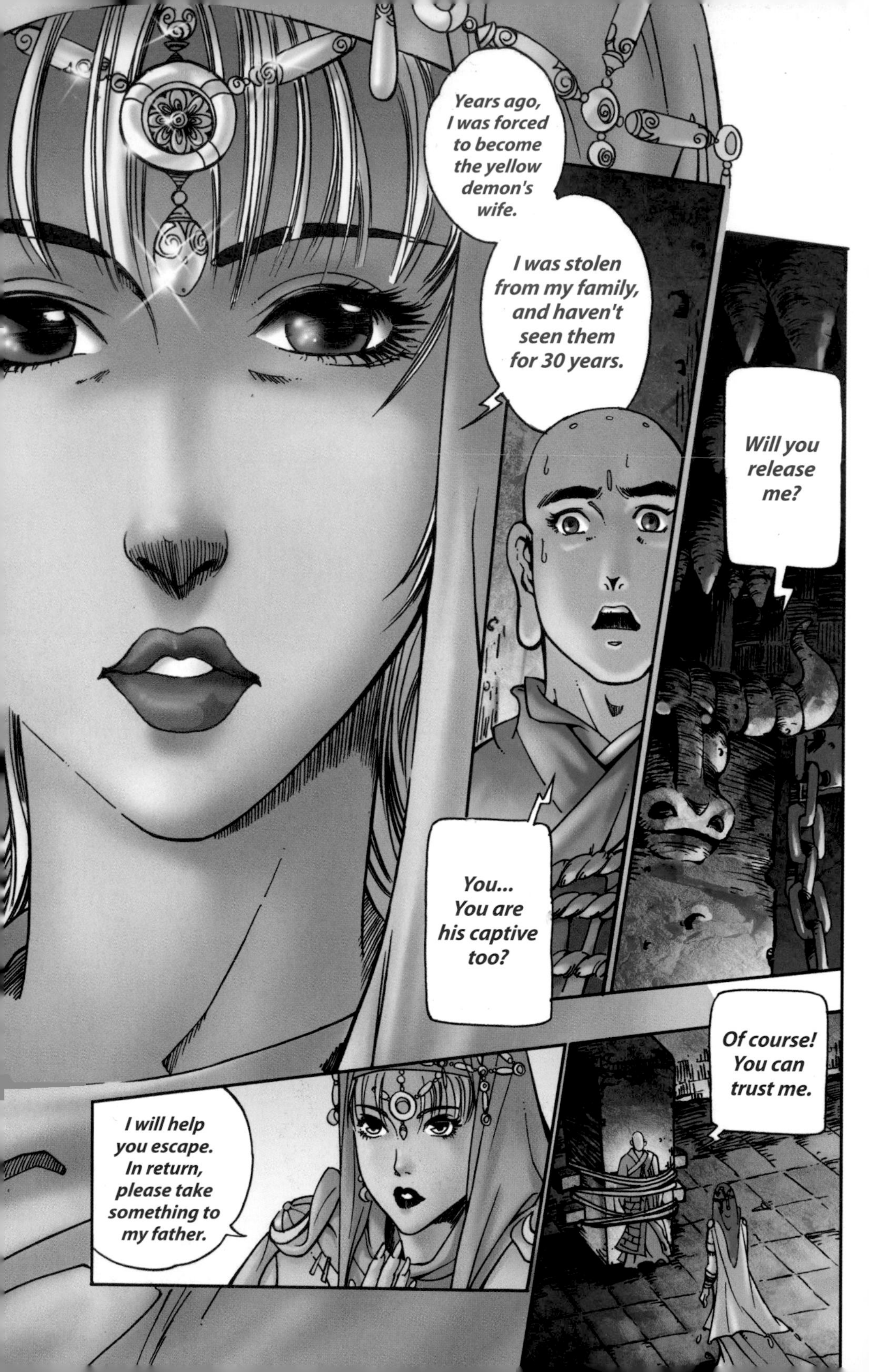
Years ago, I was forced to become the yellow demon's wife.
I was stolen from my family, and haven't seen them for 30 years.
Will you release me?
You... You are his captive too?
Of course! You can trust me.
I will help you escape. In return, please take something to my father.

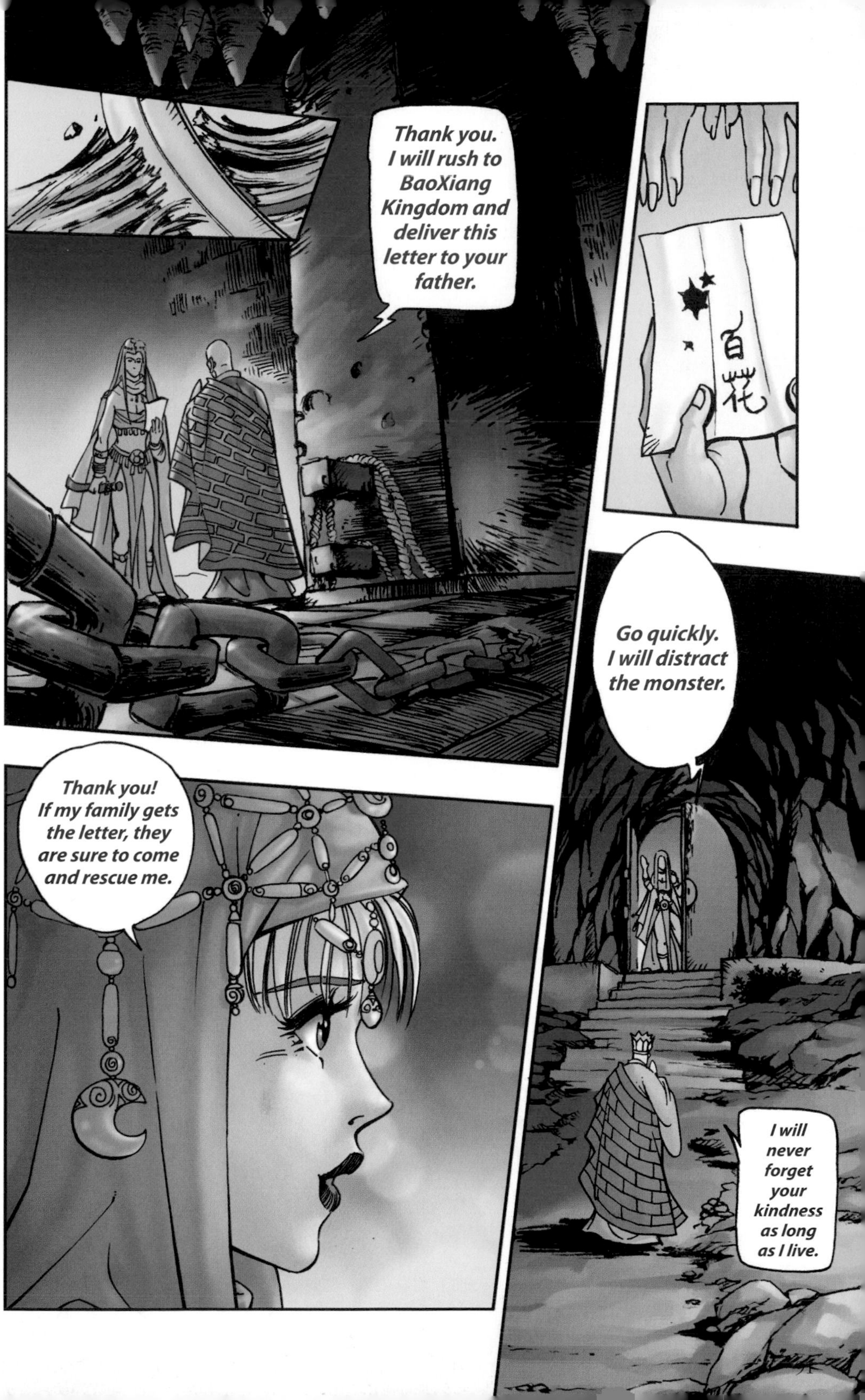
Thank you. I will rush to BaoXiang Kingdom and deliver this letter to your father.
百花
Go quickly. I will distract the monster.
Thank you! If my family gets the letter, they are sure to come and rescue me.
I will never forget your kindness as long as I live.

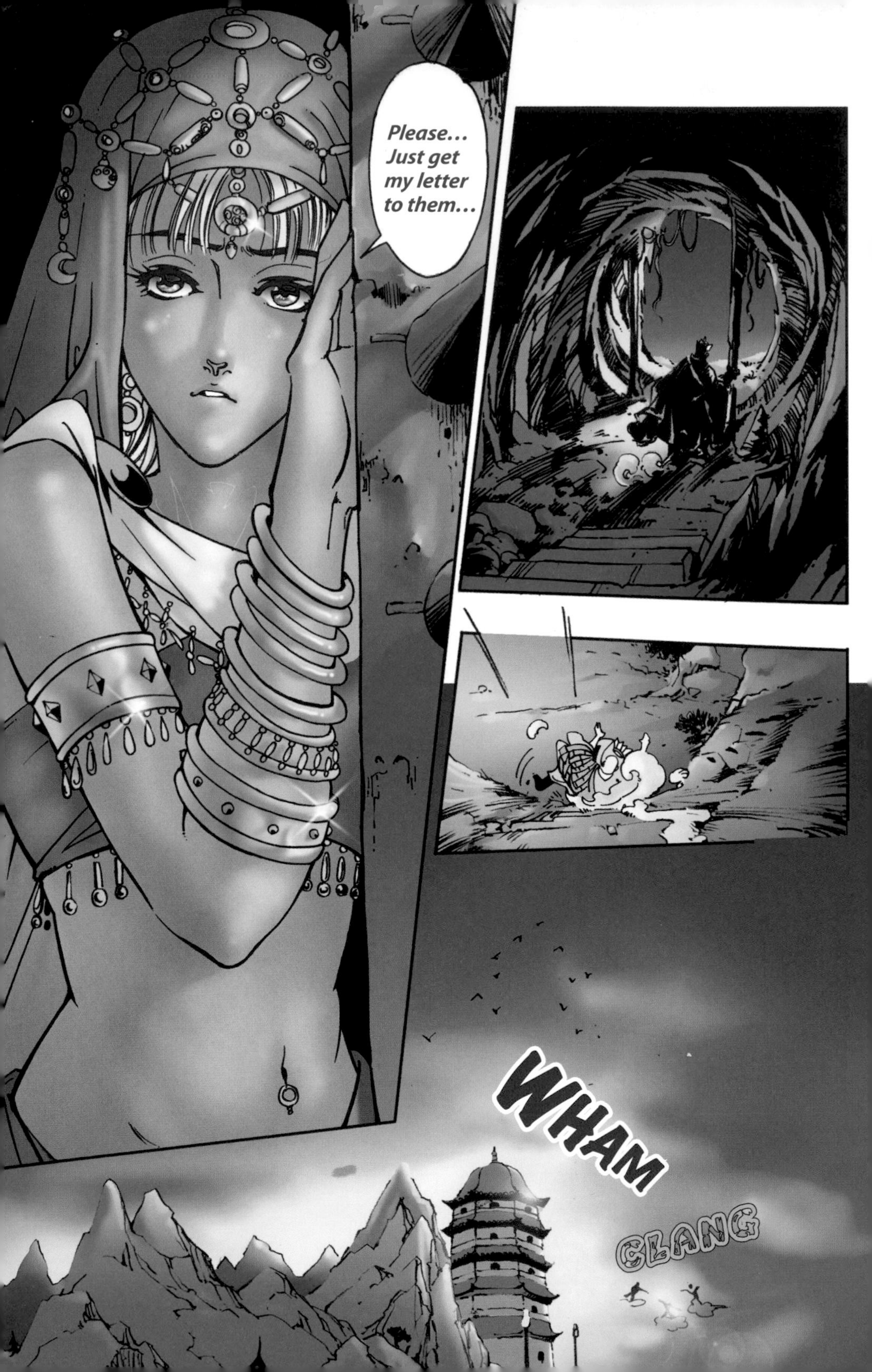
Please… Just get my letter to them…
WHAM
CLANG

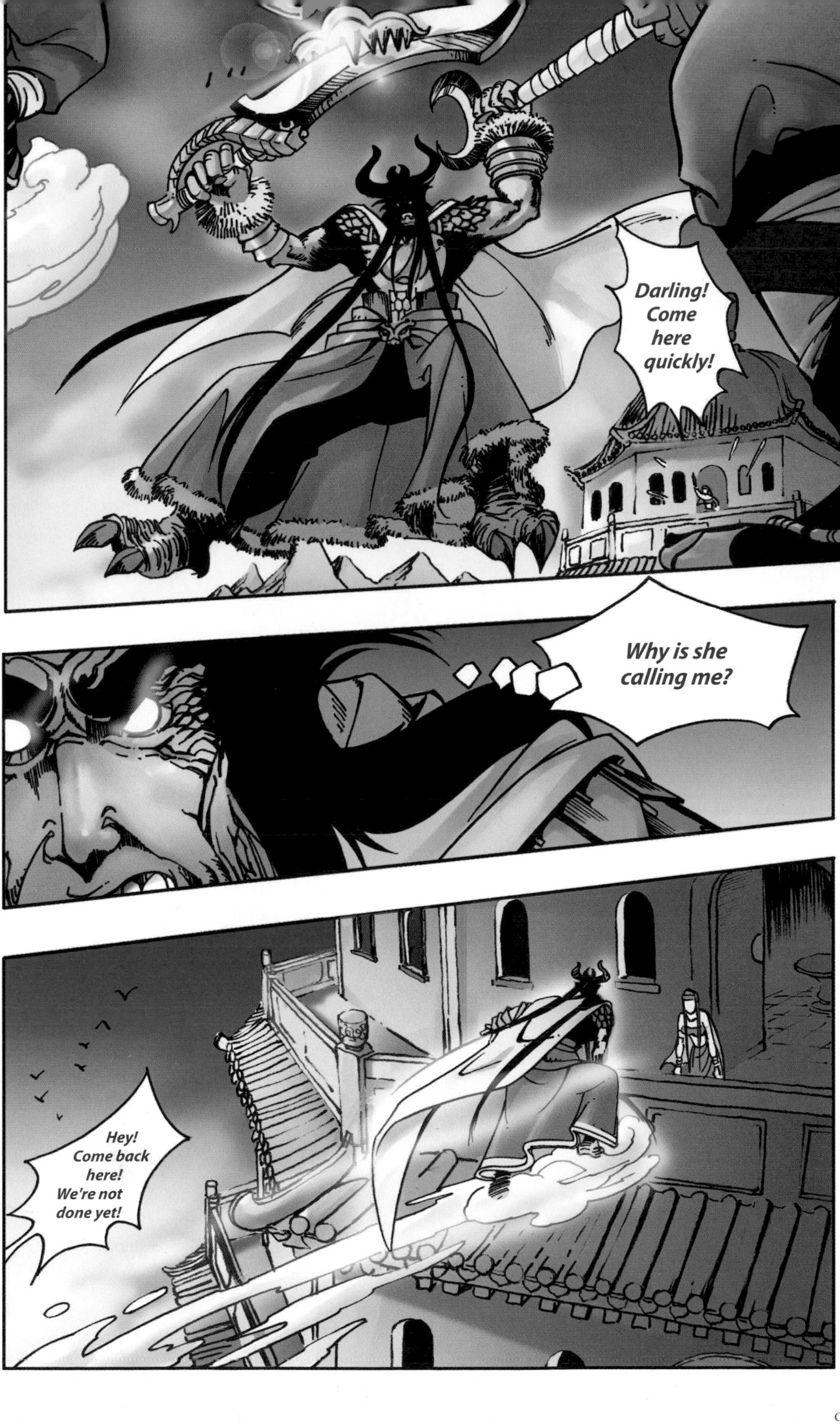
Darling! Come here quickly!
Why is she calling me?
Hey! Come back here! We're not done yet!

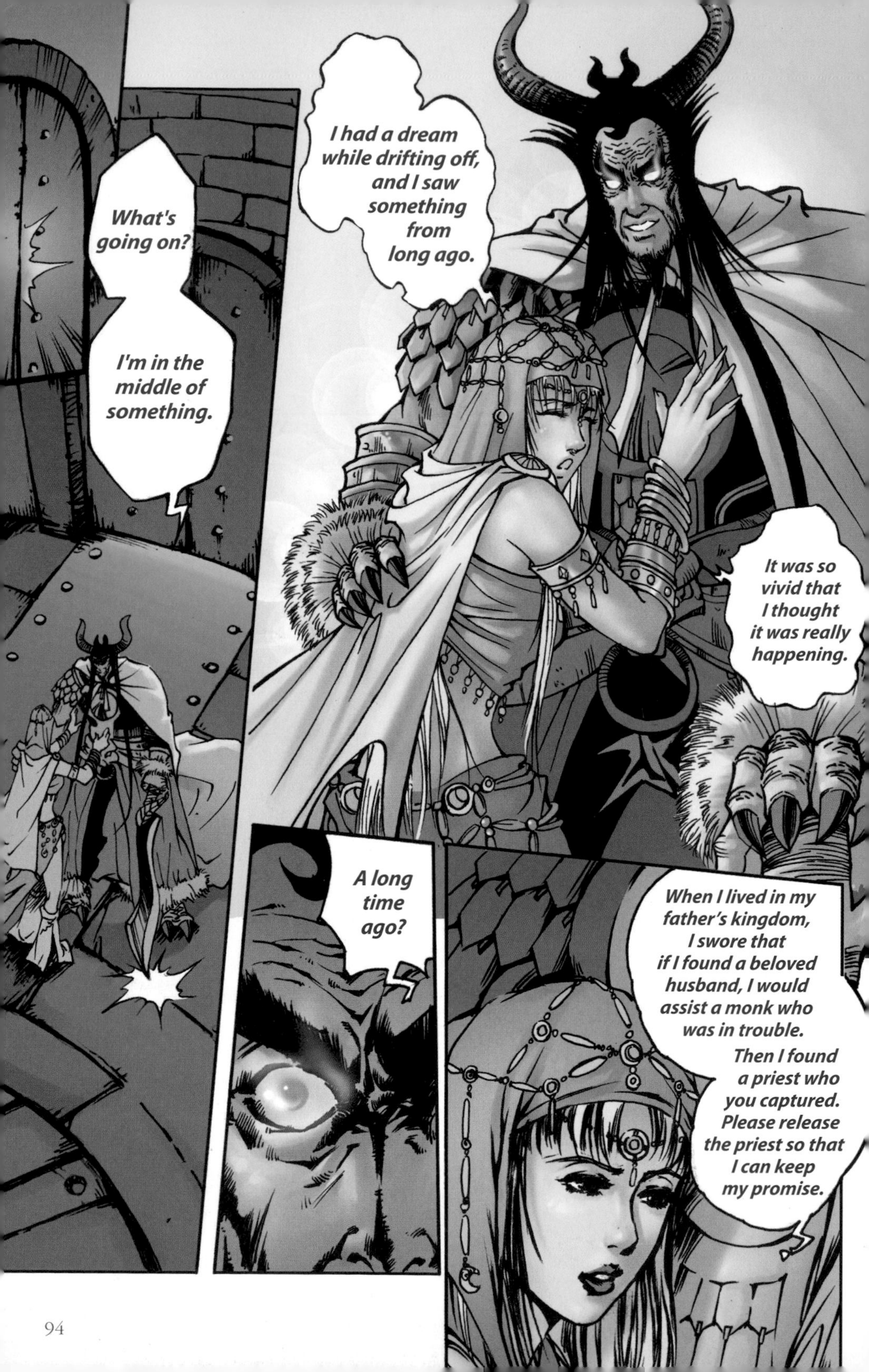
I had a dream while drifting off, and I saw something from long ago.
What's going on?
I'm in the middle of something.
It was so vivid that I thought it was really happening.
A long time ago?
When I lived in my father's kingdom, I swore that if I found a beloved husband, I would assist a monk who was in trouble.
Then I found a priest who you captured. Please release the priest so that I can keep my promise.

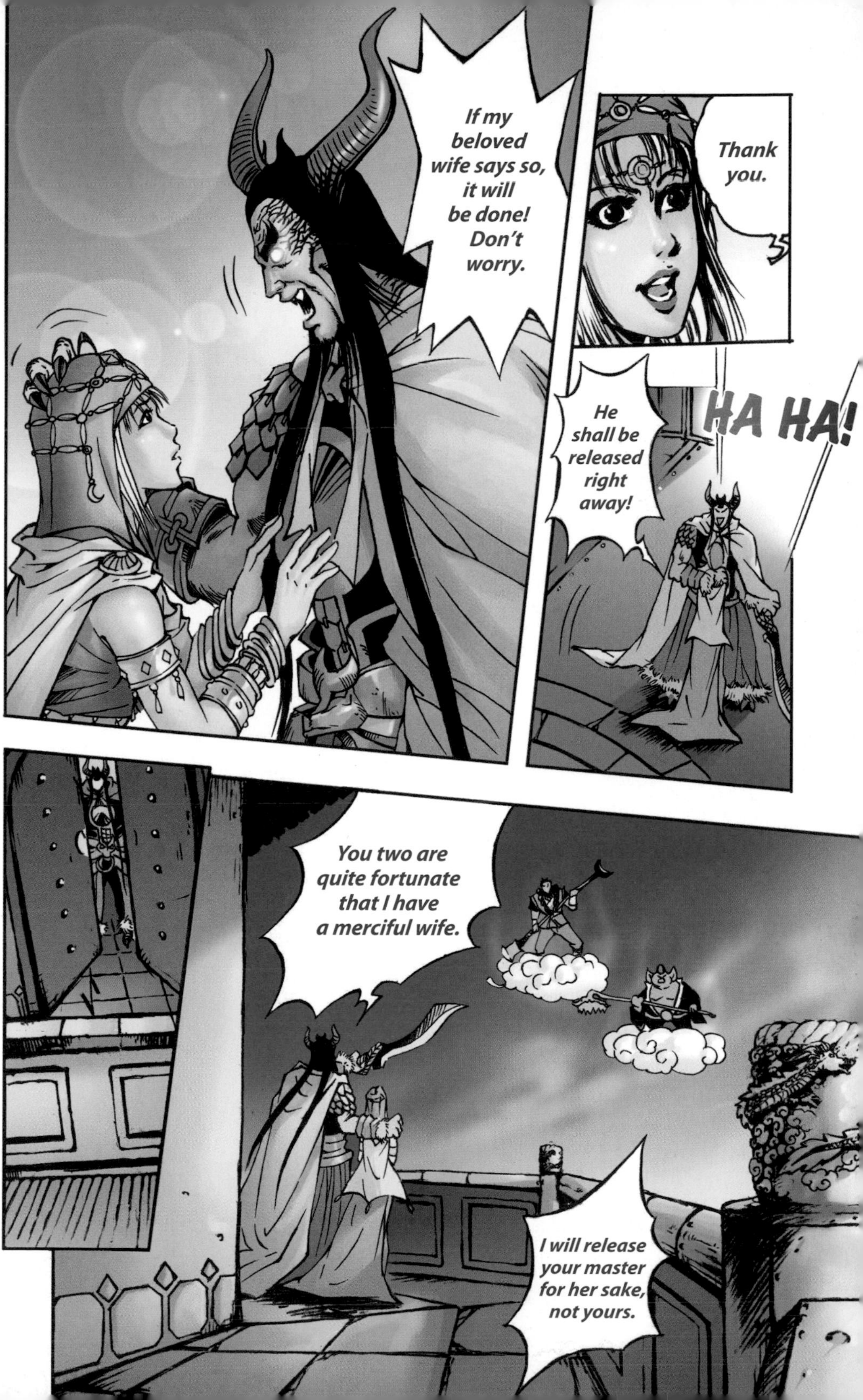
If my beloved wife says so, it will be done! Don't worry.
Thank you.
He shall be released right away!
HA HA!
You two are quite fortunate that I have a merciful wife.
I will release your master for her sake, not yours.

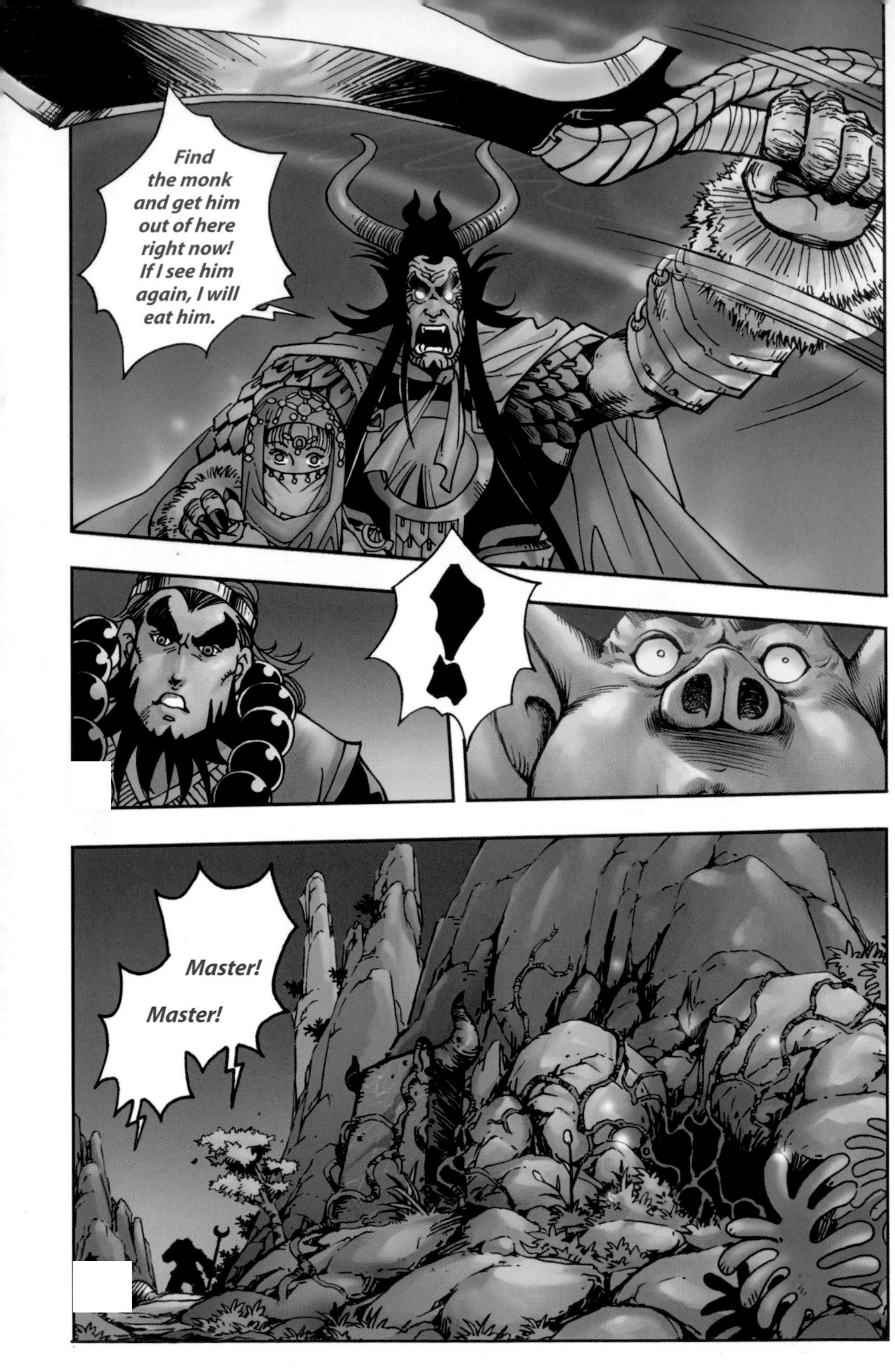
Find the monk and get him out of here right now! If I see him again, I will eat him.
!
Master!
Master!

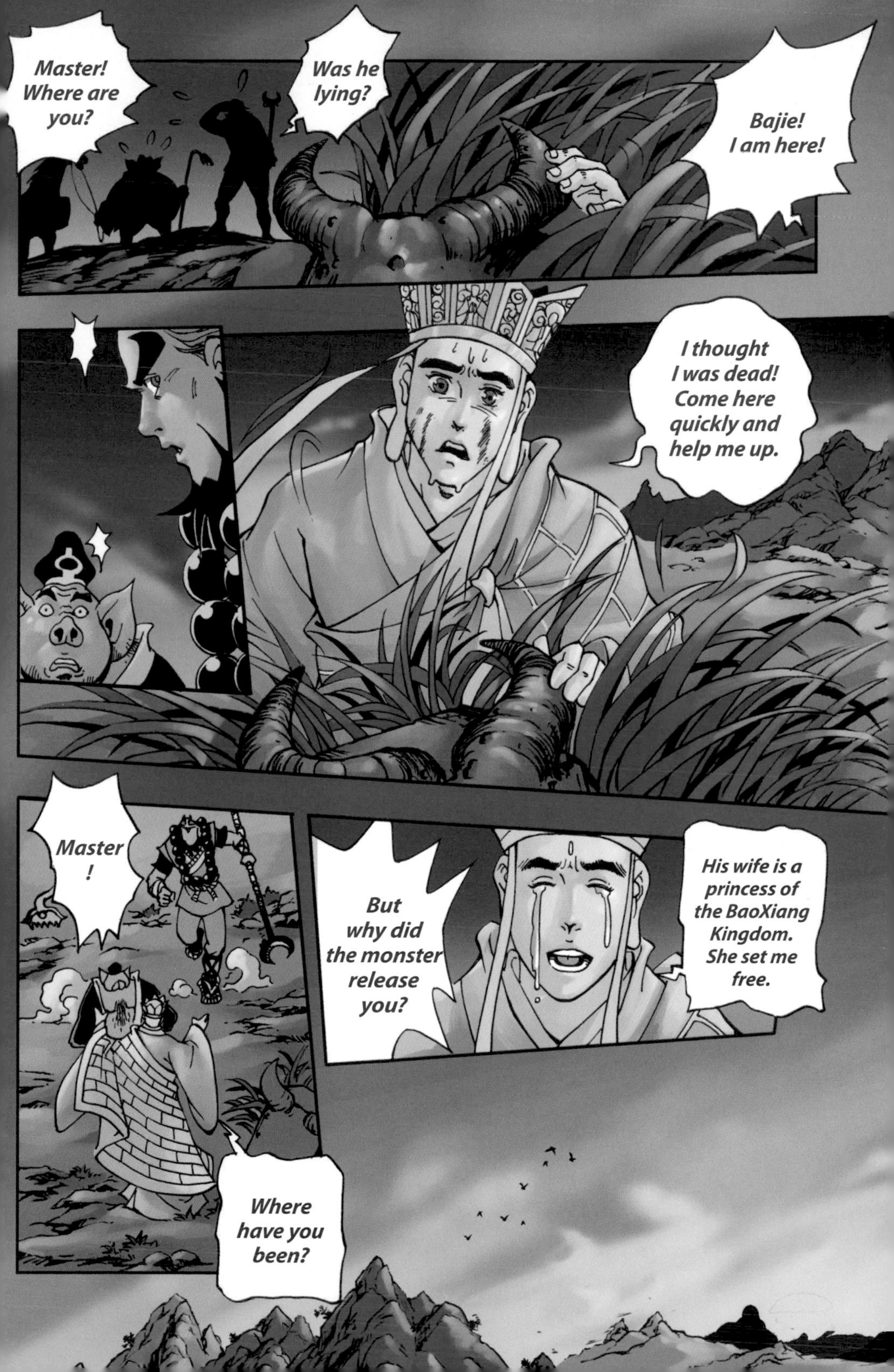
Master! Where are you?
Was he lying?
Bajie! I am here!
I thought I was dead! Come here quickly and help me up.
Master !
Where have you been?
But why did the monster release you?
His wife is a princess of the BaoXiang Kingdom. She set me free.

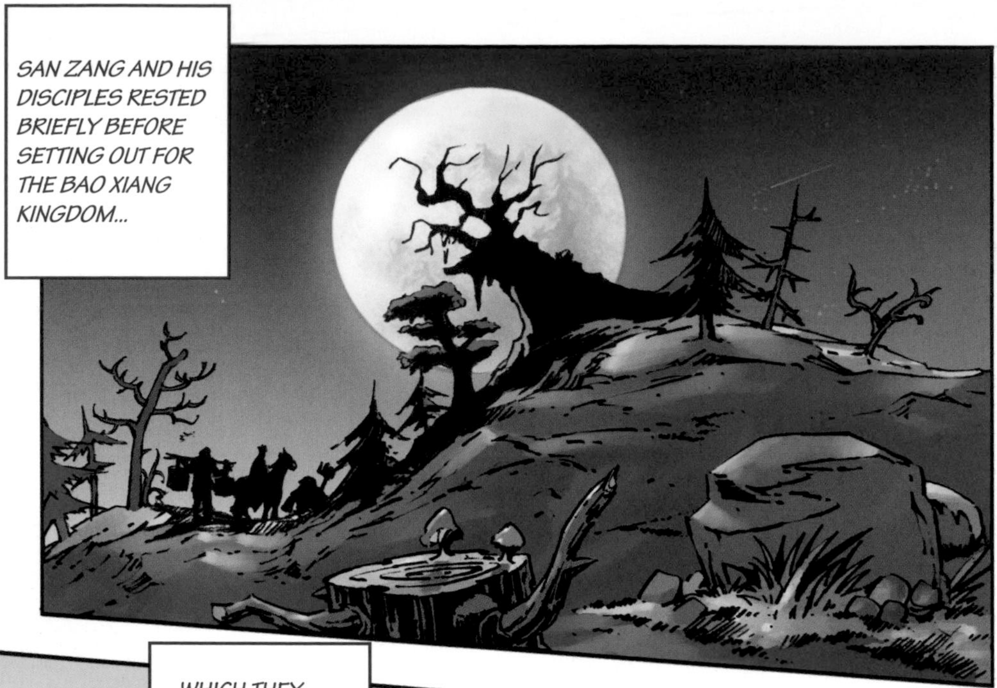
SAN ZANG AND HIS DISCIPLES RESTED BRIEFLY BEFORE SETTING OUT FOR THE BAO XIANG KINGDOM...

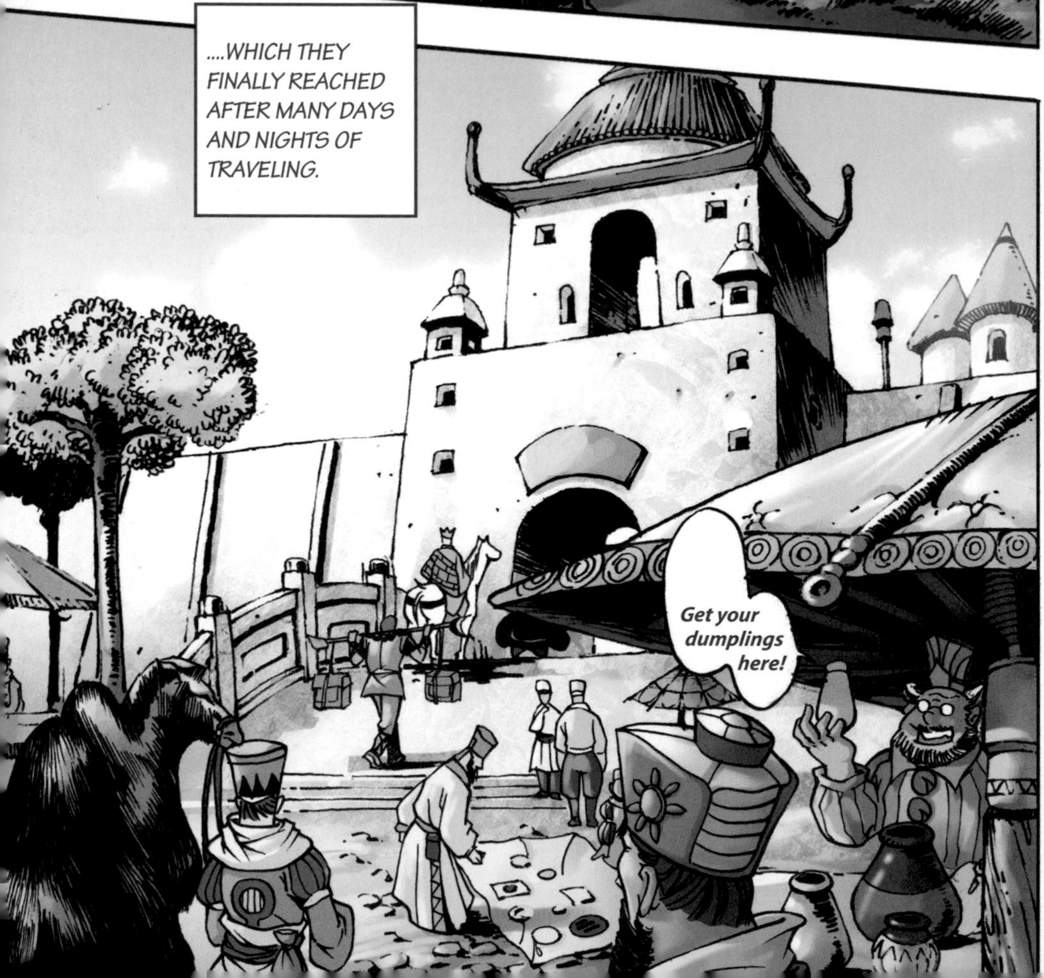
....WHICH THEY FINALLY REACHED AFTER MANY DAYS AND NIGHTS OF TRAVELING.
Get your dumplings here!

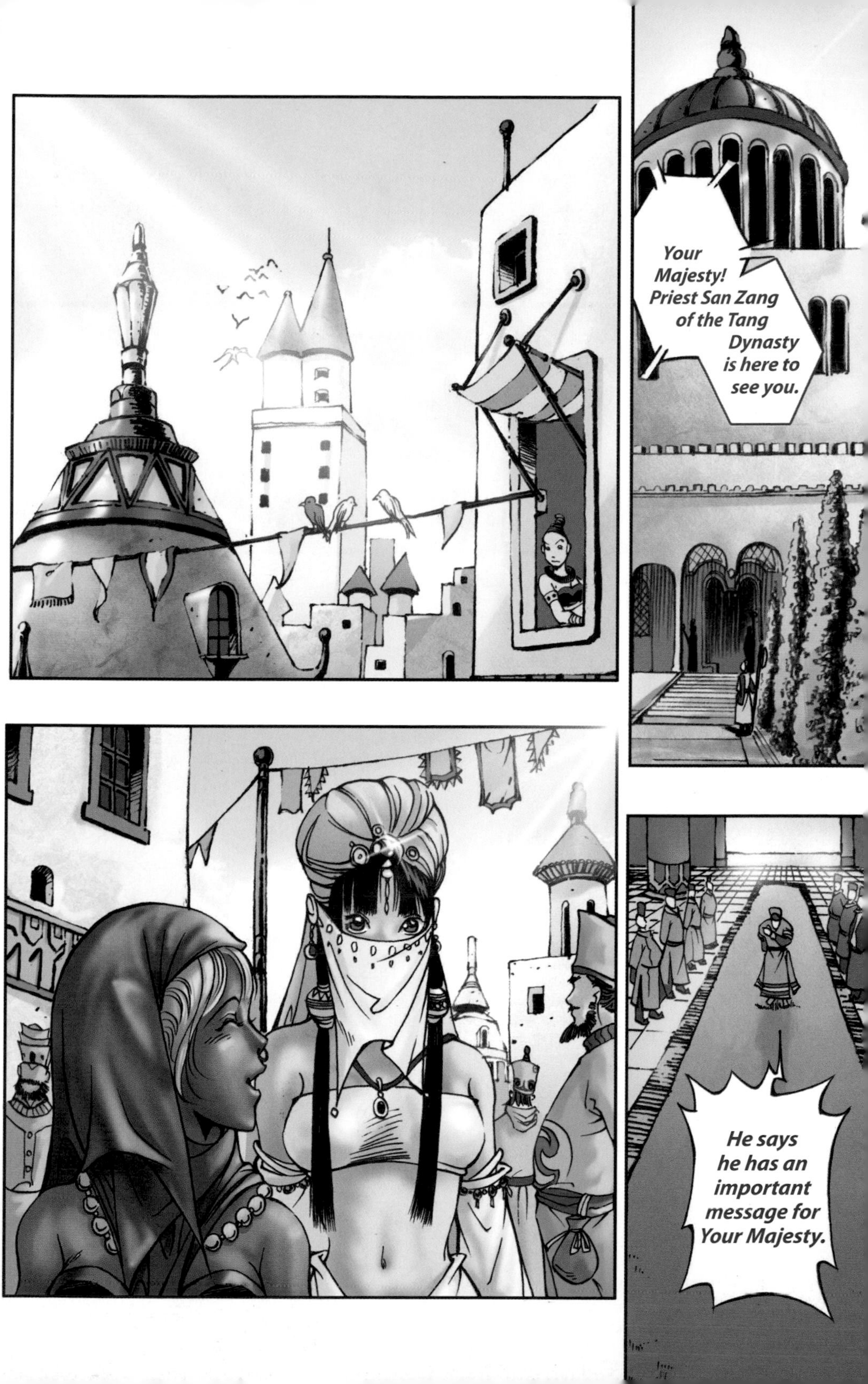
Your Majesty! Priest San Zang of the Tang Dynasty is here to see you.
He says he has an important message for Your Majesty.

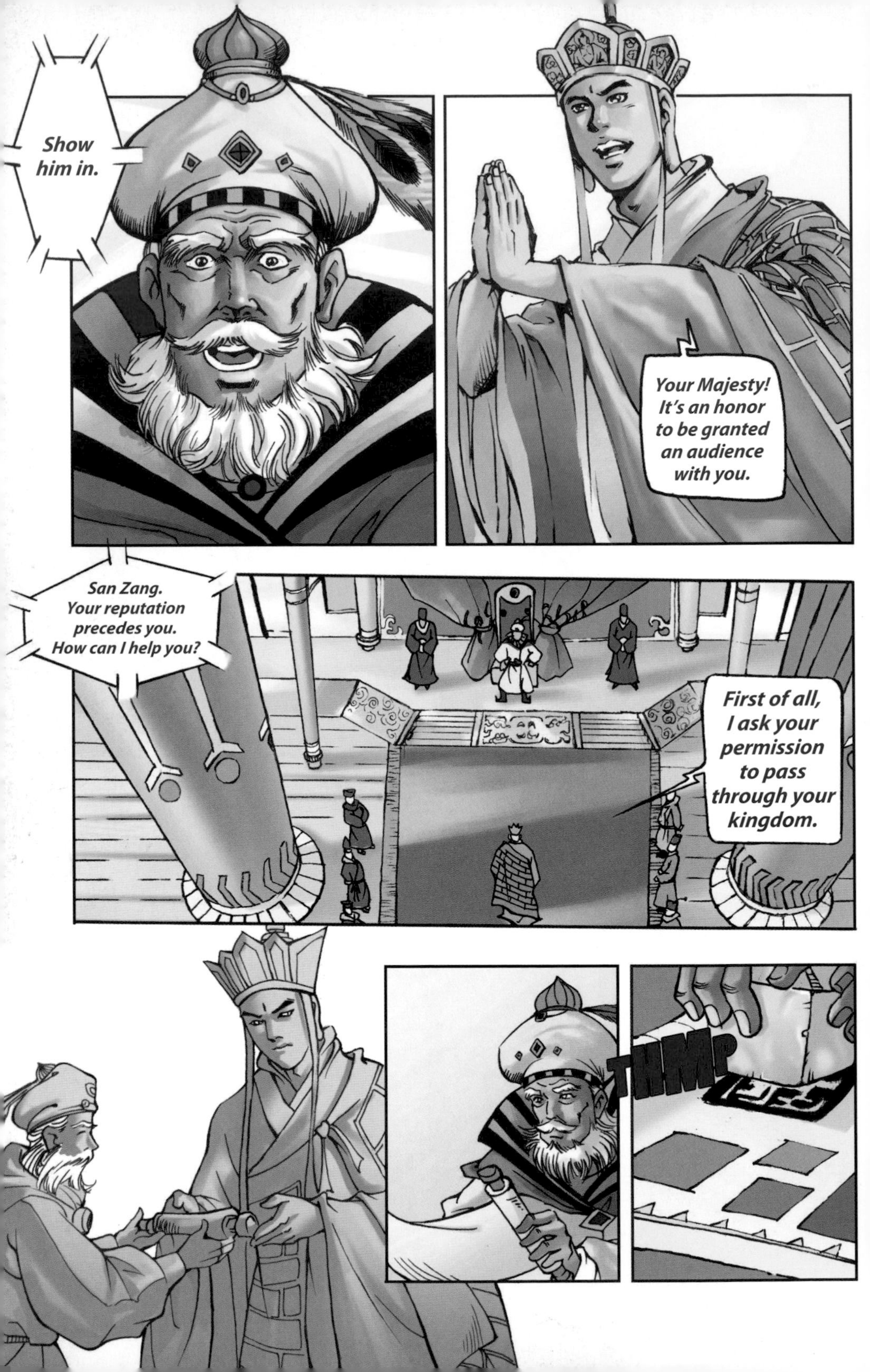
Show him in.
Your Majesty! It's an honor to be granted an audience with you.
San Zang. Your reputation precedes you. How can I help you?
First of all, I ask your permission to pass through your kingdom.
THMP

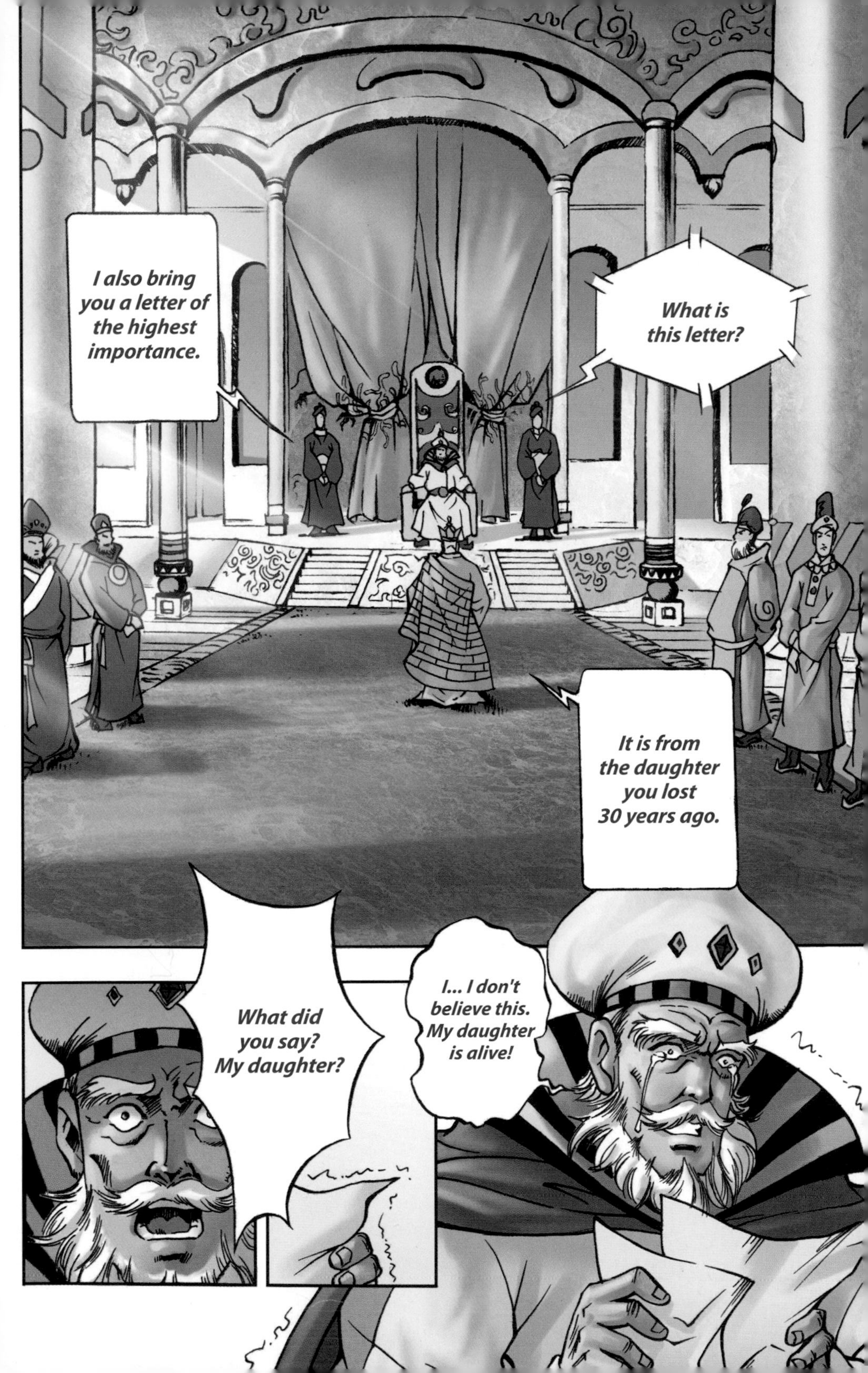
I also bring you a letter of the highest importance.
What is this letter?
It is from the daughter you lost 30 years ago.
What did you say? My daughter?
I... I don't believe this. My daughter is alive!

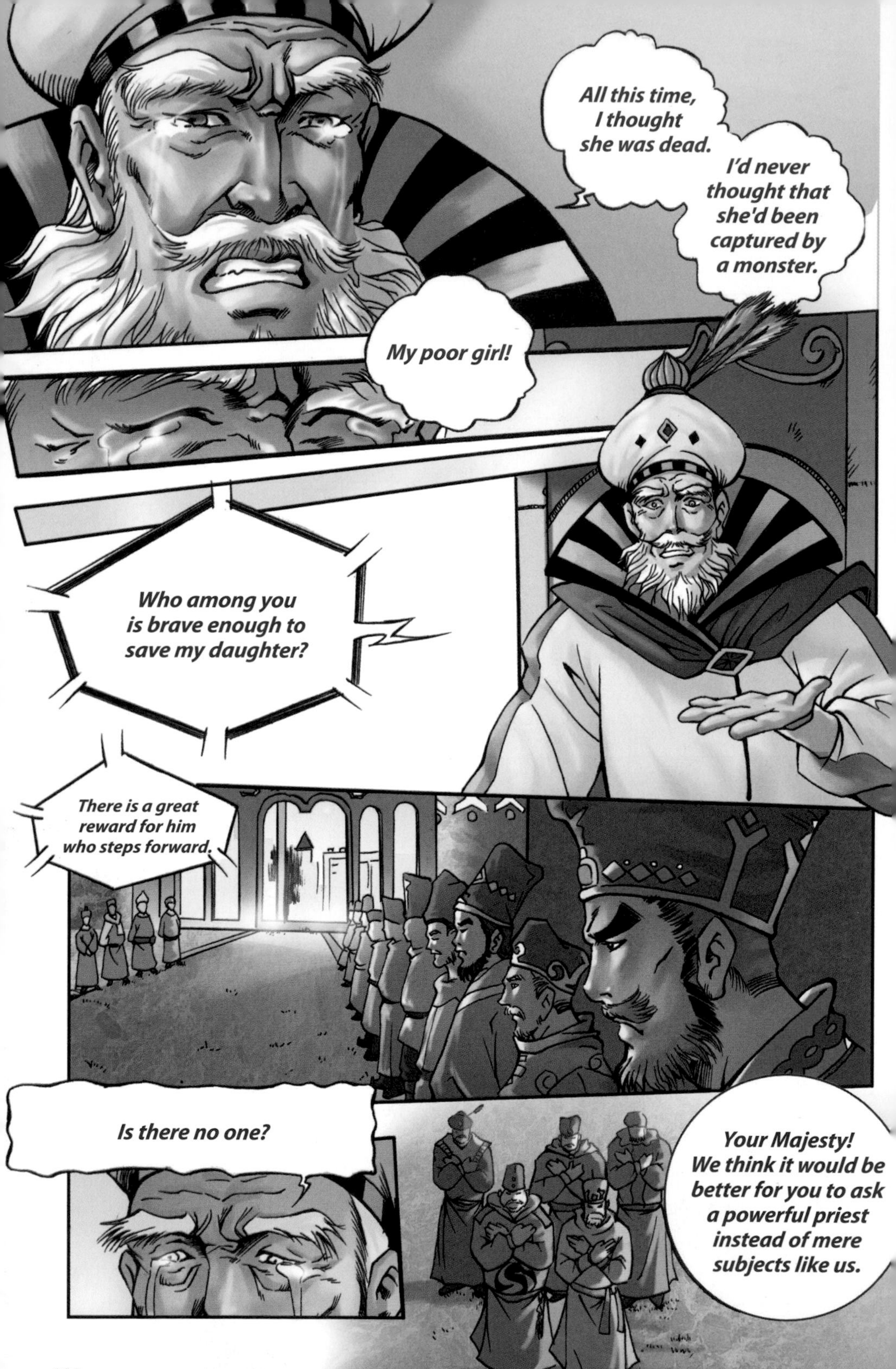
All this time, I thought she was dead.
I'd never thought that she'd been captured by a monster.
My poor girl!
Who among you is brave enough to save my daughter?
There is a great reward for him who steps forward.
Is there no one?
Your Majesty! We think it would be better for you to ask a powerful priest instead of mere subjects like us.

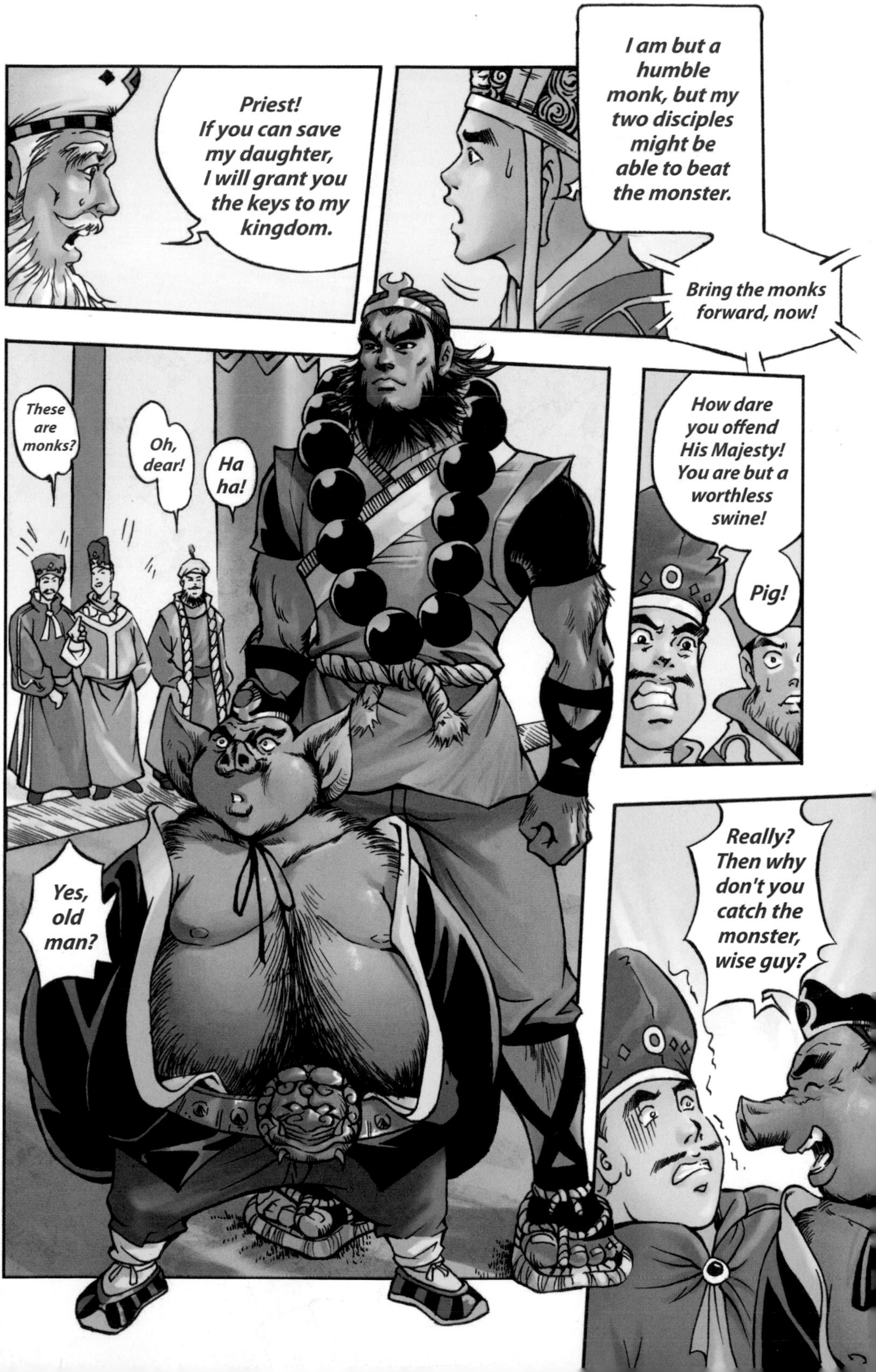
Priest! If you can save my daughter, I will grant you the keys to my kingdom.
I am but a humble monk, but my two disciples might be able to beat the monster.
Bring the monks forward, now!
These are monks?
Oh, dear!
Ha ha!
How dare you offend His Majesty! You are but a worthless swine!
Pig!
Yes, old man?
Really? Then why don't you catch the monster, wise guy?

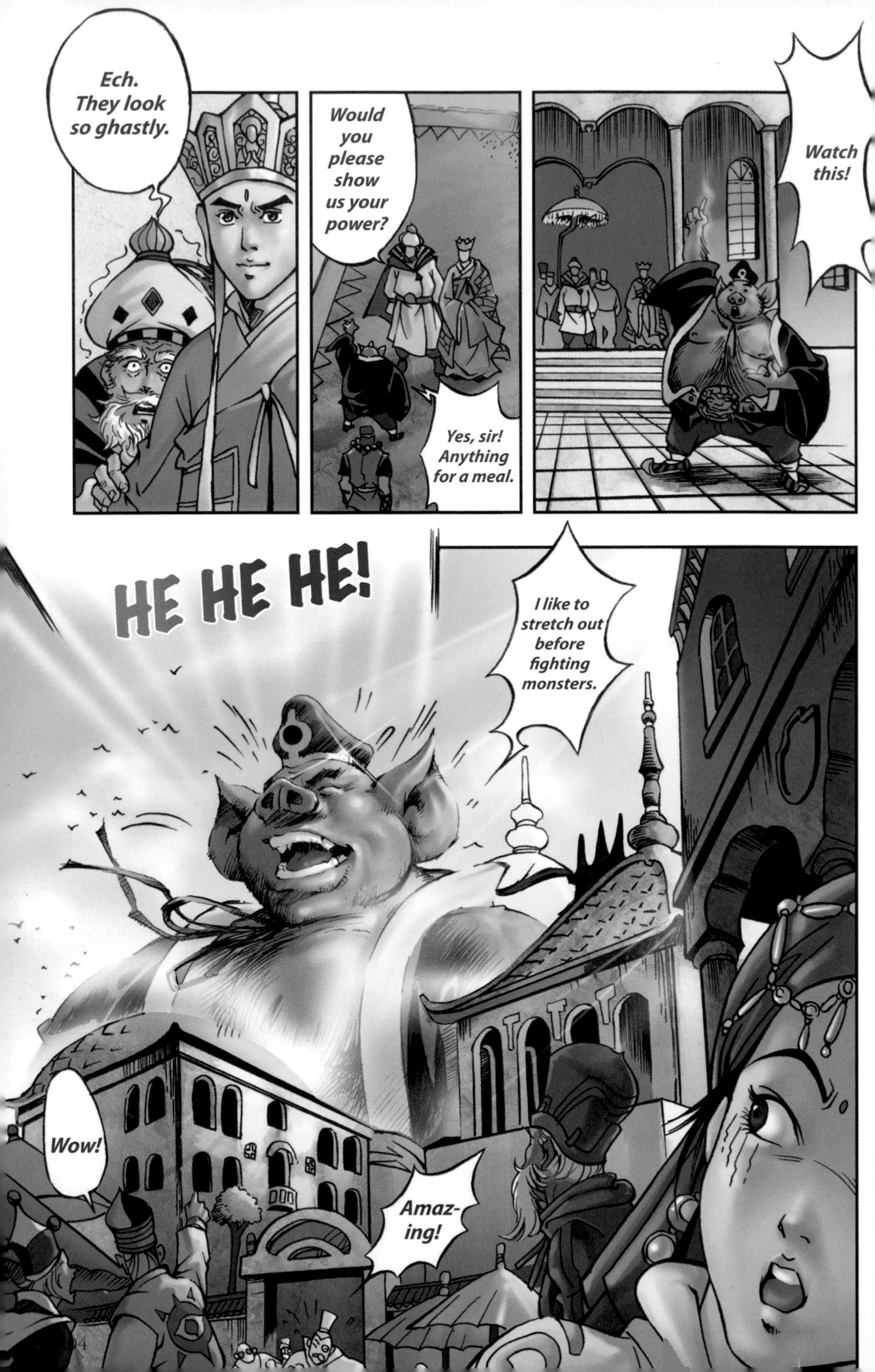
Ech. They look so ghastly.
Would you please show us your power?
Yes, sir! Anything for a meal.
Watch this!
HE HE HE!
I like to stretch out before fighting monsters.
Wow!
Amaz-ing!

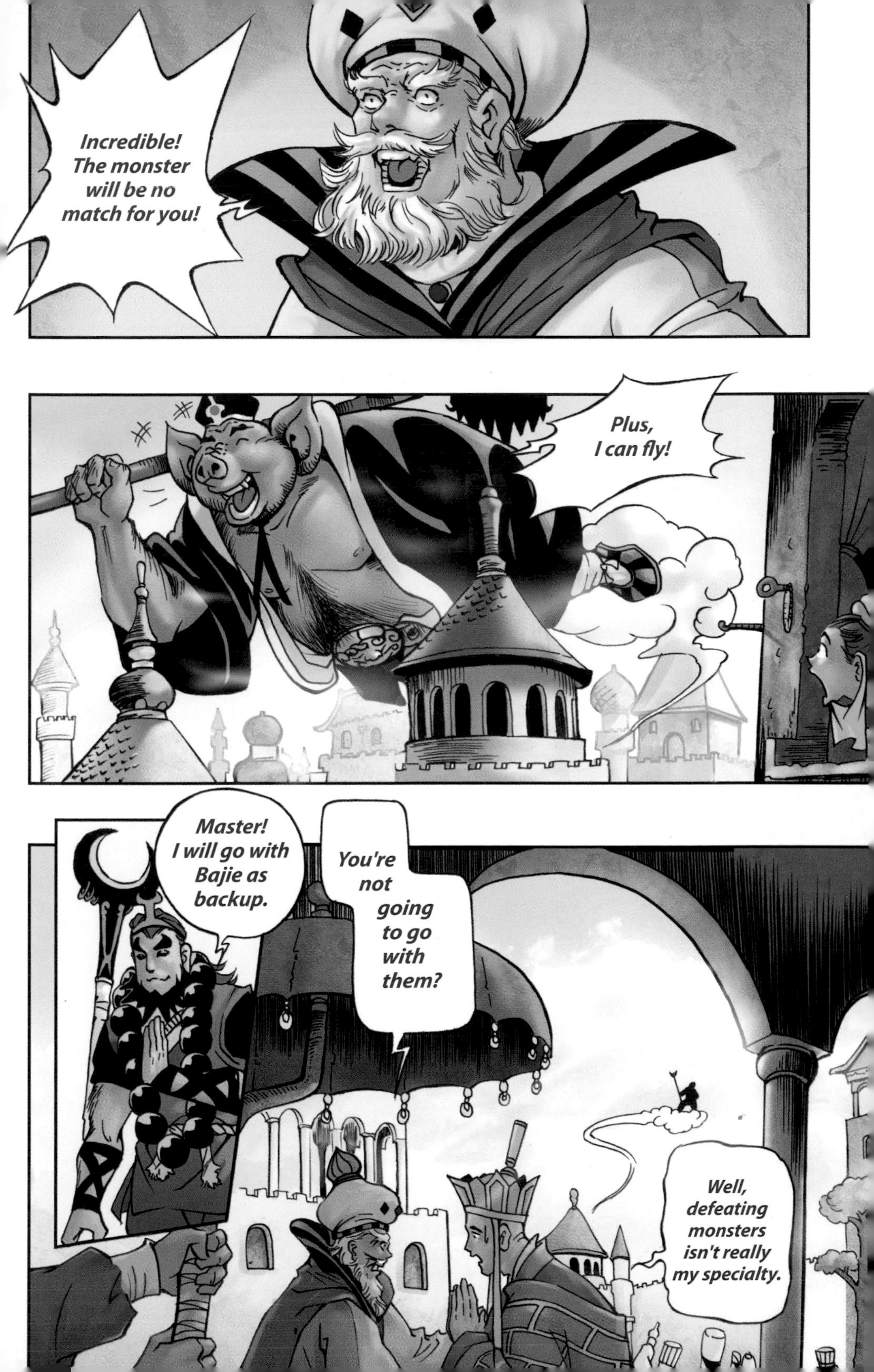
Incredible! The monster will be no match for you!
Plus, I can fly!
Master! I will go with Bajie as backup.
You're not going to go with them?
Well, defeating monsters isn't really my specialty.

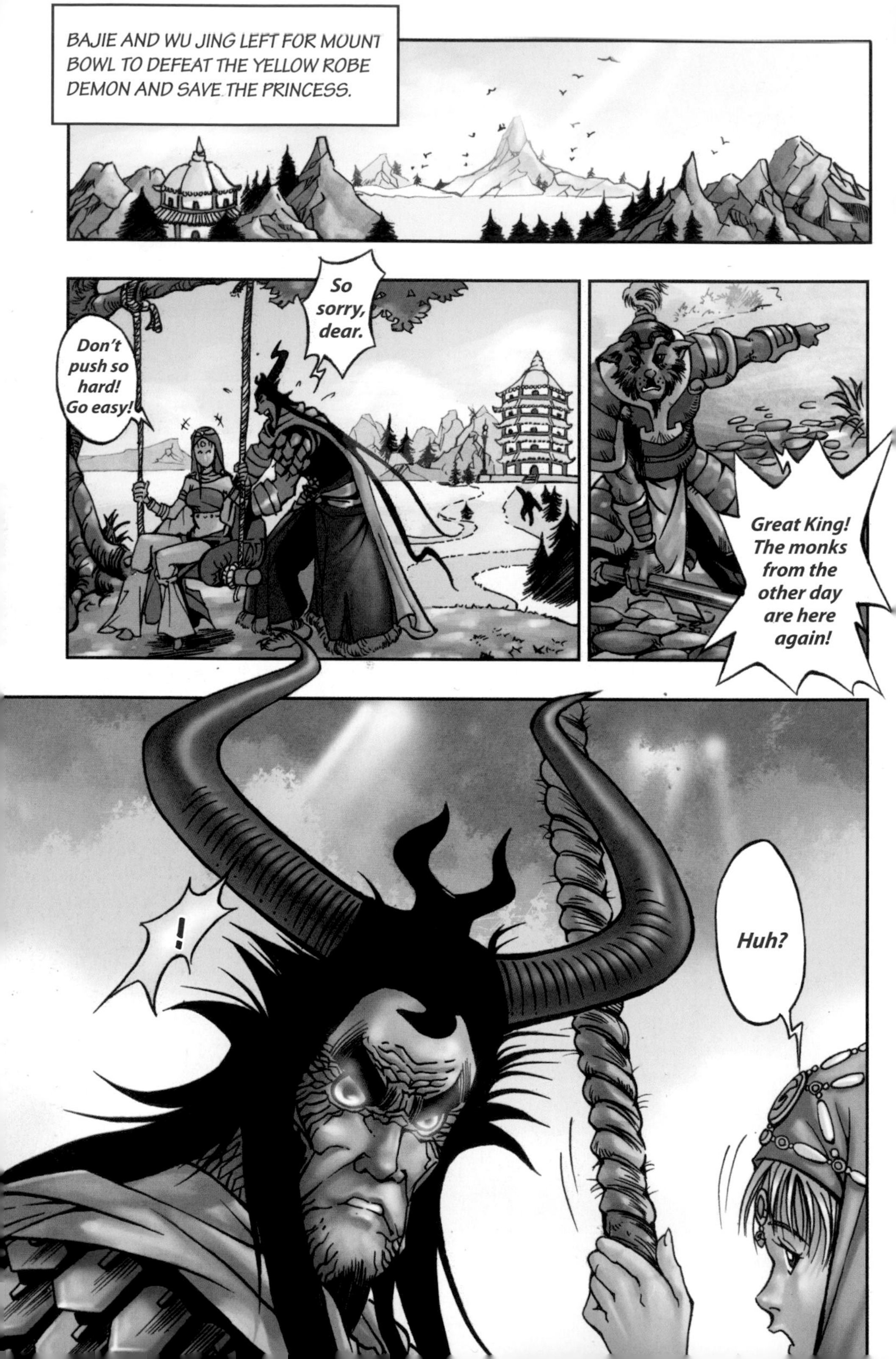
BAJIE AND WU JING LEFT FOR MOUNT BOWL TO DEFEAT THE YELLOW ROBE DEMON AND SAVE THE PRINCESS.
So sorry, dear.
Don't push so hard! Go easy!
Great King! The monks from the other day are here again!
!
Huh?

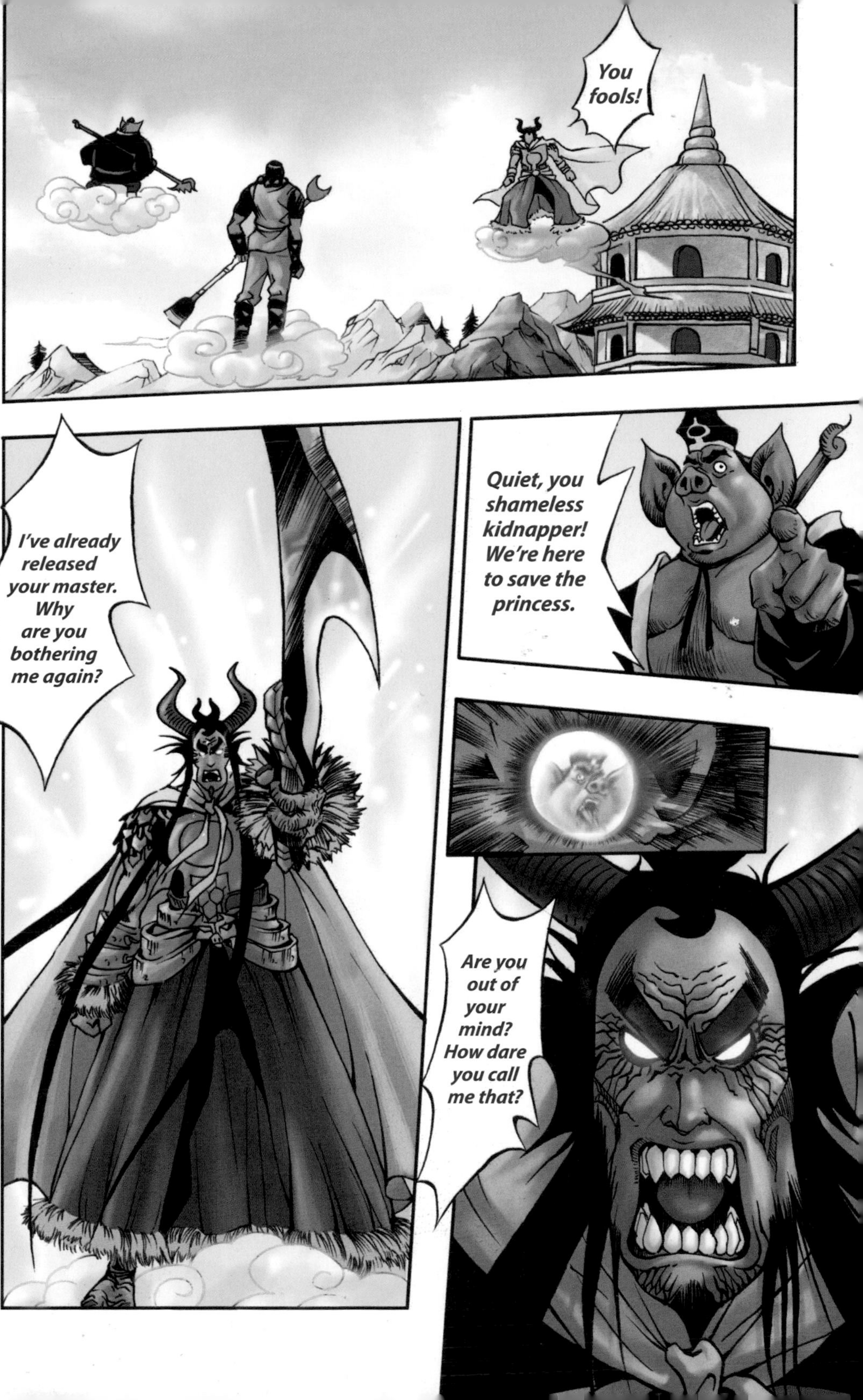
You fools!
I've already released your master. Why are you bothering me again?
Quiet, you shameless kidnapper! We're here to save the princess.
Are you out of your mind? How dare you call me that?

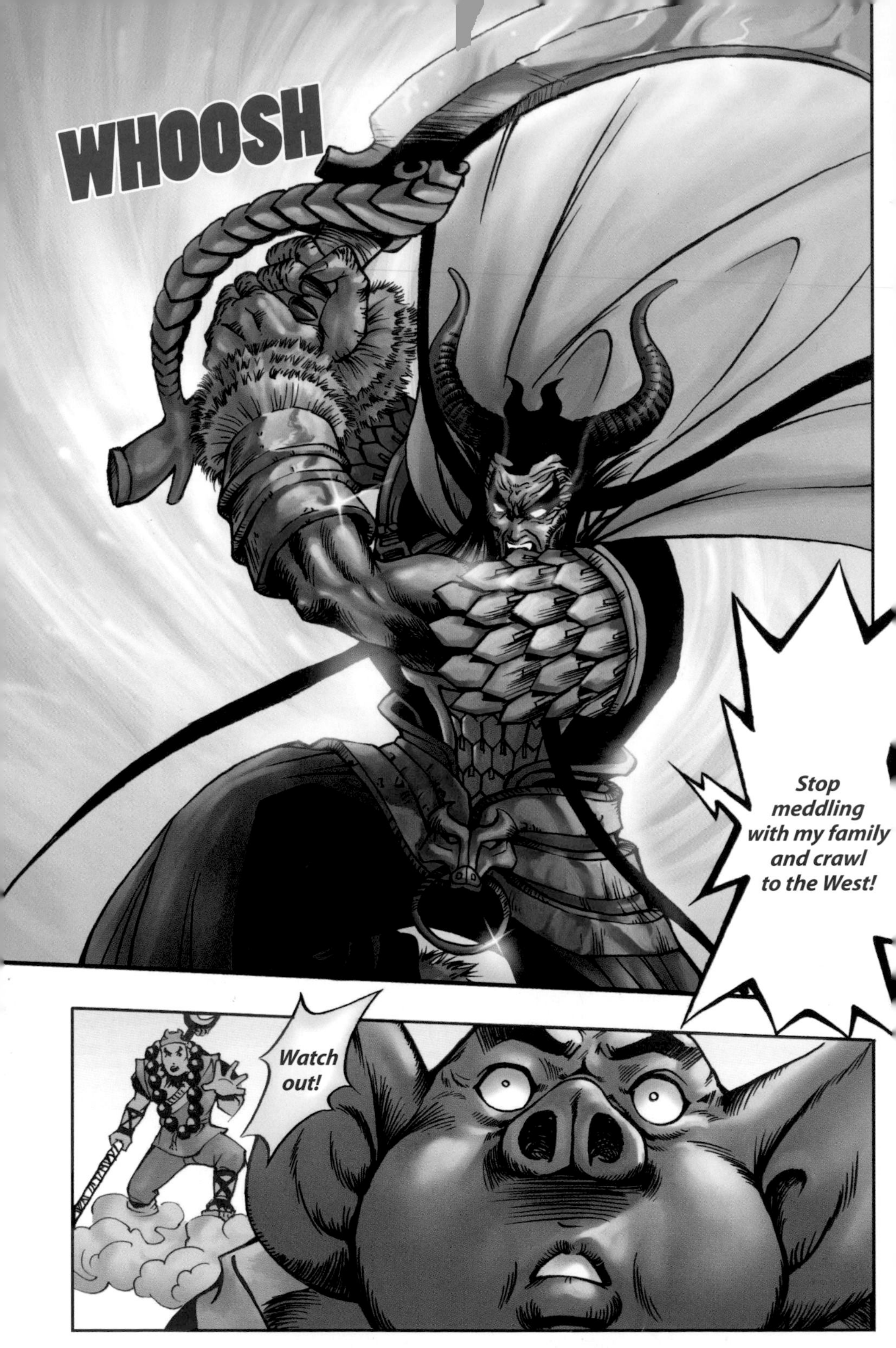
WHOOSH
Stop meddling with my family and crawl to the West!
Watch out!

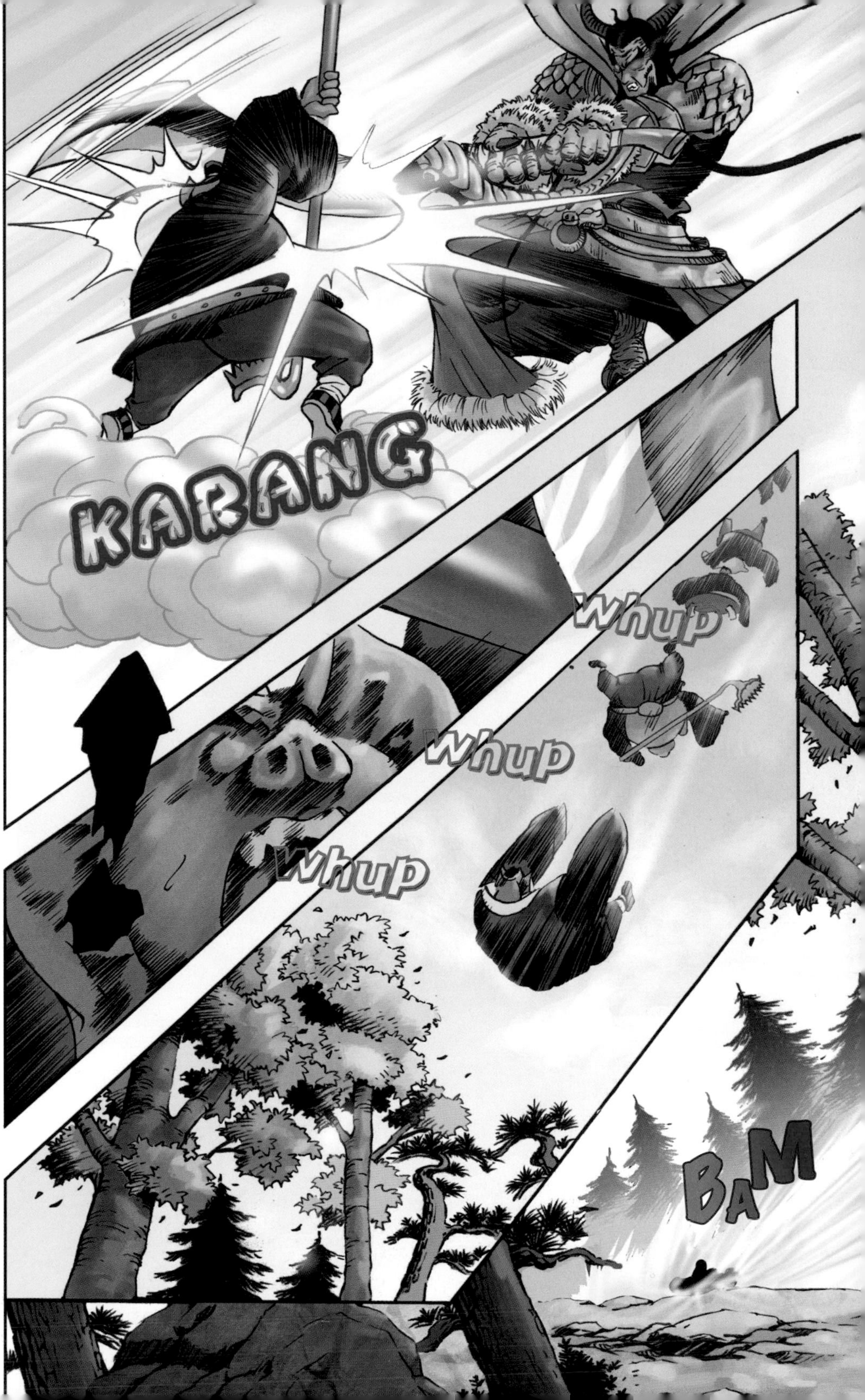
KARANG
Whup
Whup
Whup
BAM

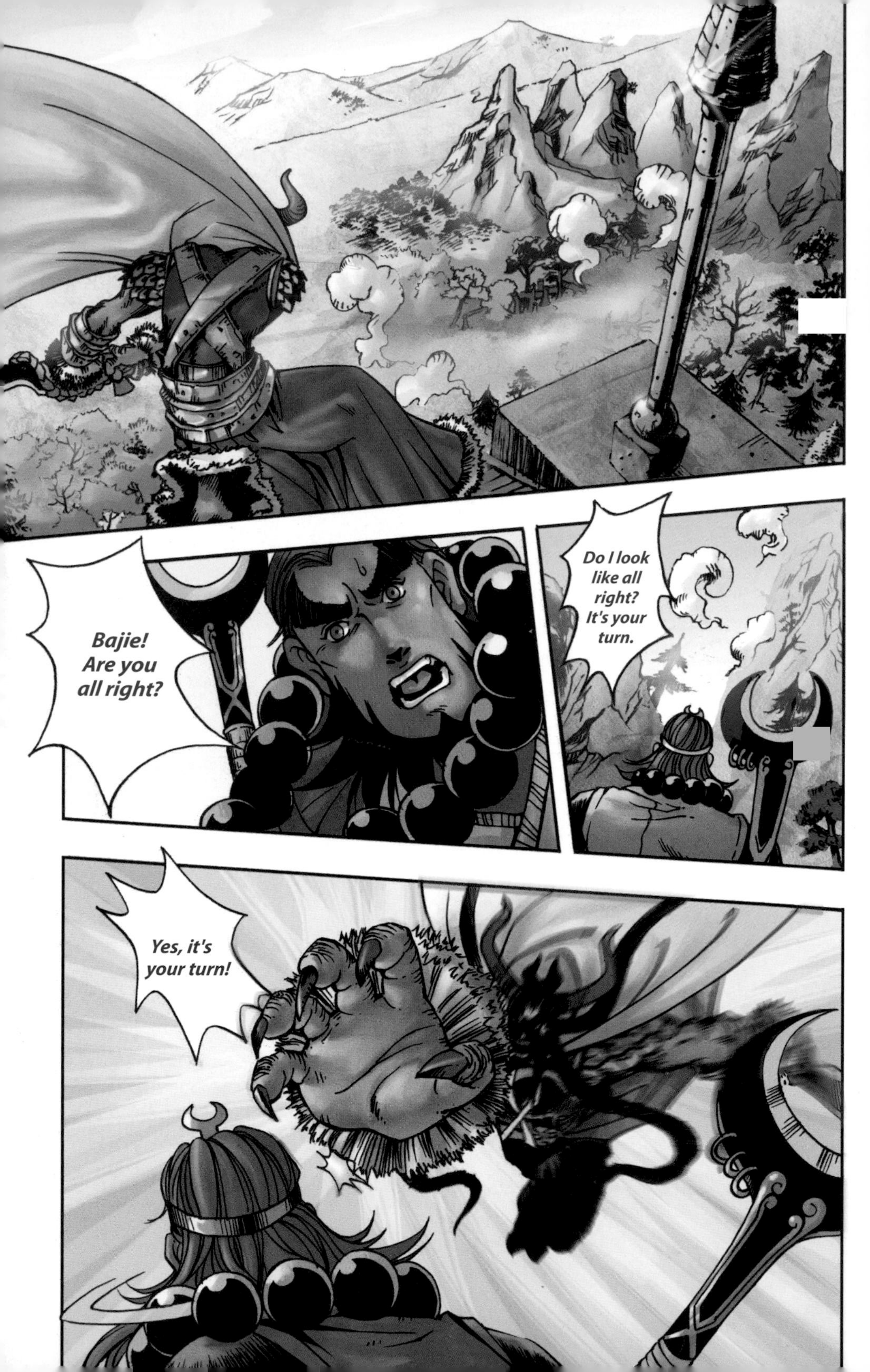
Bajie! Are you all right?
Do I look like all right? It's your turn.
Yes, it's your turn!

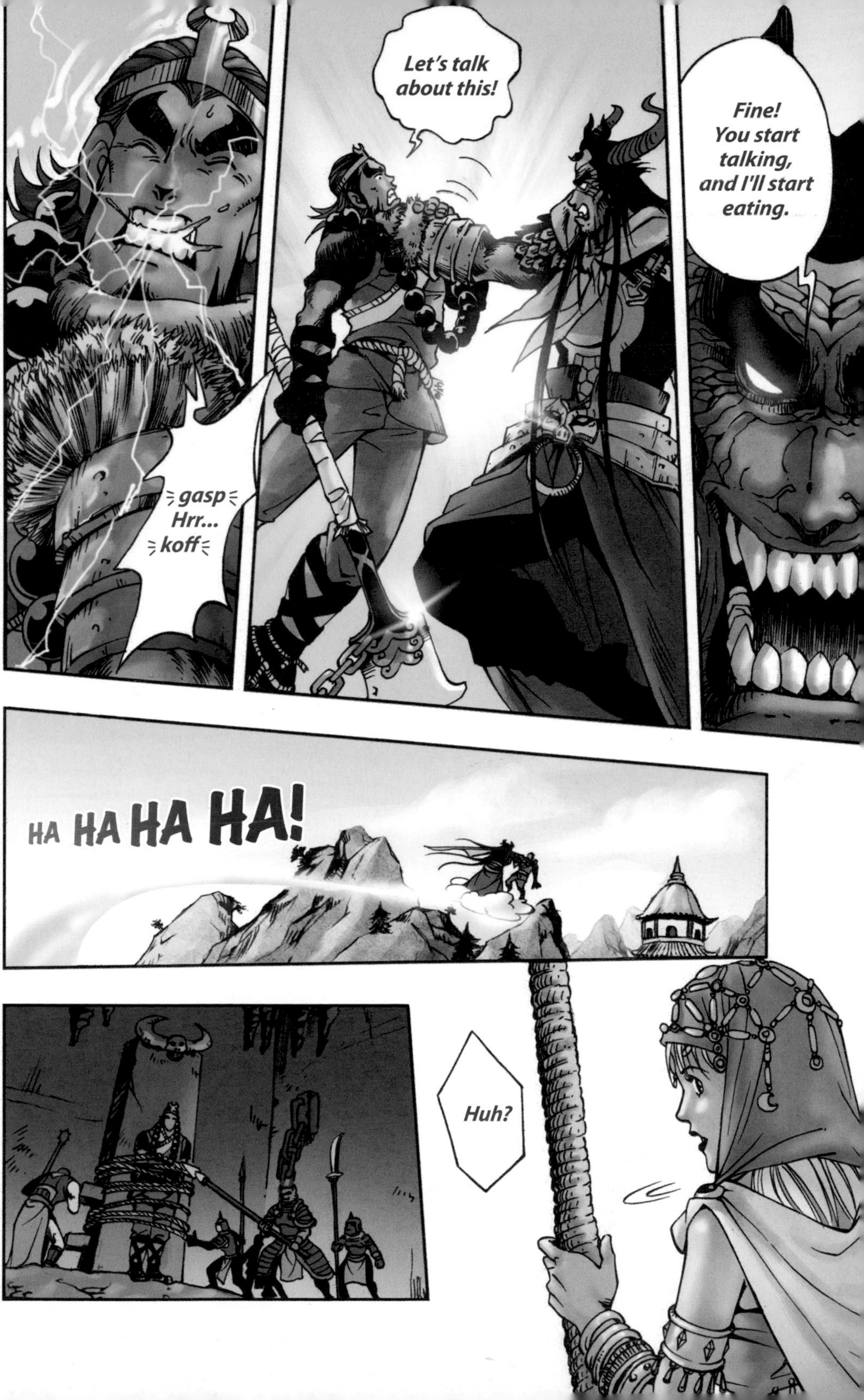
≡gasp≡
Hrr...
≡koff≡
Let's talk about this!
Fine! You start talking, and I'll start eating.
HA HA HA HA!
Huh?

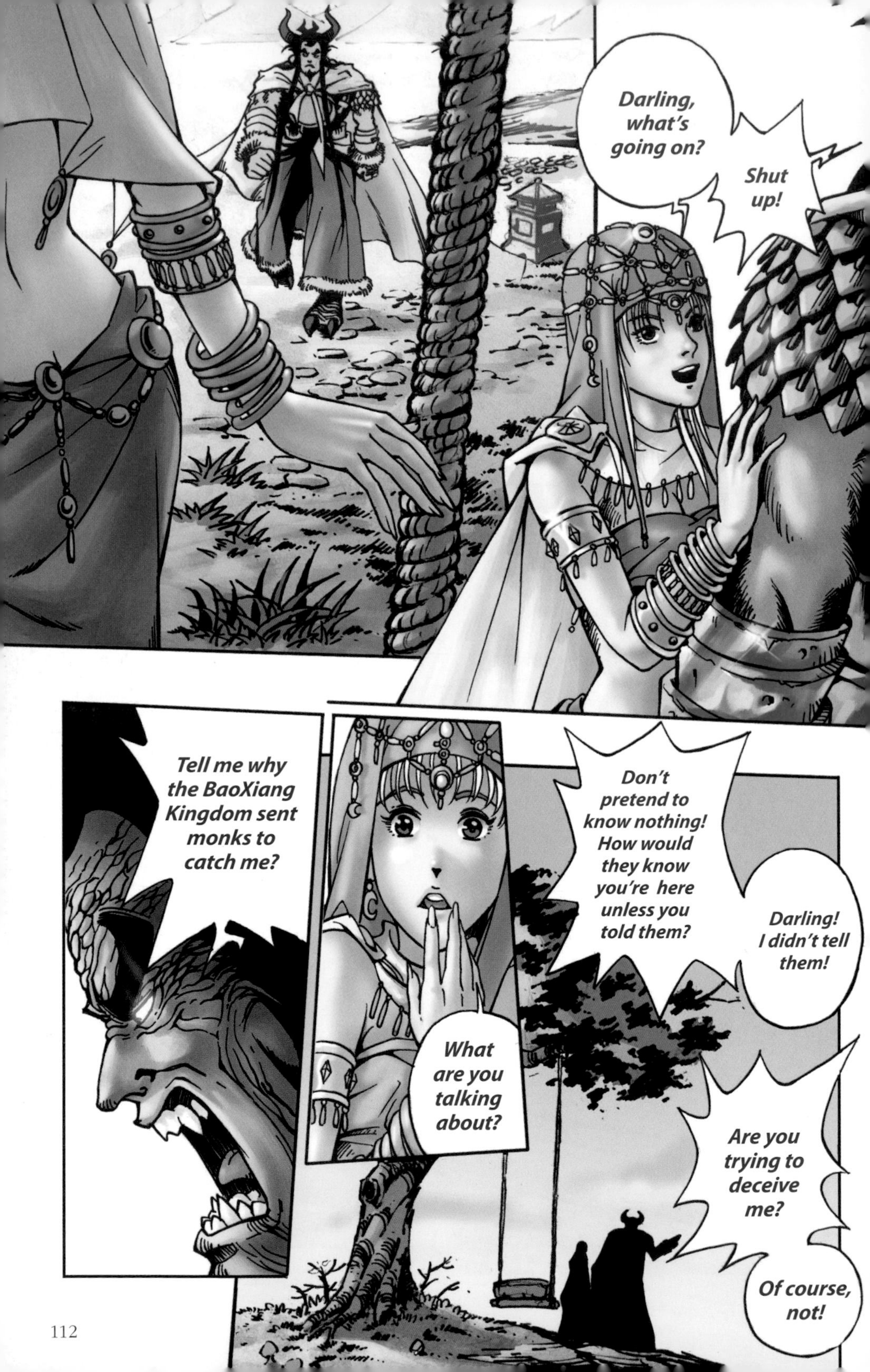

Darling, what's going on?
Shut up!
Tell me why the BaoXiang Kingdom sent monks to catch me?
What are you talking about?
Don't pretend to know nothing! How would they know you're here unless you told them?
Darling! I didn't tell them!
Are you trying to deceive me?
Of course, not!

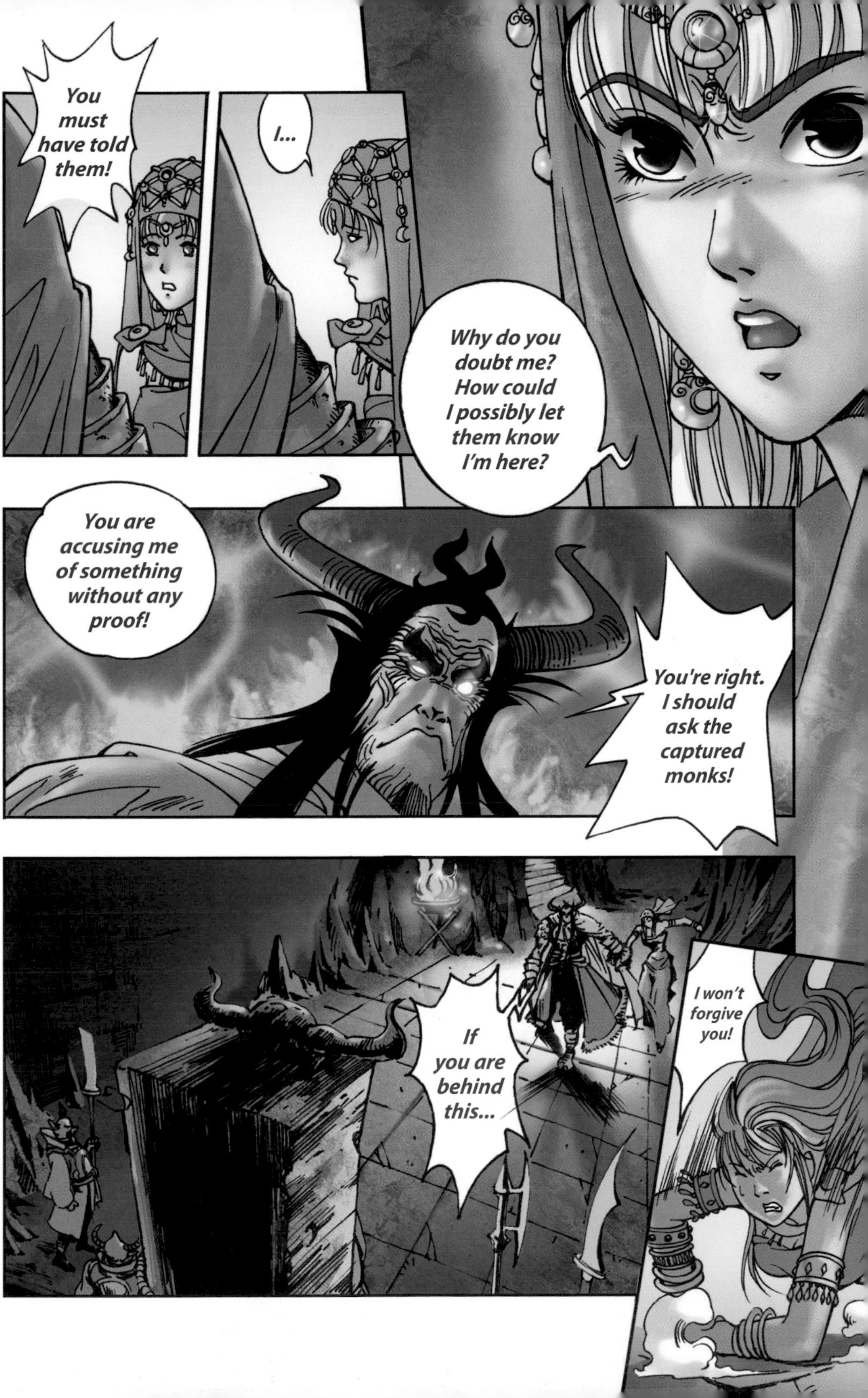

You must have told them!
I...
Why do you doubt me? How could I possibly let them know I'm here?
You are accusing me of something without any proof!
You're right. I should ask the captured monks!
If you are behind this...
I won't forgive you!

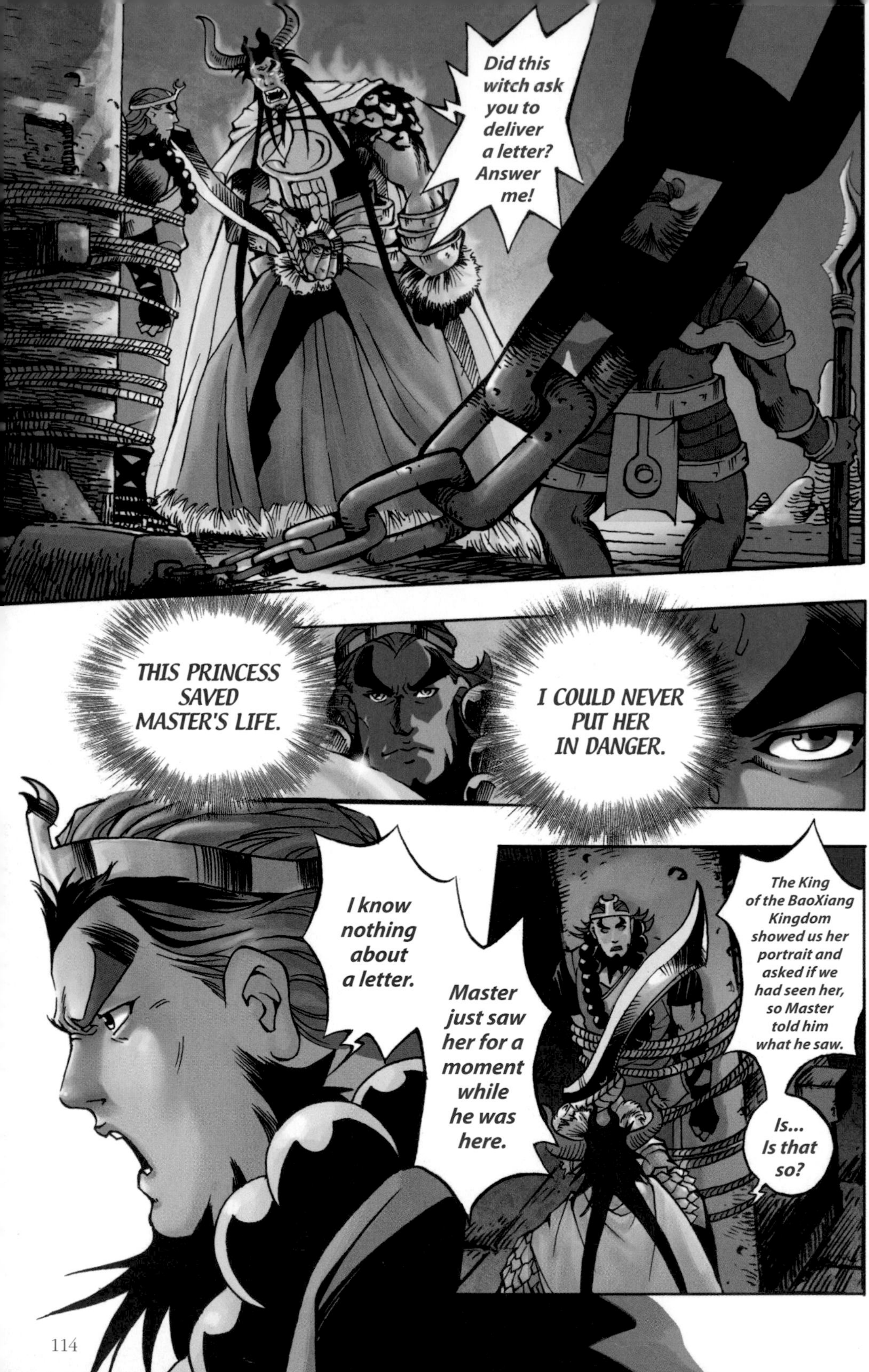
Did this witch ask you to deliver a letter? Answer me!
THIS PRINCESS SAVED MASTER'S LIFE.
I COULD NEVER PUT HER IN DANGER.
I know nothing about a letter.
Master just saw her for a moment while he was here.
The King of the BaoXiang Kingdom showed us her portrait and asked if we had seen her, so Master told him what he saw.
Is... Is that so?

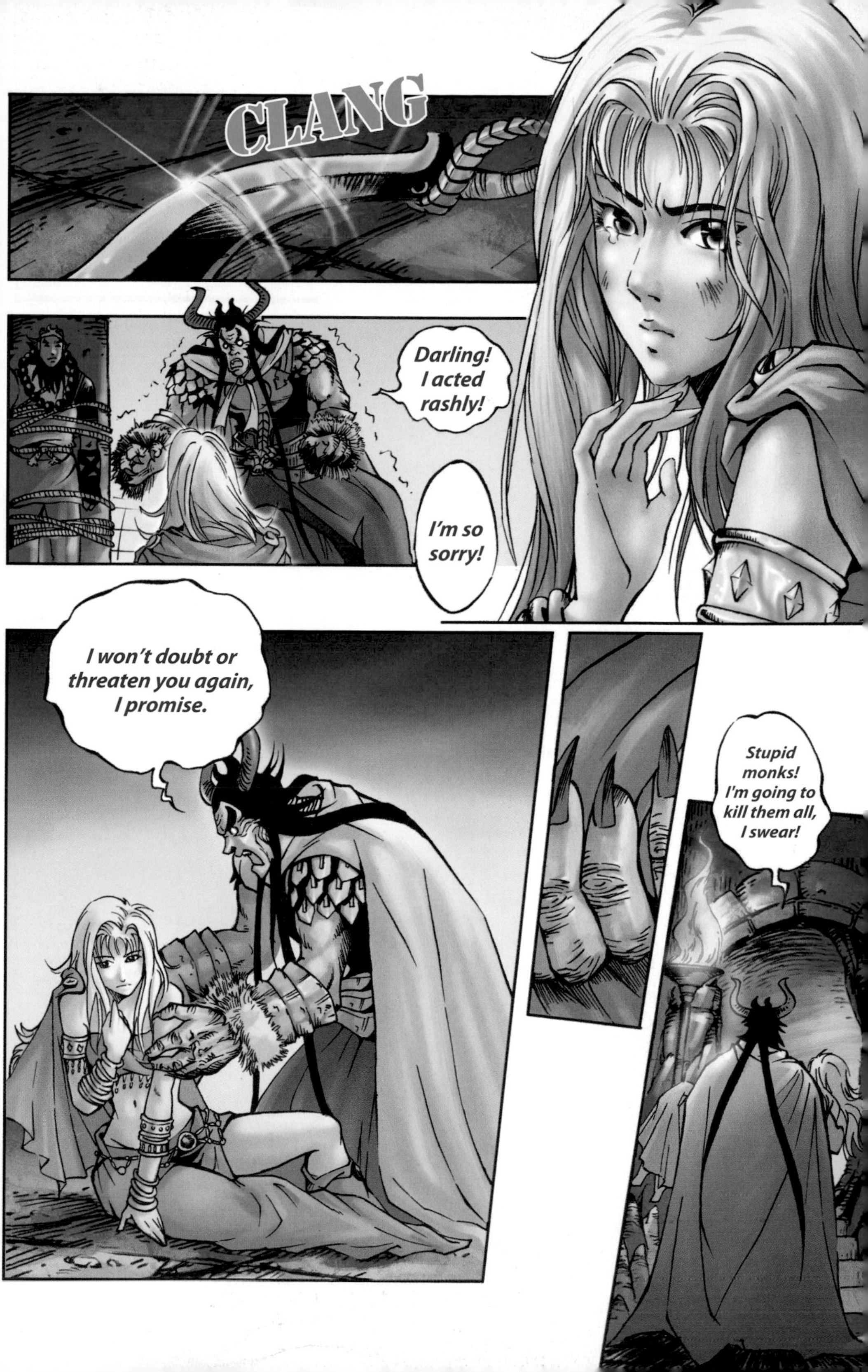

CLANG
Darling! I acted rashly!
I'm so sorry!
I won't doubt or threaten you again, I promise.
Stupid monks! I'm going to kill them all, I swear!

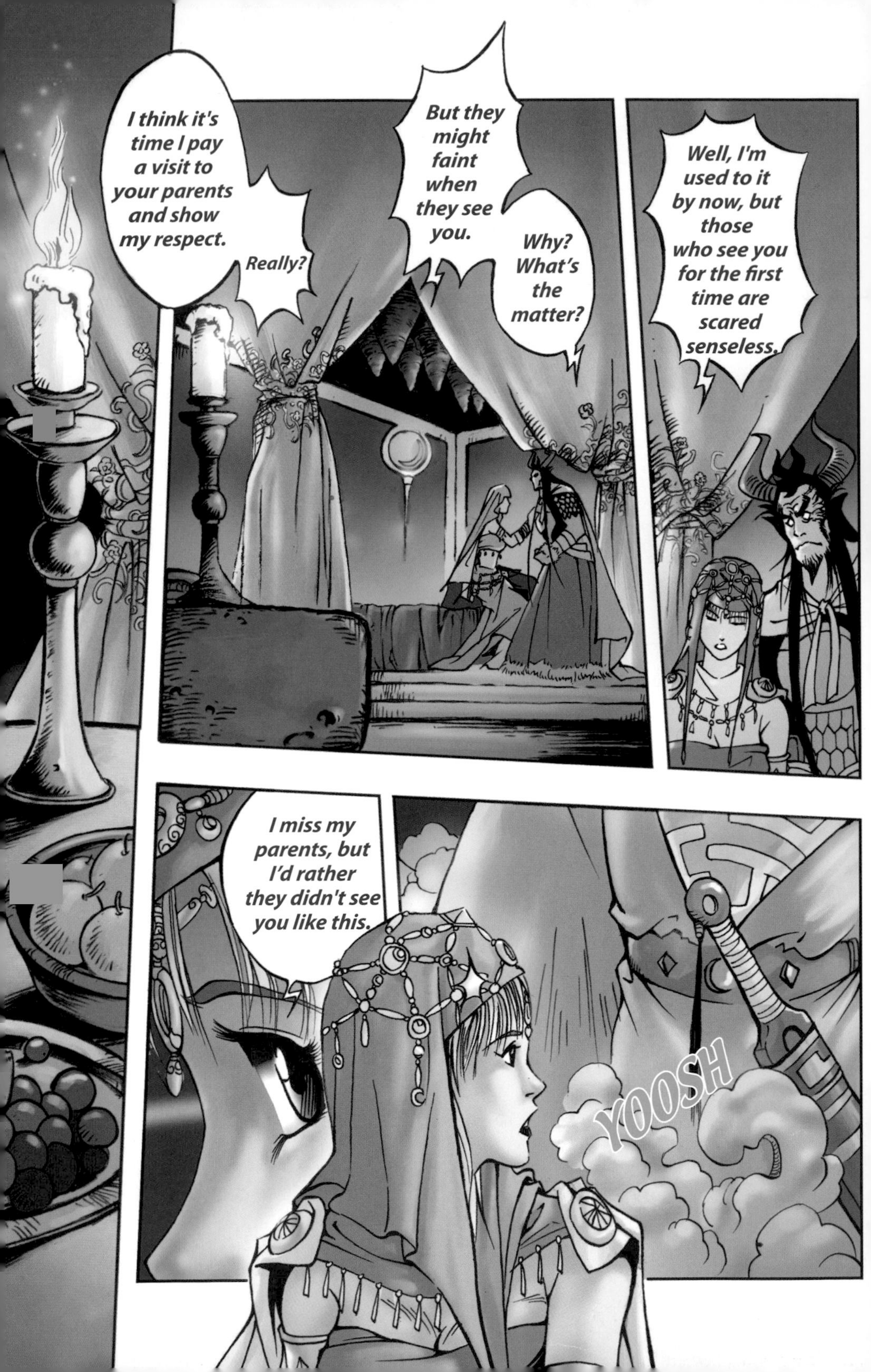
I think it's time I pay a visit to your parents and show my respect.
Really?
But they might faint when they see you.
Why? What's the matter?
Well, I'm used to it by now, but those who see you for the first time are scared senseless.
I miss my parents, but I'd rather they didn't see you like this.
YOOSH

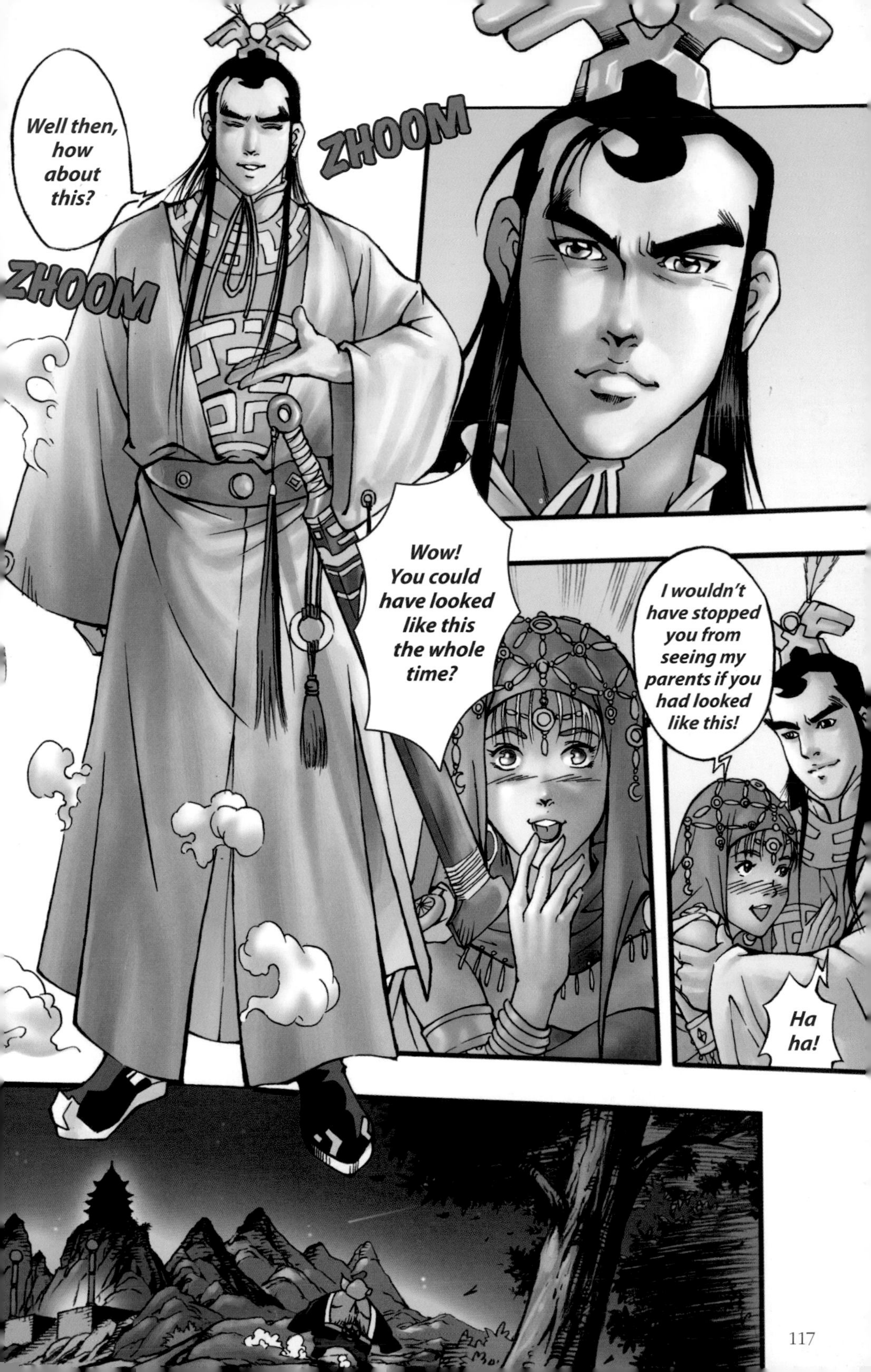

Well then, how about this?
ZHOOM
ZHOOM
Wow! You could have looked like this the whole time?
I wouldn't have stopped you from seeing my parents if you had looked like this!
Ha ha!

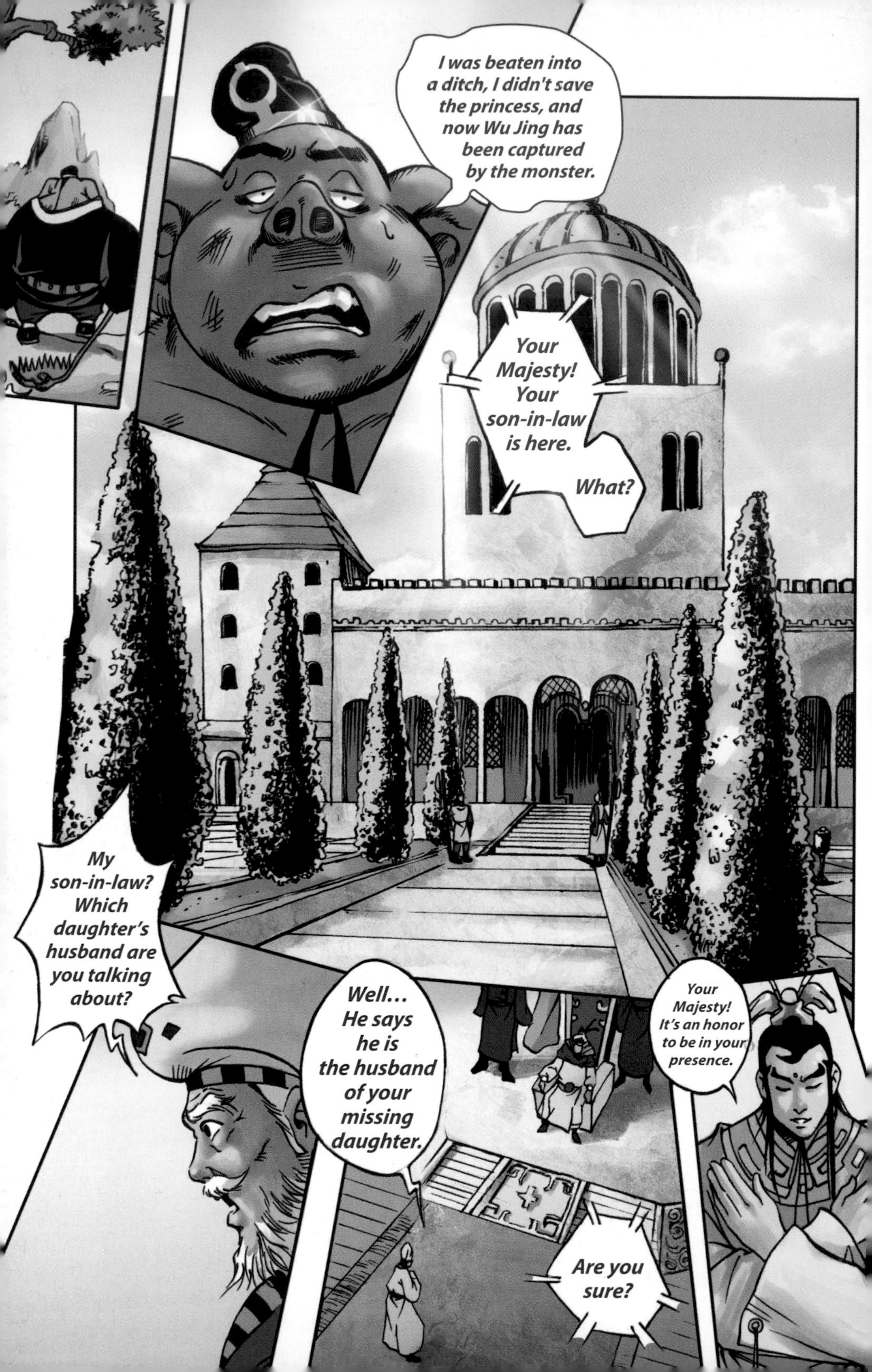

I was beaten into a ditch, I didn't save the princess, and now Wu Jing has been captured by the monster.
Your Majesty! Your son-in-law is here.
What?
My son-in-law? Which daughter's husband are you talking about?
Well... He says he is the husband of your missing daughter.
Your Majesty! It's an honor to be in your presence.
Are you sure?

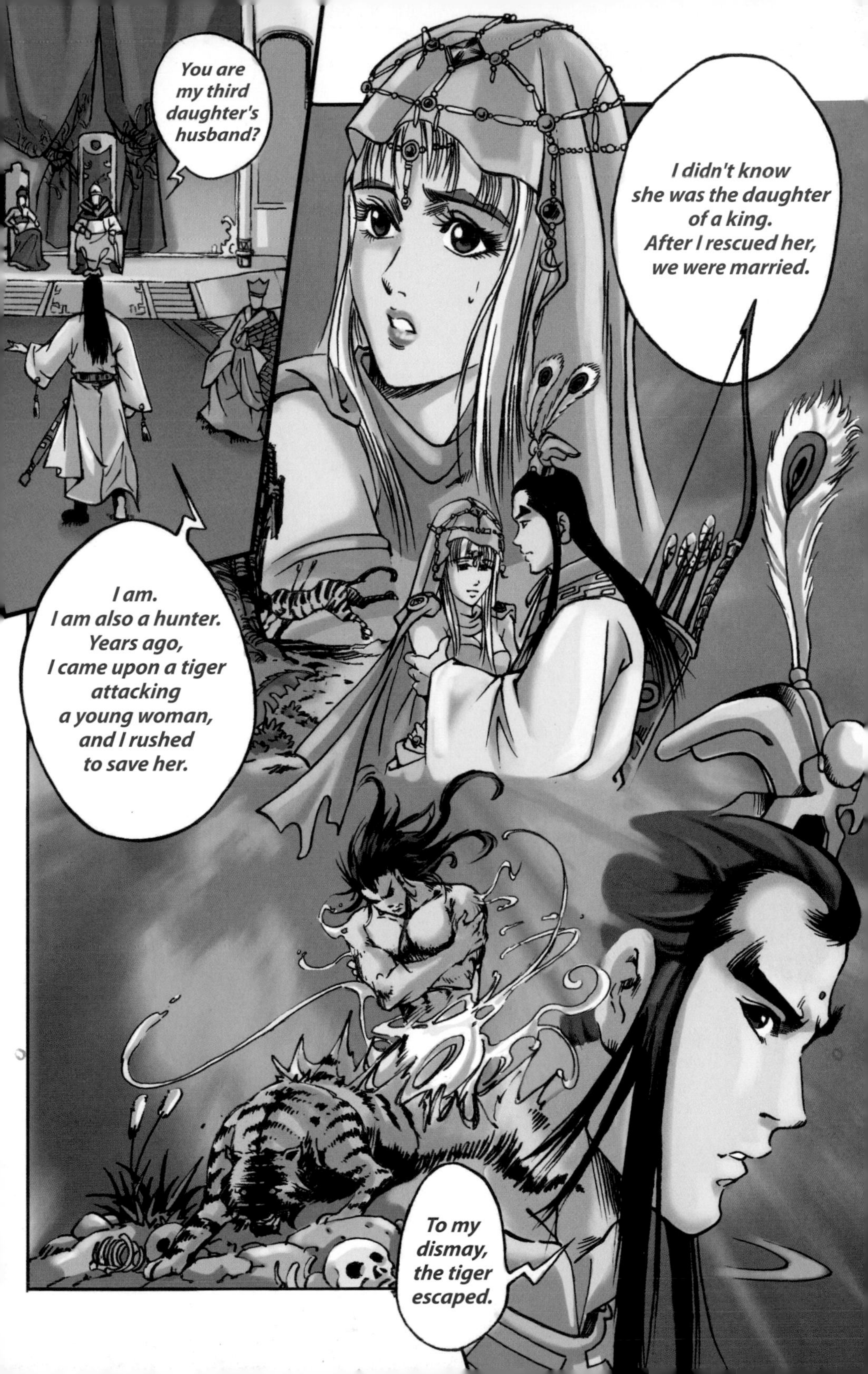
You are my third daughter's husband?
I didn't know she was the daughter of a king. After I rescued her, we were married.
I am. I am also a hunter. Years ago, I came upon a tiger attacking a young woman, and I rushed to save her.
To my dismay, the tiger escaped.

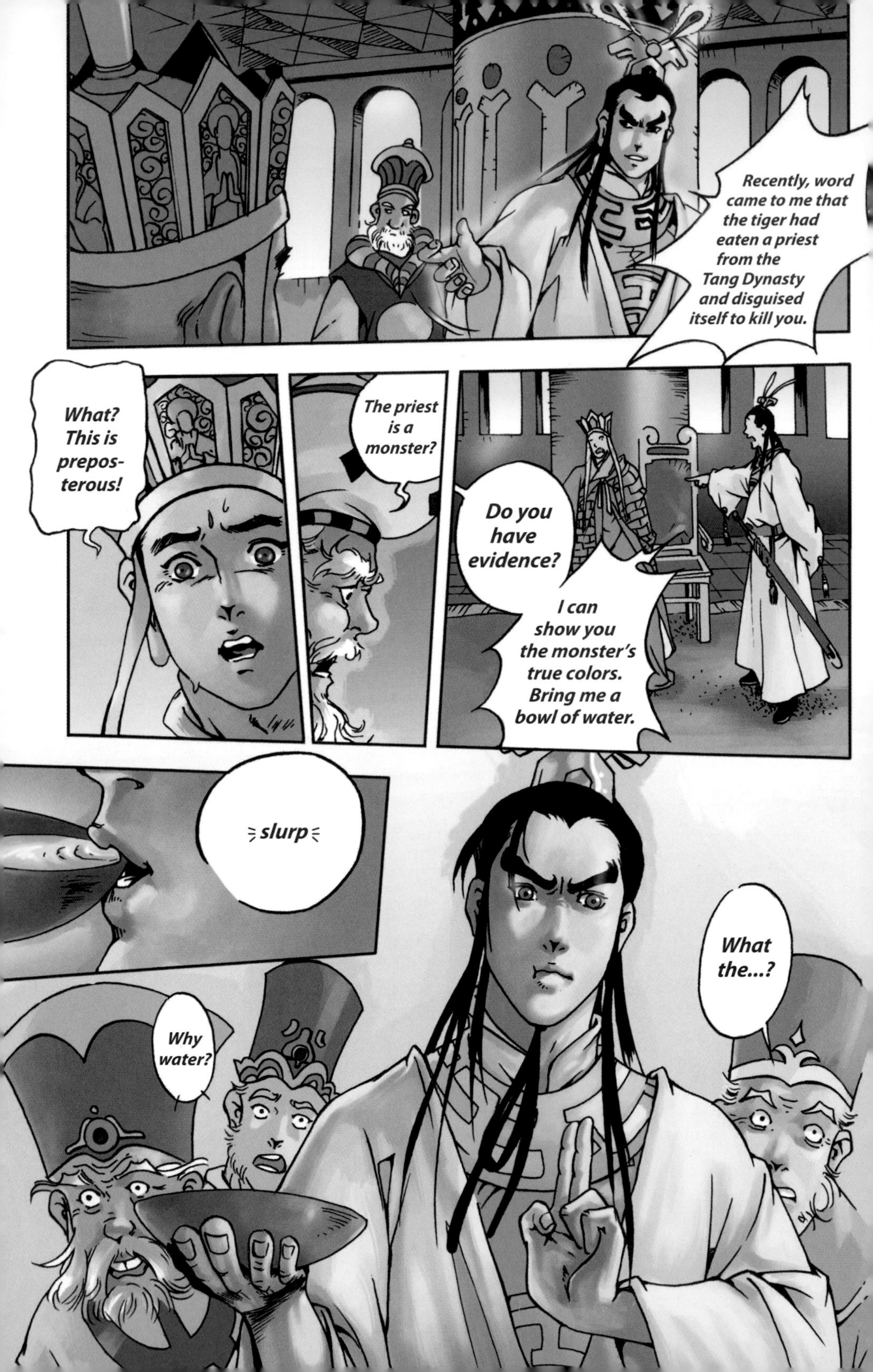

Recently, word came to me that the tiger had eaten a priest from the Tang Dynasty and disguised itself to kill you.
What? This is prepos-terous!
The priest is a monster?
Do you have evidence?
I can show you the monster's true colors. Bring me a bowl of water.
slurp
What the...?
Why water?

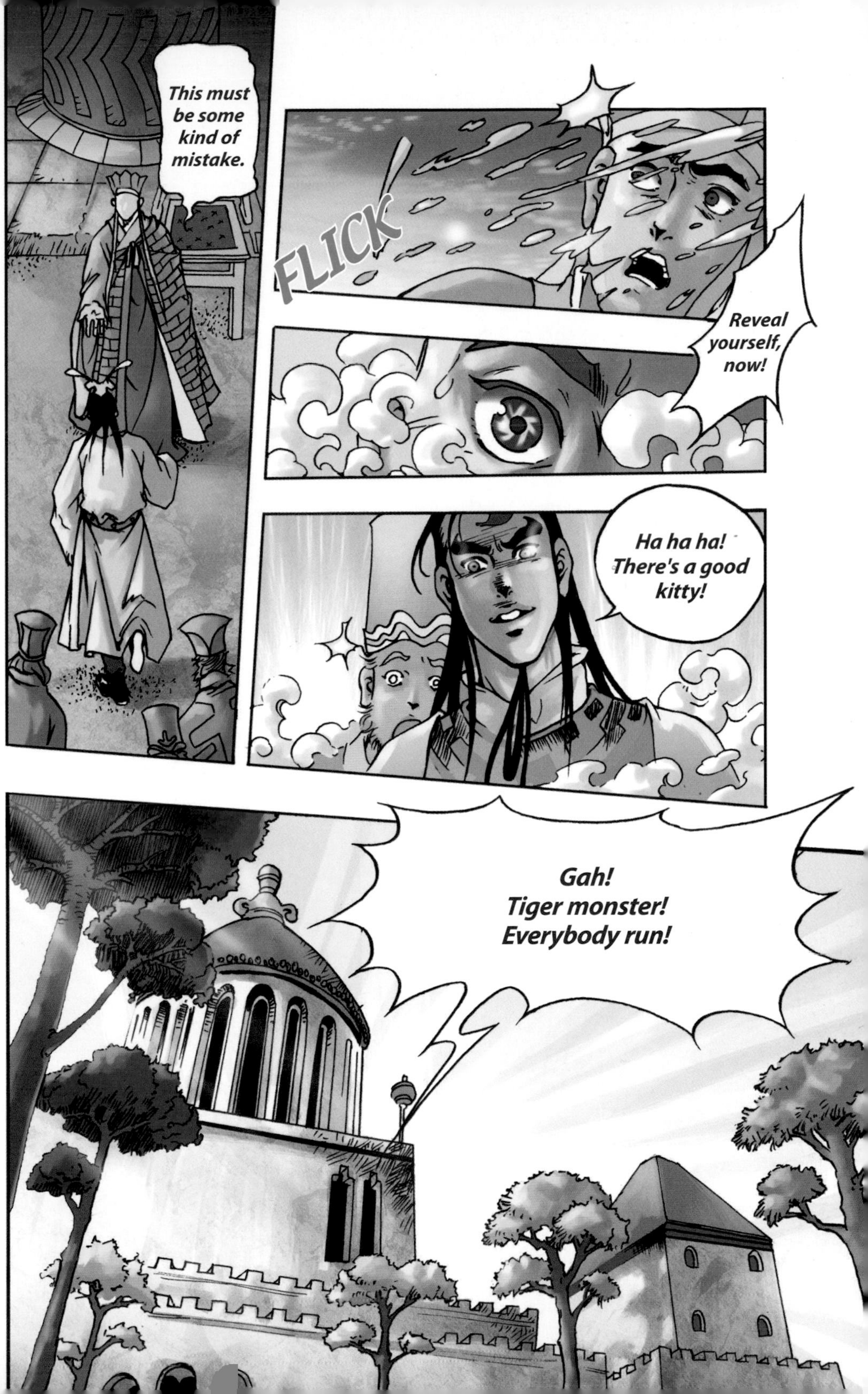
This must be some kind of mistake.
FLICK
Reveal yourself, now!
Ha ha ha! There's a good kitty!
Gah! Tiger monster! Everybody run!

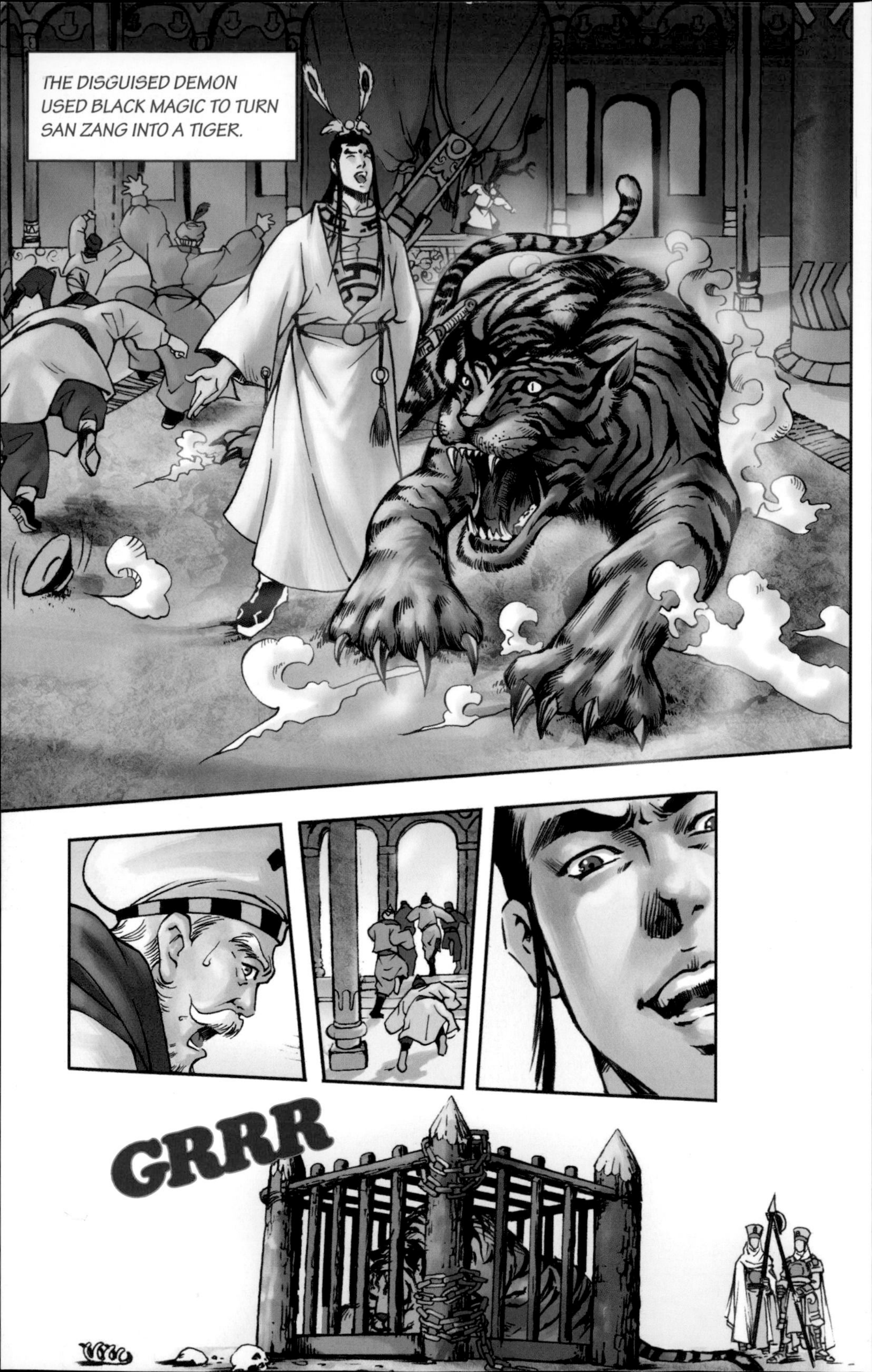
THE DISGUISED DEMON USED BLACK MAGIC TO TURN SAN ZANG INTO A TIGER.
GRRR

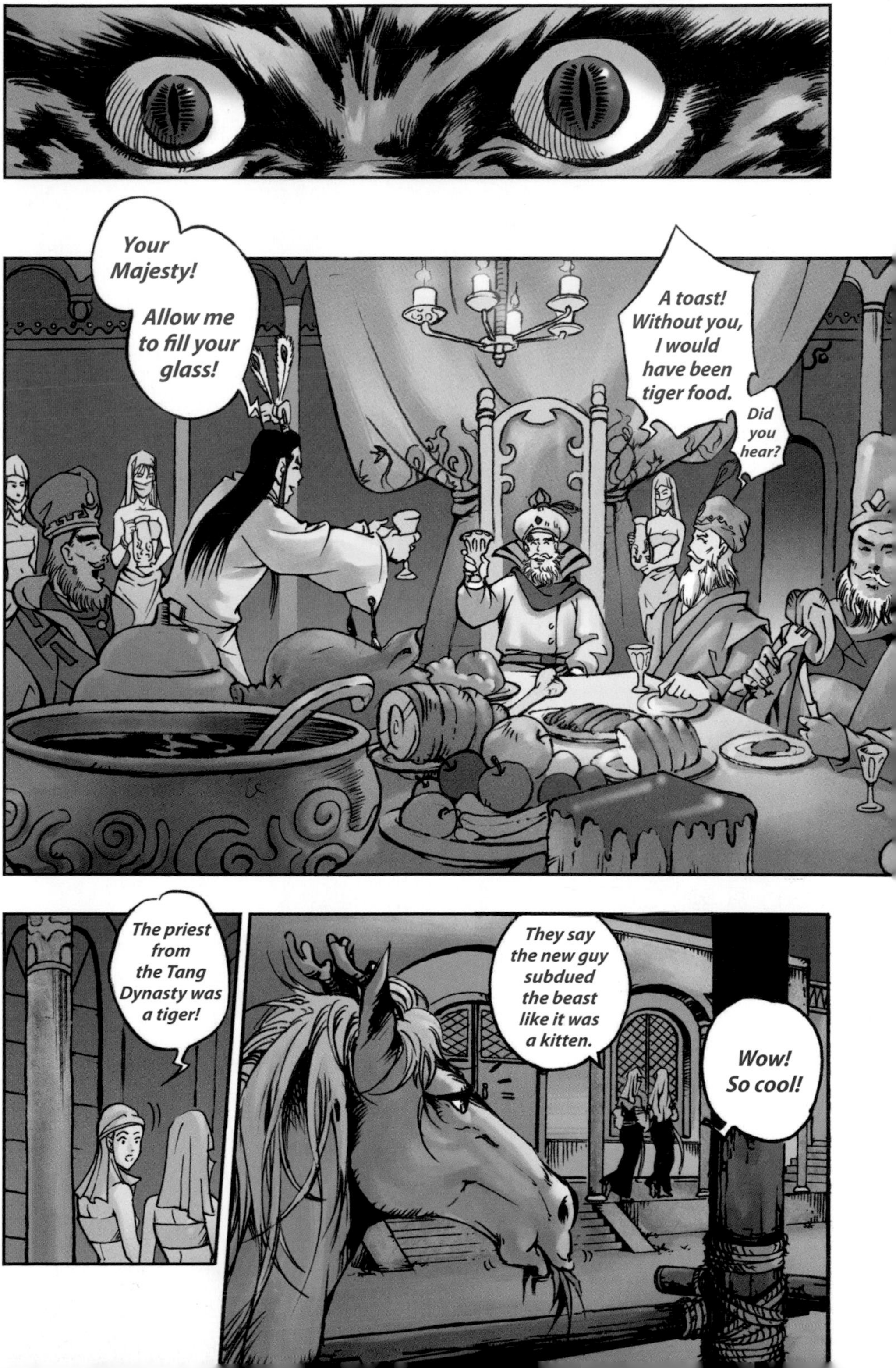
Your Majesty!
Allow me to fill your glass!
A toast! Without you, I would have been tiger food.
Did you hear?
The priest from the Tang Dynasty was a tiger!
They say the new guy subdued the beast like it was a kitten.
Wow! So cool!

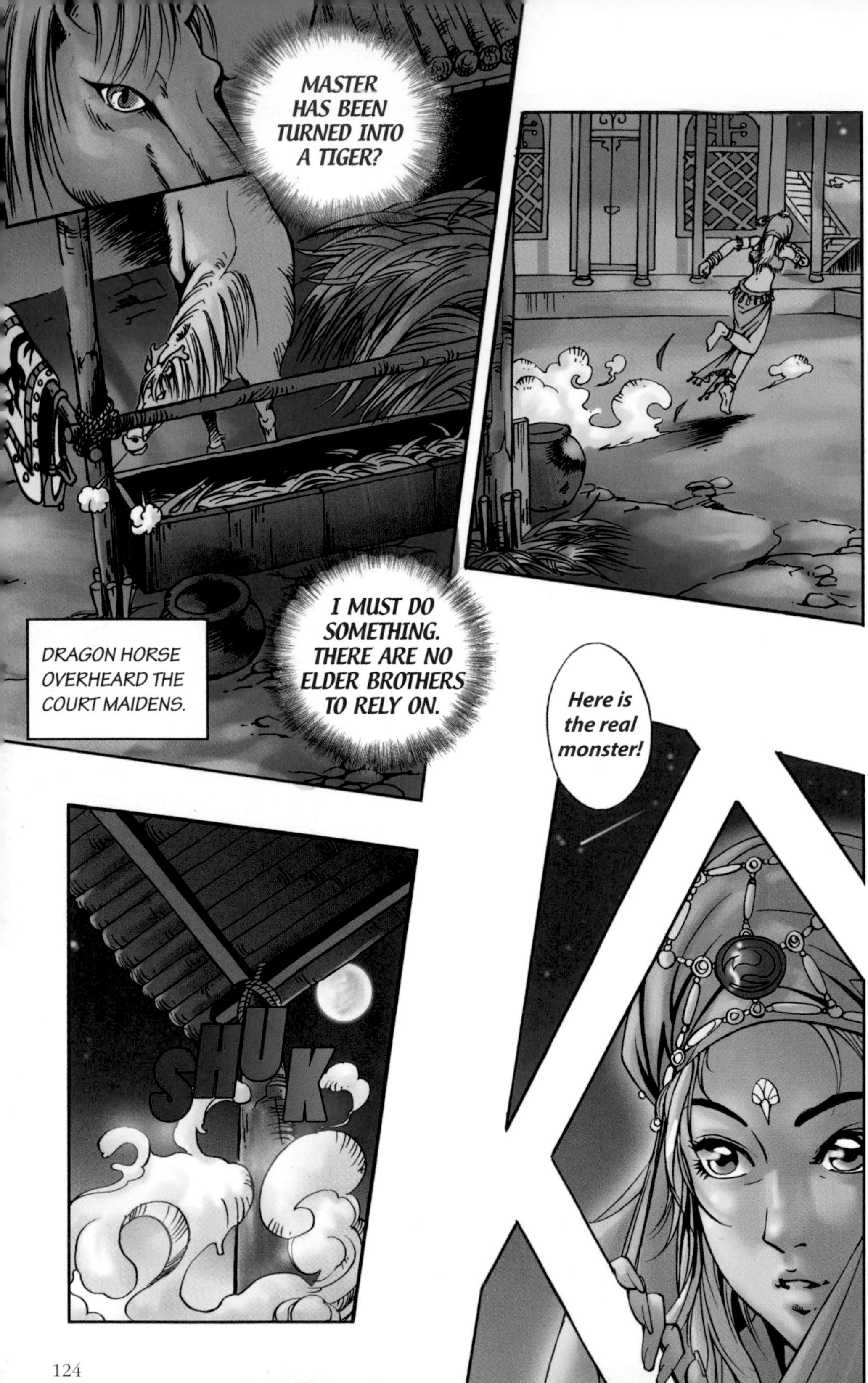
MASTER HAS BEEN TURNED INTO A TIGER?
DRAGON HORSE OVERHEARD THE COURT MAIDENS.
I MUST DO SOMETHING. THERE ARE NO ELDER BROTHERS TO RELY ON.
SHUK
Here is the real monster!

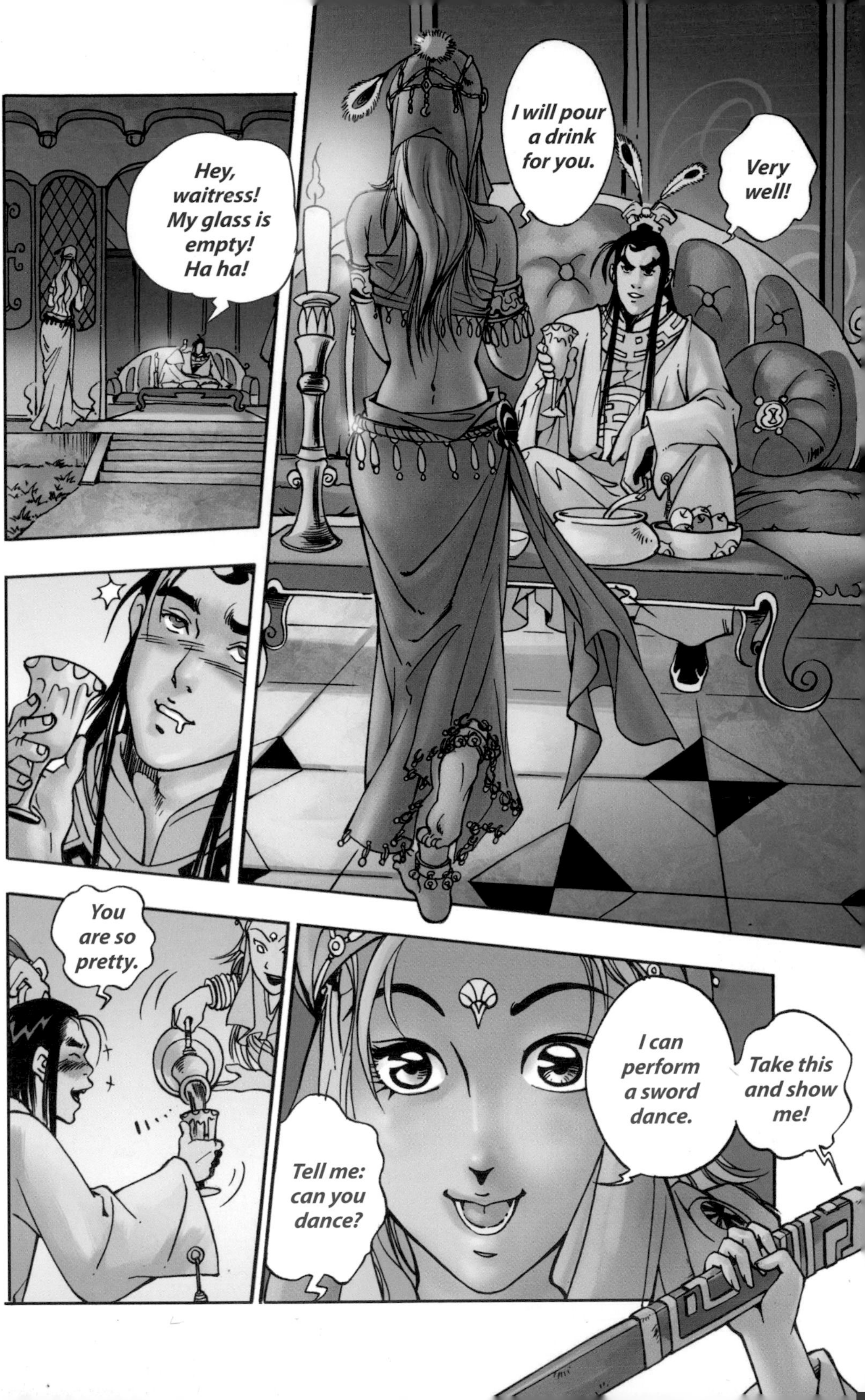

Hey, waitress! My glass is empty! Ha ha!
I will pour a drink for you.
Very well!
You are so pretty.
Tell me: can you dance?
I can perform a sword dance.
Take this and show me!

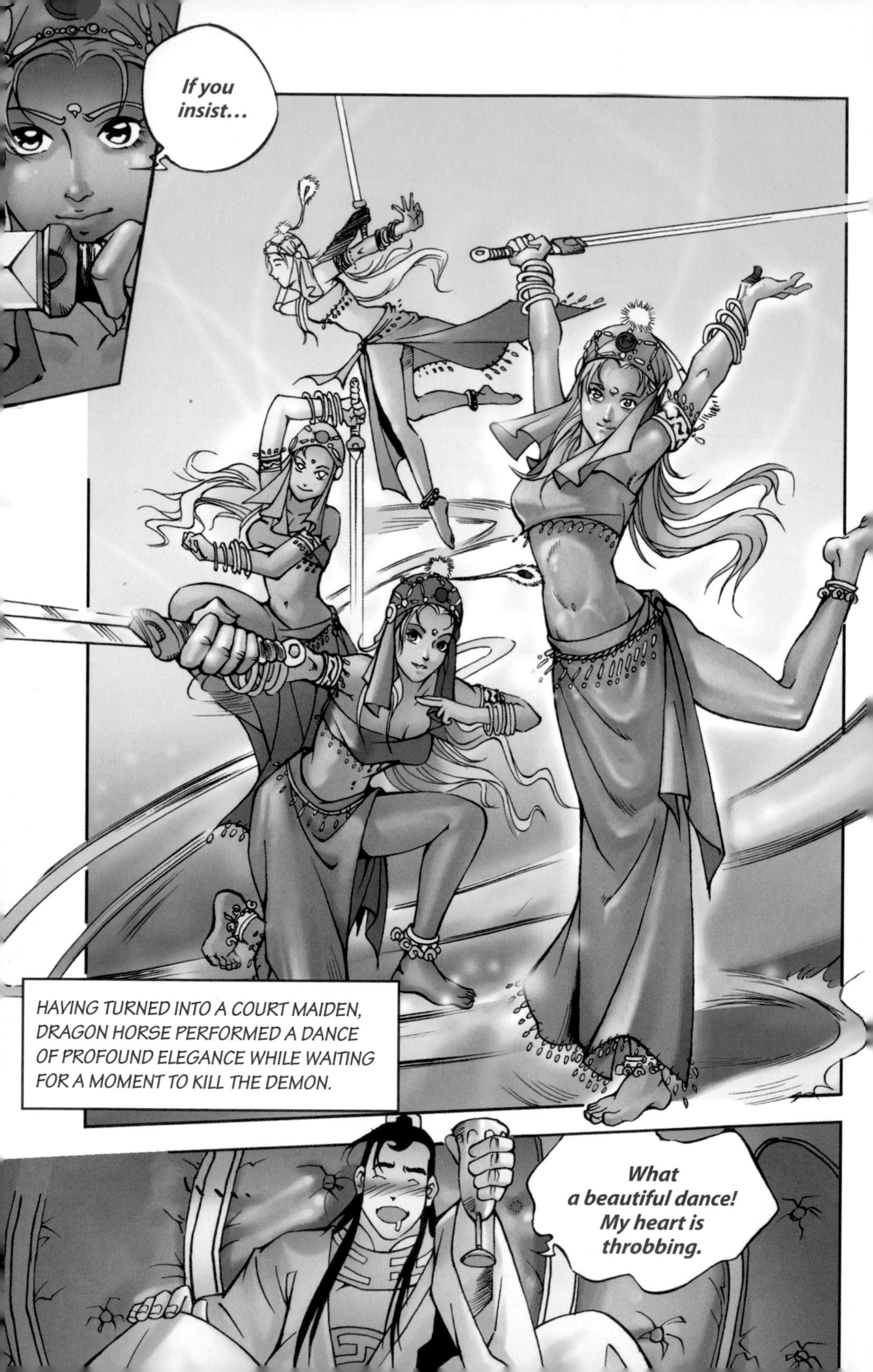
If you insist...
HAVING TURNED INTO A COURT MAIDEN, DRAGON HORSE PERFORMED A DANCE OF PROFOUND ELEGANCE WHILE WAITING FOR A MOMENT TO KILL THE DEMON.
What a beautiful dance! My heart is throbbing.

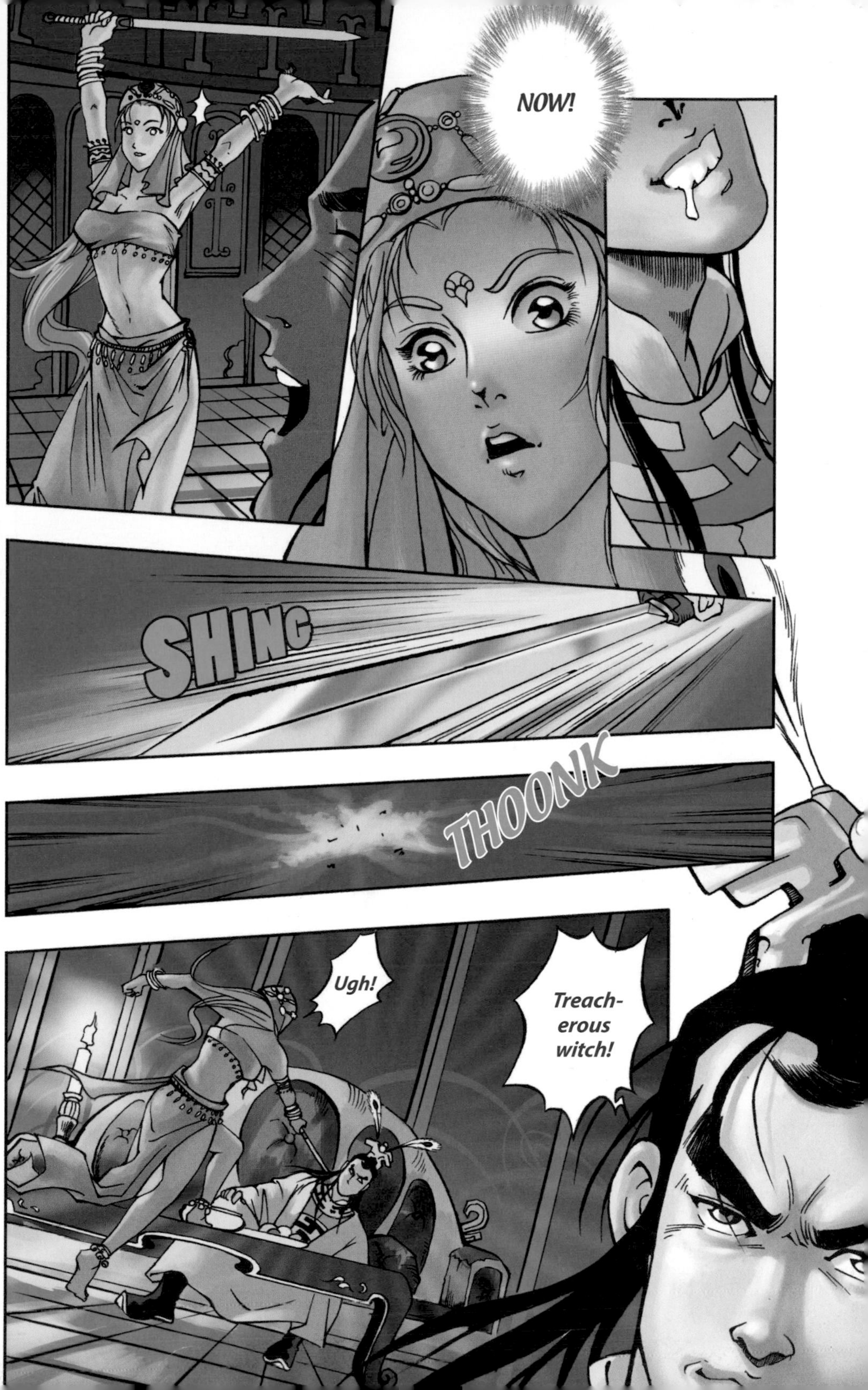
NOW!
SHING
THOONK
Ugh!
Treach-
erous
witch!

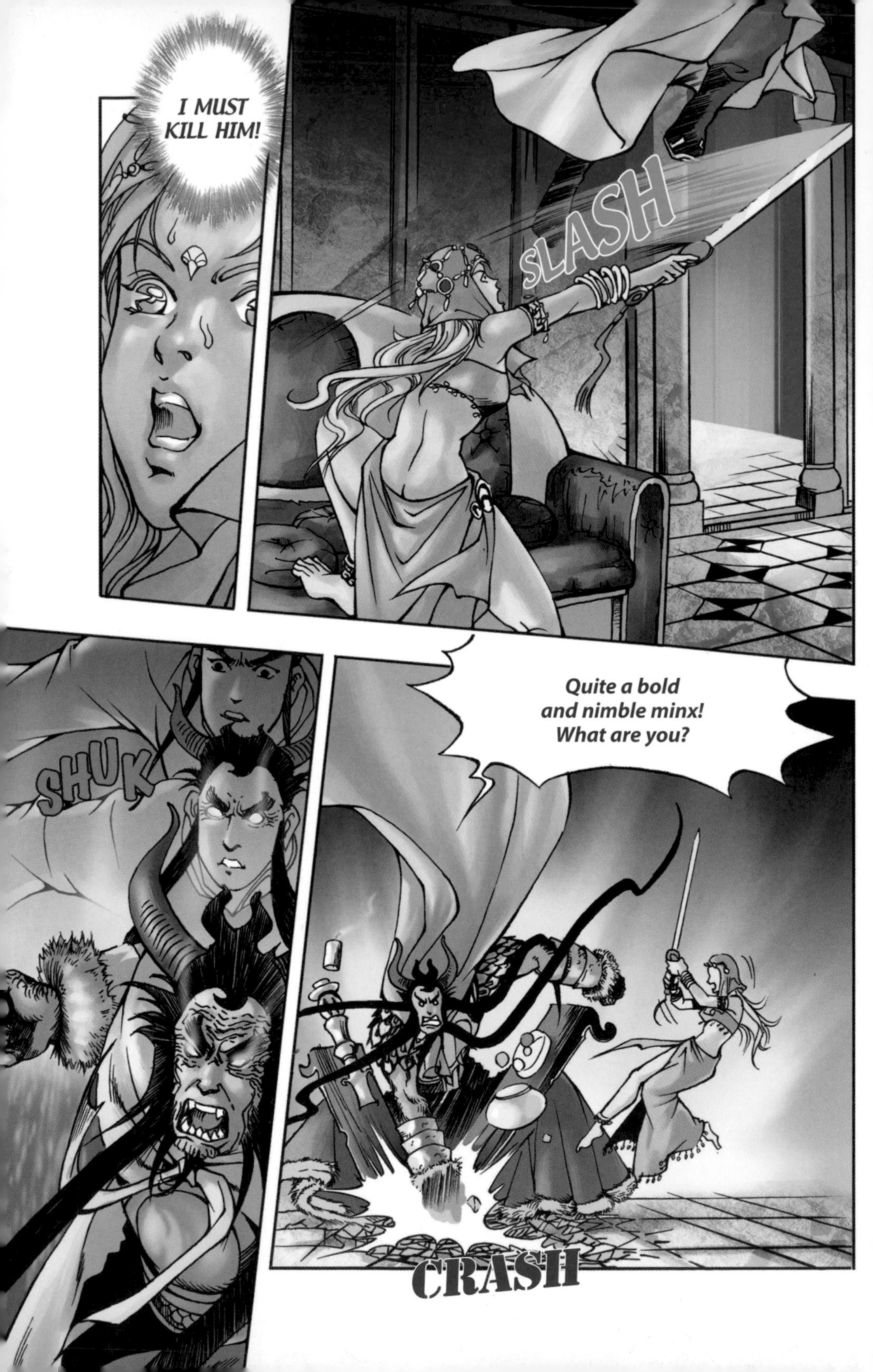
I MUST KILL HIM!
SLASH
SHUK
Quite a bold and nimble minx! What are you?
CRASH

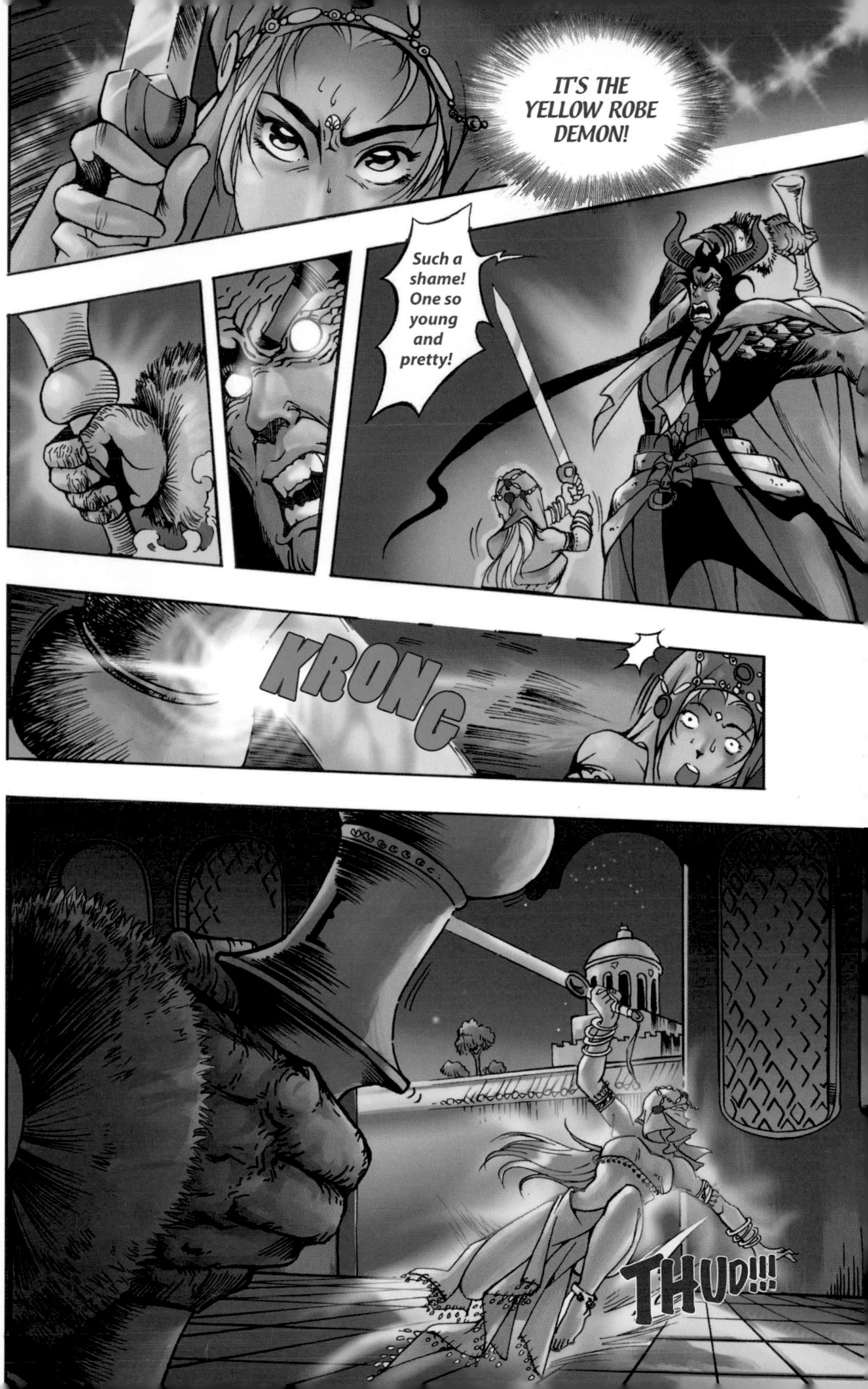
IT'S THE YELLOW ROBE DEMON!
Such a shame! One so young and pretty!
KRONG
THUD!!!

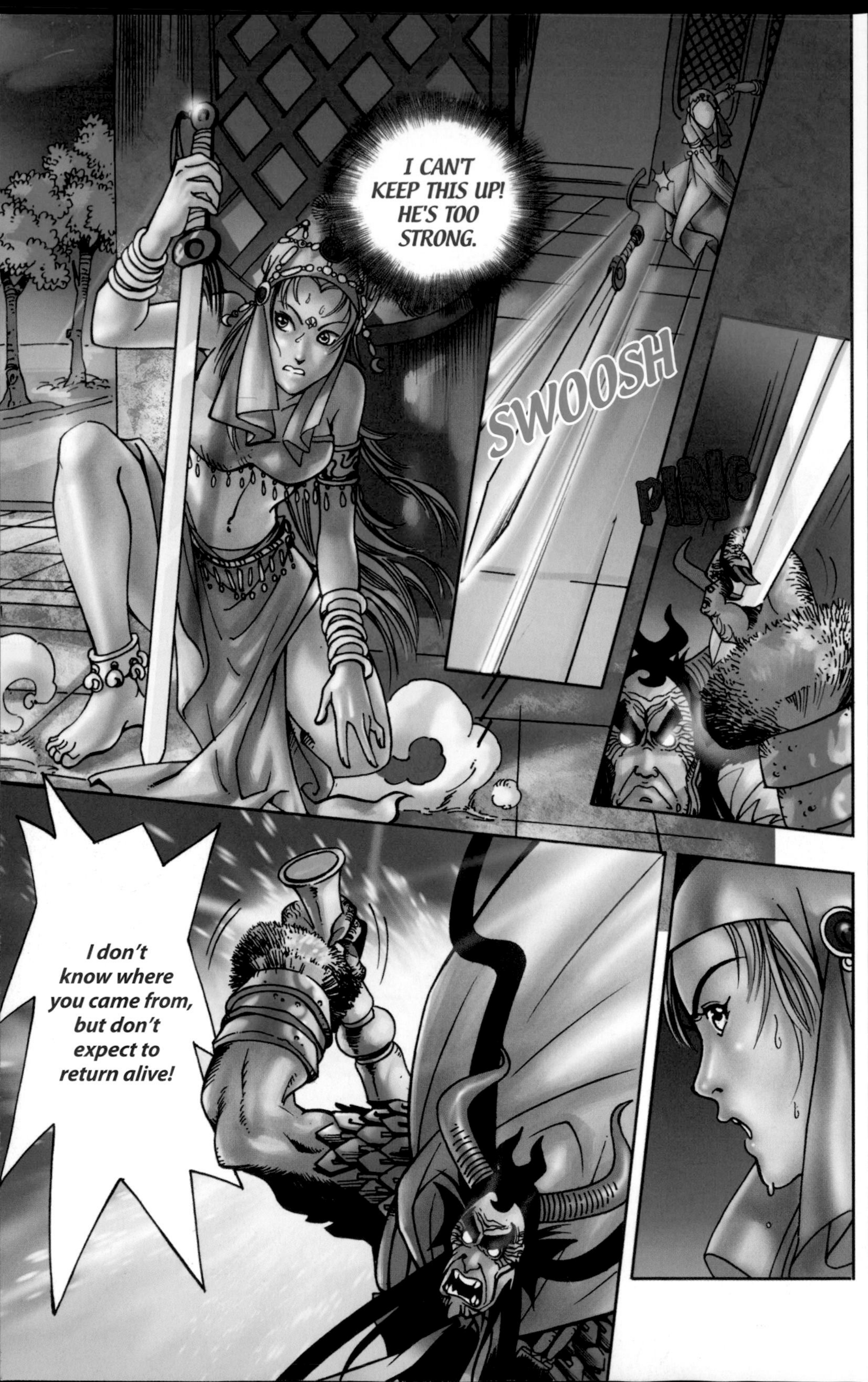
I CAN'T KEEP THIS UP! HE'S TOO STRONG.
SWOOSH
PING
I don't know where you came from, but don't expect to return alive!

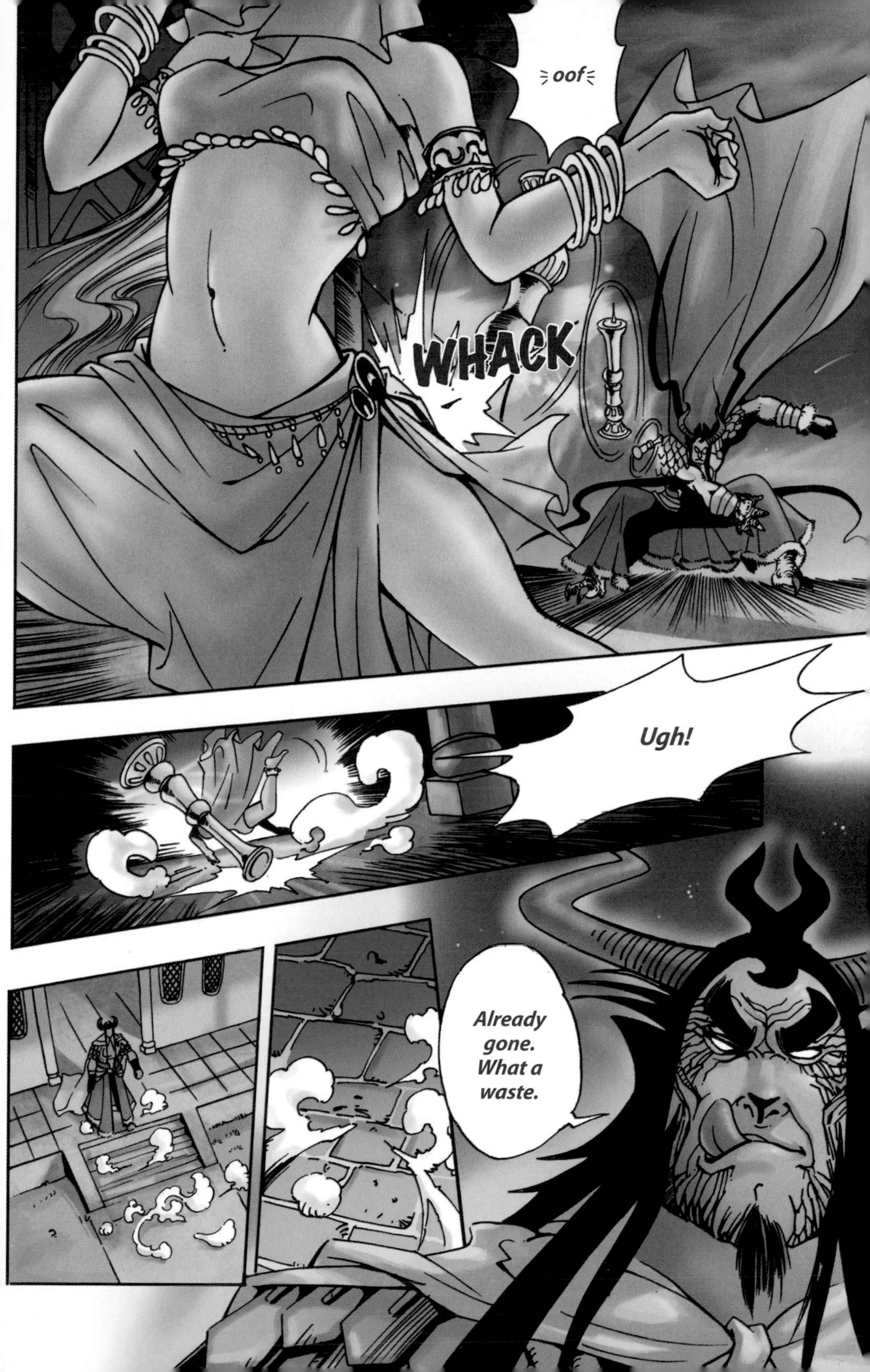
oof
WHACK
Ugh!
Already gone. What a waste.

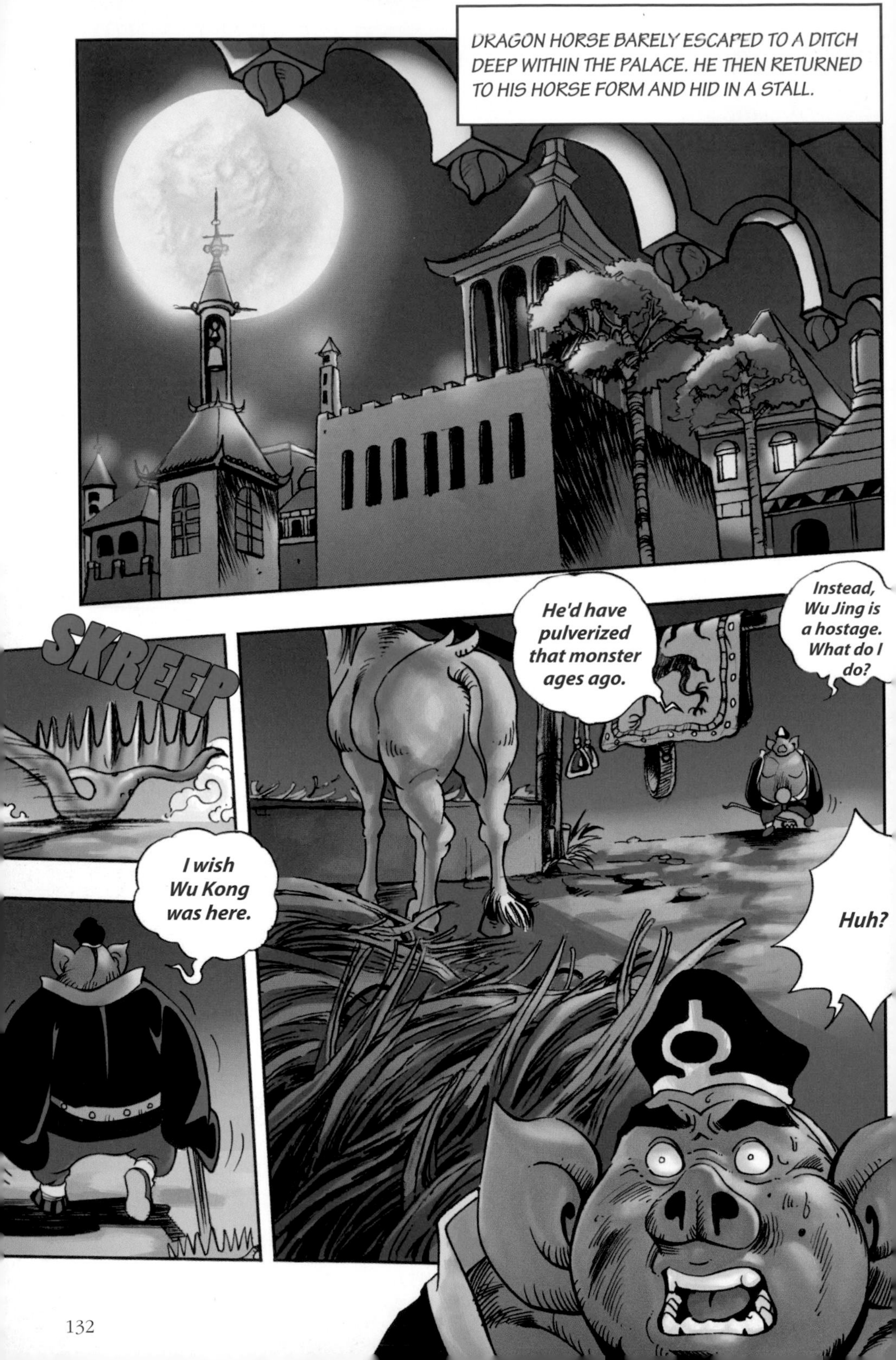
DRAGON HORSE BARELY ESCAPED TO A DITCH DEEP WITHIN THE PALACE. HE THEN RETURNED TO HIS HORSE FORM AND HID IN A STALL.
SKREEP
I wish Wu Kong was here.
He'd have pulverized that monster ages ago.
Instead, Wu Jing is a hostage. What do I do?
Huh?

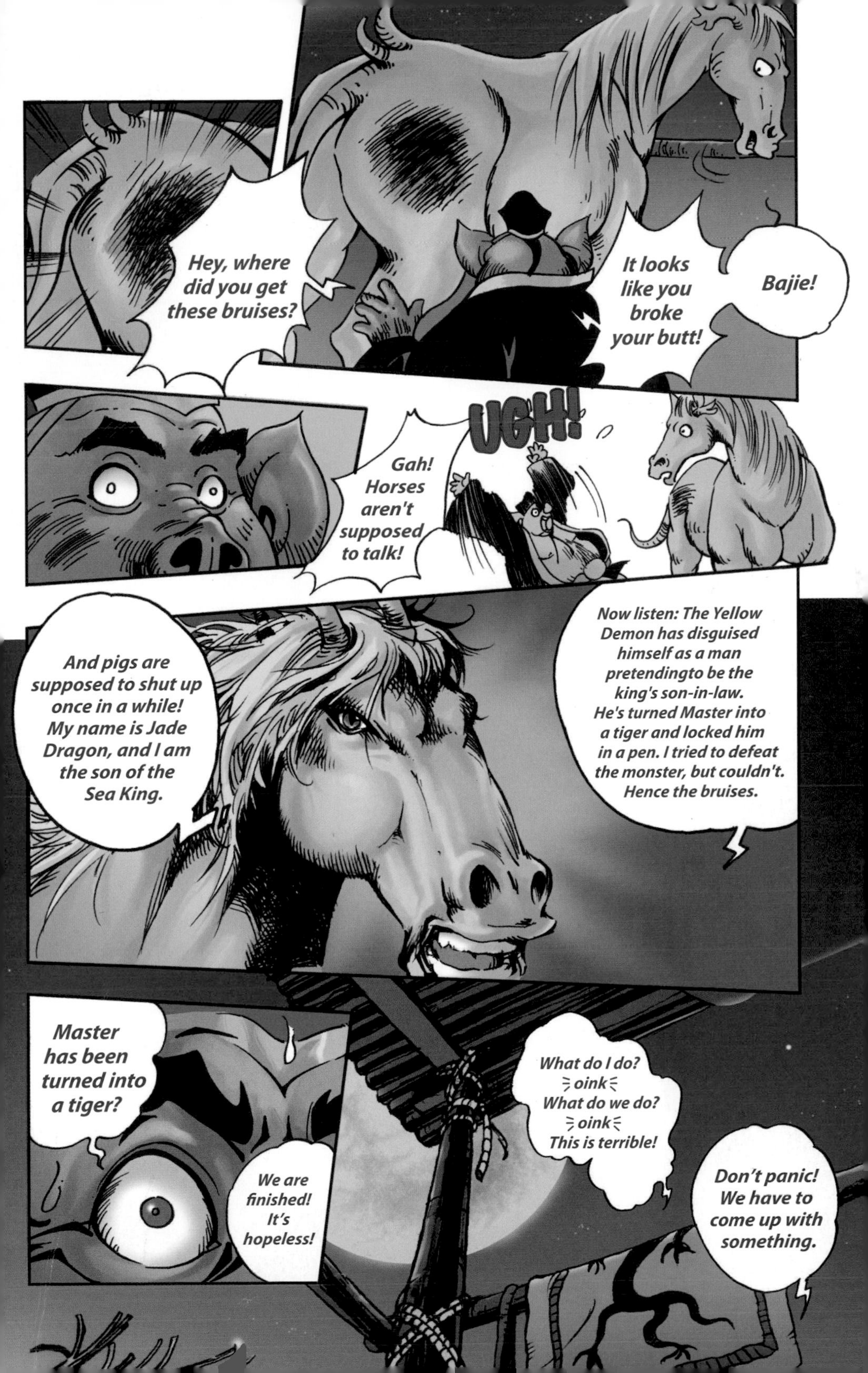
Hey, where did you get these bruises?
It looks like you broke your butt!
Bajie!
UGH!
Gah! Horses aren't supposed to talk!
And pigs are supposed to shut up once in a while! My name is Jade Dragon, and I am the son of the Sea King.
Now listen: The Yellow Demon has disguised himself as a man pretendingto be the king's son-in-law. He's turned Master into a tiger and locked him in a pen. I tried to defeat the monster, but couldn't. Hence the bruises.
Master has been turned into a tiger?
We are finished! It's hopeless!
What do I do? oink What do we do? oink This is terrible!
Don't panic! We have to come up with something.

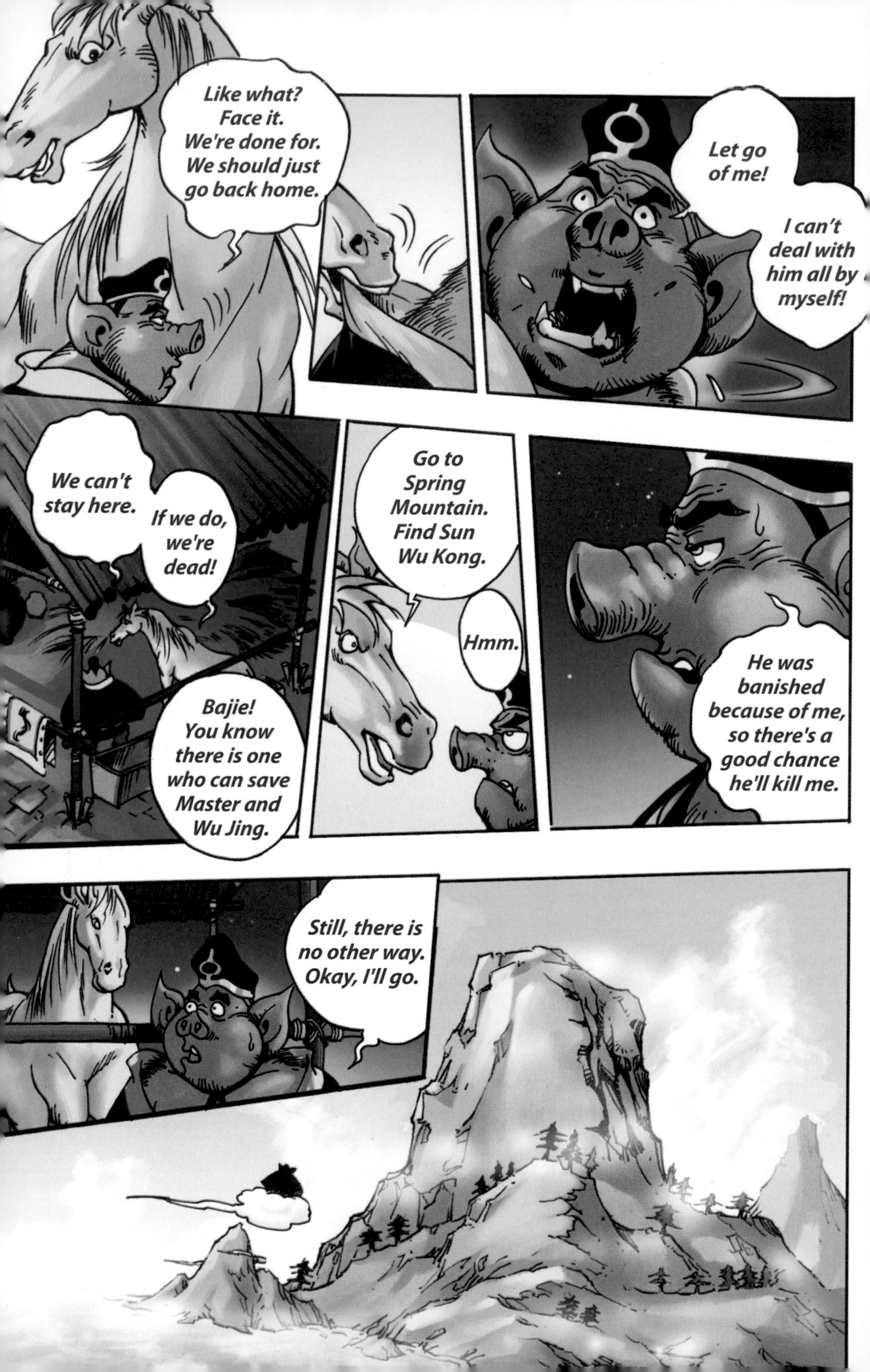
Like what? Face it. We're done for. We should just go back home.
Let go of me!
I can't deal with him all by myself!
We can't stay here.
If we do, we're dead!
Bajie! You know there is one who can save Master and Wu Jing.
Go to Spring Mountain. Find Sun Wu Kong.
Hmm.
He was banished because of me, so there's a good chance he'll kill me.
Still, there is no other way. Okay, I'll go.

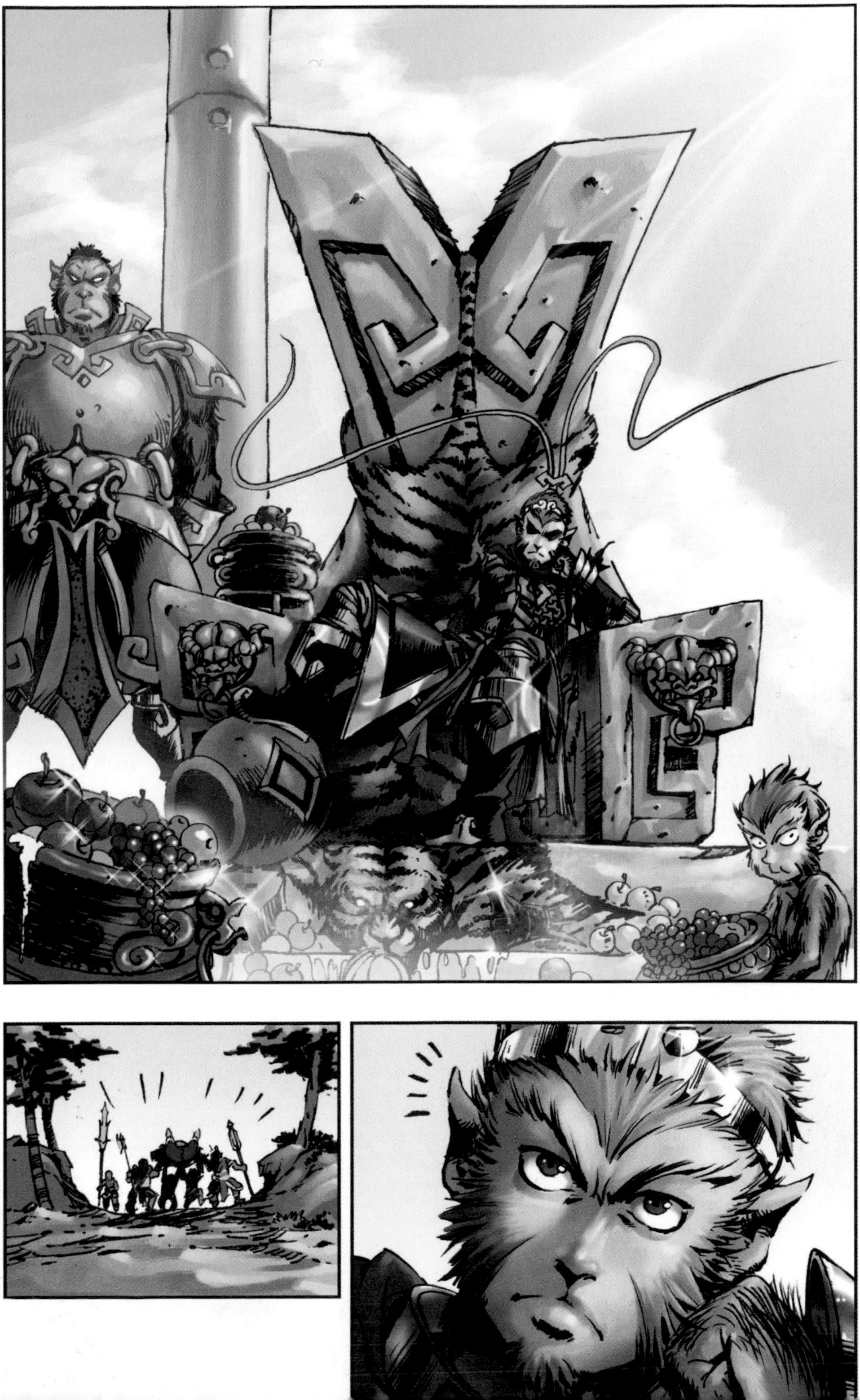

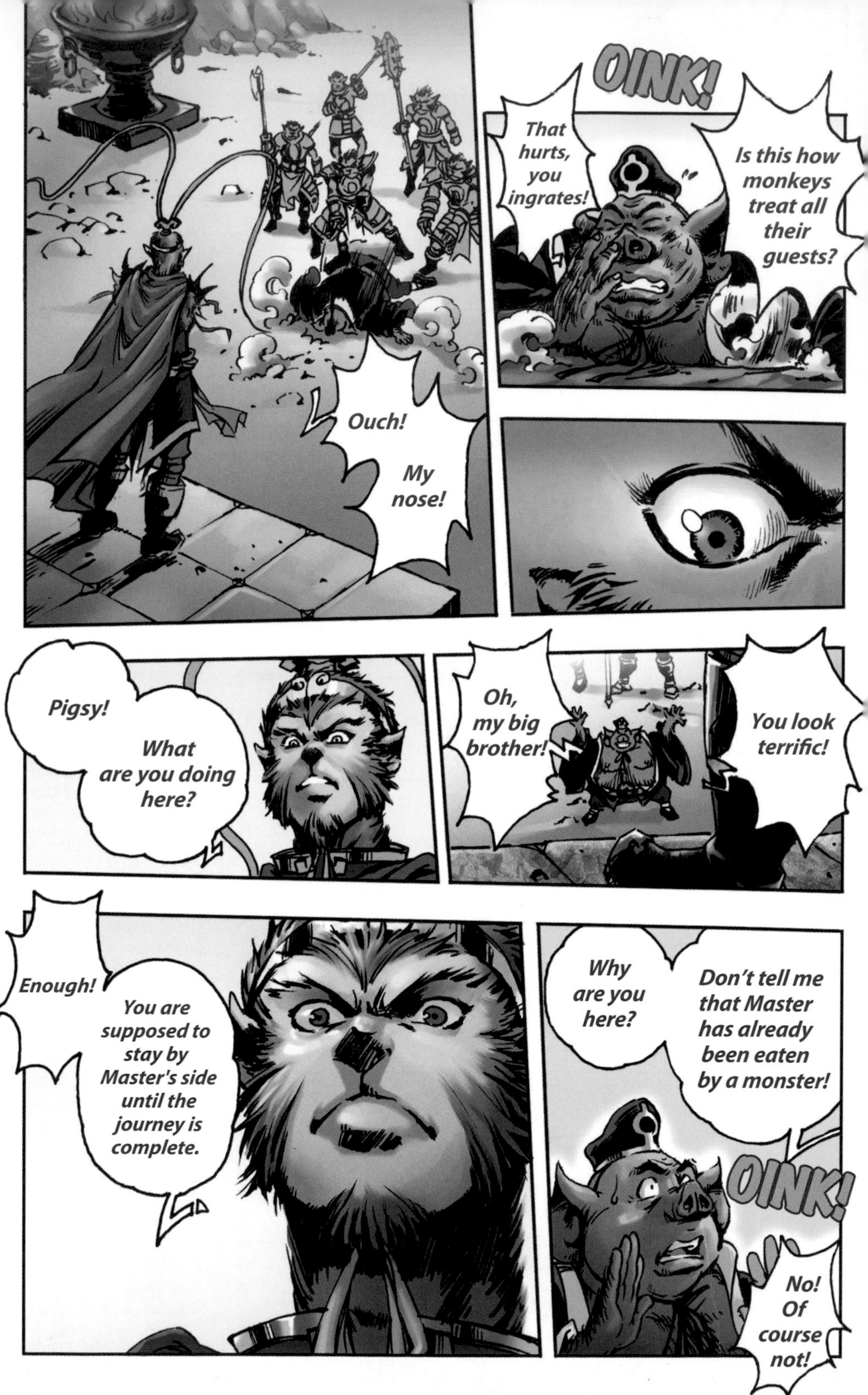

Ouch!
My nose!
OINK!
That hurts, you ingrates!
Is this how monkeys treat all their guests?
Pigsy!
What are you doing here?
Oh, my big brother!
You look terrific!
Enough!
You are supposed to stay by Master's side until the journey is complete.
Why are you here?
Don't tell me that Master has already been eaten by a monster!
OINK!
No! Of course not!

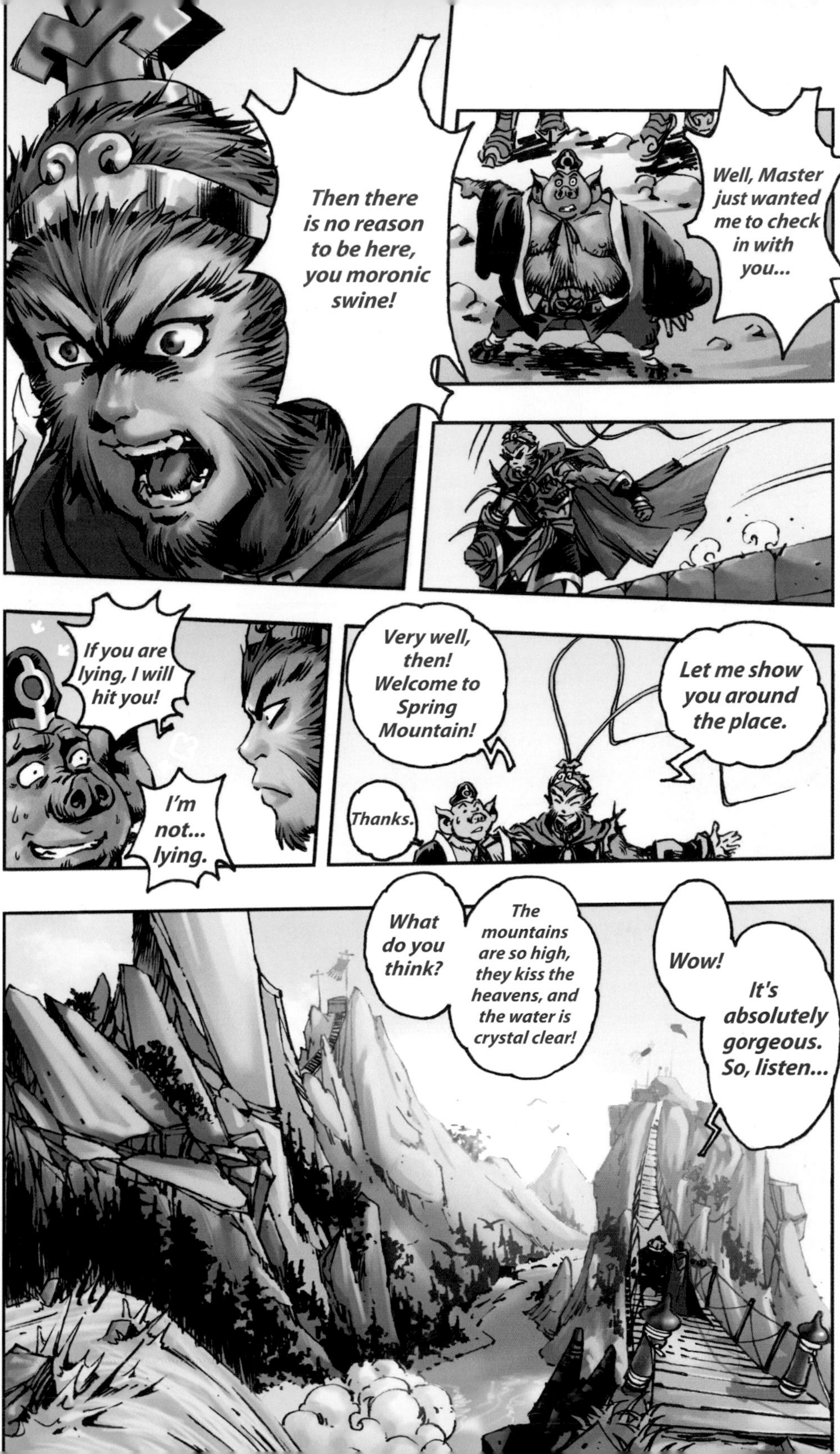
Then there is no reason to be here, you moronic swine!
Well, Master just wanted me to check in with you...
If you are lying, I will hit you!
I'm not... lying.
Very well, then! Welcome to Spring Mountain!
Let me show you around the place.
Thanks.
What do you think?
The mountains are so high, they kiss the heavens, and the water is crystal clear!
Wow!
It's absolutely gorgeous. So, listen...

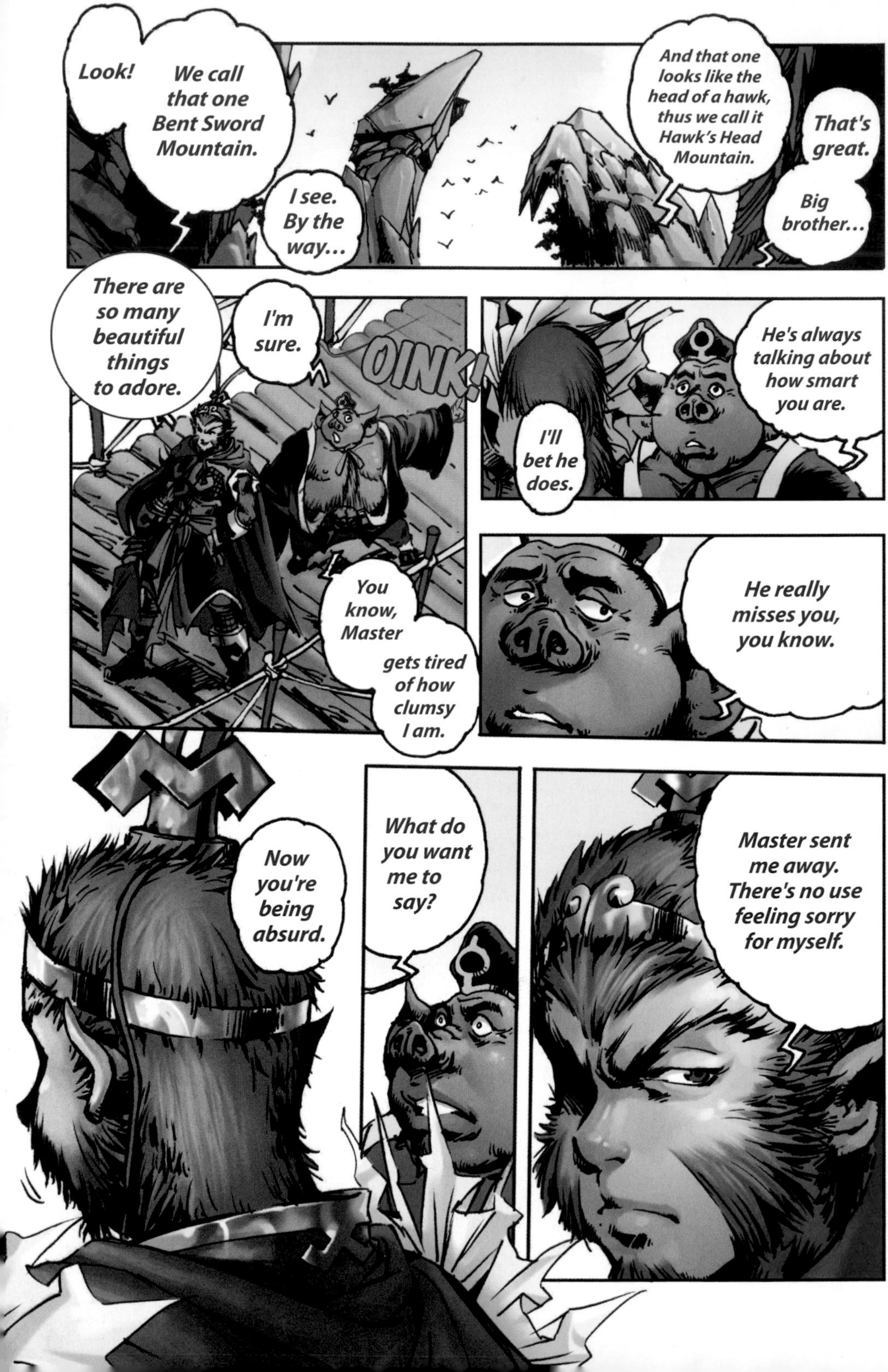

Look!
We call that one Bent Sword Mountain.
I see. By the way…
And that one looks like the head of a hawk, thus we call it Hawk's Head Mountain.
That's great.
Big brother…
There are so many beautiful things to adore.
I'm sure.
OINK!
You know, Master
gets tired of how clumsy I am.
He's always talking about how smart you are.
I'll bet he does.
He really misses you, you know.
Now you're being absurd.
What do you want me to say?
Master sent me away. There's no use feeling sorry for myself.

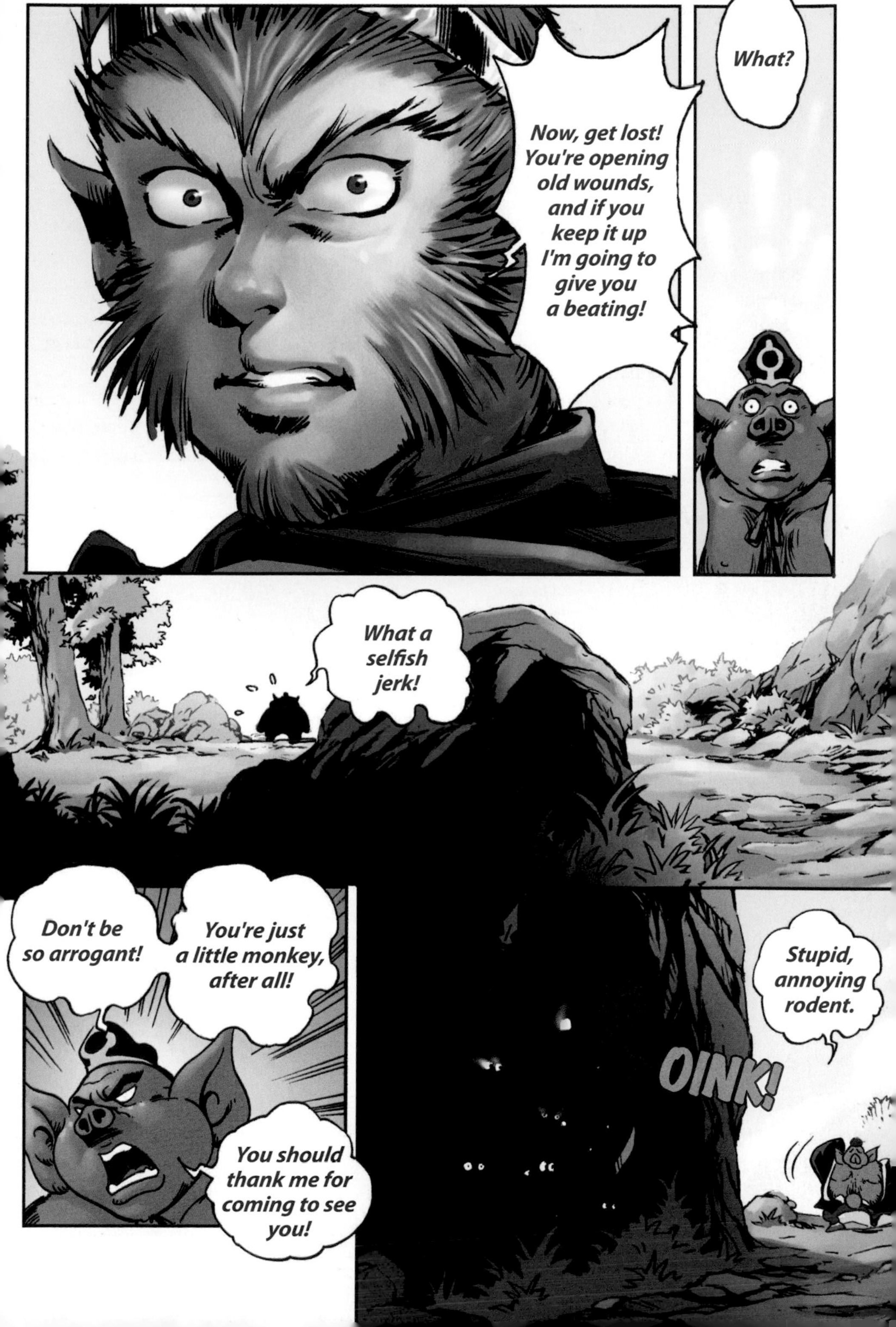
Now, get lost! You're opening old wounds, and if you keep it up I'm going to give you a beating!
What?
What a selfish jerk!
Don't be so arrogant!
You're just a little monkey, after all!
You should thank me for coming to see you!
Stupid, annoying rodent.
OINK!

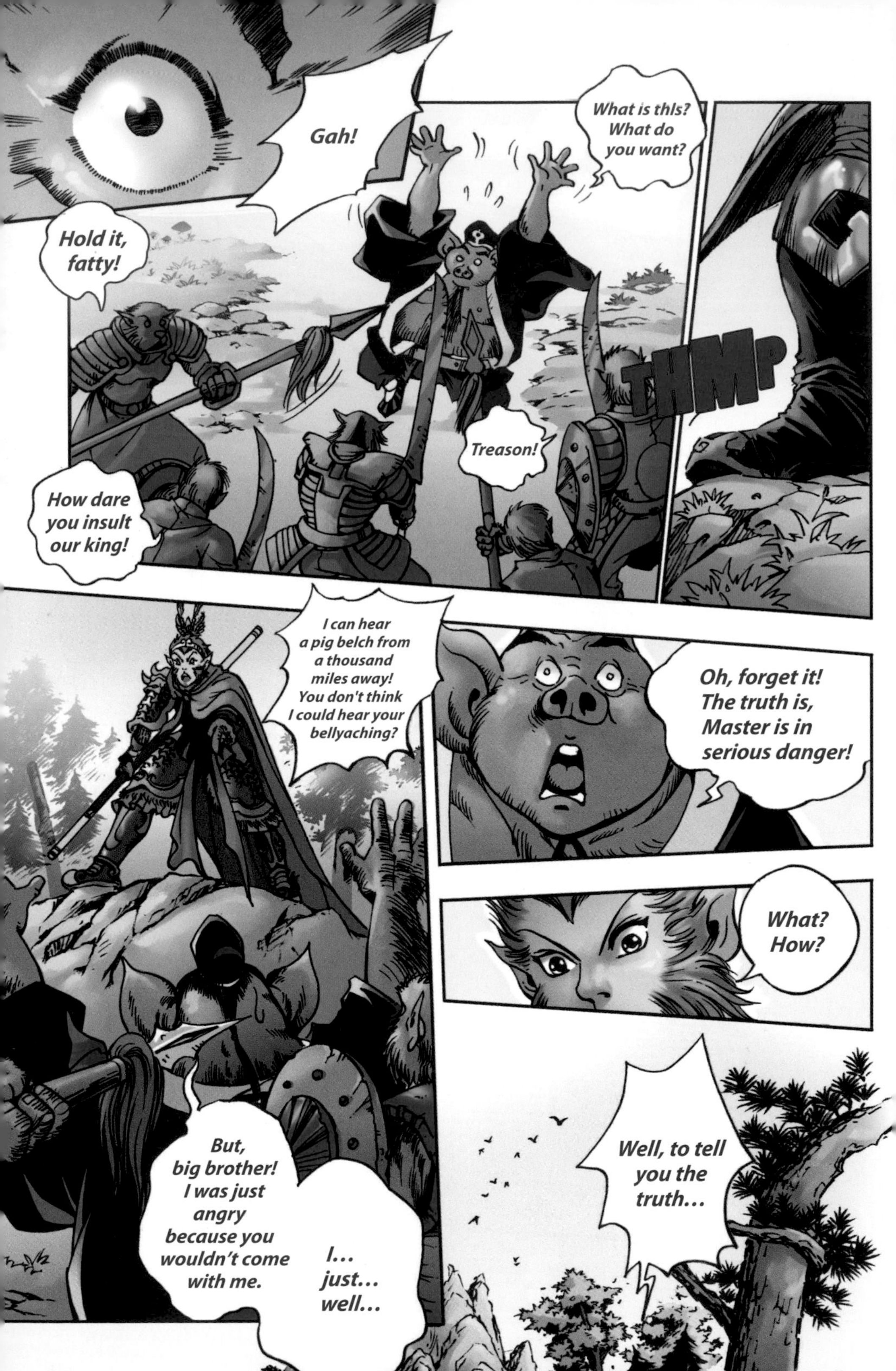
Gah!
What is thls? What do you want?
Hold it, fatty!
THMP
Treason!
How dare you insult our king!
I can hear a pig belch from a thousand miles away! You don't think I could hear your bellyaching?
Oh, forget it! The truth is, Master is in serious danger!
What? How?
But, big brother! I was just angry because you wouldn't come with me.
I... just... well...
Well, to tell you the truth...

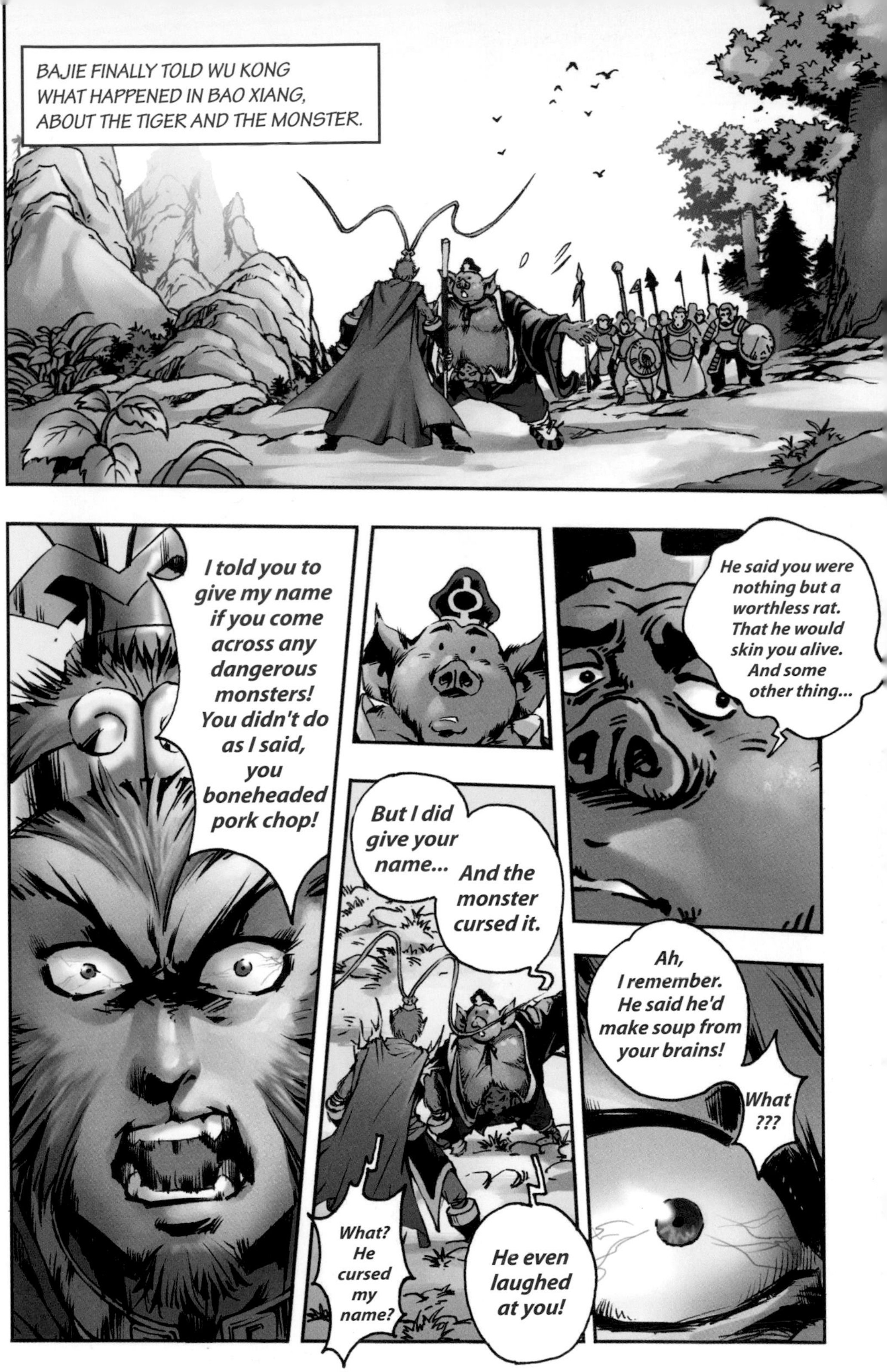
BAJIE FINALLY TOLD WU KONG WHAT HAPPENED IN BAO XIANG, ABOUT THE TIGER AND THE MONSTER.
I told you to give my name if you come across any dangerous monsters! You didn't do as I said, you boneheaded pork chop!
He said you were nothing but a worthless rat. That he would skin you alive. And some other thing...
But I did give your name...
And the monster cursed it.
Ah, I remember. He said he'd make soup from your brains!
What ???
What? He cursed my name?
He even laughed at you!

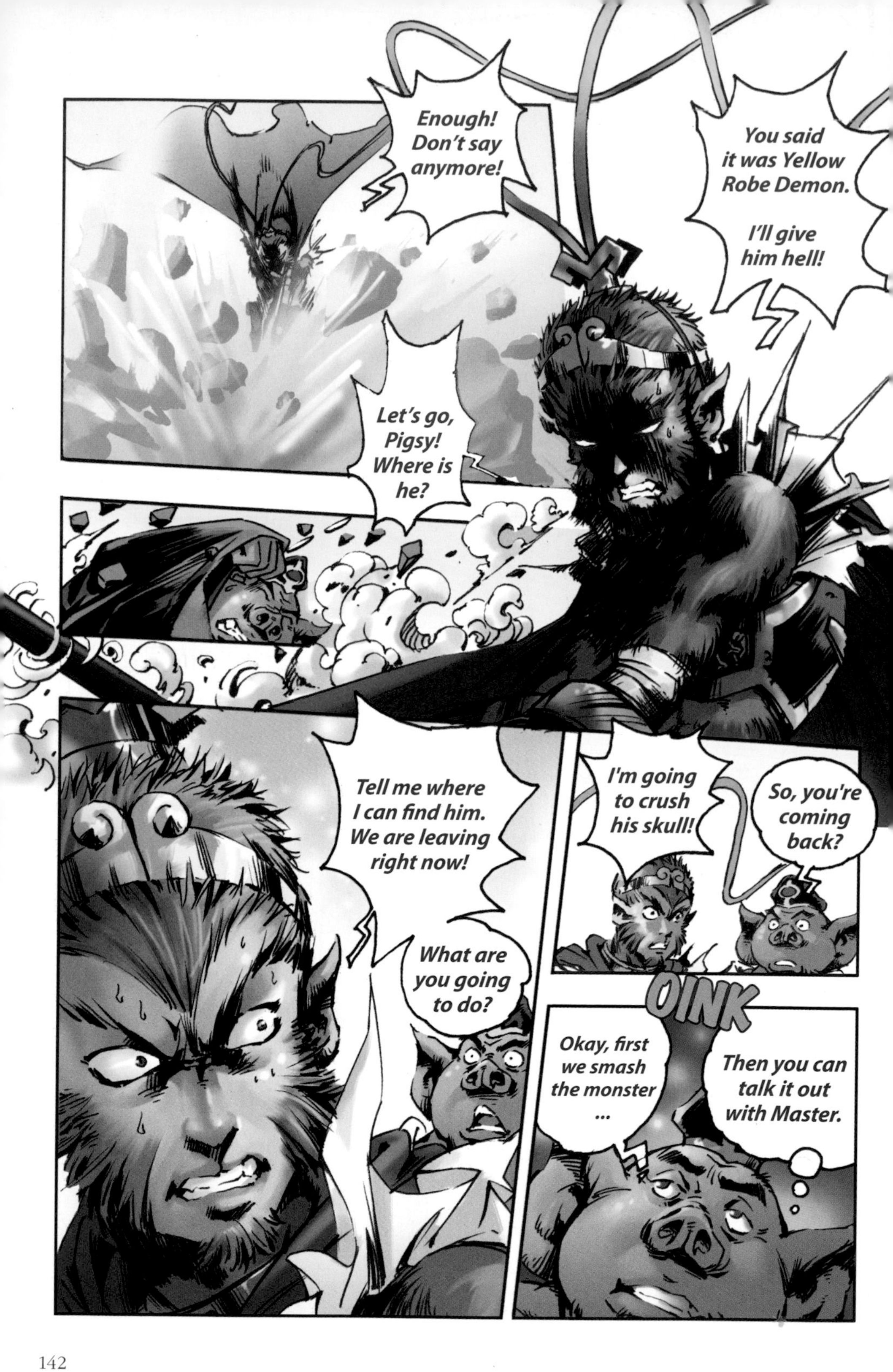
Enough! Don't say anymore!
You said it was Yellow Robe Demon.
I'll give him hell!
Let's go, Pigsy! Where is he?
Tell me where I can find him. We are leaving right now!
What are you going to do?
I'm going to crush his skull!
So, you're coming back?
OINK
Okay, first we smash the monster ...
Then you can talk it out with Master.

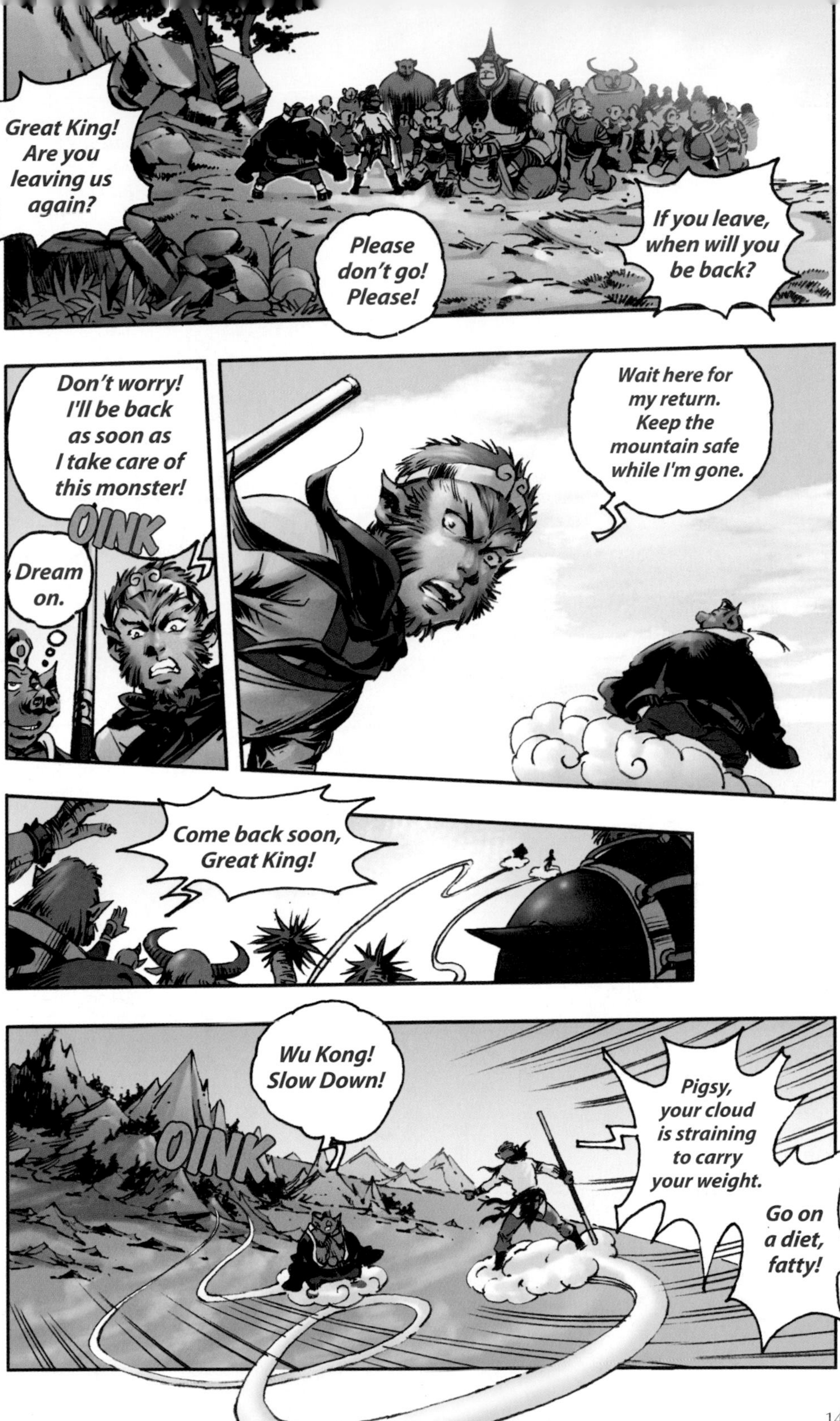
Great King! Are you leaving us again?
Please don't go! Please!
If you leave, when will you be back?
Don't worry! I'll be back as soon as I take care of this monster!
OINK
Dream on.
Wait here for my return. Keep the mountain safe while I'm gone.
Come back soon, Great King!
Wu Kong! Slow Down!
OINK
Pigsy, your cloud is straining to carry your weight.
Go on a diet, fatty!

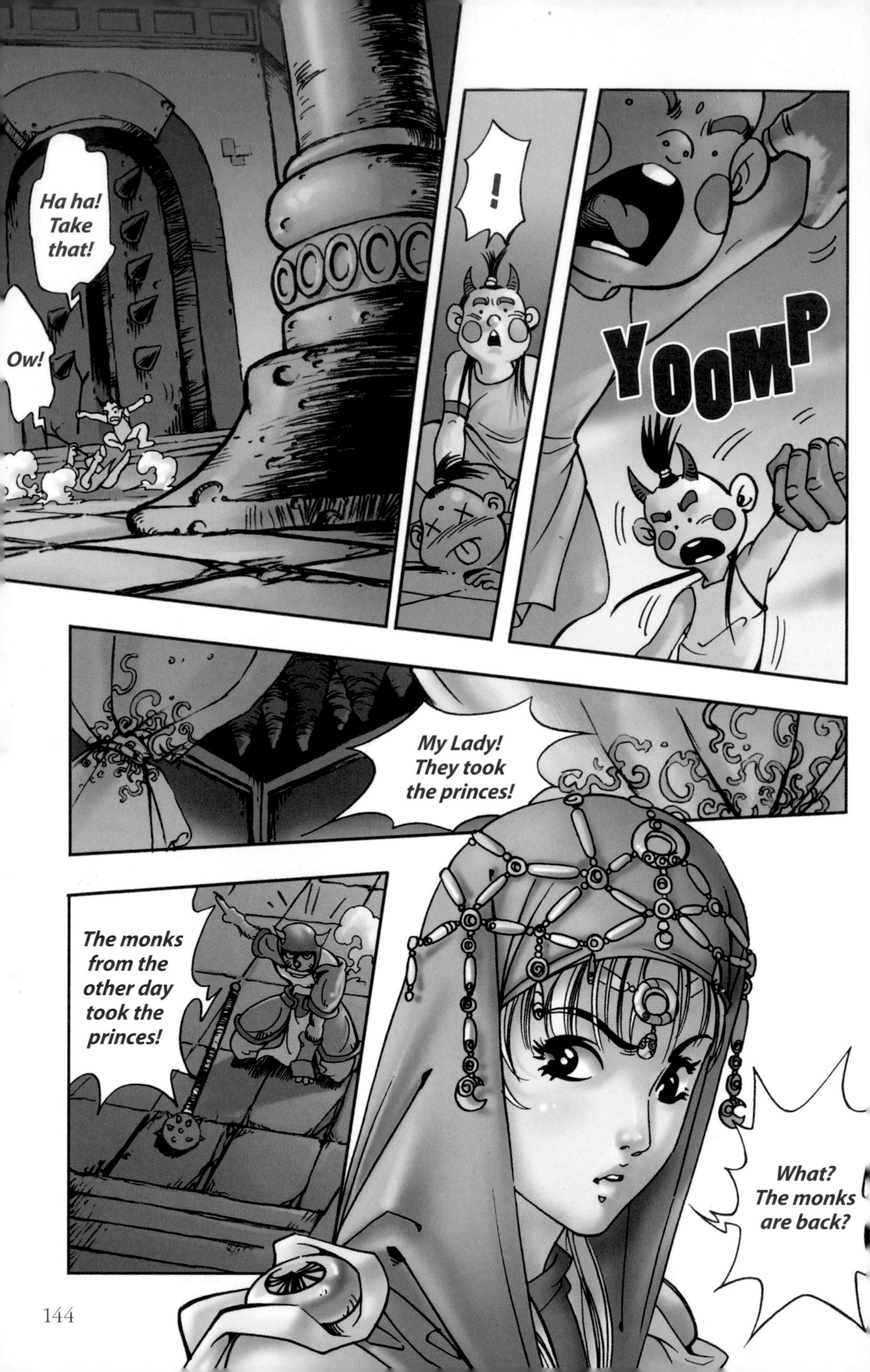
Ha ha! Take that!
Ow!
!
YOOMP
My Lady! They took the princes!
The monks from the other day took the princes!
What? The monks are back?

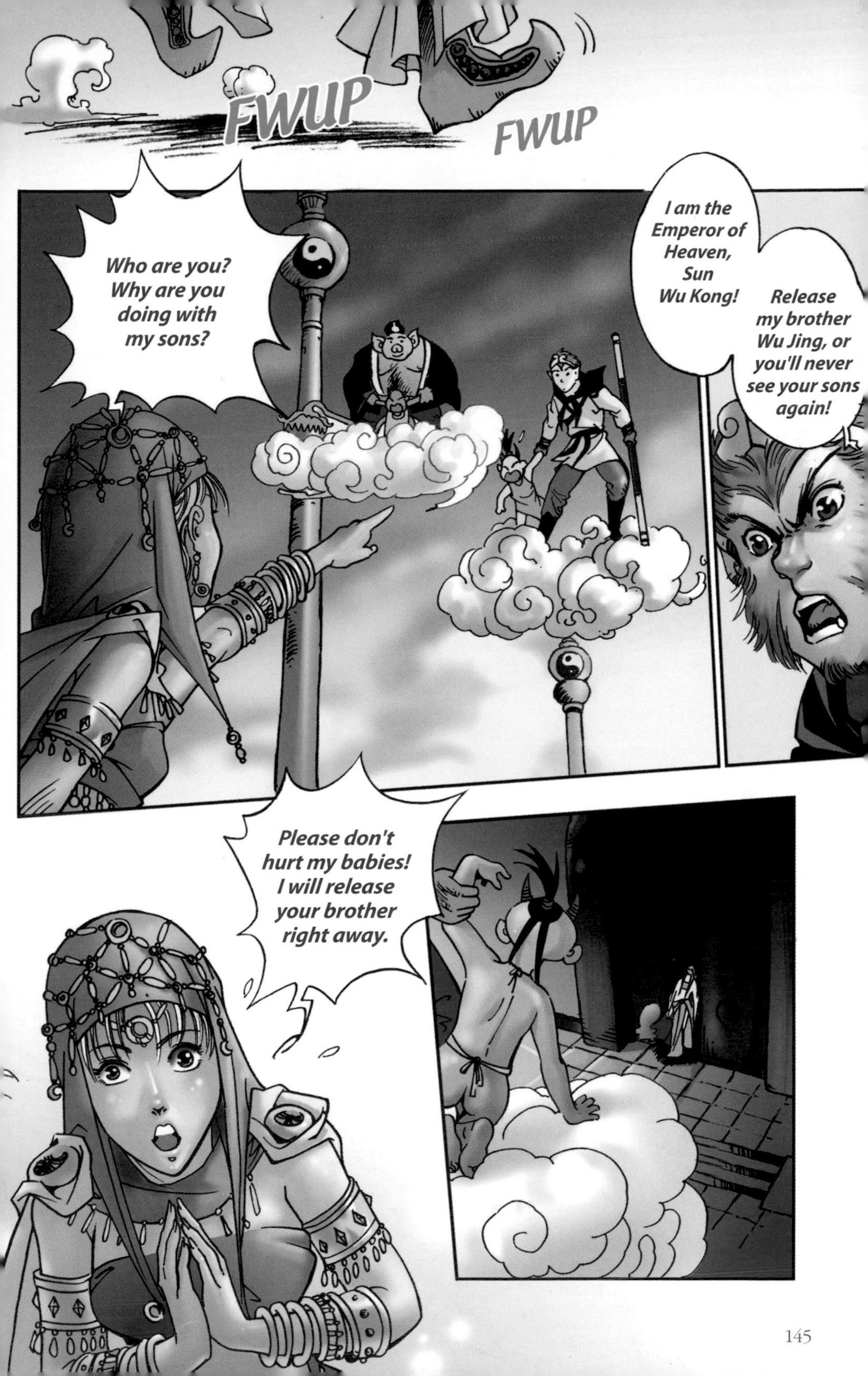
FWUP
FWUP
Who are you? Why are you doing with my sons?
I am the Emperor of Heaven, Sun Wu Kong!
Release my brother Wu Jing, or you'll never see your sons again!
Please don't hurt my babies! I will release your brother right away.

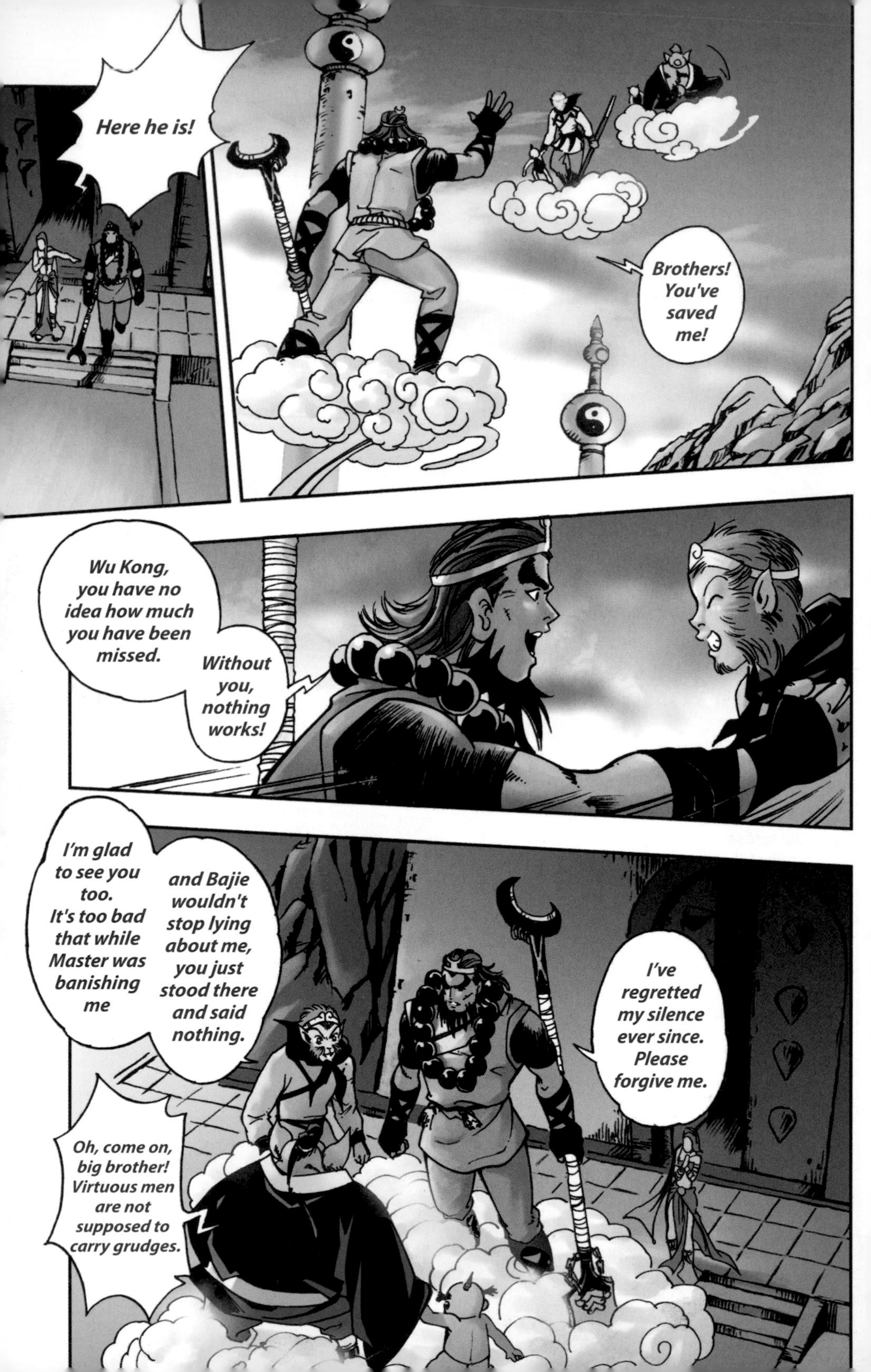
Here he is!
Brothers! You've saved me!
Wu Kong, you have no idea how much you have been missed.
Without you, nothing works!
I'm glad to see you too. It's too bad that while Master was banishing me
and Bajie wouldn't stop lying about me, you just stood there and said nothing.
I've regretted my silence ever since. Please forgive me.
Oh, come on, big brother! Virtuous men are not supposed to carry grudges.

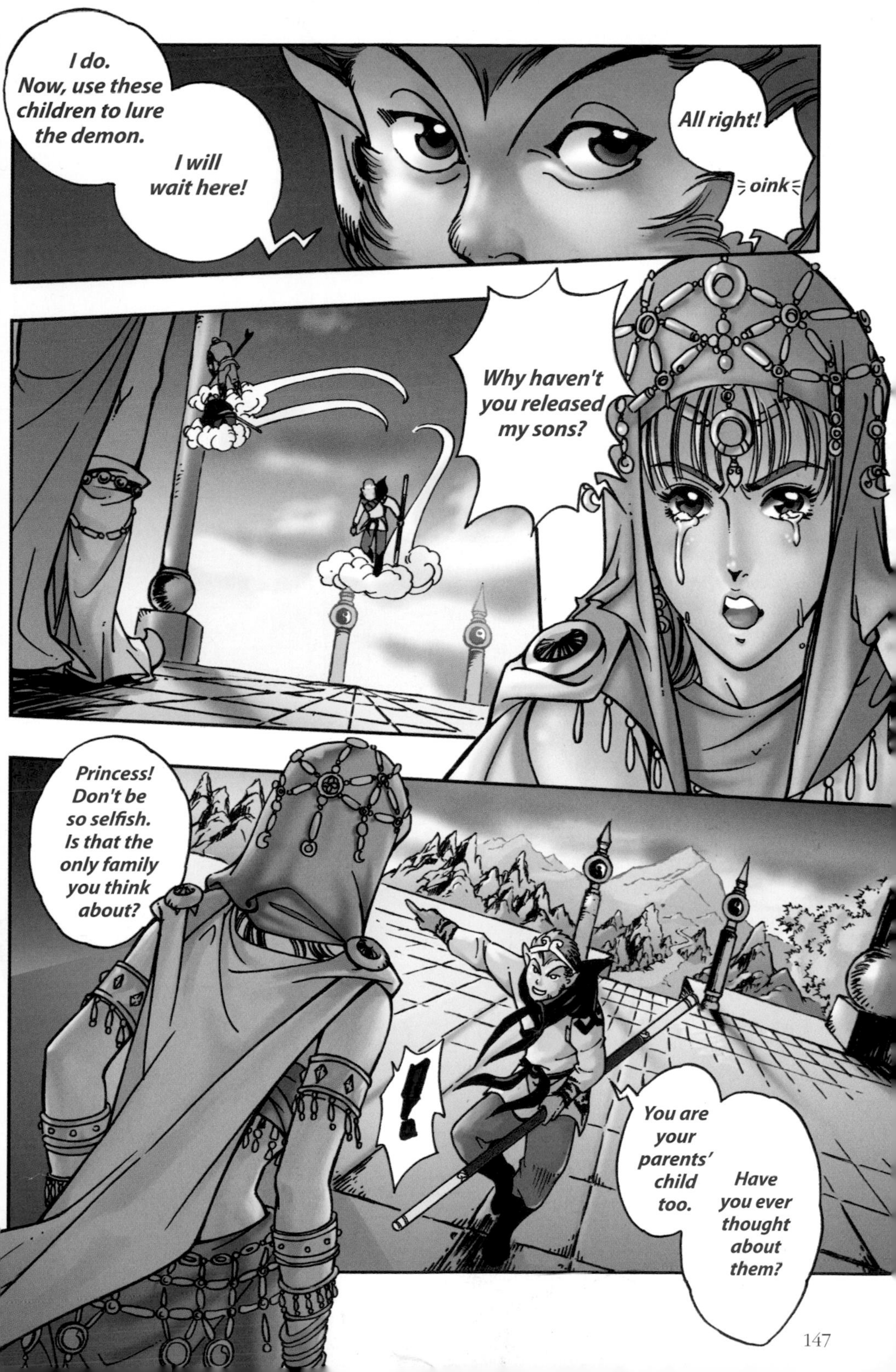
I do.
Now, use these children to lure the demon.
I will wait here!
All right!
oink
Why haven't you released my sons?
Princess! Don't be so selfish. Is that the only family you think about?
!
You are your parents' child too.
Have you ever thought about them?

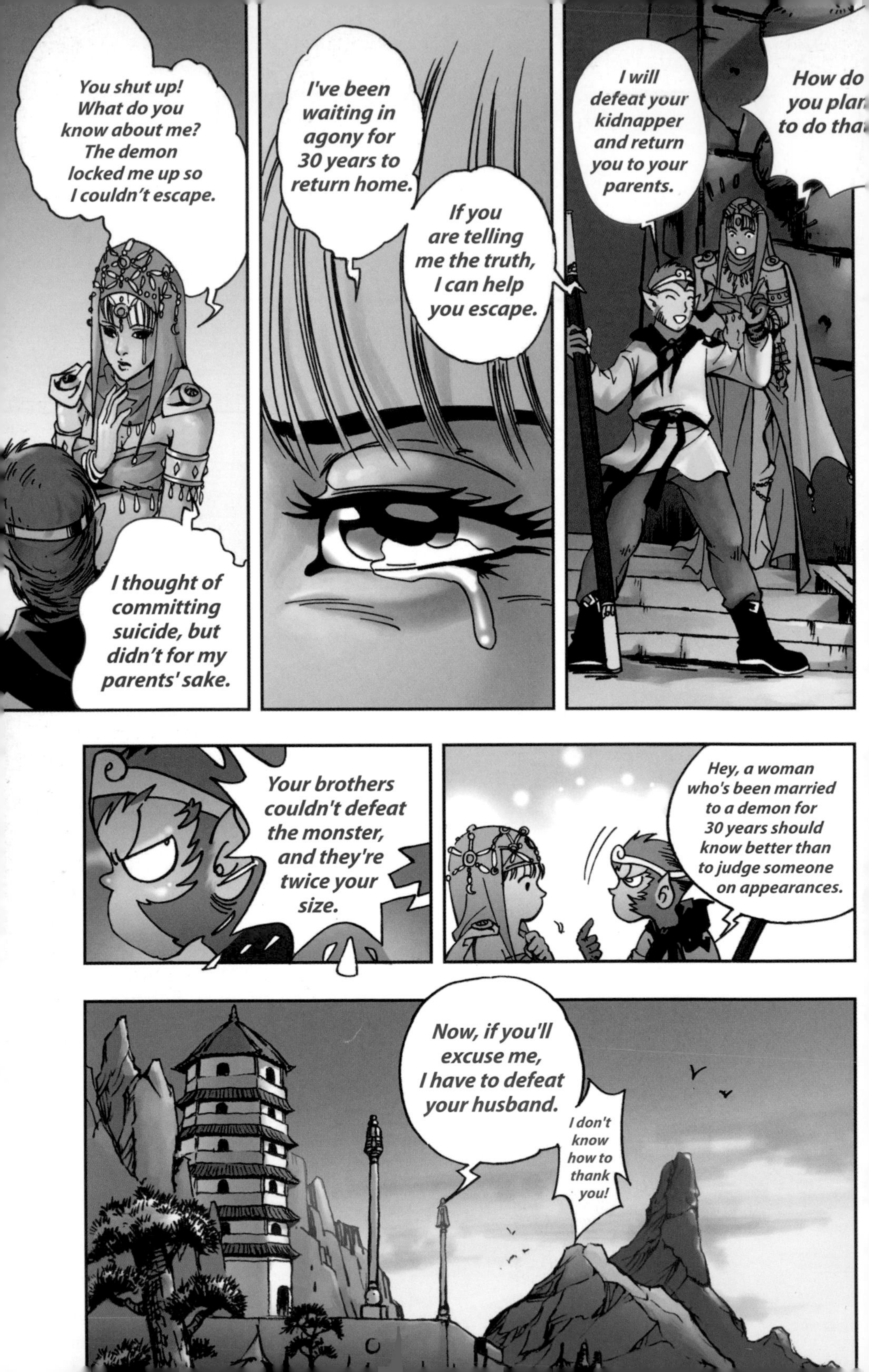
You shut up! What do you know about me? The demon locked me up so I couldn't escape.
I thought of committing suicide, but didn't for my parents' sake.
I've been waiting in agony for 30 years to return home.
If you are telling me the truth, I can help you escape.
I will defeat your kidnapper and return you to your parents.
How do you plan to do that
Your brothers couldn't defeat the monster, and they're twice your size.
Hey, a woman who's been married to a demon for 30 years should know better than to judge someone on appearances.
Now, if you'll excuse me, I have to defeat your husband.
I don't know how to thank you!

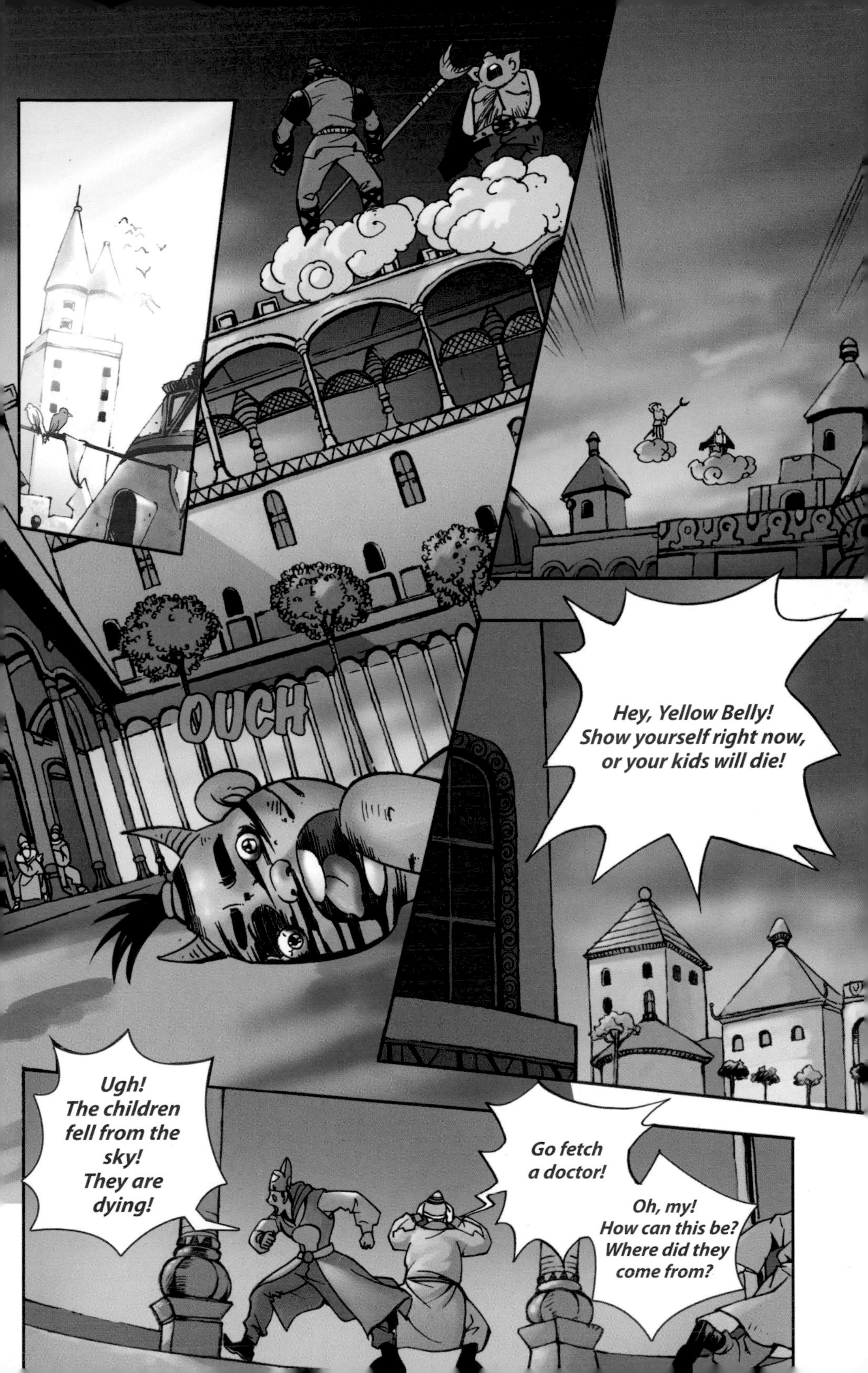
OUCH
Hey, Yellow Belly! Show yourself right now, or your kids will die!
Ugh! The children fell from the sky! They are dying!
Go fetch a doctor!
Oh, my! How can this be? Where did they come from?

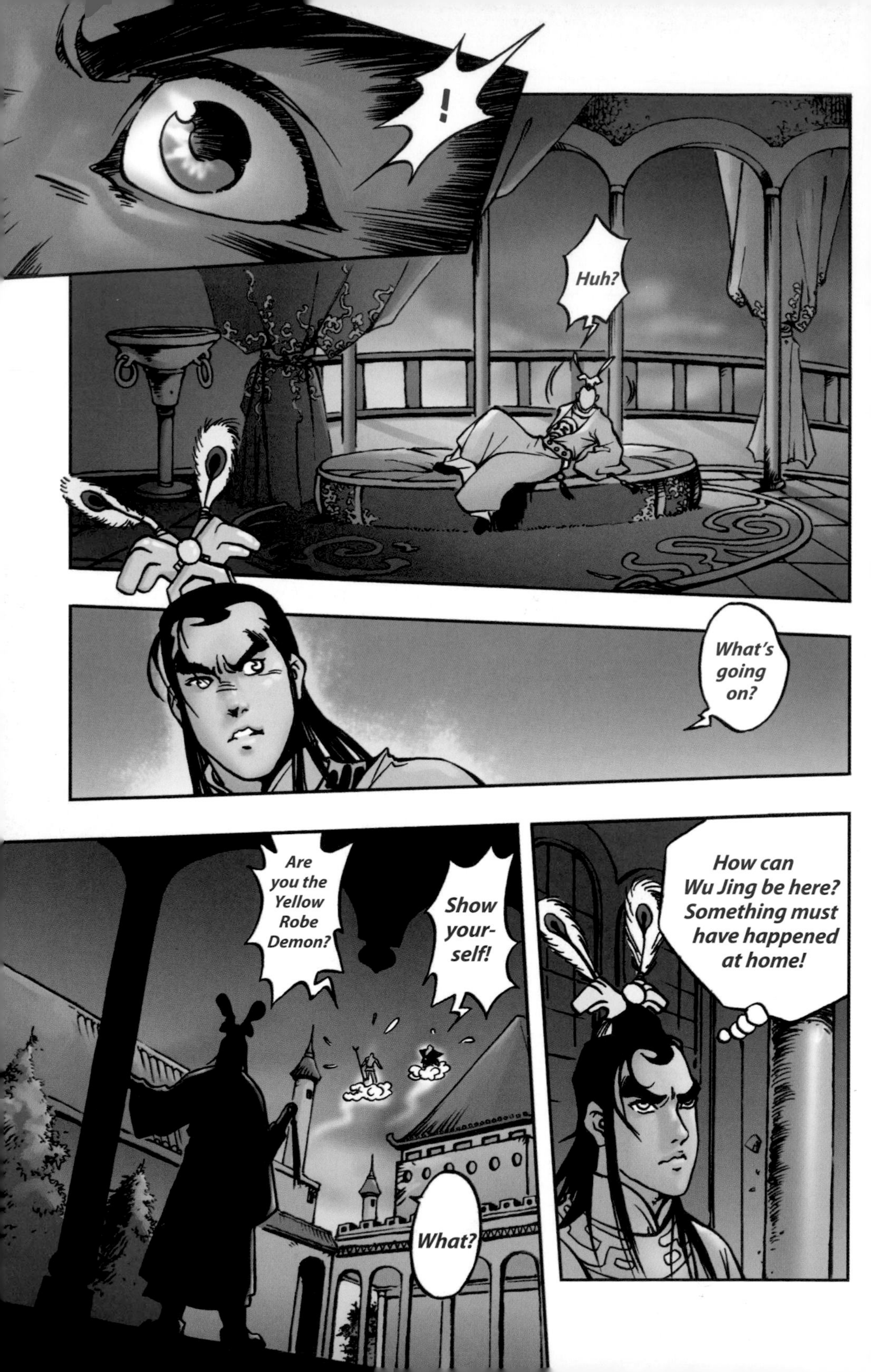
!
Huh?
What's going on?
Are you the Yellow Robe Demon?
Show your-self!
What?
How can Wu Jing be here? Something must have happened at home!

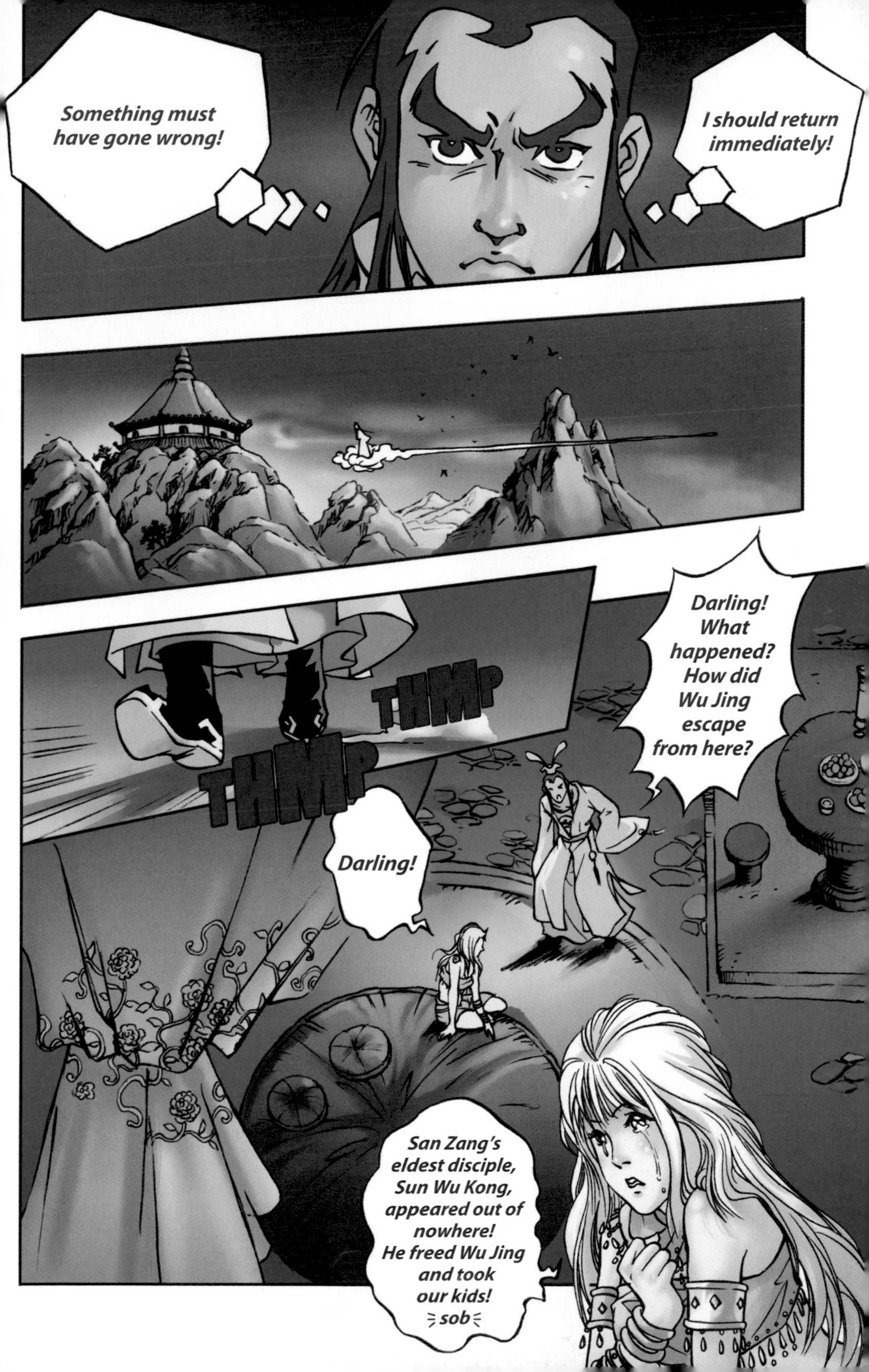
Something must have gone wrong!
I should return immediately!
THMP
THMP
Darling! What happened? How did Wu Jing escape from here?
Darling!
San Zang's eldest disciple, Sun Wu Kong, appeared out of nowhere! He freed Wu Jing and took our kids!
sob

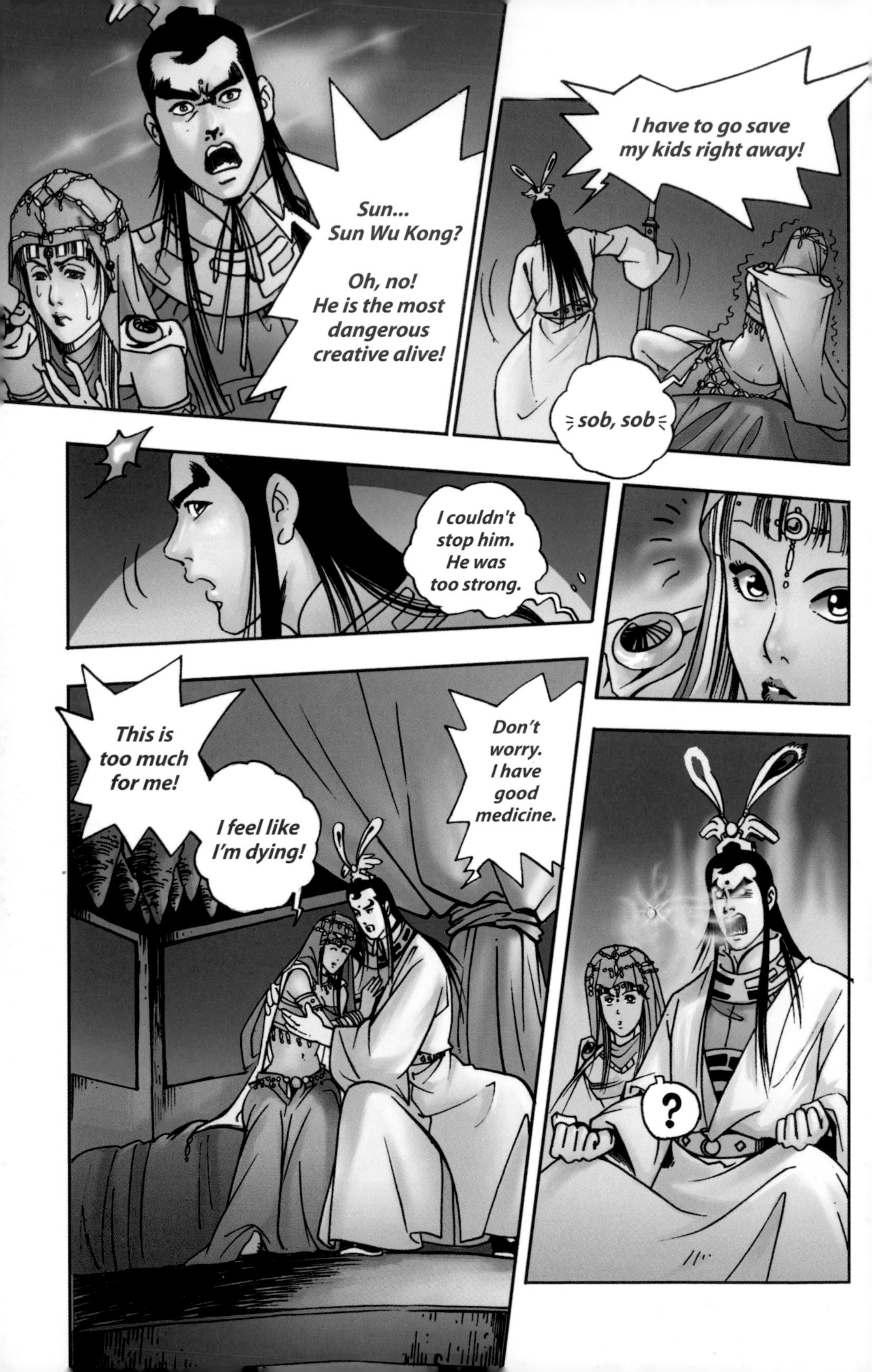
Sun...
Sun Wu Kong?
Oh, no!
He is the most dangerous creative alive!
I have to go save my kids right away!
sob, sob
I couldn't stop him. He was too strong.
This is too much for me!
I feel like I'm dying!
Don't worry. I have good medicine.
?

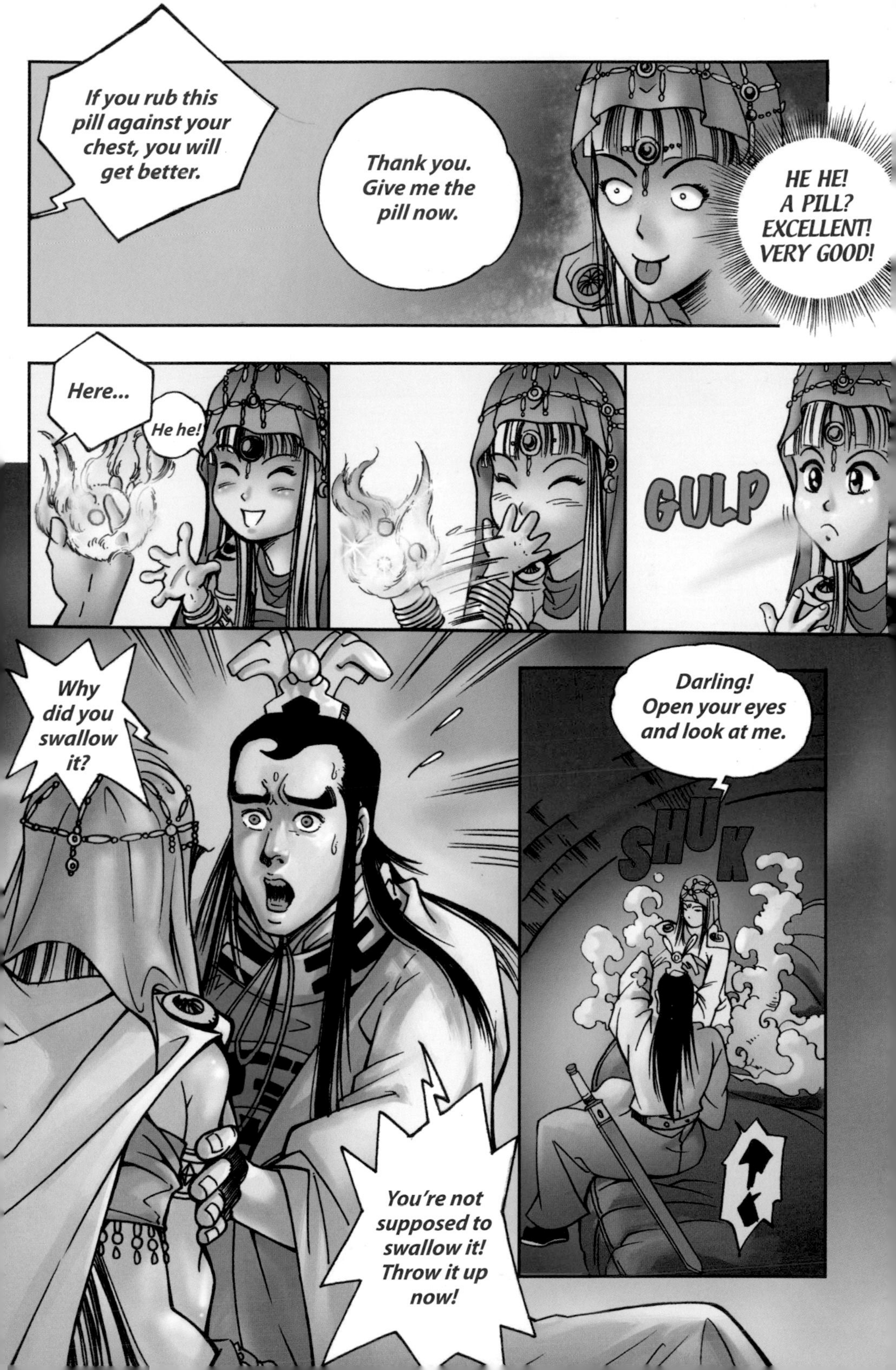
If you rub this pill against your chest, you will get better.
Thank you. Give me the pill now.
HE HE! A PILL? EXCELLENT! VERY GOOD!
Here...
He he!
GULP
Why did you swallow it?
You're not supposed to swallow it! Throw it up now!
Darling! Open your eyes and look at me.
SHUK

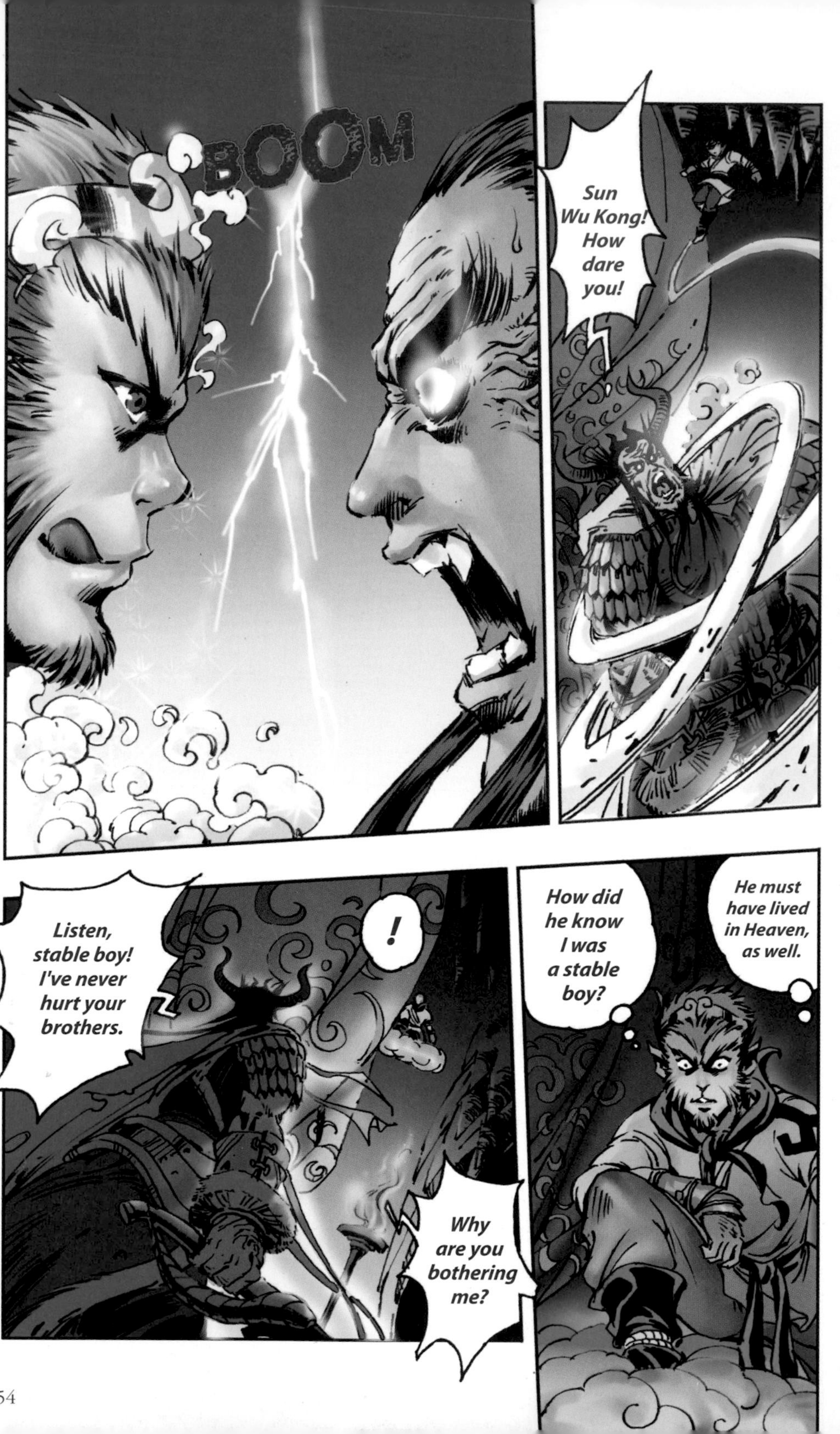
BOOM
Sun Wu Kong! How dare you!
Listen, stable boy! I've never hurt your brothers.
!
Why are you bothering me?
How did he know I was a stable boy?
He must have lived in Heaven, as well.

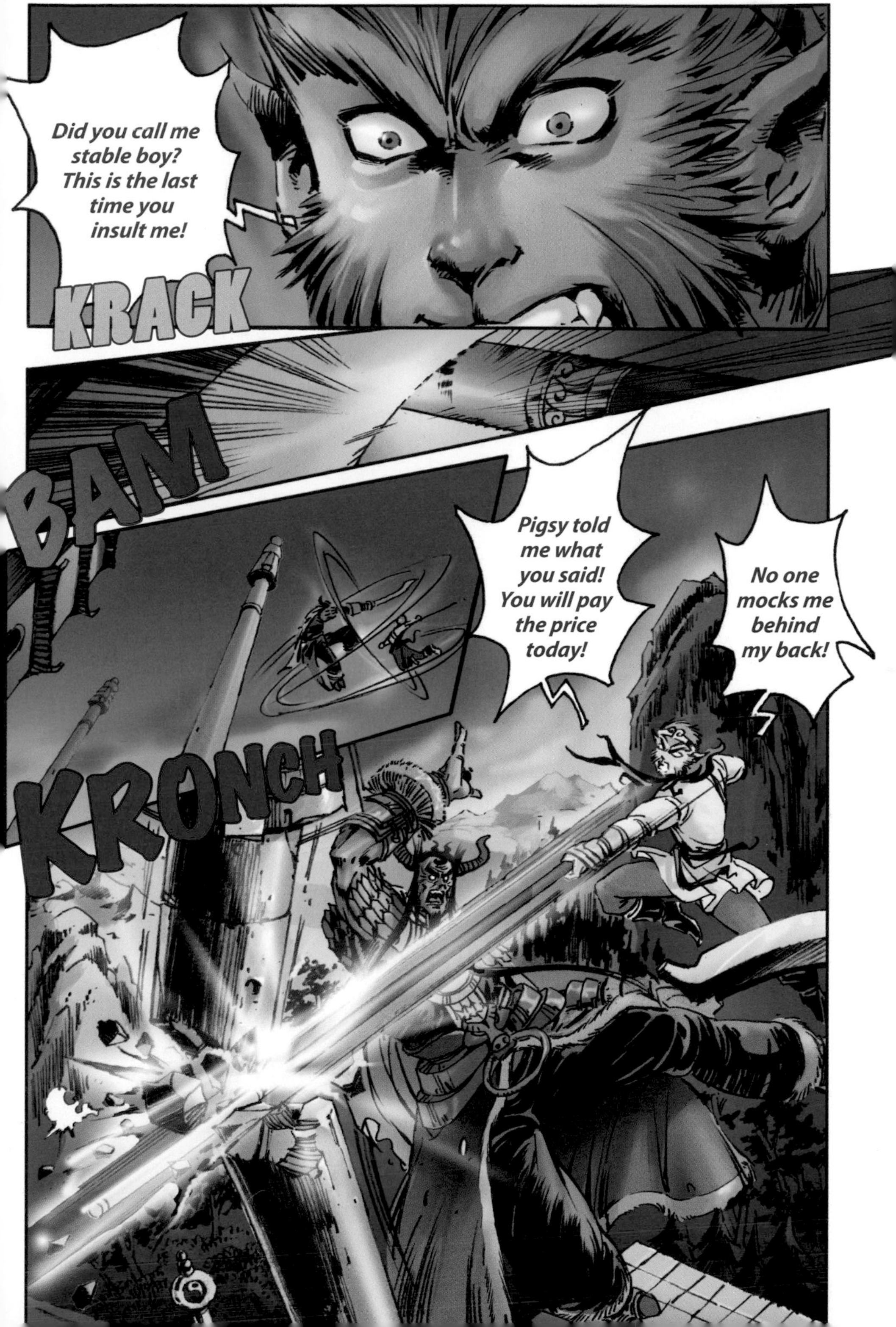
Did you call me stable boy? This is the last time you insult me!
KRACK
BAM
Pigsy told me what you said! You will pay the price today!
No one mocks me behind my back!
KRONCH

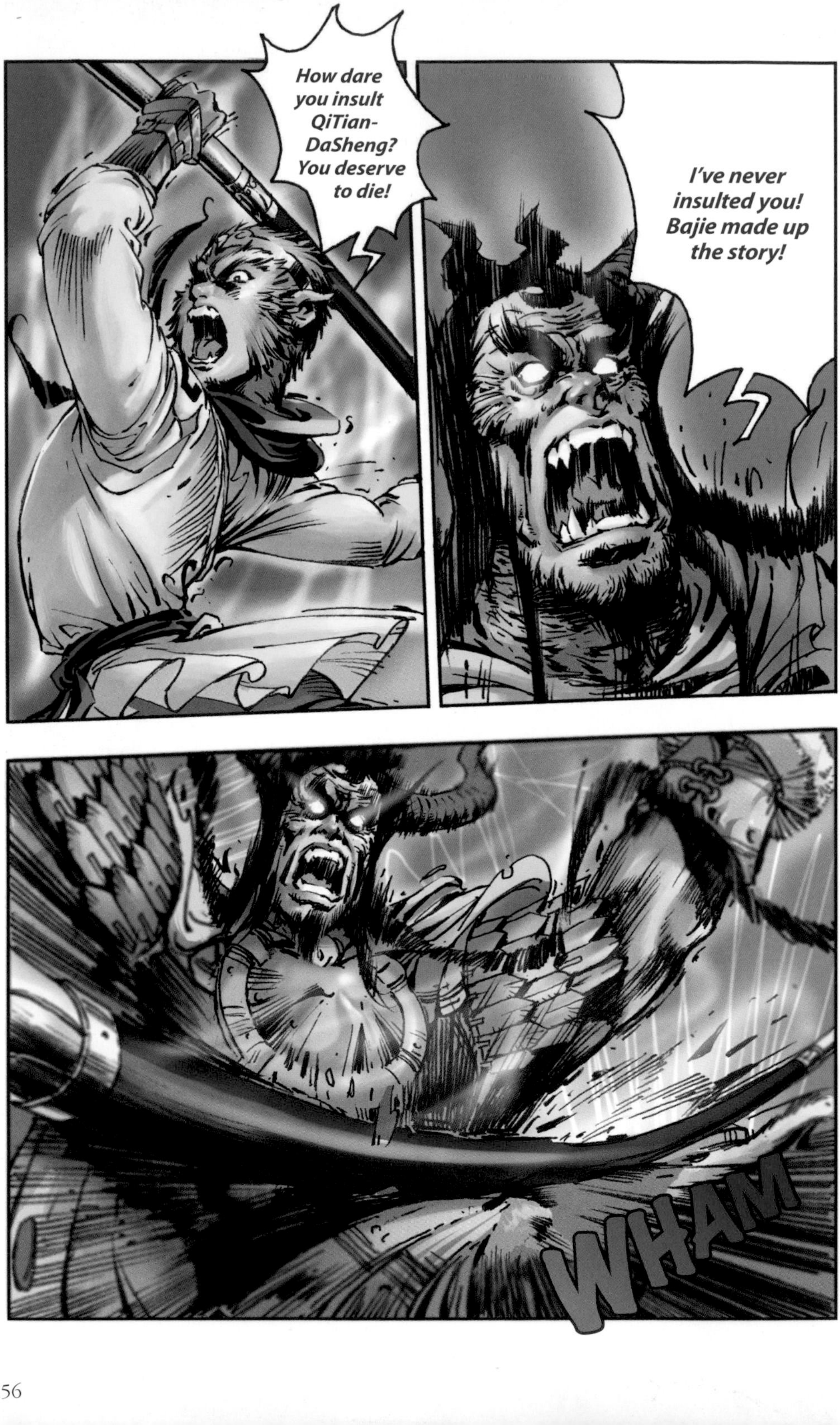
How dare you insult QiTian-DaSheng? You deserve to die!
I've never insulted you! Bajie made up the story!
WHAM

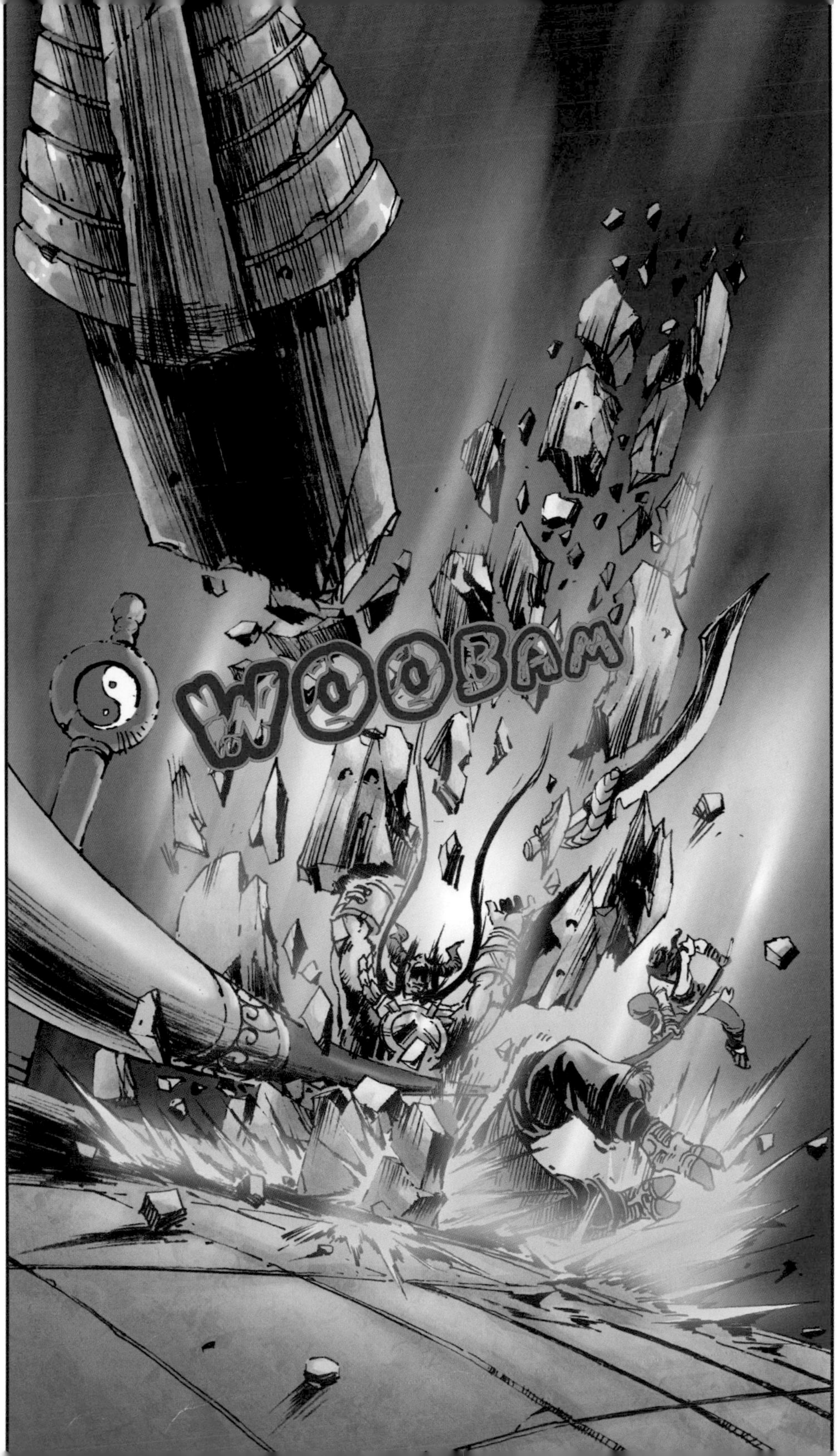
WOOBAM

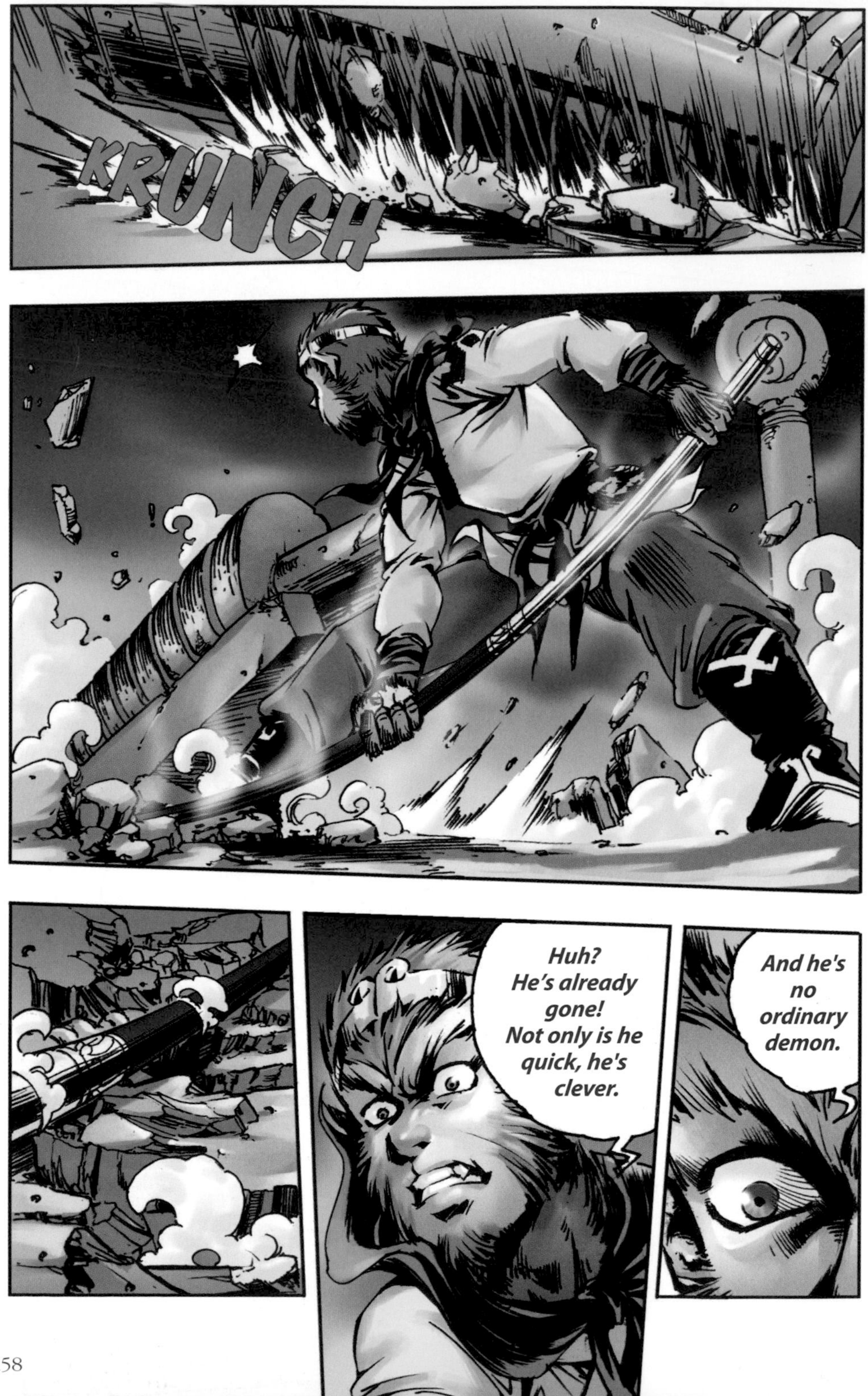
KRUNCH
Huh?
He's already
gone!
Not only is he
quick, he's
clever.
And he's
no
ordinary
demon.

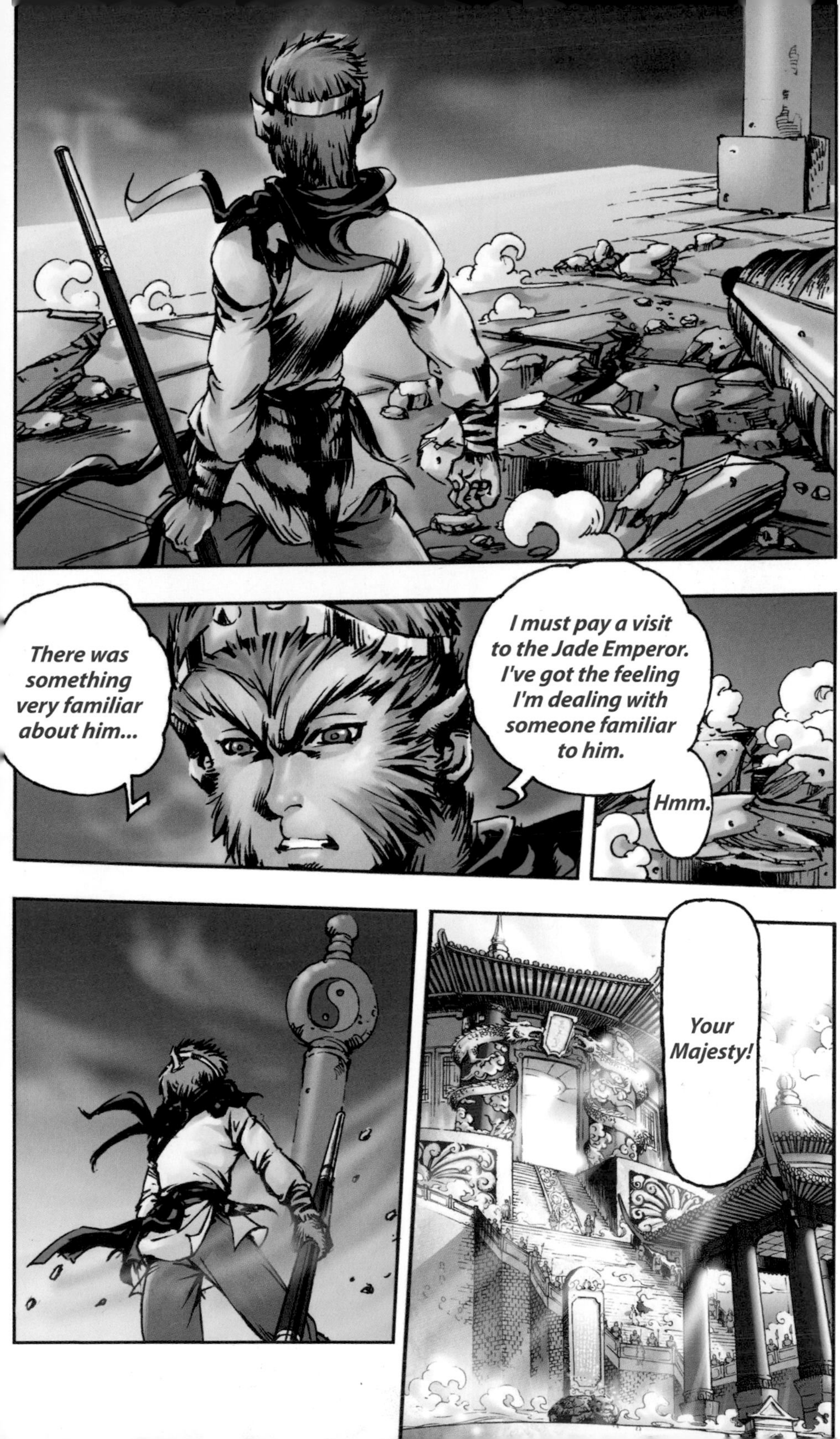
There was something very familiar about him...
I must pay a visit to the Jade Emperor. I've got the feeling I'm dealing with someone familiar to him.
Hmm.
Your Majesty!

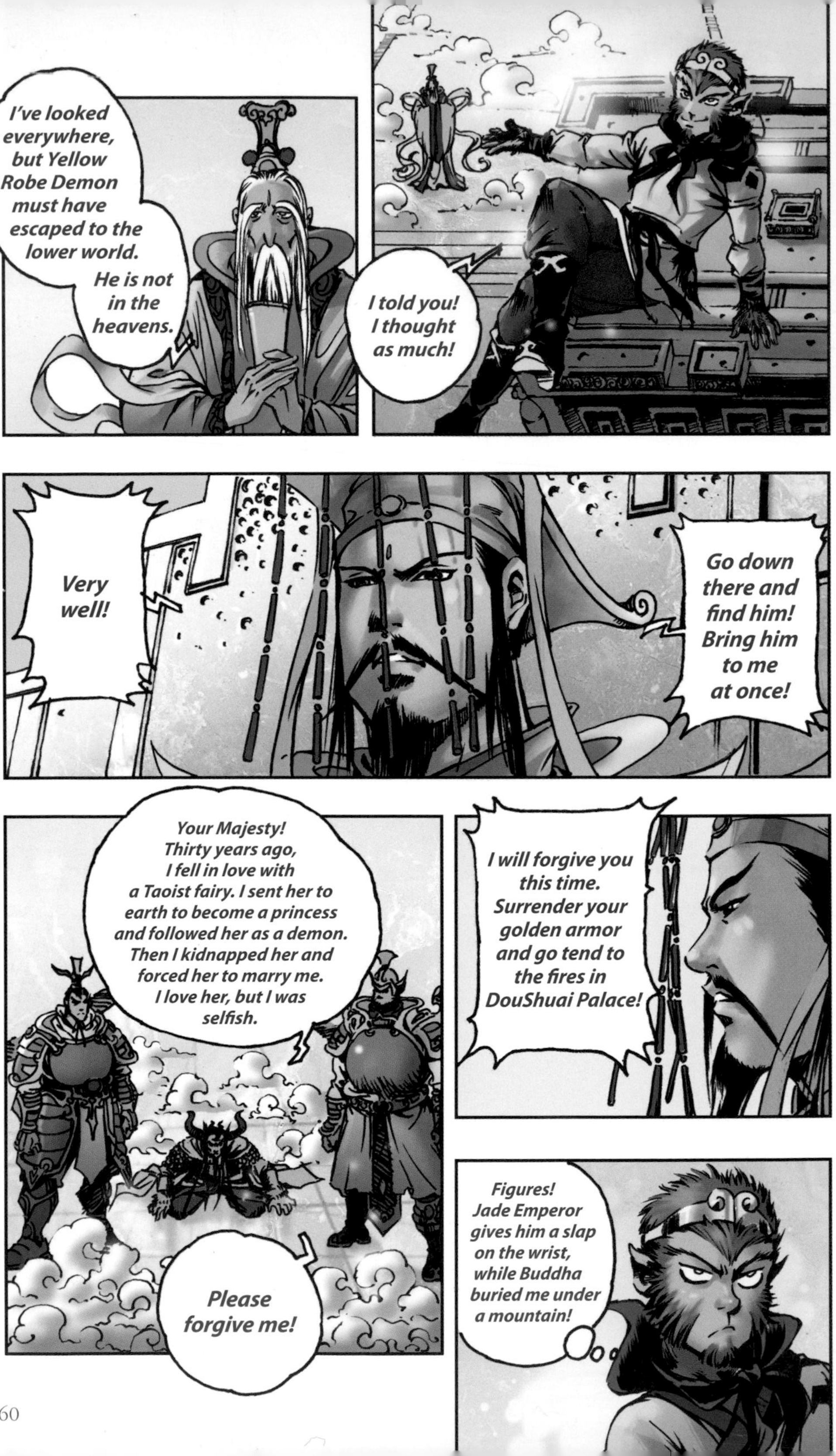
I've looked everywhere, but Yellow Robe Demon must have escaped to the lower world.
He is not in the heavens.
I told you! I thought as much!
Go down there and find him! Bring him to me at once!
Very well!
Your Majesty! Thirty years ago, I fell in love with a Taoist fairy. I sent her to earth to become a princess and followed her as a demon. Then I kidnapped her and forced her to marry me. I love her, but I was selfish.
Please forgive me!
I will forgive you this time. Surrender your golden armor and go tend to the fires in DouShuai Palace!
Figures! Jade Emperor gives him a slap on the wrist, while Buddha buried me under a mountain!

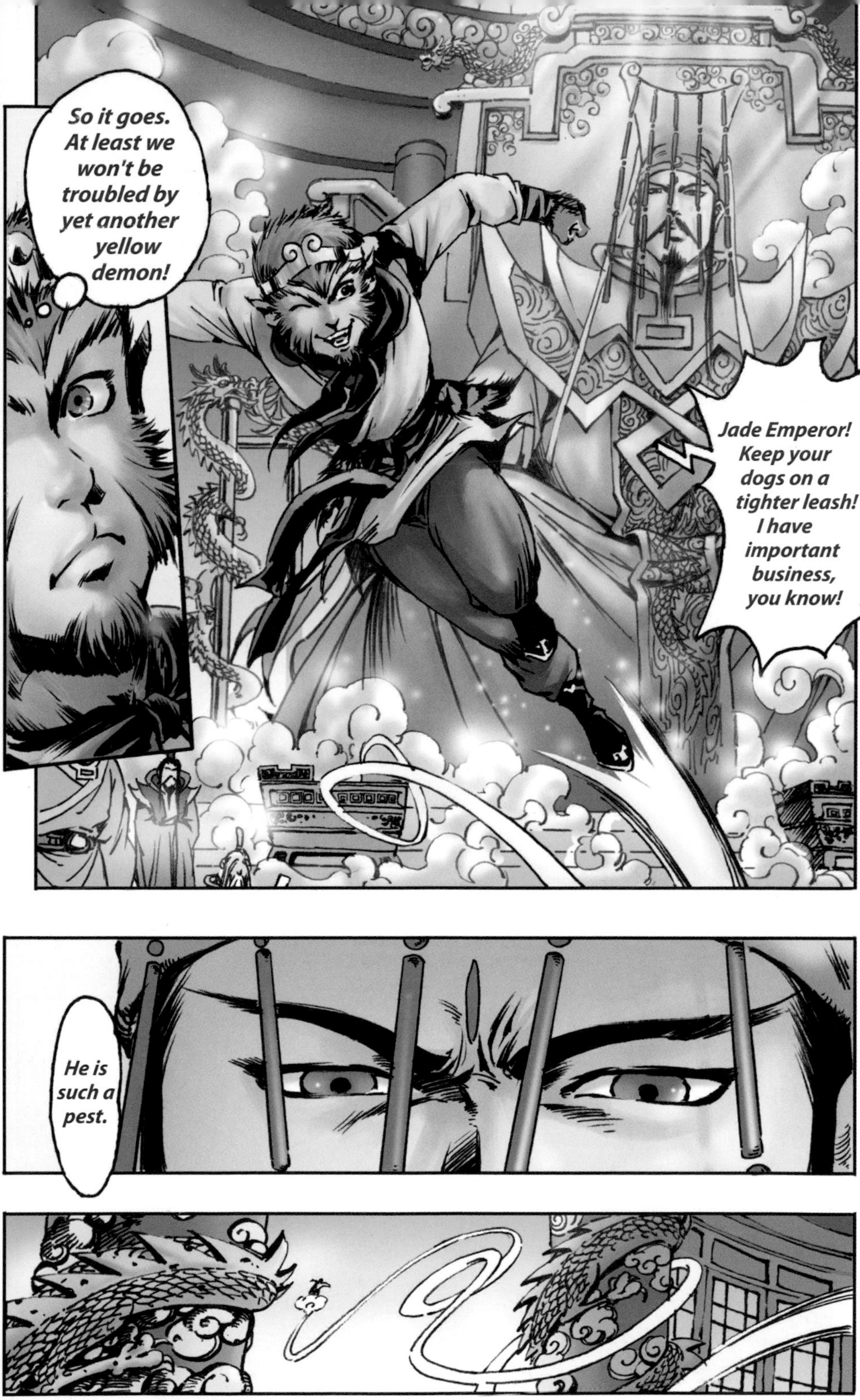
So it goes. At least we won't be troubled by yet another yellow demon!
Jade Emperor! Keep your dogs on a tighter leash! I have important business, you know!
He is such a pest.

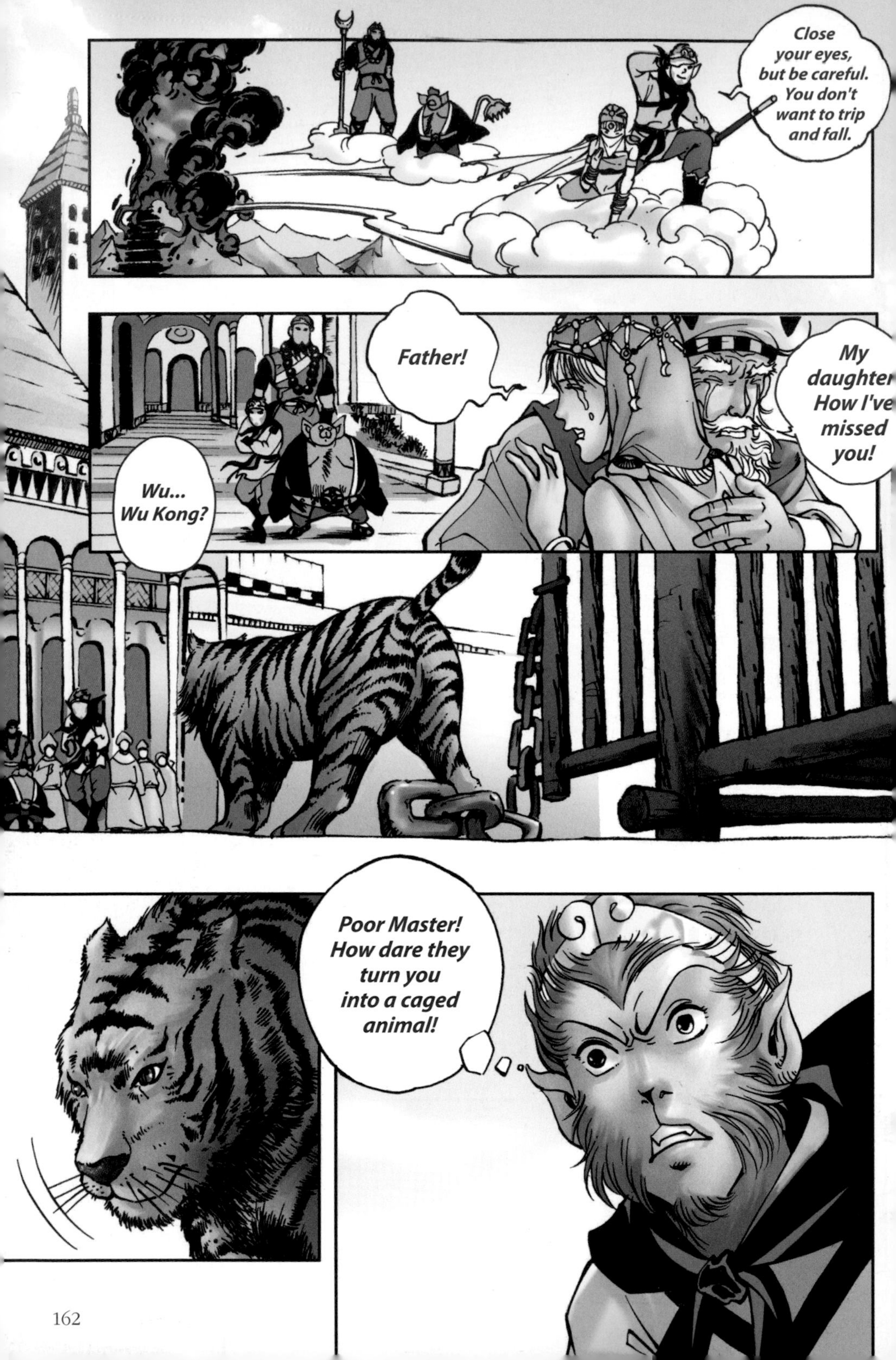
Close your eyes, but be careful. You don't want to trip and fall.
Father!
My daughter How I've missed you!
Wu... Wu Kong?
Poor Master! How dare they turn you into a caged animal!

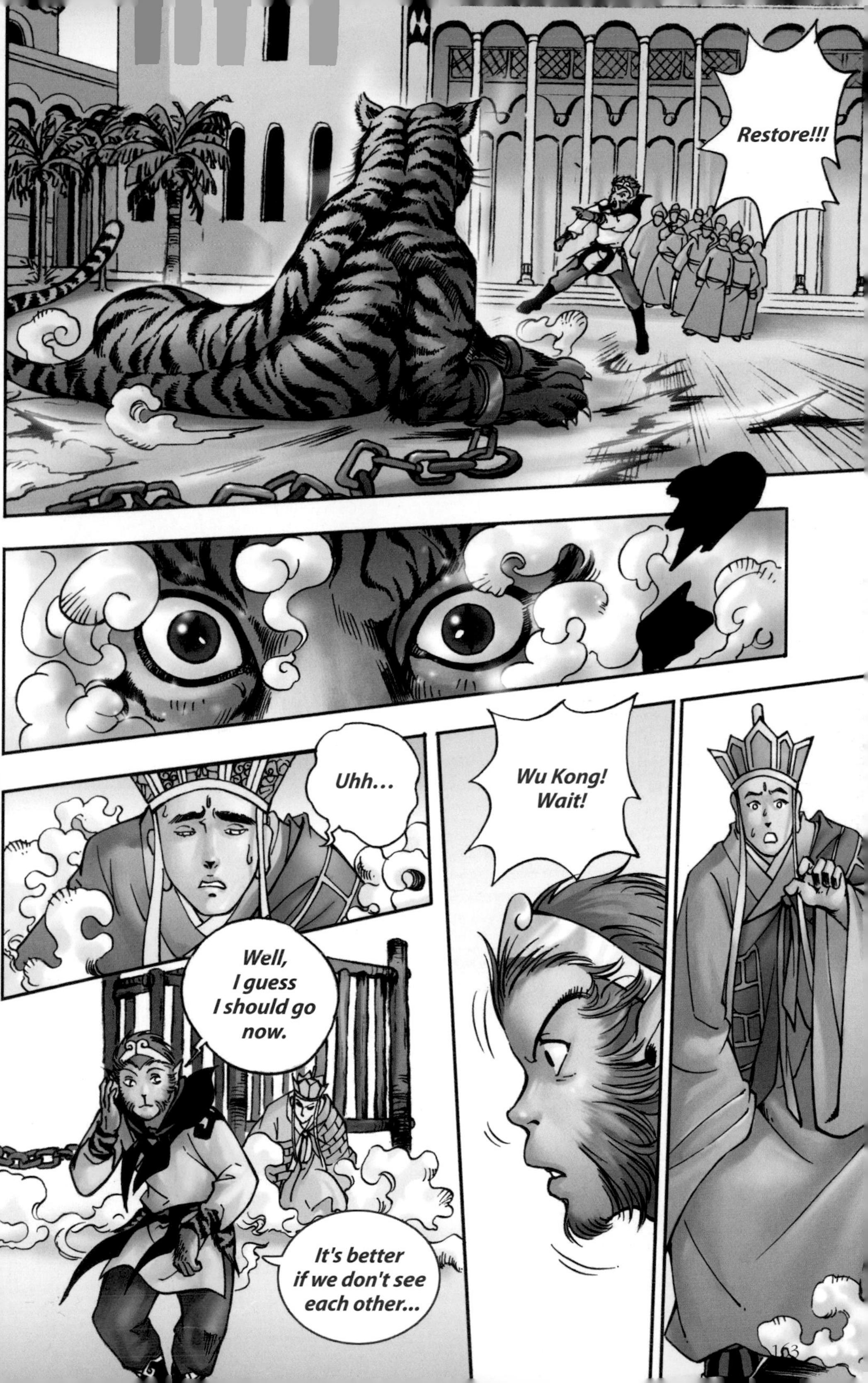
Restore!!!
Uhh…
Wu Kong! Wait!
Well, I guess I should go now.
It's better if we don't see each other...

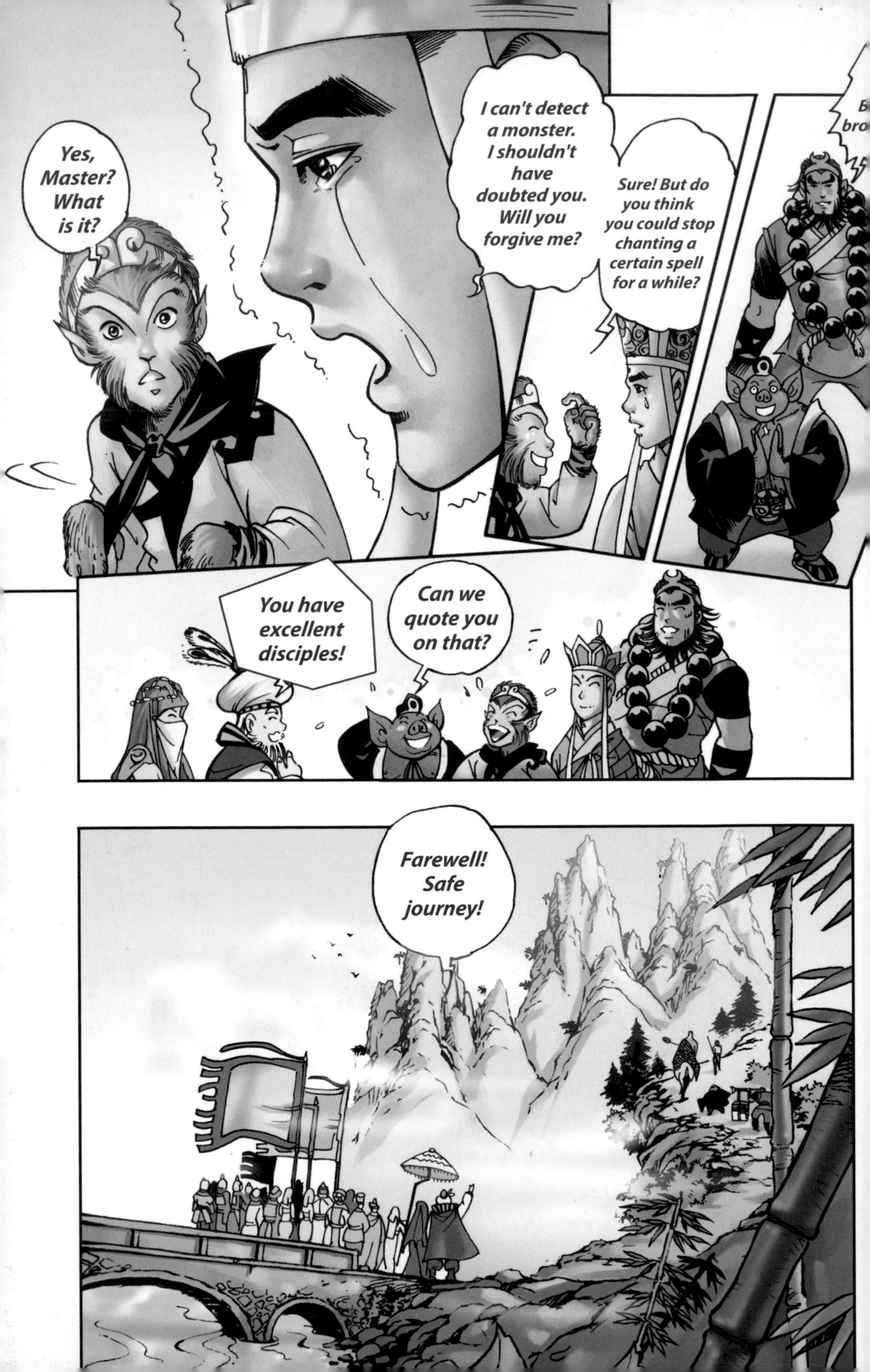
Yes, Master? What is it?
I can't detect a monster. I shouldn't have doubted you. Will you forgive me?
Sure! But do you think you could stop chanting a certain spell for a while?
You have excellent disciples!
Can we quote you on that?
Farewell! Safe journey!

MONKEY KING

Appendix

THE EXPULSION OF SUN WU KONG

● Having made amends for Sun Wu Kong's destruction of the sacred RenShen tree, San Zang and his disciples continue west. After a few days, though, the replenishing effects of the RenShen fruits they ate to celebrate the tree's restoration begin to wear off, and the priest asks Sun Wu Kong to search for food. While the eldest of San Zang's disciples is away, the White Bone Goblin, who sleeps deep within the mountains, disguises herself as a young woman, approaches the traveling companions, and tells them she wishes to make an offering to Buddha. She has heard that eating San Zang's flesh will grant eternal life, so she tries to offer the priest poisoned food in order to capture him. At first she is denied by San Zang's piety; the priest refuses to eat food that the woman claims is for her husband. Shortly thereafter, Sun Wu Kong returns and immediately recognizes that the young woman is a monster in disguise. Wu Kong strikes the young woman, but not

before the goblin is able to escape the body and leave behind a fake corpse. Outraged by Wu Kong's violence, San Zang chants a spell that causes the monkey tremendous pain. The priest wants him to depart the group, but Wu Kong convinces San Zang to let him remain.

A short time later, the goblin appears again, this time disguised as an old woman claiming to be the mother of the woman Wu Kong struck down. Once more, Wu Kong sees through the Goblin's disguise and strikes her, but again the goblin escapes. San Zang punishes Wu Kong, but the monkey is able to convince the priest to forgive him for a second time. San Zang warns Wu Kong that there won't be a third time. Not long after, the goblin appears for the third time, this time disguised as an old man. Wu Kong recognizes the goblin, only this time his aura slips away to the heavens and enlists a group of gods to help him capture and destroy the goblin's spirit. Back on Earth, Wu Kong strikes the old man, while up in the sky the goblin's spirit is destroyed, and it falls to the ground in the form of a skeleton. Despite the proof of the bones on the ground, San Zang refuses to believe the monkey was defending his master from a goblin and expels Sun Wu Kong from the group.

As San Zang and his remaining disciples continue to the West, Sun Wu Kong returns to Spring Mountain to find that his former kingdom has been overrun by monsters who have killed or enslaved his monkey brethren.

Wu Kong defeats the monsters and restores Spring Mountain to its former glory.

Meanwhile, San Zang must rely on Zhu Bajie for the things Wu Kong used to do, and the journey becomes difficult. While looking for food, Bajie decides to take a nap. San Zang then dispatches Wu Jing to find his brother, and while the two disciples are away, San Zang notices an enormous temple. He goes to the temple to perform a service, but when he enters he discovers the Yellow Robe Demon; it turns out the temple is actually a demon's lair. San Zang is recognized and captured by the demon, who imprisons the priest and waits for the two disciples to come looking for him.

Wu Jing finds Bajie, and the two return to the site of their parting. When they discover their master has been kidnapped, the two disciples head to the temple and fight the yellow demon. Although the monster is too powerful for the brothers, the fight ends in a draw when the demon's wife, the Jade Lady, interrupts them and begs her husband for the priest's release. Unknown to the demon, the Jade Lady visited San Zang in his cell and revealed herself to be a princess of the BaoXiang Kingdom who was kidnapped by the demon and taken for his wife thirty years before. She offers to plead for his release if he will promise to deliver a letter to her father that explains what happened to her.

Once San Zang is released and reunited with his disciples, the priest

makes good on his promise and delivers the letter to the king of BaoXiang, who had thought his daughter was dead. The demon immediately suspects his the Jade Lady of treachery, but Wu Jing protects her by insisting that his master delivered no letter on her behalf. Regretting his accusations, the yellow demon offers to transform his monstrous appearance and pay a visit to her father in the guise of a handsome tiger hunter. When the demon arrives in BaoXiang, he tells the king that he rescued the princess from a tiger attack and married her. He then accuses San Zang of being the tiger in question, and uses magic to transform the priest into a tiger and trap him in a cage.

Outside, in the king's stable, Jade Dragon overhears what has happened to San Zang and, knowing that all his elder brothers are gone, convinces Bajie to go to Spring Mountain and find Sun Wu Kong. Convincing the monkey to return won't be easy, though. After all, it was Bajie's antagonism that contributed to Wu Kong's dismissal. Still, Bajie knows there is no other option.

When he reaches Spring Mountain, Bajie won't admit that San Zang is in trouble, and instead tries to lure Wu Kong back with flattery. When Wu Kong angrily rejects the flattery and sends Bajie away, the pig finally comes clean and tells Wu Kong what has happened to their master, even going so far as to make up a story about the demon laughing at and cursing Sun

Wu Kong's name. Enraged, Sun Wu Kong departs quickly for the BaoXiang Kingdom, and immediately begins laying a trap for the monster. Wu Kong convinces the Jade Lady to betray her husband by promising to reunite her with her father. The monkey then lures the demon by pretending to kill his children. The monster returns to console his wife, but does not realize that she is actually Wu Kong in disguise. The monkey quickly defeats the demon, who slips away to the underworld. Wu Kong then seeks the help of the Jade Emperor, who captures the demon and punishes him by ordering him to maintain the fires at DouShuai Palace.

Satisfied that the monster has been justly punished, Wu Kong returns to BaoXiang to see the princess reunited with her father, and to restore his master to human form. When he does this, San Zang apologizes for not believing Wu Kong earlier, and swears that he will no longer utter the pain spell when he's angry at his eldest disciple. Once the travelers are reunited, they depart BaoXiang Kingdom to continue their journey.

TRANSFORMATION AND THE NATURE OF EXISTENCE

● *A goddess takes human form so she can ask a priest to undertake an incredible journey. The son of a sea king transforms into a horse to assist the priest. A naval commander is expelled from the heavens and becomes a pig who will play a pivotal role in the journey. A demon transforms into a handsome tiger hunter so that he can meet the father of the woman he kidnapped and married thirty years ago. And a stone monkey, who learned the secrets of eternal life and seventy-two different kinds of transfigurations from Master Puti, transfigures into the wife of a monster to trick and then defeat his adversary. Twice.*

There are so many transformations and transfigurations in The Journey to the West that it might easily be titled The Journey of Countless Transformations. So often does Sun Wu Kong rely on his ability to transfigure when fighting off demons and monsters that the reader might be reminded of The Matrix. There are obvious differences: the Matrix character who transforms the most, Agent Smith, is a villain, whereas Sun Wu Kong, the invincible creature enlisted to help save the world, more closely resembles Neo. But there is a similarity between Smith and Wu Kong that, ironically, highlights one of the biggest differences about the significance of transformation in the two stories.

In each story, it is the character who is closest to and most under-stands the nature of the world who is the most accomplished transformer; in each story, it is the character who is literally created from the elements of the world who is able to manipulate those elements into almost any form, because nature dictates that all things, living and dead, are one in the same. Agent Smith is a program created within the digital world of the Matrix; he is literally composed of ones and zeroes, and therefore can change into anything within the Matrix. Sun Wu Kong was born from a stone atop Spring Mountain, a stone that was infused with the heavenly power of creation, and therefore is neither completely natural nor entirely heavenly—but because he is somewhere in between he can act like and transform into either one of those things.

The fact that these two characters occupy opposing ends of the hero/villain spectrum is indicative of each story's attitude toward nature and transfiguration. In The Matrix, transfiguration is a terrifying ability that makes the heroes paranoid and fearful, because anyone they meet in the Matrix could become Agent Smith at any time. The world of the Matrix, sameness is a menace that endangers anyone who enters, deployed tactically to subdue anyone who wishes to become an exception to the Matrix's code of conformity. That is why the characters in the story long to be free and join the "real world"; even if the world outside the Matrix is cold, dead, and inhospitable to human life, it is a place where each person is unique, where no one can be possessed or cloned, and where no villain can transfigure into the likeness of a friend. (Well, at least not until Agent Smith is able to escape into the real world, but we don't want to spoil the movie.)

Contrarily, in the fantasy world of Journey to the West, transformation is one of the highest forms of enlightenment, achieved only by those elite deities (as well as ambitious monkeys and the occasional fallen demon) who have come to recognize that all things—animal, mineral, and vegetable— are one in the same. As was discussed in previous volumes, one of the reasons transfiguration isn't as threatening in Journey to the West is because the story itself is not presented as a binary conflict between good and evil. Therefore, transfiguration is not simply employed as a weapon of war or oppression by the forces of evil, but rather as a tool utilized only by the wisest to attain a desired goal. This is another important distinction: because both villains and heroes are capable of transfiguration, Journey to the West is once more making the argument that even if incredibly wise beings are capable of great treachery, that does not inherently make them villains. (Remember how San Zang reacted to Sun Wu Kong killing mountain bandits who were threatening their lives?) In fact, several adversaries encountered by San Zang and his cohort are ultimately spared a deathly fate and returned to Heaven to act as servants, because it is recognized by the wisest of deities that anyone could end up falling into villainy. It would be hard to imagine Agent Smith being pardoned at the end of The Matrix and becoming Neo's ally.

Ultimately, the opposing portrayals of transfiguration in The Matrix and The Journey to the West indicate opposing perspectives on the inability to distinguish between beings in nature. In The Matrix, transfiguration is the tool of an enemy who would otherwise be easy to distinguish, used only to endanger those who would seek to know the truth. In Journey to the West, transfiguration is a power that can be used by a goddess to impersonate a monster, because the truth is that there is very little difference between the two.